THE
STONE
GIRL

THE STONE GIRL

A NOVEL

DIRK WITTENBORN

W. W. NORTON & COMPANY
Independent Publishers Since 1923

Copyright © 2020 by Dirk Wittenborn

Map on page 16 courtesy of the Adirondack Experience.

For information about permission to reproduce selections from this book, write to Permissions, W. W. Norton & Company, Inc., 500 Fifth Avenue, New York, NY 10110

For information about special discounts for bulk purchases, please contact W. W. Norton Special Sales at specialsales@wwnorton.com or 800-233-4830

Manufacturing by LSC Communications, Harrisonburg
Book design by Fearn Cutler de Vicq
Production manager: Anna Oler

Library of Congress Cataloging-in-Publication Data

Names: Wittenborn, Dirk, author.
Title: The stone girl : a novel / Dirk Wittenborn.
Description: First edition. | New York : W. W. Norton & Company, [2020]
Identifiers: LCCN 2019050533 | ISBN 9781324005810 (hardcover) |
ISBN 9781324005827 (epub)
Subjects: LCSH: Psychological fiction. | GSAFD: Suspense fiction.
Classification: LCC PS3573.I924 S76 2020 | DDC 813/.54—dc23
LC record available at https://lccn.loc.gov/2019050533

W. W. Norton & Company, Inc., 500 Fifth Avenue, New York, N.Y. 10110
www.wwnorton.com

W. W. Norton & Company Ltd., 15 Carlisle Street, London W1D 3BS

1 2 3 4 5 6 7 8 9 0

For
Kirsten and Lilo

PART I

———

POWERS THAT BE

A t the end of the summer of 2018, high atop a nearly inaccessible gorge deep in the Adirondack forest of New York State's North Country, three women had an unusual monument set in place. Elegantly tapered, nearly ten feet tall, a hand-chiseled obelisk of native bluestone inscribed with brass capitals caught the light of the sun. Weighing in excess of two thousand pounds, it had the solemn presence of a memorial to war dead. A marker worthy of a state courthouse or a city square made no sense in the middle of nowhere. And yet it did.

To the others, Evie Quimby referred to it as a *calling lure*—an old-fashioned expression, commonly used by trappers. A calling lure draws a beast out of its lair and tempts it into a snare. Usually such lures are scents: barkstone, civet, skunk, blood, and the like. They're messages carried on the wind; beckonings so potent and pungent and closely related in the animal's mind to sex and/or prey that they trigger urges the creature cannot resist. That obelisk's inscription had no smell, but the words spelled out in brass were guaranteed to get inside the head of one man. Its message was simple: *We know what you are.*

But the truth was when those three women first put up that stone none of them knew the true nature of what they were after or up against.

A month after the stone was put in place, Evie Quimby, her mother Flo, and Lulu Mannheim convened in the vegetable garden behind Flo's cabin. Misfortune had galvanized the bond between them by then into something that went beyond the categories of daughter, mother, friend. The women were finding out the truth about themselves. How far were they willing to go? How much were they ready to risk, when there was no making things right, just a remote chance of making them a little less wrong? Their troika was a democracy; the particulars of the damage that had been to done to each made them equals. All three were in agreement, but each saw the necessary reckoning in a different light.

Flo told her daughter and Lulu straight out, "All you're doing by this is asking to get yourselves killed." She was outvoted.

The garden lay neatly fenced behind a cabin built of logs squared by a double-bladed ax at the end of the Spanish-American War. Silvered by weather and time, it perched precariously halfway up a mountain steeply conifered in fragrant shades of green: spruce, balsam, and pine. Six miles north of the village of Rangeley, New York, pop.: 438, it sat back up in the woods at the end of a rocky dirt switchback with a 30-degree incline at an elevation of over two thousand feet.

The true purpose of their meeting, like that of the stone, was not discussed outside the three. The women told themselves if anyone was watching (a remote but real possibility), or the sheriff stopped by unannounced to see what they were up to (he did so regularly since Evie had come back to Townsend County), it would appear as if they were doing nothing more suspicious at that cabin than conspiring to harvest pumpkins a week early. The women had reason to be both cautious and paranoid.

Evie was the first to arrive. Wearing the uniform of her youth, work-worn Carhartt coveralls and steel-toed boots, she could've passed for a local, but she wasn't . . . not anymore. Getting out of the rental car, walking through the wet grass and puddled mud, she saw more rain in the distance blowing in across the Sister Lakes: Lucille and Constance to the west, and Millicent, the largest and most homely, just to the south. Each was its own shade of blue. A family of half-feral cats, collared by Flo with tiny bells to give the songbirds a chance, tinkled as they slunk out from under the skinning shed to see what Evie was up to.

The Quimby homestead, like the Adirondacks, was wilder and more primitive than simply rural. The stump she used to stand on as a girl to dazzle a pet crow with the shine of a dime was still there, but the tilted meadow was now littered with rusting machine parts, outboard motors beyond repair, and the remains of a '62 Willys Jeep that had died because there was no one in residence to rebuild its crank case. Buddy Quimby, her father, had been better at taking things apart than figuring out how to make them work again. Puzzling out how the pieces of what was broken fit together had always been Evie's job. At thirty-four, Evie was no longer the girl that had grown up in that weathered gray cabin, the one who had once told herself she would never come back to Townsend County.

Flo had told her more than once over the years that she was not responsible for what happened to Buddy, but Evie knew that was not entirely true. Pausing to scratch the back of a cat who had lost its tail to a fox, Evie headed up to what was left of the skinning shed and searched among the cobwebs for a pickax and spade. If there had been no *hunting accident*, if she had never run from the Sister Lakes, the Willys would still be on the road, the outboards repaired, and her father would have been there next to her. It was Buddy who had taught her about calling lures and the setting of traps.

Lulu's Range Rover spun its wheels up the dirt track to the Quimby cabin. Windows down, stereo on max, the Grateful Dead's anthem "Box of Rain" echoed up the mountainside. Evie could hear them coming. It was her father's favorite tune. He'd often croon the lyrics as a warning, just before someone started a fight he would feel obliged to finish. Her mother only played it when she was feeling more hopeless than sad.

Lulu came in fast with Flo riding shotgun. Braking too hard and too late, the Range Rover skidded across the soggy meadow and came to a full stop just before colliding with the remains of the Willys. As Lulu got out the car, Evie reminded her, "The idea is we're trying to be discreet."

"Your mother wouldn't get in the car unless I played the song. I've been listening to it on repeat for almost an hour."

Evie called out, "You coming, Mama?" But Flo just sat in the front seat, staring straight ahead, grimly puffing on one of her nasty cigarillos. She used to hate the smell when Buddy lit up, but now inhaled deeply to remind her of the man that was gone. Flo insisted on listening until the last of his sad song played out.

Lulu, at fifty, was small, girlish, and had a sashay in her step. Except for hair hennaed a shade of cherry red that a twenty-five-year-old would have thought too youthful, she looked like what she was: a very rich woman who exercised too much, believed in Botox, and had more important things on her mind to worry about than the brand-new pair of $1,800 green crocodile loafers she ruined as her feet slopped through the mud.

"I told my lawyer the legal parts of what we're doing." Having made a fortune on top of the one she inherited by buying and selling big-city commercial real estate, Lulu had lots of lawyers.

"What'd he say?"

"We're insane." Lulu said it with a laugh to let Evie know she hadn't changed her mind.

Flo was out of the Range Rover now but she still hadn't said hello. She looked older than seventy-four. Part Mohawk, she was dark-eyed, her face wrinkled as a raisin. Flo had blue jay feathers woven into her bone-white braids that day. Head capped by a red bandanna tied close to her skull, knee-high black boots, ankle-length skirt pulled up and cinched under a man's belt. To ease the tension, Evie volunteered, "You look like a pirate, Mama." Evie was blond, blue-eyed, and pale as skim milk. The total lack of physical resemblance between mother and daughter was puzzling to anyone who didn't know Evie had been adopted by Flo and Buddy on the third day of her life.

Flo ignored the comment and growled, "Let's get this over with."

The gate to the vegetable garden was secured by a rusty padlock. It began to drizzle as Flo searched through the keys strung on the lanyard around her neck. Gate opened, Evie shouldered the pickax and Lulu picked up a spade. When Evie offered her mother a shovel, all Flo had to say was, "I'm not going to help you two dig yourselves into a hole you can't get out of."

Faded seed packets tacked to stakes, neatly demarked rows of carrots, sweet peas, tomatoes—both cherry and heirloom—sweet peppers, Brussels sprouts, potatoes, and butter beans; all but the pumpkins had already been harvested. As they followed Flo back through the garden, Evie found it comforting to think there was still a sliver of the universe so tidy and well ordered.

Her mother pointed to a furrow where sweet potatoes had already been taken from the ground. Lulu put a crocodile loafer to the shoulder of the spade and Evie brought down her pick. The drizzle turned into cold, pelting rain.

Four feet down they found what they came for. It took all three of them to pry a five-foot-long duffel bag out of the earth. Wrapped in polyurethane, duct-taped watertight long ago, it clinked as Evie hoisted its weight onto her shoulder and staggered back to the cabin through fading light.

Flo kindled a fire in the Franklin stove with pinecones. Evie dropped the duffel on the kitchen table and Lulu began to cut away the plastic with a paring knife. Evie was just about to unzip it when Flo suddenly slammed her fist down on the kitchen table so hard the salt and pepper shakers jumped, and shouted, "This is a mistake!"

Lulu reminded her gently, "We voted."

"I know we voted. I'm old, not senile!" Evie reached out to take her mother's hand, but Flo wasn't interested in gestures. "If you go up on that mountain, he's not going to come for you by himself."

"That's what I'm counting on."

Flo muttered an obscenity as Evie unzipped the bag and took out parts of what would soon be a trombone-action 12-gauge shotgun, sawed off at twenty inches. The serial numbers on it and the rest of the weapons in the bag had been removed with a file by her father long ago. The guns were lovingly packed in Cosmoline to prevent rust. Evie wiped off the grease, worked the action, and dry-fired at a light-bulb. Flo looked at her daughter as if she were handling snakes.

Buddy had buried the guns in the garden the night before they came for him. Guns were another thing her father had taught her about. Evie reached back into the bag and began to assemble a second gun, attaching barrel to action, action to stock. Flo didn't give up. "You kill him, and you'll spend your life in jail."

"I'm not going to shoot anybody, and neither is Lulu." Lulu was relieved to hear that, but Flo wasn't worried about Lulu pulling the trigger.

"What are the guns for, then?"

Evie wasn't trying to be funny when she answered, "They're a conversation starter."

"Bullshit." Lulu backed away from the argument and turned on the TV. It was hooked up to the satellite dish on top of the skin-ning shed. CNN was replaying the president mocking a woman who had recently testified on national television about the terror of being pushed into a darkened room by a pair of young men she thought were her friends. Held down on a bed, she heard them laugh as a hand was clamped over her mouth to smother her screams for help. There were more guns in the bag waiting to be assembled.

Flo grabbed Lulu's arm. "You know important people, Lulu! You have money and lawyers. You can go to the FBI. You don't have to do it this way."

The news cut to sound bites of outraged and indignant US senators challenging the veracity of the woman's sworn statement, questioning her memory and motives for waiting so long to name her assailants. What right did a woman have to sully the reputation of a man whose success proved he was beyond suspicion? Lulu turned off the TV.

"Flo, if they don't believe that woman, why the hell would you think they're going to believe us?" Evie stopped oiling the guns and waited for her mother's answer.

Flo turned her back and opened the refrigerator. Evie wasn't expecting her mother to hand her the .22 semiautomatic pistol her father used to stash in the crisper under the celery no one ever ate. It was strangely romantic that after all these years her mother still kept the gun in her husband's favorite hidey-hole. "You might as well take the Ruger."

Evie took the pistol from her mother, pulled out the clip, saw that it was loaded, and handed it back. "Keep it, you might need it before we're through with this."

PART II

PARTS BUT LITTLE KNOWN

CHAPTER 1

W hen I was little I believed my mother could fix anything. My faith
in her ability to make all things right had to do with her profession.
Evie Quimby was a "restaurateur artistique"—a woman whose hands were
trusted enough to repair statues for the Louvre. She could reassemble the
pieces of a dropped figurine I knew I shouldn't have touched with an artistry
that bordered on witchcraft; make the cracks in precious things that had
been mistreated disappear so completely it was easy to pretend no permanent
harm had ever been done. Of course, being the one that hid the cracks, my
mother knew better.

Her studio was in Paris, on Rue Daguerre in a converted garage on the
edge of Montparnasse. We lived above in a gabled attic. When the bell rang
downstairs, a pale yellow pit bull, Clovis, and I would run to the window
and look down and watch museum curators and antiquity dealers nervously
unload the broken remains of goddesses, demons, saints, and forgotten
statesmen, all swaddled in bubble wrap. Her specialty was repairing sculpture, ancient mostly, but once I remember seeing a man in a convertible
Bentley accompanied by the singed remains of a sculpture of Michael Jack-
son that had been struck by lightning.

Sometimes, when the bell rang in the middle of the night, Clovis
growled and we'd spy from the shadows. In the morning, I'd discover a
wooden box the length of a coffin with something beautiful but broken inside
that, depending on your point of view, had either been looted or rescued from
a war zone. Whether the damaged statue was made of marble, bronze, limestone, diorite, granite, ivory, or unfired clay, my mother always began by
laying out the different broken parts of the figure on a steel table as if it were
a person who had just suffered great bodily harm. A pair of lips frozen in the
promise of a smile cleaved from a face, legs torn from a torso, a nymph's

breast smashed to shards—I would sit in the corner with Clovis and watch her pick up the pieces one by one, memorizing the edges with her fingertips as she puzzled out how to make them whole.

Perhaps because she kept so many other parts of her life secret, she was transparent about her work and installed a glass window in the door so I could always see what she was doing. The epoxies and polymers she used were toxic; when it came time to assemble the broken pieces, she shooed the dog and me out of her studio. Turning on the exhaust fans, she'd pump up the volume on Dorothy Dandridge or Amy Winehouse, then pull on black rubber gloves that came up above her elbows and don a rubber gas mask with canisters sticking out from her cheeks. She looked like an alien.

Through that small window into her solitary pursuit, I would watch her slowly add one part epoxy to two parts hardener. If she got the mix wrong, smoke rose as if from a cauldron. If the damage to a piece was severe, she installed the same kind of titanium rods a surgeon uses to pin broken bones. It didn't occur to me until much later that the thing she was really trying to fix was herself.

When asked how she became a restorer, she gave different answers depending on her mood. Once I heard her say, "When I was young I worked for a very rich woman who liked to break beautiful things." Which sounded like the opening line of a scary fairy tale.

My mother was similarly elusive when pressed for specifics about anything having to do with her life before she came to Paris. I knew only that she was adopted as a baby by a couple named Buddy and Flo and grew up in the woods outside what she referred to as a "flyspeck of a village" called Rangeley. Not knowing flyspeck meant fly shit, I asked her if it was "nice." She answered with a smile and a hug and told me stories about the Adirondacks: lakes and waterfalls with Indian names, forests carpeted with wild orchids called lady's slippers, black bears with a taste for blueberries, and a pet crow named Jimmy.

I pestered her to tell me more about this remote paradise I pronounced "Rang-e-lee"; demanded to know why Buddy and Flo never came to visit like my friends' grandparents. And why, on those rare occasions when my grandmother Flo called, was Grandpa Buddy never with her? And why did my grandfather always ring up on a pay phone? I can still hear the clatter and clink of quarters going into the box every three minutes. My mother told me her parents didn't have much money.

When I volunteered to forgo my allowance and all my Christmas presents so we could buy them tickets to come see us, my mother added that her parents didn't like cities. When I refused to let it go, she grew exasperated and told me that even though they'd never been to France, my grandparents didn't like French people.

Unable to stifle my enthusiasm for the Rangeley of my imagination, she finally gave up and bought me an old water-stained map of the Adirondacks she found in a flea market and we hung it on my bedroom wall. It was printed in 1757 during the French and Indian War, and what I liked most about it was that it was all out of proportion and full of inaccuracies. Lakes and rivers and towns were in the wrong latitudes. Mohawks was spelled "Mohoks." And there were villages and forts that had vanished so completely they could not be found on Wikipedia.

I have a faint memory of her tucking me into bed one night and seeing her point to a blank spot on the map labeled "Parts but little known," and hearing her say, "That's me, Chloé." But perhaps she only said that in a dream.

I lost interest in meeting my grandparents or Jimmy the crow or ever setting foot in the Parts but little known when my mother let it slip that my grandparents trapped and skinned animals for a living. But by then, Buddy and Flo had stopped calling.

When it came to questions I had about her life after she arrived in Paris, my mother was more forthcoming. She came to France in November 2001 to work for an art restorer named Jacques Clément. At the end of a dinner party in the Adirondacks three months earlier, Jacques had written his name and telephone number on the back of a matchbook and had offered her a job in Paris. All she knew about the man was that he was renowned for being able to salvage beautiful things others thought were beyond repair.

It must have been weird. My mother was seventeen years old and unable to speak a word of French when she knocked on his studio door. Jacques Clément was forty-one and had no memory of ever offering her a job. She

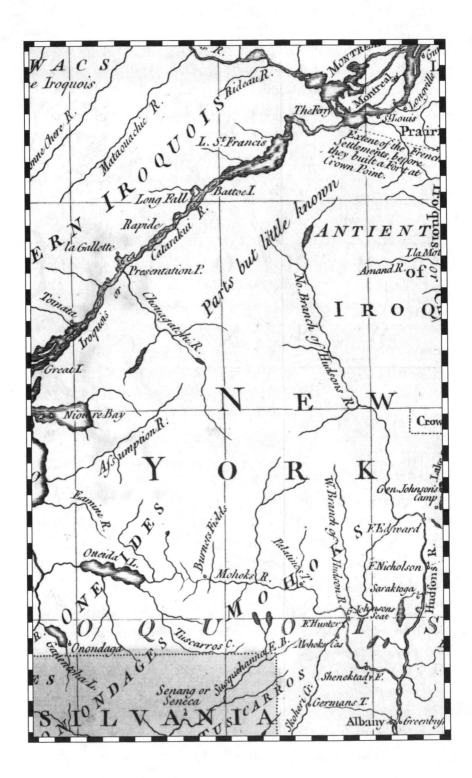

started out as his unpaid assistant and slept on the couch. A month later she moved into his bedroom. A year later she was his wife. His name is still next to hers on the brass plaque attached to the studio door.

She told me that at first the marriage was just a way for her to work legally in France. When it became more than that, she was warned that Jacques Clément was a notorious womanizer, a hound of the worst sort, and not to take any of his promises seriously. My mother laughed when she told me all the awful things she heard about my father. It was said, when it came to his tastes in women, my father's attitude was, "If it walks . . ." As it turned out, except for the time he fed her an oyster that gave her hepatitis, my father surprised her and everybody else by turning out to be loyal, loving, and devoted . . . until he deserted us.

I was six months old when he was run over while bicycling to meet us at the flower market. Except for that, my mother kept the sad parts of her life story to herself. But I always knew it wasn't easy being her.

Strangers looked twice at my mother when we went out together, especially men. Tall, square-shouldered, she had hair the color of wild honey, even features and a mouth that turned up at the corners as if she were smiling at a private joke. If you were standing to her left, she had the wholesome glamour of a Grace Kelly, but when she turned her face, even people who know it's not polite couldn't resist staring at her.

Like most people, I thought that my mother had retreated into her studio and the world of broken things because of the birthmark she once had on her face—a port-wine stain that unfurled across the right side. More red than purple, the blood vessels were so close to the surface of her skin, it seemed to have its own pulse.

She waited until I was twelve to tell me that she fell in love with my father because he was the only man that ever made her feel beautiful. That was the year she had her birthmark removed with laser surgery. Men eyed her differently after that, seeing a simpler creature than I knew her to be. The trouble was, when she looked in the mirror now, she had trouble recognizing herself. But I didn't know it wasn't just the way people looked at her that made my mother wary of the world.

By the time I was fourteen, like most teenagers, I was more interested in the unfolding mystery of my own life than delving into the shadows of hers. I was creating a past for myself in the ways all young people do. On the night of January 6, 2018, I took off all my clothes and lay down in a narrow bed with a boy who was on my debating team. We didn't go all the way, but I can still feel the warmth of his body in the darkness. When he walked me home in the rain that night, he told me he'd been in love with me since Christmas. The next morning, I woke up with a cold that wouldn't go away. Ten days later, we knew that I had acute lymphatic leukemia.

~ ~ ~

A spinal tap gave us the good news—the cancer hadn't spread to my brain. After explaining to me that the chemo would make me infertile, my oncologist asked me, age fourteen years six months, if I wanted to have children; and since I didn't know, we harvested my eggs, which was weird. Then I got an intravenous chemotherapy cocktail of cyclophosphamide and methotrexate. For the next week, all I did was vomit, have diarrhea, and watch my hair fall out. My mother never left the hospital.

Nights were the worst. The meds made it easy to fall asleep, but failed to sedate my recurring nightmare. In the dream that played inside my head, I was already dead, yet somehow alive and trapped next to my corpse in a coffin lined with white silk, unable to escape or do anything other than watch myself rot.

I woke up terrified, gasping for air, drenched in sweat. My mother held me in her arms and told me it was just a bad dream. With an intensity that can only be described as ferocious, she swore to me, "You are not going to die! I promise you we can fix this!"

Because googling "acute lymphatic cancer" had told me 68 percent of girls between the ages of thirteen and nineteen with my "subtype of lymphocyte" survive, and because I was desperate for hope, but most of all because my mother was a restorer and could fix anything, I chose to believe she would find a way to make good on her promise.

Of course, I had moments of doubt. Once when my nightmare jerked me awake, as she helped me into dry pajamas, I told her, "Just in case I don't *get better I want you to know if I find out there's something after all this, I'll send you a message."*

My mother shook her head no and repeated her mantra, "You are not going to die." But I could tell she had her doubts, too, when, a few heartbeats later, she asked me, "What kind of message?"

"Email." She thought that was funny even though she was crying.

When we got home from the hospital, I started to feel better. I was hungry again. My hair was growing back and my white blood cell count was normal two blood tests in a row. April 1, I was officially in remission. And then I wasn't.

The doctors didn't sugarcoat it: the best and only chance I had was an allogeneic stem cell transplant, a.k.a. a bone marrow transplant. If we could find someone whose HLA—human leukocyte antigens—were compatible with mine and was willing to have a needle stuck in their pelvic bone and give me a couple hundred milliliters of their healthy marrow, we might be able to trick my body into stopping producing the cancerous white blood cells that were killing me. The HLA tests showed my mother's marrow would have worked, but the oyster that had given her hepatitis C ruled her out. The virus lingering in her blood would kill me before her marrow could save me.

My oncologist took her into his office to tell her my HLA was difficult to match. The chances of finding a compatible donor who was not a blood relative were one in one thousand. My late father was an only child and his parents were dead. My mother was adopted, had no idea who her birth parents were, and no desperate desire to find out until now.

For the next forty-eight hours I could hear her in the hall outside my hospital room on her cell phone. My mother's adoption records were sealed, and according to New York State law, even in a case when a fourteen-year-old girl needs a bone marrow transplant, they could not be unsealed without a court order. And even then the names of my mother's birth parents could not be released unless they had already registered in writing that they did not object to being contacted, which was a legal process guaranteed to take longer than my oncology team said I had to live.

My mother inundated every New York State official she could think *of with calls and emails begging for help. What she needed was a miracle. If I had known what it meant to be Buddy Quimby's daughter, I wouldn't have been surprised that when she found out the originals of her adoption records were stored in the Townsend County courthouse, she cold-called the town clerk and offered him a $10,000 cash bribe to unseal her records. When he said, "That would be against the law," she jumped her offer to $50K. My mother had no idea where she would get that kind of money, but the silence on the other end of the line was promising, "Believe me, ma'am, I'd like to help you out here, but when the Mink River flooded our basement last spring, the Sheriff's Department loaded all our records up and dumped them in the town hall in Rangeley." My mother asked for the name of the sheriff. She got her miracle.*

When my mother came into my hospital room that afternoon to tell me she was taking me to the Adirondacks, I was still too groggy to make sense of what she saying. America? Rangeley? Next week? She said she had to leave me alone for a few hours and would be back after she saw a woman at the US consulate about speeding up the renewal of my passport and the forms we'd need to take my medications through customs. All I could think to say before I nodded off was, "So I guess I'm going to meet Jimmy the crow after all. . . ."

I don't know how long I slept, but when I woke up, I was startled to see an elegantly dressed man in a chalk-stripe blue suit with a rosebud in his lapel standing at the foot of my bed holding the biggest bouquet of flowers I had ever seen. Calla lilies, roses, birds of paradise all wrapped in pink tissue paper and cellophane, bowed with silk ribbon. Friends of my mother's had brought me flowers, but not like these.

The bearer of this unexpected bouquet was in his fifties, American, and fit. Most of all what I recall was the way he just stood there, unnaturally still, smiling at something I couldn't see. He introduced himself. I was still trying to figure out if he was part of a dream. By the time the nurse came in and put the flowers in a vase, I knew he was real. His voice was boyish, and his manner had a courtly bashfulness that pulled me in as he said, "Your mother and I are old friends. I heard you weren't feeling well and I wanted to stop by, see how you're doing."

"Yeah, I've been sick for a while." I didn't like to say the C-word out loud.

I was surprised when he took hold of my hand in his and sighed, "You're as lovely as she was, at your age." He said a few more words, but nothing that seemed important at the time. Then he was gone.

When my mother got back to my room that night, I could tell she was nervous. Slipping into my hospital bed, she wrapped her arms around me. "There's some things you need to know about me before we go back to Rangeley." I was only half listening until she said, "When I was seventeen, I walked into the woods and shot a man."

"What do you mean?" I wasn't sure I'd heard her right.

My mother's voice caught as she told me, "It was a hunting accident."

"Why are you telling me this now?"

"I didn't want you to hear it from someone else. Rangeley's a small town."

"Did he die?"

"No."

I was shocked, but not as much as you might expect. Cancer has a way of putting the unexpected into perspective. I thought my mother's confession solved the mystery of her reluctance to talk about her past. She didn't notice the flowers until then.

"Who sent the bouquet?"

"A friend of yours brought them. He said his name was Scout."

I never suspected that as soon as I fell asleep that evening, she eased herself out of my hospital bed, slipped on her shoes, and took the elevator down to the first floor. My mother waited until she was out on the street to scream.

CHAPTER 2

The people coming in and out of the block-long medical center on Rue du Faubourg Saint-Jacques on that balmy spring night stopped and stared. Somebody shouted, "As-tu besoin d'aide?" Do you need help? When the security guard at the hospital entrance heard her cry out, he thought a woman was being attacked. He wasn't far off. Evie's scream was a howl of rage spiked with pure panic. The sound of it shocked her. Having spent her girlhood working traplines that ran the length of Townsend County, she recognized it as the wail of a creature that has just discovered it's caught in something that's never going to let go.

The security guard ran toward her, calling out, "Est-ce que tu vas bien?"

She wasn't remotely all right, but it was too complicated to explain. When the guard came out and asked what had happened, all Evie could think to say was, "I'm not sure." And that was what scared her the most. She had no idea why after seventeen years of complete silence, no contact of any kind, Scout had suddenly appeared at the foot of her daughter's hospital bed with a bouquet from the most expensive florist in Paris. The possibility that at that moment he might be standing in the shadows watching her was all that kept her from screaming again.

Why now? What did he want? How had he found out Chloé was sick? Known which hospital to go to? What if he waited for her to leave for the night so he could come back to Chloé's room and . . . Evie began to run. The guard shouted after her, "Qu'est ce qu'il se passe?" Evie had no time to translate her dread into French.

Darting through the electric doors, ignoring security's request for photo ID, she cursed the elevator for stopping at every floor. Evie ran through the oncology ward at a sprint. The night nurse looked up from her desk.

Evie threw open the door to her daughter's room but found only a painfully thin teenage girl dewy with night sweat, who would be dead in a few months if her mother didn't find a way to keep her alive. The worst is always relative.

Evie spent that night on two chairs pushed together in the corner. As moonlight fell through the curtains and shadows danced across the wall, she kept herself awake watching Chloé breathe. The next morning Evie said nothing about Scout. Chloé had enough to worry about without knowing cancer wasn't the only monster knocking on their door.

Slipping out of the room, Evie hurried downstairs and checked the hospital's visitors' log. She had assumed Scout had snuck into the building, or given a false name. That he had signed in as himself was more frightening. Providing both his NYC address and his Paris hotel, it was almost as if he dared her to make contact. In the box marked "relationship to patient," Scout had written "old family friend."

It all made a sick kind of sense. Like a magician that distracts you with a flourish of a handkerchief, Scout had always hidden his malevolence with calculated gestures. His visit was both a threat and a reminder that she and her daughter were at his mercy—but why now?

When Chloé was first diagnosed, Evie googled everything having to do with acute lymphatic leukemia. Now she typed Scout's name into her search box. This was a malignancy that walked on its hind legs. Ninety-three pages of items appeared, and she scrolled through the minutiae. Parents' names, the educational institutions he attended, jobs he had held, and the many awards he'd been granted. Of course, the life on the computer screen bore no resemblance to what she knew him to be. Most of the items were drawn from the financial pages of the *New York Times*, the *Wall Street Journal*; magazines, blogs, and servers related to the world of money, acquisitions, and the liquidation of assets. There were more references to involvement in philanthropic organizations and worthy charitable causes than Evie would have expected, but nothing that gave a clue to why he had stepped back into her life.

For Evie to understand why Scout had suddenly felt the urge to remind her of his existence, she would have had to know about events that happened before she was even born. One in particular that was not listed on Scout's résumé.

CHAPTER 3

Scout landed in New York City in the summer of '82, lean, neat, and twenty-one years old. Erect and watchful as a hungry egret, he belonged to what was then the almost exclusively white male subspecies of American go-getter that flocked to Wall Street every June to apprentice in the dark arts of turning others' losses into personal gain.

At White Stone Trust they were called "summer analysts"—which meant Scout was one of twenty glorified interns, all of whom were overachieving rising seniors from the most selective universities in the country. White Stone was an institution that had a reputation on the Street for only being interested in "the best of the best." At the end of their eight-week summer audition, nineteen of the twenty would be told, "Thanks, but no thanks," and one very lucky bastard would be informed he had a six-figure job and a golden future awaiting him when he graduated.

On his first day, Scout passed through the revolving brass door of the White Stone Trust building on the corner of Wall Street and Broad an hour before the candidates were instructed to arrive. Sporting a seersucker suit as crisp, clean, and unwrinkled as a freshly made bed in a five-star hotel, he introduced himself by asking, "What can I do to be useful?" He was only five foot ten, but seemed taller. He had hair the color of butterscotch, and the rosiness of his cheeks made him appear more boyish and wholesome than he was. More than a few of his fellow summer analysts teased him about his nickname, and several younger members of the all-female secretarial pool made flirtatious inquiries as to its origin. But he saved that tale for Alice, the Brit expat office manager with a caustic, matronly manner. It was a curious choice of confidant given that Alice had greeted the summer analysts by announcing, "I am not your friend. Any attempts to ingratiate yourself or curry favor with me will be reported to my superiors." But that was just the point—for how he came to be called Scout was the kind of story you wanted repeated behind your back.

As he told it to Alice while staying late to fix the Xerox machine for her, he was raised in the woods of Michigan's Upper Peninsula by a single mom who was both a Lutheran minister and legally blind. The winter he turned seven, while walking home after ice-skating on a frozen pond in the forest, they disagreed over which trail to take. Dutifully listening to his mother, he let her lead him down the wrong path. By the time it was dark they were hopelessly lost. Then Mother tripped and fell. Ankle broken, she could walk no further.

When it began to snow, he was forced to choose between staying with her in the hope that their prayers would be answered and setting off into the darkness by himself. He made sure Alice understood that leaving his mother behind was the hardest decision he ever had to make. When he finally led the state police back to her four and a half hours later, he was dubbed "Scout."

Alice didn't believe the story, but having worked at White Stone Trust for nearly twenty years, she recognized that someone capable of such shameless self-promotion just might be her boss in a year. She passed Scout's sad story on to the senior male executives of the firm as if it were gospel. It was part of the truth about Scout, it just wasn't the whole story.

The first months of Scout's life were remarkably normal considering that his father, a doctoral candidate at a large midwestern university writing his dissertation on Foucault, had abandoned his mother in the eighth month of her pregnancy and run off to Brazil with a visiting poetry professor named Inês shortly after emptying his wife's bank account.

It was around the time of his first birthday that his mother made the decision that would alter Scout's life. In search of a higher purpose, she enrolled in the Wisconsin Lutheran Seminary in Mequon five hours downstate. Monday through Friday, her son was cared for by his maternal grandmother in the Upper Peninsula town of Marquette. If Scout hadn't had the same eyes as his father, pale and watery gray like something that lives in a shell, it might have gone differently for the child. As it was, every time his grandmother looked at him, she saw the bastard who had left her daughter pregnant, penniless, and brokenhearted. She kept the boy clean and fed but avoided touching him more than was absolutely necessary. When he cried, she closed the door to the spare room and turned up the TV. Scout's mother had no idea Granny was in the early stages of Alzheimer's.

When his mother came home on weekends, she tried to make up for the lost time with her "little man." Suddenly there was so much pampering, hugging, and tickling he felt like the mice that lived under the stove had crawled up into his clothes.

Her sudden closeness made it hard to breathe. Forty-eight hours of too-much followed by five days of not-enough; his inability to control the women in his young life filled him with such outrage and humiliation it hollowed out a void inside himself that he filled with dreams of omnipotence. As he got older and the prison of the crib turned into solitary confinement in the spare room, he would pick a scab until it bled to remind himself he was real.

It was shortly after she was ordained and they had moved into a small parish on the shore of Lake Superior that his mother stood at the kitchen stove scalding milk for cocoa. Stirring in the dark chocolate, she told her son, age five, to wait and let it cool. Eager for the bittersweet taste on his tongue, he took a sip, burned his mouth, and began to weep. When his mother chided, "That's what you get for being greedy," he threw the cup of cocoa in her eyes.

Infection followed. The child had not meant to blind her, of course, but by then remorse did not come naturally to him. He quickly noticed that now that his mother could not see him, he could do no wrong in her eyes. It seemed to Scout his mother was happier blind, but he kept that thought to himself.

In the long winter of his youth, he focused on schoolwork and hockey. Blessed with a slap shot as monstrous as his id, he never failed to credit the team and Jesus Christ when the sports reporters from the local papers interviewed him about his uncanny ability to score goals. More than a few headlines in the Upper Peninsula read, SCOUT TO THE RESCUE.

From Scout's curriculum vitae, all White Stone Trust knew about the young man was he had spent twelfth grade at a boarding school in Massachusetts that had educated presidents and valued hockey, and that he had been admitted early decision to an Ivy League university, both on a full scholarship. He had a 3.9 grade point average with a major in economics and a minor in classics, scored enough goals to be scouted by the pros, and found time for amateur theatrics.

He applied for summer internships at a number of financial institutions. Morgan, First Boston, Kuhn Loeb, Goldman Sachs, White Stone, Dillon Read, among others. All of them would have wanted Scout on their team were it not for an "incident" that occurred during spring break of that junior year in college.

He had begun dating the drama major who directed him in *The Tempest*, unwittingly typecasting him as Caliban. She thought he was a sensitive soul because he could cry on cue. Scout was decidedly more conservative, at least in appearance, than her previous beaus.

With her parents' knowledge and blessing, she had invited Scout to spend an off-season romantic week, just the two of them, at her family's summer cottage on an island off the coast of Maine. Three cozy days into the holiday, she had called her parents to say she was having a wonderful time. Scout would later remember overhearing her tell her mother, "He's the one, Mom." But the next day her parents got a very different kind of call from their daughter: tears verging on hysteria. She had taken the ferry back to the mainland by herself and was in a phone booth. Too upset and embarrassed to get into specifics, she told her father she had passed out and Scout had done things to her.

Her outraged father, being a lawyer, told her to call the police and flew up and joined her. The police took note of the fact that she had been having consensual sex with Scout for several months prior to the incident. Her medical exam showed no bruising or physical indications of rape, though the doctor did comment that her pubic hair had been recently shaved. Not that that precluded sexual assault, it just made the men, and curiously the one female member of that small-town constabulary, inclined to believe she had gotten what she had asked for.

Since it happened out of state and no criminal charges were filed, the incident would have gone away if the girl's father hadn't been a tenured professor at the university's esteemed law school. The president of the university was called; disciplinary committee notified. Because there were no corroborating witnesses and the incident boiled down to "he said/she said," Scout's record remained blemish-free, but a nasty residue of salacious rumor lingered around his name.

Unable to get justice for his daughter, the father/law professor contacted every one of the financial firms Scout had interviewed with. One by one the rejection letters appeared in Scout's mailbox. No one was more surprised than Scout when White Stone accepted him into their summer analyst program—except, of course, for the poor girl's outraged father, who had written a letter detailing the sexual assault for the benefit of a senior managing director at White Stone by the name of Moran.

Once Scout got to New York, he had every reason to think his troubles were behind him. But that first week on the job, more than once when he looked up from his desk he saw Porter Moran, the grand wizard of the Private Wealth department, staring at him just the same way people back in the Upper Peninsula would scrutinize a fox that showed signs of being rabid.

Moran, as a partner and head of Private Wealth, operated in a different universe than most investment bankers. His clients weren't publicly held companies; they were private individuals with a net worth of $250 million at the very least. Porter's specialty was handling multigenerational wealth—families whose collective assets pushed the billion mark, which was a lot of money in 1982.

He was a big man in his fifties, partial to double-breasted vests and peaked lapels; six foot three, two hundred and fifty pounds at least, but surprisingly light on his feet. He moved with a grace that brought to mind both John Wayne and Jackie Gleason. A lifetime of wining and dining rich clients had left him puffy, but beneath all that muscle marbled with fat, it was obvious that once upon a time Porter had been a very handsome man.

Some of the families who were clients of Porter had recognizable brand names seen on the shelves of supermarkets and drugstores; others you would never have heard of. Often they were intermarried. The real dividend from the Private Wealth department came from the stockpile of connections and assets these families had banked over the years, and which Porter could, at auspicious moments, draw upon and leverage to give White Stone an edge.

It wasn't anything Porter Moran said to Scout—in fact, they had never exchanged a word—it was the way the rainmaker for Private Wealth eyeballed him that worried Scout. Two weeks into the job, Scout was convinced that Porter Moran had already decided his talents were superfluous.

Finishing work just after 9 p.m. on the last Wednesday in June, Scout ducked into a deserted men's room on the fifth floor before heading to the night elevator. As he aimed at the piss biscuit, Scout's brain was railing at the unfairness of the shadow that incident with the girl over spring break had cast over his future. He hadn't hurt her. He'd simply borrowed her body for a few hours. Done things he'd been thinking about doing since they first met. What galled him most was that he probably could have talked her into it, but she would have asked why and he knew his answer would have bothered her. Sharing the experience would have spoiled it.

Suddenly, out of nowhere, Porter Moran stepped up to the urinal next to him. The fly of Porter's trousers had buttons rather than a zipper. The big man waited until he had his stream going. "So what really happened with the girl? . . . And don't bullshit me."

Dick in hand, Scout summarized the incident in three short sentences with the clinical precision of a veterinarian. Then added, "She was passed out. I had some fun of my own with her. No permanent damage."

Porter shook himself and flushed. "Boys will be boys . . . no harm, no foul." More unexpected, as they washed their hands at adjoining sinks, Porter inquired gruffly, "You have a dinner jacket?"

"Yes." He didn't, of course.

"It's my niece's birthday tomorrow. There's a party for her at the Carlyle. It starts at seven p.m. See you there."

"Thank you . . . sounds great!"

As he headed toward the door, Porter added, "One more thing. Don't mention this to any of the others. You're the only one I invited."

"I understand."

"You don't, but that's okay for now."

Having rented a tuxedo, Scout paused to admire his reflection in store windows as he walked up Madison Avenue; he liked what he saw. He stepped into the Carlyle at 7:15 p.m. expecting to be shown to a table for ten or twelve at the restaurant. Instead, he was directed upstairs to a gilded ballroom, where a hundred and fifty people had gathered. Two-thirds of the mob were in their twenties; the rest were their parents' and grandparents' age. And although he didn't know a soul, he knew they all had one thing in common.

When Scout finally caught a glimpse of Moran across the room, he was hobnobbing with a group that included names he recognized from the headlines of that morning's *Wall Street Journal*. When their eyes met, though, he had no acknowledgment from Porter other than a glance that said *Not now*. Scout retreated to the bar. He was wondering why Porter had invited him when the big man stepped over to him. "I didn't bring you here to drink."

"It's Coca-Cola."

"You see that girl over there?" Porter nodded to a blond woman in her early twenties sitting on a banquet with two girlfriends, laughing and smoking cigarettes. "Her father's the third-richest man in Palm Beach."

"Lucky her. Are you going to introduce me?"

"We're in the business of making believers of people who don't know shit about us."

"So you want me to go over and talk to her?"

"No, I want you to go over and make her think you're a scholar and a gentleman. Show me I'm right about you." The last part was what his hockey coach had said before the start of his first varsity game. Scout focused on the goal.

Moving close enough to the girls to eavesdrop but not to appear to be lurking, he overheard just enough to ascertain that they had been roommates at Brown, spent the previous weekend at Maidstone, and that after the party they were going to Area. He didn't know Maidstone was a private golf and tennis club on the beach in East Hampton or that Area at that moment was the hippest nightclub on the planet, but he did pick up that one was named Priscilla and the one he'd been told to impress had played the part of Miranda in a summer Shakespeare workshop in the Berkshires.

"Can I possibly bum a cigarette from one of you ladies?" He didn't smoke, but they didn't know that. It was as good an excuse as any to push his butterscotch hair out of his eyes, lean in, and give the bashful grin that made women feel special and safe.

He took a Marlboro, accepted a light, and was about to turn away when he exclaimed with truthless enthusiasm, "You know, I think we've met . . . you went to Brown, right? You're Priscilla." Everyone likes to be remembered.

Scout was swimming in known waters now. He asked them questions about themselves, but more importantly he listened to their answers as if he had been waiting his whole life to hear what they thought. Because Scout had gone to the right schools, looked smart in a tuxedo, and most of all because somebody had invited him to the party, the three young women on the banquet assumed he was a nice guy.

In less than a minute he had them talking about college as if they were old friends. When Scout got around to introducing himself, he gave them the name he was burdened with at baptism and didn't mention hockey just in case one of them had heard a rumor about the hockey player named Scout and the girl who had woken up shaved.

When they started talking about hotels in Europe Scout had never heard of, much less stayed in, he volunteered a self-deprecating story about waking up in the middle of the night at a hotel in Venice. Curtains drawn, total darkness, and suffering from jet lag, he opened the door to what he thought was the bathroom, only to have it close behind him, and discover he was locked out in the hall naked. Worse, he had to wrap a doormat around himself to go down to the lobby for a spare key and, being less than fluent in Italian, asked for a spare sock. He had heard the story from a fraternity brother.

It had the desired effect. He was sitting on the banquette with them now, leaning ever so gently into the daughter of the third-richest man in Palm Beach.

Moran watched and liked what he saw. Most men Scout's age would have been distracted by the physical proximity of so much femininity, but Moran perceived that Scout's only interest was to please him. The girl had her arm around Scout's shoulder now. She was flirting; Scout simply demonstrating his ability to turn himself on like a heat lamp.

Moran moved closer. A passing waiter dropped a tray of champagne glasses. Moran didn't get it when Scout stage-whispered in an English accent, "Be not afeard, the isle is full of noises—"

"That's Caliban! I just played Miranda at summer stock."

One of the others asked, "So you're an actor?"

Scout smiled shyly. "Sort of . . . I'm a summer analyst at White Stone Trust."

The daughter of the third-richest man in Palm Beach put her

tanned arms around his neck, pulled him close, and said, "You're a funny guy." The kiss she planted on his cheek left a lipstick mark. As Scout proudly wiped it away with his handkerchief, he was disappointed to see Porter Moran had stopped watching.

It wasn't until the end of the evening when they brought out the birthday cake that he found out that the pretty girl he was ordered to charm was Porter's niece and that her father was already a client. Scout wasn't sure what to think. It was a test, but of what?

There were other invitations after that, always offered at the last minute and never discussed or acknowledged at the office. A charity benefit for a museum where the price of a table was a six-figure donation; a golf scramble at a club that had thirty-six holes; a member-guest tennis tournament played on grass. Usually there were other people his age in attendance, but not always. Business was never discussed and Porter rarely bothered to introduce him. Scout was left to fend for himself. Porter watched.

~ ~ ~

Moran waited until the last week of August to invite Scout to stop by his home after work and talk about his "future." It was an insufferably hot and humid evening. The city smelled like a clogged drain but the light was golden. At least that's how it seemed to Scout.

He got off the subway at 72nd and Lex and walked up and over to a thirty-foot-wide Beaux Arts mansion, slightly grander than the consulate across the street. When he saw a single buzzer at the door, he realized that Moran occupied the whole house. When the bell rang, dogs barked. A pair of German short-haired pointers sniffed Scout's crotch as Moran shook his hand.

Down a hallway checkerboarded in black and white marble, Moran led him into a living room featuring walnut paneling that had once graced the walls of a seventeenth-century château. When Scout looked up he saw uncircumcised putti and naked nymphs carved into the cornices. Porter plopped into a gilt armchair; Scout sat on the couch and waited for the rainmaker to speak.

"Want a drink?"

"Coke would be great."

"That's right, Scout doesn't drink. Commendable. Of course, I have to warn you, in this business, you'll run into clients who won't trust you if you don't imbibe . . . in moderation of course."

"In that case, I'll have what you're having."

"That's the spirit. While I make us a daiquiri, look around."

Scout was drawn to a painting that was six feet tall and depicted a pair of raw and fleshy not-quite-human forms engaged in an intimacy that looked painful. Scout had never seen a Francis Bacon before. He was still trying to figure out who was being fucked by whom when Moran reappeared with the daiquiris. Scout hadn't had a real drink since the incident. Alcohol hadn't played a part in what happened, he just knew that people would be more inclined to believe his side of the story if they thought he was a teetotaler. Moran watched Scout's eyes try to disentangle the snarl of body parts in the painting.

"You remind me of me."

Scout saw no similarity between himself and the bloated rain-maker, nor did he want to, but said, "I'm flattered."

"I bought this house when I was twenty-seven years old." Porter sipped thoughtfully, giving Scout time to absorb the magnitude of that accomplishment.

"That's impressive." Scout said what he thought Porter wanted to hear.

"Want to know the secret of how I pulled it off?"

"Got to admit, I'm curious."

"I married a very rich girl." It wasn't what Scout expected him to say. Porter gestured to a silver-framed photograph on the mantel of an attractive woman with a widow's peak who looked to be around twenty-five. Next to it were photographs of a pair of teenagers who had the same hairline. Their children, no doubt.

"Your wife's beautiful. You're a lucky man."

Moran nodded in agreement. "Of course, being married to a rich woman isn't as easy as people like to think. It's hard work . . . a job in and of itself. Truth is, not every man is suited to the challenge of marrying up. Requires special talents to make it work for you. To see, as they say, the big picture." Moran drained his glass. "Though there is one thing that makes tying the knot to money easier than your average ball-and-chain marriage . . . no one ever feels sorry for a rich girl, especially if she's pretty."

Moran gave the photograph of his wife a sympathetic smile. "It's not fair or right, just the way it is. Trust me, it's the only prejudice nobody will ever fault you for." Moran was telling him something, but he wasn't sure what.

"Is your wife here in town?" He couldn't think of anything else to say.

"Sadly she passed away a few years ago. Cirrhosis of the liver. Drink got to her. She tried to fight it but . . . sad, in the beginning she was a fun drunk." For several minutes, the only sound in the room was Moran thoughtfully crunching ice cubes. Then the big man opened a humidor and lit a cigar. "So, Scout. You want to come on board?"

Porter handed him two contracts. The first was White Stone's standard employment agreement. The second was a twenty-four-page contract on Porter Moran's personal letterhead that featured a draconian confidentiality clause. "When you graduate next June, you'll come to White Stone as a junior associate directly under my supervision. To give the illusion that you are more solvent than I know you to be, I'll arrange a $250K loan, interest-free, payable in twenty-five years or on demand."

"A loan from White Stone Trust?"

· "It'll come from a foreign bank. This is a separate arrangement, just between you and me. White Stone's not involved nor privy to our agreement."

Scout's eyes darted across the pages of the second contract. The wording was unusual, the services required vague. "What do I have to do?"

"For the moment, nothing. In a year or two we'll talk about it.

Live up to your potential and we'll pick up the tab for an MBA or law school. I suggest both."

"Why?"

"To make you more useful to me and the men who will become your friends."

Scout started to sign the contracts, then paused.

"Under one condition."

Porter looked at him like something dirty stuck to the bottom of his shoe. "This isn't negotiable."

Scout smiled. "Everything's negotiable, but I don't think you'll have a problem with this . . . I don't want to be called Scout anymore."

"Fair enough."

After Scout signed the contract, they talked about fly-fishing. It had been done this way for a long time, and there were reasons.

CHAPTER 4

I got out of the hospital thirty-six hours after Scout brought me the flowers. Before giving the final okay for me to fly to America, my oncologist insisted that we spend the next five days at our apartment in Paris to make sure my body could handle the new meds I was on. Chemo had made me so radioactive, the head nurse told me not to share a toilet with anyone who might be pregnant and alerted us to the possibility that when I passed through the airport security scanner I might be mistaken for a dirty bomb.

After thirteen days in the oncology ward, I had hoped coming home would make me feel more normal. But like I said, I was radioactive and knew it.

Though I had spent my entire life in the cozy attic apartment above my mother's studio, when I came back from the hospital, home felt like a haunted house and I was the ghost.

The familiar spooked me. Sitting on the swing my mother had hung from the rafters in our living room when I was little; gazing up through the skylight she had cut into the roof above my bed so I could fall asleep looking at the stars: all that had made my life special suddenly reminded me of how much I would be leaving behind, how much I wished I had been more appreciative of it all when I was well.

Trying not to surrender to morbid thoughts, I searched Netflix in the hope of finding a feel-good movie my mother and I could watch under the covers of her bed. It's harder than you think to find a movie where the girl isn't murdered or tortured or dies young.

It was broad daylight, but I could feel nightmare sweat coming out of me. Desperate to distract myself from thinking about the future, I pulled my mother into my bad dream by asking about the darkness in her life.

"What was the name of the man you shot?"

My mother nervously began to water dead houseplants. "His name wouldn't mean anything to you. It's not important."

"What if we run into him when we go to Rangeley?"

"He doesn't live in Rangeley. You don't have to worry about him."

"I'm not worried. Just curious."

"Can we talk about something else, Chloé?"

"What did it feel like?"

"What did what feel like?"

"Shooting a person? I mean, did you freak out when you saw the blood?" Like I said, I wasn't feeling normal.

I thought my mother was trying to change the subject of the conversation to a pleasanter topic when she asked me, "Did the man who brought you those flowers say anything about me?"

CHAPTER 5

Evie tried to make her question sound more casual than it was. Chloé was bent over her phone, and impatience crept into her mother's voice. "Can you stop for a minute and answer me? What did Scout say exactly?"

"How am I supposed to remember?" The text was from the boy on the debating team. Everybody at school knew she had leukemia by then.

"You talked to him. . . . Think." Evie saw Chloé wince as she put in her earbuds. The doctor had warned the bone ache would get worse.

"I wasn't paying attention." As Chloé texted back heart emojis, she thought about how urgent and slightly scary the boy's nakedness had felt in the dark.

Evie unbudded her daughter's right ear. "Try to remember." Evie's voice had an edge to it. Chloé heard it.

"Why is it suddenly so important?"

"It's not important. I was just wondering what Scout had to say for himself. We haven't seen each other in a long time. Does he still need a cane to get around?"

"Didn't notice."

"How did he seem?"

Chloé sensed her mother was hiding something. "Were you and Scout lovers?"

"Christ no!" Evie felt like she'd been kicked in the stomach. "Why the hell would you think that?"

"Because your face is turning red, and the way he said it."

"Said what?"

Chloé was a good mimic. Her voice captured just the right note of ersatz sincerity. "'Tell your mother I miss her in ways she can't imagine.' Trust me, he definitely has a thing for you."

Evie felt her throat closing. "Did he say anything else?"

"Something like . . ." Chloé sounded just like him when she mimicked, "'Let your mother know I'll be checking in.' Don't worry, you'll hear from him."

Having to hide both terror and rage left Evie feeling scorched and blistered; the kind of raw there is no salve for. As she started dinner, Evie turned Scout's words to Chloé over and over, hoping to shake loose some clue to his intent. In truth, she had no evidence that would indicate anything more than casual sadism on Scout's part. But having grown up in the forest, she knew a predator roamed far afield when its needs weren't met in the usual hunting ground.

She prepared Chloé's favorite meal that night, *poulet à la fermière*. Jacques had taught her how to braise the chicken in shallots and white wine and then add a splash of cream. Usually while she cooked, Evie could hear her husband whispering in her ear in French. "More butter . . . don't forget the tarragon." But tonight, it was Scout inside her head: *I'll be checking in.*

At dinner, Chloé took two bites of the *poulet* and pushed her plate away. "I'm sorry, Mom, it's really delicious, but I feel like I might vomit."

After the meds knocked Chloé out for the night, Evie stood alone in the living room staring down at the darkness of the empty street below. Her daughter's cancer wasn't her fault, but Scout was.

Part of Evie wished her monster would step out of the shadows, come to the door, and tell her what the fuck he wanted. Another part of her longed for him to ring the bell simply so she could put the muzzle of the shotgun she kept in the bedroom to his head and pull the trigger. It was no idle fantasy. She had told Chloé there was a 12-gauge on top of her clothes closet in case art thieves tried to steal the antiquities entrusted to her care. But the truth was that Evie had been waiting seventeen years for Scout to show up.

Knowing that killing the monster wasn't going to keep her daughter alive, Evie splashed cold water on her face and went down to the studio to rummage for the pack of cigarettes she had hidden when she gave up smoking a year ago. She had promised Chloé she'd quit for good, but she needed something to keep her hands from shaking.

Lighting up and feeling guilty, she opened her laptop and consulted her bank account. She was trying to calculate how much money she could borrow on her credit cards in case the lost relative she was in search of wanted cash in return for their marrow, when an incoming Skype chimed.

Evie accepted it and the lower half of a man's face appeared onscreen—a Dr. Radetzky. Chloé's oncologist had said he'd put them in touch with a doctor in America who could harvest the marrow if they found a relation who was a viable donor, but she thought the timing was strange—11:30 in Paris was 5:30 in the morning in New York. Had he been up all night or started work early? The doctor was rumpled, about forty, and wore a white hospital lab coat. Tired eyes, graying beard, sitting in a cluttered office. His hand reached out to adjust the angle of the camera as if he were trying to touch her.

"I'm Nick Radetzky . . . I was hoping to speak to Evie Quimby." None of Chloé's doctors called her by her maiden name.

"I'm her."

His image flickered, his voice a half-beat behind the movement of his lips. It was as if he were speaking from another galaxy. "I'm sorry, I didn't recognize you . . . you've changed."

"You know me?"

"We spoke briefly once, a long time ago."

"Who are you?" The cigarettes were making her dizzy.

"I'm a psychiatrist. I've been in contact with your mother and she suggested we speak. I'm sorry to ring so late, but when I called you earlier your voicemail was full."

Evie's face brightened. She was thinking one of the emails she fired off must have touched somebody's heart at the Adoption Registry, and their luck had finally turned.

"You know where my mother is?"

The doctor looked puzzled. "She's in Rangeley. At least she was a few days ago. She mentioned that she hadn't spoken to you in a long time." But Flo wasn't the mother Evie needed to find. Radetzky continued, "I was hoping you might be able to answer some questions I had about my brother. We weren't close but I've recently discovered some things that—"

Evie cut him off. "I don't know what my mother told you, but I never met you or your brother and don't have time to—"

It was the doctor's turn to interrupt. "You and your father found my brother's body."

Evie recognized him now. He didn't have a beard seventeen years ago. She remembered he was wearing sneakers and a rumpled black suit. Evie's brain coughed up a memory of a corpse submerged in a swirl of white.

The psychiatrist leaned into the screen. "I know it's been a long time, but I was wondering if over the years you might have remembered something, heard something that could help me understand exactly what happened that night. How he fell? How he drowned? I've spoken to everyone else who was mentioned in the sheriff's report. Except for you and your father."

Evie pulled back from the screen as if she'd been slapped. She felt small hairs on her arms and the back of her neck stiffen and rise. It was as if Scout were in the room breathing on her. The only thing she was certain of was that Scout had surfaced at the foot of her daughter's bed two days ago because he knew she would be getting this call.

Onscreen the pixelated psychiatrist held up a piece of paper close enough for her to make out the letterhead: it was from a bank in Cyprus. He was saying something about his brother getting an interest-free, unsecured loan for $250,000 when he was still a college student. The doctor said, "Who gives a kid who can't qualify for a credit card that kind of money? Any idea?"

"I barely knew your brother. All I know is what everybody else knows. He committed suicide. I'm sorry but—"

"You're sure of that? No doubts whatsoever?"

Evie was drowning in doubts, but not about that. Scout was breathing on her and she wanted him to stop. Her voice turned shrill when she told Dr. Radetzky, "I don't have anything to tell you. Don't call me again." She hit end call. The screen went black, but the memory of the corpse shrouded in white lingered.

Turning her computer back on, she typed a few terms into the search field. She'd forgotten how much newspaper coverage the drowning had received, not at first when everybody said it was a swimming accident, but later when the tabloids got ahold of a photograph of the corpse in the bottom of a boat—Buddy's boat—lying among the smaller mammals they had trapped that day.

In the press, Scout was quoted at length about the tragedy and was entirely accurate in every statement he made. But other than that, Scout had nothing to do with the drowning, not that she knew of. He was three hundred miles away when it happened; had flown up to the lake that morning. She saw him and the other men get out of the seaplane.

By 2 a.m., she had smoked half a pack of stale Marlboros and felt more confused than ever. Her mouth tasted like an ashtray and she was ready to call it a night. Scrolling back through what the Internet knew about Scout one last time to see if she had missed anything, an article Scout had penned in an obscure fly-fishing periodical back in the nineties caught her eye. She wouldn't have bothered opening it if the title hadn't pissed her off.

"A Bachelor Party on the Mink River." Evie had always thought of the Mink as her river. Though she had far more serious problems, it galled her to see Scout's name attached to the legendary trout stream that linked the Sister Lakes. The Mink was where Buddy had first taught her to cast a fly, tutored her in the art of teasing rainbows to the surface and setting the hook. The river was fifty yards wide in some places, a rushing, narrow torrent in others. Hurriedly snaking its way ever downward, it passed through vast tracts of mountainous forests closed off to the public and patrolled by a small army of game wardens.

For over a hundred years the Mannheim family and a private hunting and fishing preserve called the Mohawk Club had held dominion over the best sixty-five thousand acres of Townsend County. Two of the Sister Lakes, twenty-plus miles of the Mink, three entire mountains, and ponds and feeder streams too small to mention on a map were all for their pleasure alone. Evie stopped thinking of all the trout she and her father had stolen from those waters when she read the first line of Scout's article.

"Two weeks before the date of my wedding, I kissed my darling fiancée goodbye and set off with my best man and groomsmen for my last fishing trip as a bachelor." Evie noted the color photograph of Scout, age thirty-five, standing on the riverbank, waders on, fly rod in hand, smiling cavalierly back at the camera as he headed out into the river to join the two other fishermen hip-deep in the current. But she didn't remember ever hearing that Scout had been married. There was no reference to a bride in Scout's bio. Had she gotten out quick with a divorce? Did he purge the marriage from his backstory?

In the photo, the rounded dome of a man-high boulder mid-stream told her the men were fishing a pool Buddy called "Big Baldy." The color of the sky, the dapple of sunlight and shadow on the riffle of the river, and most of all the way one of the fisherman held up two fingers to make the peace sign all felt weirdly déjà-vu familiar.

She knew the place, knew the way that stretch of river felt and smelled and fished. But it was more than that: enlarging the photograph, peering into it with the help of a magnifying glass, Evie was startled to see her own face, age twelve, looking back at her through a tangle of deadfall garlanded with honeysuckle at the edge of the forest.

Scout had his back to her in the photo. In fact, she'd never even seen his face that day—nor did she even meet him until five years later. The eeriness of brushing up against something so dark, as the young girl she'd been at the time—never realizing it—made her wonder what else she had seen but not seen.

The photo was credited to a P. Moran and dated June 27th, 1996. In the text of the article published four months later, Scout described Moran as his "mentor" and "best man." The two younger fishermen standing in the river were to be his groomsmen. The names were meaningless to Evie, but as she stared at the photograph, the shadow in the forest she recognized to be herself summoned memories so visceral and vivid it was as if she were still crouched in that tangle of deadfall and flowering vine.

The precariousness of that moment in time flooded back to her. That stretch of the Mink belonged to the Mohawk Club. If those men had seen her, she and Buddy would have been arrested, charged with trespassing, and worse. She remembered being cold and wet and noticing a silky white poisonous mushroom called a destroying angel sprouted at her feet just before the fishermen appeared. But what struck her most as she studied the barely visible face of the twelve-year-old girl peering back at her was simply that she, unlike grown-up Evie, showed no fear. Back then, Evie still believed the forest belonged to her.

Evie sat alone in her studio in Paris, twenty-two years later, wondering where that fearless Adirondack girl had gone. Missing her, she turned off her computer, closed her eyes, and tried to remember what it used to be like to be Evie Quimby.

G rowing up in Rangeley, Evie lived in a world made up of two
kinds of people—those who felt sorry for her because of her
birthmark and those who pitied her for being adopted by Flo and
Buddy Quimby. Whether you believed the Quimbys to be weird,
feral, dangerous, or simply aging hippies with a fondness for guns
depended on what rumors you believed.

Buddy was a hollow-eyed local boy with a smile known for breaking and entering hearts. He also possessed an unnatural gift for avoiding capture when hunting, fishing, and trapping on private property
posted with signs that guaranteed TRESPASSERS WILL BE PROSECUTED
TO THE FULLEST EXTENT OF THE LAW. Buddy seemed on course to
become, like his father, a park ranger who augmented his income
by cultivating pot in out-of-the-way corners of the six-million-acre
Adirondack State Forest. But just before he turned twenty, Buddy
drove a rusted-out Dodge pickup with mismatched fenders north to a
Grateful Dead concert in Montreal. Though he promised to be home
day after next, no one saw or heard of him again until he appeared out
of nowhere at his father's funeral five years later.

As soon as Buddy pulled up to the cemetery driving a tricked-out
four-wheel-drive AMG silver Mercedes-Benz with California plates
that had recently been rolled, speculation started to swirl. Then Flo
got out of the Benz. The North Country was used to seeing women
who were part-native Mohawk; but Flo's appearance was additionally
striking. Bangled ankles and wrists, perfumed with patchouli, long
sari skirt, pink shawl, people paid attention to Flo even before they
noticed her halter top exposed scars that looked to be the entrance and
exit wounds of a 9-millimeter slug or perhaps a .38.

Flo was good-looking, jet-black hair, skinny and voluptuous all at the same time. Everybody saw the chemistry. In the midst of grave-side conversation with mourners, she interrupted Buddy with a kiss on the mouth, then during the Lord's Prayer she licked the whorl of his ear with the tip of her tongue—unusual behavior for any funeral, but especially in Rangeley. And then there was the fact that she was thirteen years older than Buddy.

When Flo was queried by curious townsfolk about how she and Buddy became a couple, all she offered up was, "We met in a library and fell in love without meaning to." She said it as if being with Buddy was against the rules.

Given that Buddy was the least likely man in the county to set foot in a library, it was generally assumed they were hiding something, especially after Buddy's cousin Billy Dunn helped them move into the old Quimby cabin. According to Billy, Flo had a diploma from Cornell hanging on the wall above the toilet and Buddy had built floor-to-ceiling bookshelves containing 396 books, which for sure didn't belong to Buddy. Cousin Billy also saw an arsenal meant for hunting people, not animals. A laser-scoped Barrett M82 sniper rifle that Buddy bragged could assassinate a deer at two thousand yards was stashed in a broom closet, a .22-caliber Ruger semiautomatic pistol with a silencer chilled in the fridge, and a snub-nosed revolver slept in the ankle holster he wore inside his boot when he left the house.

The dark and nefarious rumors that quickly circulated about what Buddy had been up to during those missing five years ran the gamut. Some claimed Buddy had been a sniper for the CIA in El Salvador. Those who were convinced Flo had been gutshot swore she and Buddy had been millionaire pot farmers in California who had lost everything in a gun battle with the DEA. Buddy neither confirmed nor denied any of it, in part because he liked to keep people guessing, but mostly because he knew the mystery made people think twice before turning him in for infractions of New York State fish and game laws.

By the time Evie was twelve, she had heard all the loose talk about her parents and given up trying to figure out what was true and false. To Evie, the unsolved mystery was why Buddy and Flo had wanted to adopt a baby who looked like her. Flo said, "It just felt right."

But the day P. Moran happened to take a snapshot that offered a glimpse of twelve-year-old Evie and the man destined to bring her so much misery was tattooed into Evie's memory for reasons that had nothing to do with Scout.

Evie was homeschooled by then. She had been de-enrolled from the seventh grade of Townsend County Middle School back in March as the result of an altercation with thirteen-year-old Carl Tillman, son of Mary Lou Tillman, the owner of the gas station and convenience store, also called Mary Lou's, which sold bait, beer, stale bread, and ammunition. Carl had added to the shame of her birthmark by burdening her in first grade with the nickname "Giblet-Face." By the spring of seventh grade, one giblet joke too many from Carl had prompted Evie to kick him with such force he had to have his right testicle removed. Carl was now saddled with the moniker "Scrotum," and "poor little Evie Quimby" was now "Batshit-Crazy Evie."

When Flo announced homeschooling meant she wouldn't be using any of her old schoolbooks, Evie thought she had died and gone to heaven. But as soon as she sat down at the kitchen table for her first lesson, Evie discovered there was another Flo hiding inside her normally ob-la-di, ob-la-da mom; that Flo was the Mohawk girl from the St. Regis Reservation who had won a National Merit Scholarship and possessed a master's degree in French mannerist fiction. Though she was also the woman who had given it all up for a man whose idea of great literature was Clive Cussler, she intended to see her daughter didn't end up the same way.

When they sat down to work that first day, Flo's North Country accent suddenly evaporated. No longer dropping the final *n*'s, *g*'s, and *t*'s of her words, she morphed into someone Evie did not recognize and wasn't sure she liked. That there were at least two people inside of everyone was one of the many things she learned from Flo.

To get a sense of what her daughter did and didn't know both in terms of vocabulary and the possibilities life could throw at a girl, Flo began by handing Evie a copy of *Pride and Prejudice* and told her to open to page one and start reading aloud. Three sentences in, Evie yawned and asked her mother, "When can I stop?"

Flo smiled. "When you get to the last page in the book."

Evie's mother turned fifty-two the year they started *Pride and Prejudice*. Her hair, once as blue-black lustrous as the barrel of a new gun, was now streaked with gray. Because she wore it long, down to the small of her back, and sometimes braided feathers into it, took in stray cats, and gathered weeds, blossoms, and roots she claimed could cure everything from piles to pleurisy, kids in Rangeley had begun to call Flo "the Witch Lady."

Whether Flo could actually cast a spell was a matter of opinion, but her mother's ability to spot a word Evie did not understand the meaning of bordered on the supernatural. Pointing to the dictionary she kept parked next to the salt and pepper shakers, Flo would say, "Let's look that one up."

When Evie whined, "Why don't you just friggin' tell me what it means," Flo got sharp. "Because I won't always be around to explain things to you. And friggin' isn't a fucking word."

Fifty pages into *Pride and Prejudice*, Flo handed her a sheet of lined paper and announced, "I want you to write on one side of the paper what the story makes you think and on the other side tell me what it makes you feel."

"What's the point of that?" To Evie the assignment bordered on cruel and unusual punishment.

"Because if a woman learns to separate what she thinks from how she feels, she has a chance of making the right decision for herself."

The morning of June 27, 1996, would stand out among other mornings in Evie's life because that was the day she and Flo finally got to the last word on the last page of *Pride and Prejudice*; it was the first of the hundred and sixty-eight books they would read together over the next five years. Closing the Penguin Classics edition, they sat in silence for a long minute, solemn as if all the characters in it had just died of the plague. Then Flo asked, "So what do you feel, Evie?"

"I'm happy it had a happy ending, but somehow, tying the story in a bow the way Jane Austen did so everybody who reads it can feel good about men and women and compromising—doesn't seem how it goes in Rangeley. Men get pissed off when women tell them they're wrong, especially when they know they are."

Flo didn't disagree. "And what does that make you think?"

"Well, I guess there are Mr. Darcys out there. But at first he seemed like a total jerk too. After a while I realized he's just uncomfortable around people. Life's taught him to expect the worst. Trust doesn't come natural."

Flo corrected her. "Naturally."

"So to get back to what it makes me think . . . Mr. Darcy's sort of like Dad."

Flo laughed. "How did I get such a smart daughter?" When Buddy stuck his head in the kitchen and demanded to know, "What's so damn special about Mr. Darcy?" as if he was jealous, which he was, Flo answered, "Ask your daughter."

Twelve o'clock, Evie scrambled into her work clothes. Carhartt coveralls with the arms cut off and a John Deere hat pulled low and to the right to hide her disfigurement. Buddy was waiting in the pickup truck with the canoe tied down in back. Mornings were Flo's time to teach Evie what she thought her daughter needed to know to change her life. Afternoons, Buddy gave her a different kind of education. Animal traps rattled in the truck bed as they headed down the mountain.

May 15 to November 15, Buddy trapped whatever was legal and sometimes not: beaver and muskrat mostly, but pine marten, fox, otter, bobcat, weasel, and mink if they obliged to misplace a paw or a snout. Lots of men in Townsend County trapped, but Buddy was the only one who had his daughter out working the lines with him.

Age ten on, every afternoon Monday through Friday, Evie could be seen heading out with her father in search of animals that could be caught and skinned for a profit. Fall and spring they'd take to the water, usually in a leaky sixteen-foot wooden boat with a 10-horsepower Evinrude, but occasionally, like today, they'd go out in a beat-up aluminum canoe. Slowly making their way along the boggy edges of lakes and ponds, they'd check, reset, and move their traps in the shallows. Rain, sleet, or shine, Buddy would sit in the stern, paddling or working the throttle of the outboard, while Evie perched over the bow, pulled up lengths of rusty chain with forty pounds of drowned rodent on the other end.

In the winter, when their world froze solid and it was pitch dark at four in the afternoon, Rangeley would hear father and daughter riding out into the snowy woods on Buddy's skimobile to bait the jaws of their traps with frozen beaver meat and calling lures made from skunk stink and bacon grease that left them smelling so foul that Flo made them leave their clothes in the shed. Prying apart the steel teeth and cocking the spring with one hand while holding onto the trap with your other—if you wore gloves in the snow and ice it was easy to lose your grip and the trap would bite back. Because that meant losing your finger, Evie didn't wear gloves.

By November, the calluses on her hands would crack open and her fingers were raw and chilblained. It was punishing work for a grown man, much less a child. Then there was the skinning.

Evie claimed she didn't mind putting on a black rubber butcher's apron on weekends and pelting out carcasses with Buddy while they listened to ball games on a blood-splattered radio. She wasn't lying. What gave her nightmares was the killing they had to do when they came across a trapped animal that was still alive. Evie's job was to calm the creature by talking to it while Buddy took out a club weighted with lead. Her father said hearing a quiet voice made a wild animal feel less humiliated to be caught, but she had her doubts.

Their first stop that day in June '96 was Perkins's Hardware. "We got to get some more traps."

"Where are we gonna set 'em?" They'd put out almost two hundred already.

"It's a surprise."

"As in you don't have permission."

Buddy answered that with a wink. Sneaking onto private property, hiding from game wardens, and getting chased was the part of trapping Evie liked best. When she was with her father, she knew bad shit could happen, but she also knew Buddy could kick its ass.

As Buddy haggled price with Perkins, Evie perused the Conibear traps they were buying. Holding up the brochure that advertised their steel embrace as "painless," Evie called out to Buddy, "Whoever wrote this never ran out of air underwater." The only person in the store who thought that was funny was her father.

As Mrs. Perkins waited on the mayor's wife, she watched Buddy weigh Evie down with a dozen traps attached to six-foot lengths of chain and send her out to the truck. Perkins's wife clicked her dentures into place and hissed, "Somebody oughta call Child Services about the way Buddy Quimby works that little girl."

Evie turned around slowly and gave the women the look Buddy had taught her. Equal parts promise and threat, twelve-year-old Evie solemnly volunteered, "You do that, ladies, and you'll be making a mistake you will come to regret."

Back in the truck, Buddy ran a stoplight and got on Route 7. Lighting up one of the cheap stogies Flo wouldn't let him smoke in the cabin, her father asked, "What was that all about?" Buddy had heard every word.

"Nothing. Just people not minding their own business."

Buddy surprised her when he said, "You know, Evie, we could just tell everyone the truth."

"About everything?"

"Not about the pot and the cigarette smuggling." Buddy augmented his income sprouting North Country Maui Wowie under grow lights and purchasing a few thousand cartons of smokes up on the Indian reservation tax-free and illegally reselling them for twice what he paid in the bars and bodegas of the five boroughs of New York City. "Just tell people the truth about why I got you working the traps for me."

Evie rolled down her window and spit out her gum. "It'd just give them another thing to tease me about."

Shortly before Evie started trapping, Buddy and Flo had taken her to see a doctor down at the hospital in Albany. The good news was a series of operations could remove her birthmark. The bad news was they would cost in excess of $25,000. Buddy had neither insurance nor that kind of cash. One dollar out of every three they grossed from the pelts went toward Evie's surgery. The math was bloody but simple for Evie: the more animals they trapped, the sooner she'd stop being "Giblet-Face" and start becoming the person she would have been if God hadn't fucked up when he made her.

Buddy circled north around the Sister Lakes on the county road. A quarter mile past a "No Dumping" sign punctuated by oo buckshot, he turned off the macadam. Shifting into low, they headed up the fire road that cut across the back side of Flathead Mountain. Four-wheel drive fighting for traction, the pickup skittered and bounced up the mountainside.

Three kidney-rattling miles into the piney wilderness, her father swung east onto an old logging road overgrown with poplar saplings thick as your thumb. As green wood splintered against the front bumper, a herd of deer bounded in and out of view. Pheasants and ruffled grouse exploded into the air, the furious flutter of their wings sounding to Evie's ear like a deck of cards being shuffled midair.

She had no idea where her father was taking her until Buddy slammed on his brakes for a porcupine that wouldn't get out of their way. Through a break in a stand of hundred-foot spruce trees two feet across at the base, she glimpsed one of the last of the palatial Great Camps the Adirondacks were once famous for on the shore of Lake Lucille four miles below. It was named Valhalla.

Vaguely Bavarian with thirty-plus rooms, it was built in 1893 by the robber baron Adolphus Benjamin Mannheim, who, according to Buddy, got rich by stealing a railroad among other things. Four-story tower, front porch as long as a hockey rink, nine-hole lakeside golf course, and enough alpine guest cottages and outbuildings to constitute a village, it looked to Evie like what Hansel and Gretel would have built if they had all the money in the world and elves for architects.

Though it had been over a decade since one of the robber baron's descendants had been seen in Rangeley, the Mannheims were still viewed as royalty in Townsend County; to everyone except Buddy, that is.

In the winter when the caretakers and gamekeepers left and Valhalla was caked in snow and ice, she and her father would ride his skimobile across the frozen lake right up to the front door. While Evie peered through the shudders at the shadows inside, Buddy would piss off the front porch just to make it clear how he felt. But this time of year, if they came any closer they'd be arrested for trespassing.

Pulling out a pair of binoculars, Evie could see gardeners on their knees weeding a flower bed in the shape of a giant *M* and gamekeepers patrolling the lake in a glistening, mahogany twenty-six-foot launch called the *Aloha*. Buddy leaned across her and pointed to the golf course. "Right there on the third hole is where that horse's ass Adolphus IV had his stroke. Fat lot of good his money does him now lying in a hospital bed like a big root vegetable."

In Evie's mind, the fact that an army of servants still labored to make it all perfect even though not a single Mannheim had set foot in Valhalla in years added an aura of spooky enchantment to the Great Camp. "You got to admit it's beautiful."

Buddy rolled down the window, spat in the direction of Valhalla, and muttered, "Fuck the Mannheims."

Her father took pleasure in recounting the inordinate amount of misery the Mannheim clan had suffered over the years. At any opportunity, he would regale her and anybody else who would listen with sordid tales of scandal, suicides, necrotic spider bites that resulted in amputation, wasting diseases, and most recently a photograph in *People* magazine of a granddaughter who was said to be a member of Leonardo DiCaprio's "Pussy Posse" getting arrested for driving a Ferrari drunk and naked in the south of France. But in Evie's mind, the possibility that all that misfortune meant the Mannheims were cursed only made Valhalla seem all the more enchanted.

When the porcupine finally got out of the way and they were rolling again, Evie asked a question she knew she wouldn't get a straight answer to. "Why do you really hate the Mannheims?"

Buddy smiled and summed up his philosophy of life. "What's the point of having a grudge if you can't hold on to it forever?" Then he added, chuckling, "Besides, I don't hate the Mannheims . . . at least not today."

"Why's that?"

"Because we're going to trap the beaver out of Dog Pond." Dog Pond belonged to the Mannheims, and by rights so did the beaver that called it home.

"Their gamekeepers catch us while we're out there in the canoe setting the traps, there's no paddling away."

"Beautiful day like today? They'll be too busy throwing fishermen off their lake to bother with Dog Pond. We put a trapline up there, we could pick up an extra thousand dollars this fall. Might get you your operation ahead of schedule."

Evie eyed her disfigurement in the rearview mirror thoughtfully. Running her fingers across the pebbled surface of the birthmark as if she were examining an imperfection in a pelt, she told him, "We both know you're not putting those traps up there for me."

Buddy squashed a hornet against the windshield with the heel of his hand. "Why the hell else do you think I'm doing it?" They rode on in silence after that, Buddy sulking and Evie feeling like the only grown-up in the truck.

Dog Pond was in fact a small lake located just below Kettle Mountain at the extreme northeast corner of the Mannheims' eighteen thousand acres. On the off chance that he was wrong about Valhalla's gamekeepers being too busy to check Dog Pond for poachers, Buddy hid the truck in a grove of balsams just north of the Mannheim property line up on state parkland. Unloading the boat, they put the traps, stakes to chain them to, and the rest of the gear inside the canoe. Tying ropes to the bow, father and daughter yoked themselves to the task of pulling it like a sledge down to the pond through a forest knee-high with ferns.

Bright sun, blue sky, at the water's edge the air was so thick with no-see-ums they put on hats that masked their faces with mesh to keep the bugs from getting in their eyes and flying up their noses. Pulling on chest-high rubber waders, they pushed off from the shore. With no wind, the glassy surface of the pond so perfectly mirrored the sky it seemed to Evie as if they were paddling among the clouds.

The near end of Dog Pond was swamp and bog. Rising up on a sandspit just offshore, they could see a five-foot mound of mud, sticks, and animal intelligence otherwise known as a beaver lodge. Evie waded along the bank, setting traps just beneath the surface of the water while Buddy hammered in the stakes, dabbing the ends of each with a viscous red-brown calling lure called barkstone that, as Buddy put it, "makes the beaver think there's a sexy rodent in the neighborhood."

By five o'clock they had put out all sixty of the traps they had brought with them. Given the Mannheims hadn't allowed anyone to trap Dog Pond since the Korean War and pelts going for twenty-five dollars apiece, if they didn't get caught they were looking at making serious money.

Evie knew the smart thing for them to do was go straight home, but being twelve, she could not resist when her father said, "You think you're a good enough fisherman to pull a brook trout out of Staircase Creek?"

"It's fisher*woman*, and last time, if I remember correctly, I caught two to your one."

They were paddling toward the opposite end of Dog Pond now where the water poured over a rock ledge, fell ten feet, and tumbled down two miles of narrow ravine before emptying into the Mink. Five waterfalls, five deep pools, white water in between; on maps, Staircase Creek was called the Cascades.

The Cascades was public land. The trouble was, for the public to fish it without stepping on Mannheim property, or worse, trespassing on the forty-seven thousand acres that belonged to the Mohawk Club, the public had to hike seventeen miles and climb two mountains.

Because of this inequity and the fact that it cost $200,000 to join the Mohawk Club, locals felt it within their rights to categorize the club's members as "a bunch of rich assholes." Being Flo's daughter, Evie wrote them off as "rich chauvinist a-holes"—one of the many peculiarities of the Mohawk Club was it did not admit women to membership, or Mohawks for that matter.

The club's domain began just beyond the tree line at the far end of Dog Pond. If the Mannheims' gamekeepers nabbed you, they were content to fine you $250 and escort you off their property. The Mohawk Club's private army of guards imposed harsher justice. If they caught you trespassing, they handcuffed you, turned you over to the sheriff, impounded your boat and your truck, and then just to keep you from thinking about doing it again, put sugar in your gas tank, slashed your tires, and claimed they found it that way. Not even Buddy messed with the Mohawk Club.

Evie and her father pulled up near the rock ledge where the pond spilled over and pounded down into the ravine. The sound of falling water filled the air. Evie didn't hear Buddy the first time he whispered, "Stay in the canoe."

By the time she looked up, the first guard had already gotten off his ATV and was cradling a shotgun. The second man was talking on a handheld radio. They were both wearing red Mohawk Club windbreakers and had badges. They were neat, clean-shaven men paid to be hard. Evie knew she was looking at catastrophe. If they found the pickup, all the money they'd saved up for her face would go to court costs, fines, and truck repairs, but what worried her most was the pistol she knew her father kept in his ankle holster.

The guard closest to them shouted, "Get out of the canoe. You're trespassing."

Buddy's voice was menacingly friendly. "I am indeed trespassing, but not on Mohawk Club land."

As Buddy pulled off his waders, the second man called out, "Mannheim gamekeepers are on their way."

Buddy began to back-paddle. The other guard lifted the muzzle of his shotgun. "If you two don't get out now, I'll put a hole in your canoe."

Buddy's voice got quiet. "You're not gonna do that, friend."

"Why not?"

Evie shouted, "Because we'll sue your asses for endangering the life of a child!" She was stalling for time, hoping her father could think a way out of trouble that didn't involve him reaching for his ankle holster.

The men eyed one another awkwardly, then the one with the radio shouted, "Fine! We'll wait until the Mannheims' men get here. Where you gonna paddle anyway?"

Evie thought it was over until Buddy pushed off straight toward the falls. Paddling hard, he shouted, "Hold on!"

The guard with the gun scrambled out onto the slab of granite that formed the spillway. Lunging to grab hold of the back end of the canoe, his feet went out from under him on the green slime and the shotgun clattered into the pond.

A heartbeat later the canoe was airborne.

On the way down, she heard her father laughing.

It stopped being funny when they hit the water. Evie screamed as the bow of the canoe slammed into the pool below. Her head snapped back and water surged over the gunnels. Buddy was shouting, "Get your waders off!"

Knowing that if your boots filled with water you drowned, Evie's fingers tore at the bib straps of her waders. Buddy tried to get the nose of the canoe pointed downstream, but the current had them wedged between two boulders. As he pried them free, his paddle snapped in half and they were at the mercy of the torrent.

She only had one leg out of her waders when they went over a second waterfall sideways. The drop was shorter but the rock they landed on ripped a foot-long gash in the aluminum belly of the canoe.

She couldn't hear what Buddy was shouting now because the canoe had turned turtle and she was under water the color of tea. The current churned her upside down and the boot she'd pulled off tangled on something that wouldn't let go. Evie used the last bit of air she had left in her lungs to let out a scream she knew no one could hear. It was eerily quiet inside her head after that. The thought *So this is what it's like to drown* was interrupted by her father's hand yanking her up to the surface.

One arm hooked around the seat of the canoe, the other holding her tight, Buddy and his daughter gagged on white water and foam as they went over the next set of falls.

It wasn't until the Cascades had delivered them into the slower drift of the Mink that she realized her father was crying. She had never seen that before. In that moment, she glimpsed a softness in the man she didn't know existed and sensed that her father was ashamed of.

Though she was the one that had almost drowned, she felt his embarrassment so keenly she heard herself say, "It's okay, Daddy, it was my fault."

All her father said was, "No it's not . . ." Buddy dunked his head in the mink, shook himself like a bear, and returned to being Buddy. "What do you say we don't tell your mother about this?"

Evie left her father holding what was left of the canoe waist-deep in the Mink and scrambled up onto the bank.

"What're you doing?"

"I got to go pee."

"Why not go in the water?"

"Cuz it's gross!"

Buddy was trying to decide whether to wait until dark before try-ing to sneak back up to the truck when he heard voices coming around the bend in the river. Knowing they now actually were trespassing on Mohawk Club land, Buddy let out a whistle that anyone else would have thought was the call of a cardinal but Evie knew meant *Hide*.

As she pulled her pants up, he gave her a nod and let the cur-rent silently carry him and the canoe out of sight downstream. Evie stepped back into the forest and crouched low just as the four men in Mohawk Club vests came into view. She was relieved they were armed with fly rods, not guns.

The oldest of the four, a big man, all chest and belly in his fifties, took out a fancy camera as the younger one with taffy-colored hair posed for a snapshot. The other two casting dry flies out onto the pool just below her looked to be in their late twenties. One held up his two fingers and made the peace sign.

With that gesture, Evie's past and present merged.

As she sat in the darkness of her studio on Rue Daguerre twenty-two years later, reliving the wonder of that long day in her head, a car alarm out on the street snapped her back to the here and now of her life. She looked at her watch and was startled to see it was almost 4 a.m. But part of her still lingered in the shadow of the forest.

The memory taunted her. Evie wasn't sure if the person she used to be actually heard what the two fly fishermen were saying just as the photograph was taken that day or if she was just imagining she could recall the shorter one asking, "Why did Scout get to wait so long before they made him get a wife? They married us off at twenty-six."

The taller one, at least in her imagination, had an English accent. "Probably wanted to give Scout time to outgrow his proclivities." Then she heard the men laughing like a dirty joke had just been told.

At thirty-four, it made no more sense to Evie than it did when she was twelve, except the part about Scout's proclivities.

CHAPTER 7

I had heard my mother down in her studio the night before but had no idea what she was trying to piece together by herself in the dark. When I woke up that morning, she was still asleep. I should have known it was a mistake to look at myself in the mirror above the bathroom sink, but it's hard not to watch yourself when you brush your teeth. Chemo had left me bald except for two wisps of hair on the top of my head that gave me the appearance of something sick that had just been plucked. Appetite was a memory. I had lost fifteen pounds. My face was pasty gray and all skull. Trying on the China chop wig my mother had bought me, putting on red lipstick, and applying rouge only succeeded in making me look like I had gotten a make-over from a mortician.

I tried to bring up Netflix on the computer but my battery was drained. My mother's laptop was lying on the living room couch. Her password was my name. When I saw twenty open tabs, I couldn't resist clicking through them. That's when I figured it out. What she hadn't been telling me.

~ ~ ~

My mother was still asleep when I stepped into her room and shouted, "Why the fuck have you been lying to me?"

She was too groggy to put it together. "What's wrong?"

"You lied!" I dropped the open laptop on her bed. When she saw Scout's face smiling back at her, her eyes widened and she cried out as if I'd stabbed her. "Why didn't you tell me that guy Scout who came to the hospital—your so-called friend—was the guy you shot?" I wanted to blame her for all that didn't make sense in the universe.

My mother's lip was trembling. "He's not my friend."

"Then why the fuck did he thank you for saving his life after you shot him?" My mother's mouth opened but her tongue couldn't find the right words. "In the newspaper article about the hunting accident, he and some sheriff said if it wasn't for you, he would've died."

Evie cut her off. "I know what they said. It wasn't an accident."

"You shot him on purpose?"

"Yes." Pain, humiliation, and rage reduced her voice to a raw whisper.

"Why didn't you tell me?"

My mother chose her words carefully. "The hardest part of being a mother comes when your child asks you questions you think you have to answer with lies. You tell yourself you're doing it to protect them, but the truth is you're protecting yourself. You're scared that if you're honest, they won't love you." We were both crying after she said that.

She led me by the hand into the kitchen and made a pot of coffee and scrambled me an egg. She was talking to herself as much as to me when she said, "If a mother doesn't trust her daughter with her story, neither one of them can ever learn anything from it."

As I gagged down my meds, she began to tell me the grotesque and miraculous chain of people and events that changed the trajectory of her life the summer she turned seventeen.

PART III

CRIMES, OFFICIAL AND OTHERWISE

CHAPTER 8

O n the evening of Evie's seventeenth birthday, Flo put candles back up in the woods, and the shadows cast by their flickering light made the forest seem dark and magical enough to be inhabited by gnomes. Buddy lit a bonfire. Given that Evie had only one real friend, a fastidious, moon-faced boy named Dill, it was a small party. In grade school, Dill was the sole member of the class that didn't laugh when the other kids called her Giblet-Face. He worked after school at his mother's beauty parlor down in Speculator, and made no secret of the fact that his life's ambition was to become Madonna's hairdresser. Locals called Dill names too.

Eighteen and bobby-pin thin, Dill was the only person besides her parents who knew she was working the traplines with Buddy to save up enough money to have her disfigurement removed. Guardians of each other's secrets, Evie alone knew that since fifth grade Dill had dreamed of "making babies with boys."

The headlights of Dill's rusted-out VW didn't bounce up the mountain until after seven because he stayed late at the beauty parlor giving himself a new hairdo in honor of the occasion. His hair was dyed platinum blonde and shaved down to bristles on the sides, and he kept the front long so he could push his hair out of his eyes dramatically every time he said, "Love it," which was his new favorite expression.

It was just the four of them. The night was warm and they sat at a picnic table eating burgers made of wild boar Buddy had poached the week before. Like everybody else in Rangeley, they were talking about the glow that had suddenly appeared on the horizon. After fifteen years of darkness, the lights were on again in Valhalla. From the Quimbys' picnic table, the log palace twinkled like a diamond cuff on the shore of Lake Lucille twenty miles to the west; at least that's how it looked to Evie.

Buddy saw it differently. "I'm telling you Old Man Mannheim left Valhalla to that nutcase granddaughter Lulu just to fuck with us."

Flo pointed out, "She's the only grandchild he had. Who was he supposed to leave everything to? You?"

Lulu was the most notorious of all the many fuckups in the Mannheim family. Evie had grown up hearing her father read aloud tabloid stories about her exploits. Famous for table dancing without any underwear and being pierced down there, Lulu Mannheim with her long red dreadlocks was a rich girl the world loved and hated. And because of all that, Evie delighted in telling her father, "I think she's kind of interesting."

Buddy put on the army surplus night-vision goggles he used to jack deer after dark to get a closer look at the offending lights and muttered, "That nympho will probably turn the place into a nude disco."

Everybody but Buddy laughed when Flo announced, "Nymphomania is a word men invented for women stupid enough to act like men."

Evie borrowed the night-vision goggles. Infrared made Valhalla look like a UFO. "I read in *Us* magazine she's engaged to some Wall Street guy. She looked happy in the picture."

"Unless he's part vibrator, she'll wear him out in a month."

"You don't even know her, why do you have to talk about her like that?"

"Because she's rich and spoiled, and when people like her get in trouble, they blame people like us."

"Maybe she's changed."

"People don't change. You are what you are."

Having toiled on her father's traplines for the last seven years in the belief that she could become someone else, Evie didn't like hearing that. Buddy reached for his fifth beer and Flo gave him a look that said, *You've had enough.*

Dill put down his boar burger, spit out a bit of bullet that Buddy's meat grinder had missed, and volunteered, "When I was giving Betsy Clinger her perm today, she told me Lulu Mannheim's having the wedding at Valhalla." Betsy Clinger's husband took care of the Mannheims' boats. "All the guests are being flown up from New York in a chartered jet. Don't you just love it?"

Buddy bellowed, "Fuck the Mannheims," and Flo announced it was time to light the candles on the birthday cake.

Her mother gave her a dress she knew she'd never wear. Dill presented her with a gift certificate for a deluxe makeover that included haircut, dye job, and makeup consultation, none of which she wanted. Then rain blew in and the party was over.

Just before she went to bed, her father handed her a roll of hundred-dollar bills. Her share of the profits from the pelt auction up in Montreal was $2,900. Doing the math in her head, she calculated she was $3,343 away from removing the capillary malformation that had marked her life. Taking out the hand mirror she kept hidden in the bottom drawer of her dresser, she pulled her hair away from her face and wondered what it would be like not to be ugly.

The next morning, Evie took the Willys down to Speculator, deposited her share of the pelt profits in her bank account, picked up new spark plugs and rings for the outboard she was rebuilding, and wasted an hour standing in the back of the beauty parlor getting depressed watching Dill dye last year's winter carnival queen Connie Brock's hair green. Connie was sixteen years old, five and a half months pregnant, and her boyfriend claimed it wasn't his. Evie could not help but see Connie as a cautionary tale. If that was what happened to girls who were pretty and popular and stayed in Rangeley, the future for Evie seemed worse than bleak. When Connie asked her what she thought of the green hair, Evie said, "Love it!"

Hoping to cut ten minutes off the trip home, she took the serpentine gravel road that wound its way through the four-mile-wide stretch of hardwood forest south of Lake Lucille.

Top down, radio blaring, she alternately felt the warmth of the sun and the cool of shade as the canopy of sugar maples and oak gave way to clear sky. The road twisted and turned as it ran parallel to a water-falled stream called Cold Brook. Summer wind on her face, Red Hot Chili Peppers on the radio, and the shifting of gears distracted her from her worries.

Evie was calculating how many years at minimum wage it would take to scrape together enough money to go to junior college when the engine began to sputter and suck fuel that wasn't there. As the Willys rolled to a stop, Evie cursed her father for not warning her that when his gas gauge said half a tank, it really meant running on empty.

Pushing the Jeep onto the verge, putting up the top in case in rained, Evie started walking. A can of gas was ten miles up the road.

A mile later, the road dipped and hairpinned to the right to accommodate a bend in Cold Brook. The noise of the wind in the branches above coupled with the racket of the fast-flowing stream were so deafening Evie did not hear the car coming down on her from behind. If she hadn't paused to watch a porcupine eating the tree limb he was sitting on, she never would have seen the vehicle that was about to run her over.

It was a Ford F-100 extended-cab pickup going fast. When it screeched on its brakes a hundred feet past her, Evie ran toward it shouting, "Thank you!" She had one foot on the rear bumper and was about to jump in the back when the truck suddenly acceler-ated away from her. When it stopped again twenty feet away, she heard laughter.

The truck windows rolled down as it backed up to her. The boys were listening to Anthrax and an empty beer can was thrown in her direction. Kevin Dolby, who everybody knew knocked up Connie but refused to admit it, was behind the wheel. Scrotum, of the one ball, was riding shotgun. Otto Kemp, the heavyweight who got kicked off the wrestling team for a hazing infraction that involved a broom-stick, was in the back of the truck's extended cab, crammed in next to his cousin from Buffalo. All Evie knew about him was that they called him "the Laugher" because when he hit you, he laughed. Sticking their heads out the window, Otto and the Laugher chanted, "Giblet! Giblet! Giblet!" Like messing with her was a local sporting event; which it sort of was.

The boys in the pickup called themselves "Morlocks." They were known for spray-painting the word on bridges, setting fire to float docks, and tagging the side of freshly painted walls with a cock and balls that featured a smiley face on the head of the penis. Evie wasn't sure whether they were aware that Morlocks were the subhuman race of cannibals in H. G. Wells's *The Time Machine* or just thought it was a cool name. They took pride in their ignorance, anyway. The Morlocks pumped up their self-esteem by ingesting steroids, binge-watching porn, and vandalizing anything or anyone who displayed an iota of what Flo called "grace" and Dill referred to as "being different."

Kevin gave her his Rob Lowe smile and reached his arm out the window with a dollar bill folded lengthwise between his fingers. "Hey, Evie, I'll give you a dollar if you let me touch it." The Morlocks snickered as he pointed to her birthmark with the folded bill.

"Five bucks for all four of us!" That was Scrotum. Evie could hear the rattle of empty beer cans inside on the floor of the truck. She was used to casual cruelty, but this was different. She smelled teen spirit mixed with dark hormones and could see the sheen of alcohol sweat on their faces; their smiles didn't match the look in their eyes. Egging each other on, they were as uncertain as Evie was about how serious they were about acting on their bad intentions.

"We're just playing, Evie . . . There's no need to be scared. . . . We're all friends." They were speaking in one voice, talking to her soft and gentle like she was an animal caught in a trap and they were trying to trick her into relaxing so they could get close enough to humiliate her even more.

The wrestler opened the truck door. "It's just a joke, Giblet. Get in. We'll give you a ride."

Evie was shaking her head *NO* when the Laugher's hand shot out and clamped hold of her wrist. As she struggled to get away, he twisted her arm. The only thing Evie was certain of was that if she hit him, he'd hit her back. Then Otto grabbed hold of her other wrist. They were pulling her into the truck and there was no more pretending it was a game.

When she screamed, "Let go of me, fuckers!" and began to kick, they shouted, "Calm down, bitch . . . what's your problem? We're giving you a ride." Then a hand reached over from the front seat and squeezed her breasts, and Scrotum screeched, "Let's see her boobies!"

It turned so ugly so fast, Evie didn't hear a second car screech to a stop.

"What the fuck do you think you're doing!" It was a woman's voice, and at the sound of it the boys in the truck froze mid-grope. "Let her go now!" It was a voice used to giving orders, and from the way the Morlocks slowly raised their hands, Evie imagined the woman was pointing a gun at them.

Scrambling out of the truck, she landed on her knees in the middle of the road. Tires spun and gravel flew back in her face as Kevin punched the accelerator and the truck fishtailed down the road. It was over for the Morlocks, but not for Evie.

When she looked up, Evie saw a waifish girl in a black hoodie and dark sunglasses that covered half her face. The girl was barely five feet tall and one hundred pounds at most. There was no gun.

The girl stared at her as she lit a cigarette. "You okay?"

"No permanent damage." Evie picked up her hat off the ground and pulled it down over her face. She didn't understand why the Morlocks had run off until the girl took off her sunglasses and Evie realized she was talking to Lulu Mannheim. At thirty-three, she looked older than she did in her photographs.

"You want to report it to the police?"

"Wouldn't change anything."

"I hear you. What are you doing out here on the road by yourself?"

"I ran out of gas."

A man was standing next to a black Range Rover holding a map. Buff, a Rangers cap, and mirrored sunglasses, Evie figured him for the husband-to-be she read about in *People* magazine.

Lulu pointed to the map. "We're lost."

"I know the feeling." Evie wasn't trying to be funny, but Lulu laughed and pushed the hoodie back off her face. The signature red dreadlocks were gone. Lulu's hair was dyed a boring shade of brown, and the bejeweled face piercings and diamond dental implants she'd seen in the photos of Lulu had been removed. Evie was surprised that without her red dreads and bling, Lulu looked average bordering on plain.

As the heiress went on about how she was late for an AA meeting she never found because her GPS wasn't working, Evie tried not to think about dirt getting into the holes Lulu had put in her body.

The man with the map called out, "You know how to get to Route 3?"

"You're looking for Valhalla, aren't you?"

"Pathetic not being able to find my own house." Lulu wrinkled up her nose like a kid who knows they're cute. "How about you get in my car, show me the way home, and I'll have somebody take you wherever you want to go?"

"Anywhere?"

"Yeah, anywhere. You name it."

Evie opened the back door and hesitated. "What if I said Paris, France?"

Lulu gave her a curious look and chuckled. "I'd say you're a clever girl. I'm Lulu by the way." She stuck her hand out and Evie shook it.

"Evie Quimby."

"You're Buddy Quimby's daughter?"

Evie nodded, wondering how the hell Lulu knew her father and why the hell her father hadn't mentioned the fact.

"Harvey, get in back. Evie's going to drive us home." Harvey did as he was told.

Evie had never been inside a Range Rover, much less driven one. The new smell of tan hide upholstery and the twelve-speaker sound system took her mind off what the Morlocks would have done to her if Lulu hadn't stopped. The awkward silence that followed was filled by the first two tracks of the R.E.M. CD on the stereo.

Harvey hadn't said a word since she'd taken over the wheel. As she turned off the gravel road onto Route 3, Evie tried to include him in the conversation. "I heard you two are getting married."

Lulu thought that was hysterical. "What do you say to us getting hitched, Harvey?"

"You don't pay me enough."

"Harvey's my minder."

"What's that mean?"

"He's my one-man posse. Helps me stay squeaky clean and stone-cold fucking sober. My fiancé hired him." Her voice was equal parts la-di-da and hipster.

Evie surprised herself when she asked, "So what's your fiancé like?"

"Charlie? Charlie is wonderfully . . . normal. Deliciously, sane-makingly normal. A hundred percent vanilla normal."

As Evie drove through the twenty-foot-high wrought-iron gates to Valhalla, she wondered what "normal" meant to someone like Lulu. Evie had only seen the Great Camp up close in winter. Now with the snowdrifts gone she could see the railings on the porch were made of tree limbs bent into the shapes of animals—a leaping stag; a bear lying on its back, paws in the air. Evie hadn't realized the boathouse down at the lake with the funny roof curved up at the corners was constructed to resemble a Japanese Shinto temple. Valhalla was more welcoming than Evie remembered it—in part because she didn't have to worry about getting arrested for trespassing.

"If you show me where I can get a can of gas, I better get back to my Jeep." It was almost 4 p.m. by then.

"Harvey will take care of all that. Come on inside. Iced tea,

Coke, you can have a beer. I'm okay with other people drinking, just not me."

Evie's father had told her so many sordid stories about the Mannheims over the years, Lulu's friendliness suddenly seemed suspect. Nervous, she blurted out, "Why are you being so nice to me?"

The question stopped Lulu in her tracks. From the expression on the rich woman's face, Evie thought the invitation to come inside was about to be rescinded. "I was pulled into a car by boys once."

"Did somebody stop?"

"No. . . . Got any other questions?"

"Well . . . that explains why you helped me, but not why you're being nice."

Lulu's eyes narrowed as she stared at Evie's face. Not at her disfigurement, but her whole face. "You remind me of someone I know."

"Well if they look like me, I feel sorry for them."

Lulu let it lie. When Evie hesitated following her up the steps, Lulu took her by the hand and led her up onto the long porch that ran the length of the Great Camp.

Everywhere Evie looked, she saw workmen and gardeners planting flowers and painting trim. The Quimbys being Quimbys, Evie wouldn't exactly have called those workers "friends," but she knew who they were and, more importantly, they knew who she was. She could tell by the way they stopped work to stare, they were thinking, *What the fuck is Evie Quimby doing here?* Which is exactly what Evie was thinking.

The front hall was vaulted, hammer-beamed and paneled in local oak. The walls were lined with antlered and snarling trophies from all the forests of the world—moose, deer, bear, rhino, elk, kudu, and what Evie hoped wasn't a stuffed snow leopard perched and ready to pounce from the rafters overhead. Interspaced with dead mammals, there were glass-eyed trout and salmon as long as your arm. Lulu paused to look up at the embalmed wildlife. "I hope you don't belong to PETA."

"My dad and I are trappers. Beaver, otter, mink. Basically, if it has fur."

"I love fur . . . but don't tell Charlie, he thinks it's cruel."

"It is."

Before Evie could take in the contents of the hall, Lulu pulled her into a living room filled with trophies of a different sort: Chinese vases, taller than a ten-year-old child, porcelain figurines she didn't know were Ming, and paintings of landscapes from another century in gilded frames. Seeing how much more-than-more Lulu Mannheim had at her disposal gave Evie a sense of vertigo.

Lulu plopped down on a couch made of moose antlers upholstered in tasseled silk, and a maid appeared. "Doris, I'd love a Diet Coke and my friend will have . . ." Lulu patted the cushion next to her and Evie sat down, feeling like a pet.

"Hi Doris." Doris was Scrotum's aunt. "I'll have a Coke too."

There was so much in the room Evie had never seen before, she didn't hear Lulu the first time she asked, "So Evie, what do you do for fun?"

"I like to fish . . . fly-fish. People who fish with live bait are pond scum."

Evie regretted saying that last bit until Lulu exclaimed, "That's just what Charlie says! He loves fly-fishing. Total addict. It's one of the reasons I opened up the camp again. That and up here there aren't as many temptations. New York has so many friends with bad habits. . . . It's cocaine and Ecstasy I miss the most." Lulu lit a cigarette. "Hey . . . maybe you can teach me to fly-fish? I'll pay you."

"You don't have to." Evie wondered if all rich people were as lonely as Lulu.

"My grandfather tried to teach me when I was a kid, but I kept getting the hook caught in the bushes."

"Got to shorten your back cast. It's all between ten and twelve." Lulu looked puzzled. Holding an imaginary fly rod, Evie demonstrated. "You have to think about it like the face of a clock."

When Lulu tried to copy Evie's flick of the wrist, she knocked over a vase. When they both laughed, it suddenly seemed as if they really were friends, and Lulu didn't seem to want her to leave, so she didn't. An hour later they were in the kitchen making sandwiches. In the adjoining breakfast room, a pair of party planners from New York were working on the seating arrangement for the wedding luncheon and one of them called out, "Do you want all the Kennedys at the same table or should we spread them around? And who gets Bloomberg?"

"Ask Charlie." Lulu gestured out the window. A four-wheel-drive ATV with a roll cage had just pulled up outside; three men got out wearing waders and carrying fly rods that cost more than a down payment on a new truck.

The way Lulu kissed the youngest of the three, Evie figured that was Charlie. He was tall and lanky, and the way he wrapped his arms around Lulu, she seemed to disappear in his embrace, which Evie guessed was what Lulu wanted. Looking boyish and puzzled, Charlie announced, "Where have you been all my life?" It was like he was playing a part in a movie, only coming out of his mouth it didn't sound phony. Black hair and violet-blue eyes, he was about thirty and handsome verging on pretty. There was a casual sincerity to his charm, a warmth that lit up the room like a well-made fire in a welcoming hearth.

Then, as if he were a magician, Charlie pulled out a handkerchief. "I almost forgot. I have a present for you." Inside the folds of his tattersall pocket square there was a monarch butterfly, and as it took flight across the kitchen the other two men applauded like it was a show; which it was.

The one wearing a Harvard Class of '89 polo shirt deadpanned in a Boston accent, "Just so you know, Lulu, I was the one that taught Charlie that trick," and everybody laughed.

Then the older guy lit his pipe as he quipped, "And I was the one that taught it to you, dear boy, as long as we're taking credit," and everybody laughed again. All three of the men were successful some-bodies and they knew it.

Evie was having such a good time watching them try to outdo each other she didn't notice her coveralls had come half unzipped until she caught the Harvard guy smiling at her boobs. Before she could fix herself, Harvard reached out and zipped her up with a wink. "You can catch a cold going around like that, darling."

Evie wasn't exactly sure what just happened, but she knew she didn't like it. The man stared at her face longer than was polite, then headed toward the door, announcing, "Sorry to be rude, but I have to call my wife before I get into trouble."

Lulu gave Evie an apologetic look, and the other man stepped for-ward. He was older, fortyish, sporting horn-rimmed glasses and a pipe. He had a windburned face and wore a tie under his fishing vest. Bowing slightly, he shook Evie's hand. "I'm Win Langley."

"Win's my lawyer," Lulu explained. "Evie's going to teach me how to fly-fish."

Charlie laughed. "Good luck! Be careful she doesn't hook you with her back cast. Muzzy nearly took my eye out."

Seeing Evie was lost, Lulu explained, "Muzzy's my nickname. Charlie gives everybody one. What will Evie's nickname be?" Evie had a bad history with nicknames.

Charlie stared at her—looked her right in the eye as if her birth-mark didn't exist. "Evie's nickname will be . . . Goldilocks."

Win helped himself to a chocolate chip cookie. "Well, Goldilocks, I guess that makes us the three bears." There was a playfulness in his voice. Mannered in an old-fashioned way, he reminded Evie of Greg-ory Peck in *To Kill a Mockingbird*. Even though he wore a Mohawk Club tie, he was almost as hard not to like as Charlie.

"I hate to break up the party, but I'm going to have to borrow Lulu for a few minutes. There are some papers she needs to look at."

"First I have to show Evie something important." Grabbing Evie's hand, Lulu led her up the back stairs.

As they headed down a long hall lined with old black-and-white photographs of dead rich people having fun, Evie asked, "Who was the creepy guy in the Harvard shirt?"

"That's Charlie's friend Ian. He thinks he's God's gift to women."

"Why?"

"He was a Rhodes Scholar. And he has a giant dick. Or so I'm told." Evie didn't know what a Rhodes Scholar was. "I have to put up with him, he's one of Charlie's groomsmen. He looks at anything female like that."

"Like what?"

"Dinner."

"Is Charlie going to be up here with you all summer?"

"I wish. He works in New York at a hedge fund. Boring, but he's the nicest guy I ever met. Plus, Win says it's important a girl like me be with a self-feeder." Lulu could tell Evie didn't know what she was talking about. "It means somebody who doesn't expect to live off my money. Win looks after me. He helped my grandfather with his charities. Now he wants me to look at some prenup he's drawn up."

Up another set of stairs, Lulu threw open the door of a bedroom with a balcony that overlooked the lake and pointed to a wedding dress on a tailor's dummy. "What do you think?" White silk satin, neckline edged with pearls, ten feet of train, and a veil that came to the floor.

All Evie could think to say was, "It's a dream."

Lulu patted her stomach. "Trouble is that I've eaten so much up here, I've got to send it back to New York to get it let out. I've gained ten pounds." Lulu looked borderline anorexic to Evie.

Evie stopped admiring the dress when her eye caught the dazzle of a yellow jewel in a velvet box on the mantel. "Is that your engagement ring?" Evie had never seen a canary diamond before.

Lulu beamed. "Charlie proposed a month after we met. So cute and old-fashioned, got down on his knee, the whole bit. Sounds corny but it wasn't."

"Why aren't you wearing it?"

"He was in such a rush he didn't have time to get it engraved. He's going to take it in to Tiffany's when he goes back to New York this week so I can wear it at the wedding." As Lulu put on the four karats of flawless diamond, Evie spotted something else on the mantel. It was a two-gram vial of what she was correct to assume was cocaine. Next to it was a silver straw.

Lulu saw where Evie's eyes had wandered. "It was Charlie's idea."

"Why?"

"Each day I don't give in to the temptation to crack it open and snort my brains out, I know I'm getting better." Evie couldn't help thinking that Lulu had looked at Charlie just the same way she was now looking at the contents of that vial.

Charlie shouted up from downstairs, "The phone lines are out again."

"Fuck-a-do! That's the second time it's happened this week. We've got a million calls to make with this wedding coming up. Got to take care of this. Harvey will bring you back." Lulu stopped halfway out the door. "I'm serious about the fishing . . ." then shouted over her shoulder, "You know the way out."

Evie didn't. She took two wrong turns down dead-end hallways and walked in on Doris taking a pee before she found the main staircase. Hurrying, she took the stairs two steps at a time. Her mind was a jumble of all the different parts of a day that didn't connect but did— she was thinking about how she would explain to her parents what a long strange trip it had been when halfway down the stairs she caught sight of a shadow, flickering down the steps just a step ahead of her, that looked to be the silhouette of a naked woman.

It stopped Evie dead in her tracks. The way her jaw dropped and gooseflesh prickled her arms, you would have thought she had seen a ghost . . . and in a way she had.

The shadow was cast by a statue, or more accurately by the remains of a statue of a girl standing atop a plinth on the landing backlit by the sun. Life-size, nude, and made of marble, the statue was missing one of its arms, a leg was broken off just below the knee, and all that remained of its face was an open mouth that appeared to have something urgent to say.

She had no idea the statue was sculpted three hundred years before the birth of Christ, or that the marble it was carved from came from a quarry on the island where Circe was rumored to have turned men into swine, or that it had been buried in an earthquake. But Evie could see that the parts of the girl that were missing, that your imagination had to fill in, made her more eloquent and painfully beautiful than she ever would have been if nothing bad had ever happened to her.

The longer she stood in front of the statue, the more certain Evie was that it had something to teach her. Not just about art or beauty, but about how to look at things. Evie felt as if a window she didn't know existed was opening inside her.

Wondering what the broken stone girl on the pedestal would say if she could talk, Evie tentatively reached out a fingertip to the marble. Cautiously running her hand over the smooth surface of her stone flanks, Evie touched the statue as if it were a wounded creature that could be spooked and run away if she wasn't careful.

Slowly, Evie's fingers explored the jagged edges where the missing arm had been ripped from her torso and the top half of her face cleaved from her head. Looking closer, she could feel gouges that had been filled with putty made of marble dust and see cracks cemented by pigmented glue that didn't quite match the faintly luminescent white of her marble flesh. Evie was just starting to wonder how and who had made it whole enough to cast a spell over the living when Harvey called up from the bottom of the stairs. "Miss Mannheim doesn't like people touching her things without permission."

Win, the lawyer, appeared behind him, "That's all right, Harvey. Goldilocks can touch anything she wants. Being flawed makes her more beautiful, don't you think?"

CHAPTER 9

My mother had been talking for an hour and still hadn't explained why she shot Scout or how an assault with a deadly weapon came to be called a hunting accident. Pain throbbed up through the hollows of my thighs. I was impatient for answers. "Why did Scout come to my hospital room?"

"I don't know."

"Should I be scared of this guy?"

My mother looked out the window and said, "Yes."

"Jesus Christ, why the hell don't you just come out and tell me what happened?"

"Because you have to know who I was to understand."

"What the fuck does he want from us?"

"I'm not sure, but I'm hoping that if I go through that summer start to finish, I'll figure out why he's come back into my life." I started to say something, but my mother put her hand to my lips and said, "Just hear me out and then I'll answer all your questions."

She stared up at the ceiling and closed her eyes to help her remember where she was in her story. "My father didn't like it when I came home and told him about meeting Lulu Mannheim and getting invited inside Valhalla. When I mentioned teaching her how to fly-fish, he told me 'no way' was he going to let that happen and went on a rant about her being a bad influence and how he'd take away the keys to the Willys if I didn't stay away from Lulu. Seeing as how he had two hundred pot plants in the shed we were standing in, I said something smart like if he was worried about bad influences, maybe I should stay away from him. For what it's worth, I wish I could take back telling him, 'It's a little late for you to start acting like you're my real father.'"

From the face she made I could see she felt the same way about saying that as I did about calling her a liar.

"As it turned out, the phones weren't working at Valhalla because the beaver had eaten through the telephone lines buried next to the lake. Cut off like that and having a hundred and fifty people coming for a wedding the next week, Lulu was in a panic."

"Why didn't she just use her cell phone?"

"No cell reception in the Sister Lakes."

"You're kidding. We're going someplace where I can't use my cell phone?"

My mother laughed. "They probably have service now, but back then, you wanted to use your cell phone, you had to climb up Flathead Mountain. Anyway, we were in the middle of it when the sheriff drove up."

"What was the sheriff doing there?"

"He had a message from Lulu Mannheim. She offered to pay us a thousand dollars to trap the beaver out of the lake before the wedding. Legally, that is. And we'd get to keep the pelts. Buddy didn't want to do it, but it was a lot of money to us. He let me know how much I'd hurt him when he told the sheriff, 'Since I'm not Evie's real father and she thinks I'm a bad influence, it's her decision.'"

"Why didn't the sheriff arrest him for the pot?"

"Sheriff was my father's cousin."

"Is that why you were able to get away with shooting Scout?"

"I didn't get away with anything."

CHAPTER 10

Evie and Buddy were up before dawn, sorting traps and loading gear into the truck. Each feeling they had been wronged by what had been said in the shed the day before, they exchanged as few words as possible. Flo sat between them in the front seat as they trailered the boat up to Valhalla. After thirty minutes of dead and awkward silence, Flo broke the ice. "I feel sorry for both of you."

They got to Valhalla just before 8 a.m. The fog swirling in off the lake made the Great Camp look like a hologram of something too big to be real. Buddy pulled the trailer behind the Japanese boathouse and backed it down into the water. As soon as Evie slid their boat into the water, Flo got in the truck, calling out the window as she drove away, "Play nice."

Laden with traps, stakes to chain them to, a cooler of ice, extra fuel tanks for the trip home, axes, calling lures, boat hook, tarps in case it rained, two fly rods, a tackle box, plus the added weight of a middle-aged father and a teenage daughter who felt like strangers—the skiff rode low in the water.

They were just about to shove off when they heard a voice behind them. "Mr. Quimby?" Evie wasn't used to hearing her father called "Mr.," much less by Lulu Mannheim.

Lulu lit her first cigarette of the day and collected herself before she announced, "I want to apologize for what my brother, Luke, did to you." Evie remembered Buddy reading a newspaper article about Luke Mannheim dying of kidney failure and smiling. "Couldn't happen to a nicer guy."

"You've got nothing to apologize for—you were like, what, seven years old?"

"Yeah, but my family and our money made it possible for him to totally fuck you and we all knew it. He stole two years of your life."

Before Evie could ask what they were talking about, Lulu announced, "In AA, we have something called the Ninth Step. We make a list of all the people we've harmed. My brother was in the program when he died. He left this for you." Lulu handed him an envelope.

"What's in it?"

"I honestly don't know."

Buddy ripped open the envelope, pulled out a check, and stared at it wide-eyed. Before Evie could see how much it was written out for, her father tore it up and tossed it into the lake. "That's insulting." Evie had never seen her father pass up free money. The gesture struck her as both noble and dumb.

Lulu looked embarrassed. "I can give you a bigger check."

Buddy shook his head. "Money doesn't mean shit to you."

Lulu took a deep breath. "You got me there, but I wanted to give you this." She held out a laminated card. "It gives you permission to hunt, fish, trap anywhere on our property."

Buddy eyed the card suspiciously, then slipped it into his wallet and surprised his daughter by telling Lulu, "When we're done taking care of the beaver problem, my daughter will teach you to fly-fish."

As they watched Lulu run like a child back through the fog to the big house, Evie asked her father, "You going to tell me what that was all about?"

"When I was nineteen, I gave Luke Mannheim a ride to a rock festival in Canada where the Dead were playing. We got pulled over outside of Montreal. I didn't see him slip a plastic bag under the seat, but when the cops opened it up they found a thousand hits of Ecstasy. Luke said the drugs belonged to me. He calls Mommy and Daddy, Mannheims' lawyers show up, I go to prison for two years, and little Luke walks."

"Why didn't you tell anybody?"

"Getting fucked over isn't something I'm comfortable bragging about."

"What was it like being in jail?" It was a stupid thing to ask and she regretted saying it until he answered, "Like being caught in a trap. . . . Then your mother showed up."

Stunned by how much her parents hadn't told her about themselves, Evie demanded, "What the hell did Mom go to jail for?"

"She didn't. She taught a class to the inmates—creative writing. Met in the prison library. Minute I saw her, I made up my mind to be the teacher's pet."

Evie flashed on all the rumors she had heard about her parents. "So what about the other three years you were gone? What really happened to you and Flo after you got out of jail?"

Buddy smiled agreeably. "We've had enough truth for one day."

As they cruised close to the shore past Valhalla, the sun began to burn the fog off. Pondering all the parts of a person there were not to know, Evie spotted Charlie standing by himself smoking a cigarette on the topmost of the Great Camp's five balconies. A beat later, Lulu stepped out and pulled him into what Evie assumed was a bedroom. As she watched the shades drop, she said, "Must be nice to be in love."

Buddy answered, "Sometimes."

Two miles past the Great Camp, Evie spotted the telephone company repair crew replacing the section of buried phone line the beaver had eaten for dinner. Nudging the bow of the boat along the edge of the slough, they took note of furrows tunneled back into the reeds and trails of trampled marsh grass indicating a favored route of a fifty-pound rodent commuting between home and food.

Warblers and dragonflies worked the shallows with them as they laid their traps. At lunchtime Lulu and Charlie appeared on a Sunfish, tacking across the lake. White sail against blue sky, they looked picture-perfect until Lulu jibbed and the boat flipped.

By four thirty, they had set the last of their eighty-seven traps they brought with them. Friday before the wedding, they'd come back, and hopefully collect eighty-seven dead beaver.

The nuisance permit the sheriff issued them not only allowed them to trap out of season, it gave them access to all waterways flowing in and out of the Mannheim property, which meant the Mohawk Club couldn't stop them from cutting across the club's private lake and heading back home to Rangeley via their stretch of the Mink.

Throttling down the mile-long gorge, they came to a sign that read NO BOATING OR FISHING BEYOND THIS POINT hanging from a chain strung from shore to shore. Ducking as they passed under it, they cut out onto Lake Constance. The wind blew up a chop and the boat pounded as the cluster of buildings that housed the Mohawk Club amenities came into view. Whereas Valhalla was a playful bark-logged folly, the Mohawk was built to withstand a siege. Twenty cabins laid out in a semicircle around a dark-shingled clubhouse the size of an armory with stone turrets built of river rock—it managed to be both spartan and ostentatious at the same time. A pair of seaplanes were tied up at a float dock, chained to the end of a long wooden catwalk that stretched out across the shallows.

Buddy pointed back in the woods. Looking through her binoculars, she saw elevated wire pens on top of towers; doors opening up and people inside scattering feed. On the far shore a flock of mallards so vast it darkened the sky suddenly took flight. "What's with that?"

"They're training the ducks for hunting season. Every morning they put out food, open the pen doors, and the ducks fly out for breakfast. At the end of the day, they open up the pens and the ducks fly home for dinner. A couple of months of that, they're fat, slow, and trained to be easy to hit, and members of the Mohawk Club can have the pleasure of shooting wild ducks that are tame." Buddy spit in the lake. "Why not just throw a TV dinner up in the air and shoot it?"

It was just before twilight when they left Lake Constance and headed down the lower branch of the Mink. Her father cut the motor and let the river's current take them so they could relish the silence as the last light of that day dappled the surface of the water with a golden shimmer. Buddy lit up an unfiltered Lucky, while Evie stood in the bow, oar in hand, to keep them off the rocks. As they drifted downstream, a hatch of insects suddenly swarmed over the pools and eddies around them and trout began to rise. When a speckled black-green shimmer of a fish leapt free of the water just ahead of them, Buddy hissed with the intensity of a shout, "That brookie was a foot and a half long if it was an inch. Give me the oar."

Back-paddling the boat as if it were a canoe, Buddy swung the bow around and pulled up onto the bank. Evie cautioned, "This is still Mohawk Club land. Nuisance permit doesn't give us permission to fish. You may have forgotten what happened the last time we were here, but I haven't."

"Yeah, and we could get hit by a meteor before we get to Rangeley, but if that happens at least we'll be able to tell Saint Peter, 'The day I died I caught a brook trout—the Cadillac of fish.' "

Buddy's enthusiasm for both breaking the rules and fly-fishing was contagious. Helping him drag the boat up into the trees and hiding it with ferns, they grabbed their fly rods. Not bothering to put on waders, they gasped as the cold water rose up to mid-thigh, and silently waded downstream.

They ducked out of sight into a crevice in the cliff face on the south side of the river where Buddy knew they couldn't be seen by anglers on the riverbank. Then he opened a small flat cedar box lined with tiny feathered hooks, "flies" Buddy had tied himself. He chose the two that were the closest match to the hatch the trout were feeding on.

Hurriedly threading the tip of the leader through the hook eye of the fly and securing it with a turtle knot, Evie was using her teeth to bite off the excess leader when they heard a voice up on the ledge above them.

"I'm telling you of all this, Charlie, because I'd hate to see you do something you'd regret." Evie looked up through a cleft in the rock and saw Lulu's lawyer, Win Langley, talking to Charlie. The charm was gone from the men's voices.

"I can't go through with it." Charlie kicked a stone off the ledge.

Langley took a step back. "What part of it?"

"The wedding." They could no longer see the men's faces, but they could hear them.

"Everybody gets nervous before they get married." That was the lawyer.

"I'm not nervous. I just don't want to marry her. I thought I could do it, but I can't."

There was a long pause before Win asked, "Have you told Lulu this yet?"

"No, I wanted to talk to you first."

"As we both know, she's in love with you. Don't be a schmuck. You know what this could do to her."

"I'll hurt her more if I marry her."

"You realize this isn't going to make you popular?"

"I fell in love with someone else."

"Listen to me . . . I want you to fly back to New York with me in my plane tonight and spend the next few days thinking very carefully about the wonderful life you could have with Lulu Mannheim—beautiful children, Valhalla, triplex in Tribeca, house in East Hampton, and all the rest of it—then I want you to tell me you've changed your mind." Win squatted to tap his pipe on the edge of the rock ledge above and added, "You're a fucking lost boy, Charlie." Evie could hear the anger in Langley's voice.

As ash fell on her head, Evie stumbled back into the river. For a moment, she was sure Langley had heard her, but when she looked up, Langley was staring at the far shore. His voice softened and became fatherly as he told Charlie, "You understand, I'm not just Lulu's lawyer. I'm her friend and she's fragile. I care deeply about her and her happiness is important to me. Don't break her heart. I hope you reconsider." A few more words were said, but out of context they made no sense. After the two men walked back into the woods, neither Buddy nor Evie felt like fishing anymore.

CHAPTER 11

The way my mother told the story, I didn't see that coming. "What a total dick!"

My mother paused thoughtfully. "If Charlie was a total dick, he would have married her, made her miserable, and then soaked her for money for the rest of her life."

350 milligrams of oxycodone had made my bone ache go far enough away for me to feel sorry for someone other than myself. "Who was the girl Charlie wanted to leave Lulu for?"

"No idea. Not even sure it was a girl."

I didn't see that coming either. "Charlie was gay?"

My mother shrugged. "I don't know what Charlie was, except he wasn't what he seemed."

"So Charlie was faking that he was in love with Lulu that whole time?"

"We'll get there after you eat some lunch."

My mother put out prosciutto and melon. The smell of pork made me queasy. "What did Lulu say when you told her Charlie had met someone else?"

I was surprised when my mother said, "I didn't ever tell her."

"Why not?"

"I was going to, but . . ."

"But what?"

"Life got in the way."

CHAPTER 12

A s soon as Evie got back to the cabin that night, she told her parents, "I'm going to call Lulu up. If Charlie's got a girlfriend, she should know."

"Don't!" Buddy and Flo said it at the same time.

"She has a right to the truth!"

Buddy took over. "What if Charlie goes back to New York with that lawyer, thinks it over, and decides to go through with the damn wedding? He comes back up here and you've told Lulu that he's got something on the side, you've screwed everything up."

"But then he's just marrying her for money. She needs to know."

"Your father's right on this one. If the man's marrying her for her money, he'll just say you're lying or misheard or whatever, and trust me, if she's in love with him, she's going to believe him, not you."

"But her lawyer heard Charlie say it. He'll back us up."

Buddy made himself a peanut butter sandwich. "Lulu Mannheim's lawyer is not going to admit he knew the guy was going to call it off but didn't warn her."

Flo took over. "You can't get in the middle of what goes on between a couple. It's their business, nobody else's."

"Is that why you never told me what you and Buddy were up to before you came back to Rangeley? How you met in prison?"

Flo's face hardened and she shot Buddy a look.

Buddy stopped eating his sandwich. "Lulu brought up her brother and the prison stuff came out."

"What do you want to know, Evie?"

"What's the right thing for me to do?"

Flo was relieved Evie didn't ask her what happened after Buddy got out of prison. "Sometimes the right thing for you is the wrong thing for somebody else. You have to decide what's more important."

The next morning, Evie was looking up the phone number for Valhalla when the phone rang. Flo picked up and said, "She's right here." Mouthing Lulu's name, she passed the receiver on to Evie.

Buddy winced when he heard Evie ask straight off, "Did you hear from Charlie?" Then after a long pause he listened to the oblique half of a conversation where all his daughter had to say was, "No. . . . Okay. . . . If that's what you want. . . . You shouldn't feel obliged. . . . I understand."

As soon as she put down the phone, Buddy asked the obvious. "What's going on?"

"Charlie sent her two dozen roses this morning."

"Guilty conscience."

"He's driving back from New York late Thursday night and bringing Lulu's wedding dress; they had to do alterations."

Buddy waxed philosophical. "Looks like the lawyer talked him into going through with it. All that money. Hard to say no."

"I could still warn her."

Buddy butted in again. "What if the guy had a come-to-Jesus moment, dumped the other girl because he realized he liked Lulu more?"

Flo gave Buddy her *Shut up* look and asked, "Did Lulu say anything else?"

"Yeah, she wants me to go to the cocktail party and 'dinner dance' they're throwing on Friday night, and then to the wedding the next day." Evie acted like it wasn't a big deal, but it was. "Charlie has a younger brother who's a freshman at Columbia, doesn't know anybody, Lulu wants me to look after him."

Flo smiled. "That's nice for you." Evie wasn't at all sure about that. Having never been on a date in her life, she didn't want to go until Buddy said, "You won't know anybody there except for the help."

"I know Win Langley. He likes me, I can tell."

"Talking to somebody doesn't mean you know them. Besides, we've got to check the traps Friday and get what we caught skinned and—"

Flo cut him off. "You can do the skinning on Sunday. I'll bring the dress we got her for her birthday up at the end of the day in the Willys. She can drive it home after the party."

~ ~ ~

When Buddy and Evie got to Valhalla that Friday morning, the party tents were up. A pink-and-white-striped one for the dance that night, and virginal white for the wedding tomorrow. As caterers arranged gilt chairs around tables for ten, father and daughter set off into the lake once again. Knowing they had to check the traps and truck the dead beaver out before the guests started to arrive that afternoon, they had to work fast. Evie's decision to say nothing and hope for the best made her feel like an accomplice.

By noon, the mist had burned off, the sky was a cloudless blue, and they had nineteen beaver and four muskrat in the boat. Forty traps still to go, Buddy cranked up the Evinrude and they headed back across the lake to ice down the carcasses they had collected.

They hadn't gone a hundred yards when Buddy throttled back the outboard and turned the boat in a tight circle. "You see that? It's the sail to that Sunfish. Somebody must have tipped it over, gotten the mast stuck in the mud, and just left it. Those rigs cost six hundred dollars. Fucking rich people."

Through the glare of the sun bouncing off the surface of the lake, Evie glimpsed something white rippling ten feet down in the murky water. "Let's get it later."

"We'll never find it." Buddy had the boat hook out and on the third try snagged the triangle of white. Sediment from the lake bottom plumed up as he pulled it to the surface. It was heavy and seemed to have a life of its own. "Jesus Christ, it's got a snapping turtle caught up in it." He could see the back of its primeval shell and webbed claws flailing in the dark water. It wasn't until he pulled the billowing white snarl to the surface that they realized it was a white wedding dress. The jaws of a snapping turtle were clamped down on a pale naked foot.

Evie gagged as she shrieked, "Oh my God. It's her!" Scrambling to get away from the body, Evie slipped and fell down among the dead beaver, knocking the boat hook from Buddy's hand. As the body sank back into the lake, pulled downward by the snapping turtle, intent on finishing its meal at the bottom of the lake, they saw it wasn't Lulu in the wedding dress—it was Charlie.

They sat there for what seemed like a long time before Buddy picked the boat hook back up and pulled Charlie's corpse to the side of the boat. His skin was the color of a frog's stomach; blood that wasn't moving made his veins stand out, ghostly and unnaturally purple. That Charlie was wearing the wedding dress seemed more shocking and impossible than the fact that he was dead. Evie's voice broke in the middle of "What . . . happened to him?"

"Looks like he drowned himself." Her father sounded calm, but wasn't.

"Why is he wearing the dress?" Evie was trembling.

"Either he was crazy or he wanted people to find him like that, which is just another kind of crazy." Buddy grabbed hold of a dead arm and started to pull the body into the boat. The madness of what he was fishing out of the Mannheims' lake rattled him. Struggling with the unexpected weight of a drowned man, Buddy forgot the boat was already overloaded with dead rodents. His foot slid on a muskrat carcass, a surge of water rushed over the gunnels. Cursing as if Charlie were still alive, Buddy shouted, "The fucker's going to swamp us. Throw the beaver overboard." Evie felt like she was having an out-of-body experience as she made room for the dead man they had rescued.

When her father bellowed, "Oh Christ!" Evie thought he was yelling at her until she saw that the jaws of the snapping turtle were still clasped onto Charlie's foot. When Buddy couldn't kick it off with his boot, he pulled out his skinning knife and cut off the snapper's head. Reptile blood spurted out, staining the silky white train of the wedding dress tangled around the corpse's ankles. Evie vomited over the side of the boat and began to weep.

When they finally got the body into the boat and were unfolding a tarp over him, Evie noticed Charlie's eyes were wide open. He seemed surprised to be dead.

As they headed back to Valhalla with the dead man in the wedding dress, Win Langley's floatplane landed at the other end of the lake. Buddy told his daughter, "We don't say anything about overhearing that conversation between Charlie and the lawyer. They hear we stopped to go fishing in the Mohawk Club's stretch of the river, they'll arrest us for poaching. You understand me?"

They tied up at the dock behind the boathouse. A conga line of party planners and florists were carrying centerpieces for the tables into the striped tent. Electric feedback echoed as the band did its sound check. The roof and railings of the Great Camp were garlanded with ropes made of gardenias. Langley was just getting out of his seaplane. With him were Ian, the Rhodes Scholar with the big dick, and a spidery, hunched, silver-haired man in his early sixties. Evie noticed him because he only had three fingers on his left hand. All three were wearing Mohawk Club blue blazers and cream-colored flannel slacks.

Clinger the boatman tied up the floatplane and told Langley through a mouthful of Red Man chewing tobacco, "Miss Mannheim's lookin' for you, and the priest and that rabbi say they need to talk about the particulars of the service." Lulu had asked Langley to play father of the bride and give her away. The lawyer apologized for being late, explaining that a headwind had delayed them on the way up from Long Island Sound.

Buddy caught up with Langley just as he was starting up the steps to Valhalla. The lawyer looked puzzled as Buddy whispered in his ear, then Langley suddenly jerked his head back as if Buddy had just bit him. Evie was watching the fantasy unravel before her eyes when the door to the boathouse flew open behind her.

It was Lulu. Her hair tied back in a chignon roped with pearls, pink silk cocktail dress, she was all dressed up for the party except for her feet. It had rained briefly the night before and she had rubber boots on so as not to ruin her shoes in the mud. "Have you seen Charlie?"

All Evie could think to do was shake her head *no*.

Lulu scrunched up her face in cute annoyance. "He got in super late last night from New York and slept in the boathouse so as not to wake the house." Charlie's four-wheel-drive BMW M5 was parked a few feet away. "He swore he'd bring my wedding dress, but I can't find it anywhere—you don't think he could have forgotten it, do you?"

Evie started to cry. "What's wrong?" Lulu could see Win and Buddy hurrying toward her.

"What happened!" Lulu was frightened and shouting. "Tell me what's wrong!"

Evie tried to stop her from looking in the boat, but Lulu pushed her away. The wind blew back the tarp covering Charlie's body as Lulu scrambled down into the boat. When she saw her fiancé was wearing her wedding dress, she began to scream and clawed his face in a rage that would have been called murderous if he were not already dead.

By the time Sheriff Dunn got there, Harvey had dragged Lulu away from the body and taken her up to a bedroom in Valhalla. She was still wailing, but softer now that the sedatives he had given her had started to kick in.

Evie listened numbly as they stood on the dock and Langley summarized for the sheriff's benefit what Buddy had told him regarding how, when, and where the body had been discovered. Lawyerly, cold, and matter-of-fact, Langley sounded heartless to Evie until his eyes suddenly watered up with tears. "I . . . know this is irregular . . . highly irregular, but given the tragic circumstances—Lulu's emotional state and the needless damage that would be done if certain details become public knowledge—I hope no one objects if we get him out of that damn wedding dress before the ambulance arrives."

The sheriff and two deputies kept the caterers, party planners, and the rest of the hired help away from the boat. Then Clinger drove the bishop, the rabbi, and Langley out to the airport to break the news to the chartered jet full of wedding guests. The boatman would later relay to Evie that Langley told the stunned guests that Charlie had died in "a tragic swimming accident." No mention was made of the wedding dress. A bridesmaid fainted and the bishop and the rabbi led them in a moment of silent prayer. Langley asked everyone to respect the bride's privacy and refrain from discussing the tragedy with anyone from the press. Of the ninety-four guests on the plane, only one chose not to reboard and fly back to NYC.

Evie saw the solitary mourner when Clinger got back from the airport. He was skinny, young, and had a backpack slung across his shoulder. His black suit was rumpled and he wore red high-top sneakers. As Langley hurried up onto the front porch to talk to the sheriff, the wrinkled young man walked out on the bulkhead like a zombie and stared at the water.

Unable to find the key to Charlie's BMW, the deputies broke the window with a claw hammer, but couldn't figure out how to turn off the car alarm.

Sheriff Dunn had set up a tape recorder in Valhalla's grand dining hall and put on a show of making it look more official than it was. When Win Langley requested to be present during statements, the sheriff acquiesced in the hope of getting a donation for his reelection campaign in the fall; at least that's what Buddy said later.

The Mannheims' gamekeeper was in and out of the room in less than five minutes. All he had to say was that it was foggy and he was a hundred yards away when he saw Charlie get out of his car carrying a cardboard box, go into the boathouse, and turn on the lights. The box contained the wedding gown. By then, one of the canoes that were stored inside the boathouse had been found in the reeds down at the far end of the lake.

When it was Buddy and Evie's turn to go on record, Sheriff Dunn started off by asking if either of them had seen or heard anything to indicate that the deceased might have been inclined to take his own life. Buddy answered glibly, "I never met the man 'til I pulled him out of the water," then lit the cigarette he had parked behind his ear. Lulu had stopped wailing upstairs but the car alarm was still screaming outside.

"How about you, Evie?"

When Buddy looked over at her, she closed her eyes and whispered hoarsely, "He acted like he loved her . . . when he was with her." It wasn't a lie. But knowing that if she had told Lulu the truth the wedding might have been called off and Charlie might not have killed himself, it wasn't all of the truth. She knew Buddy wanted her to leave it at that, but that wasn't who she wanted to be.

Evie was about to confess what she'd overheard on the river when Langley reached over and turned off the sheriff's tape recorder. "Because I'm Miss Mannheim's attorney, there's certain information I'm not at liberty to reveal. But off the record, I've known for some time that Charlie was . . ." Win paused to collect himself. "I don't know if gay or bi would describe what Charlie was, but let's just say that he felt conflicted. Trapped. He told me several days ago he was in love with someone else and wanted to call off the wedding. Maybe I shouldn't have urged him so strongly to go through with it . . . I don't know. I honestly thought they could make a good life together. What I'm saying is I don't think one has to be a psychologist to see that committing suicide in a wedding dress was poor Charles's way of coming clean."

That's when the deputy came in with the letter they found in Charlie's BMW. The alarm finally stopped wailing as the sheriff read it aloud. It was written out in hand on a sheet of copy paper.

> *Dear Lulu,*
>   *I'm not the person you thought I was. I hope you find it in your heart to forgive me for doing this. I can't live this lie any longer.*
>   *Charlie*

As Langley put on his glasses to confirm it was Charlie's handwriting and signature, Evie announced, "I need some fresh air," and ran out onto the porch.

The grounds were deserted; the tents empty. Everyone had been sent home. Squirrels were eating the salted nuts that had been left out on the banquet tables. Evie was about to get in the pickup truck when she saw the guy in the black suit sitting on the edge of the dock, staring down into the boat, weeping. Figuring the guy must have thought the blood on the floorboards of the skiff came from Charlie, she said, "That's not your friend's blood. It's from a turtle."

"Good to know."

Evie was wondering if he was the "someone else" Charlie was in love with. "You guys were close?"

"Couldn't stand him."

"Then why are you—"

"I'm Charlie's brother, Nick Radetzky."

CHAPTER 13

I was still reeling from the idea of my mother finding a dead man in a wedding dress floating in a lake when she jumped back to the present and told me that this same guy, Nick Radetzky, had Skyped her last night.

"Charlie's brother just calls you out of the blue?" I felt like I was talking to a stranger that just looked like my mother. It unnerved me how much I didn't know about the woman who had brought me into the world.

"He's a psychiatrist. He wanted to talk about his brother's suicide."

"What did he ask you?"

"Nothing important."

I knew she was holding something back. Not wanting to call her a liar again, I reminded her, "If a mother doesn't trust her daughter with her story, neither one of them can ever learn anything from it."

Embarrassed, my mother looked away. "I didn't want to worry you with it."

"I'm already worried. Why did he call you now?"

"He discovered somebody had loaned Charlie $250,000 when he was a senior in college. He wanted to know if I'd heard anything about it. I told him I didn't know anything and hung up."

"But the psychiatrist thinks there's something suspicious about the suicide."

"He didn't say that. You're jumping to conclusions."

"What if Charlie didn't pay back whoever loaned him the money or didn't do what he agreed to do, and they killed him?"

"If he owed people money, they wouldn't have killed him the day before the wedding. Not that I'm saying anyone killed him. Once he was married, it would have been easy for Charlie to get cash. Lulu was crazy about him, she would have given him anything he asked for."

"*Do you think Scout had anything to do with it?*"

"*No.*"

"*Then why did you hang up on Dr. what's-his-name?*"

"*Because I have enough to worry about.*"

"*How can you be so sure it was suicide?*"

"*Charlie was alone when he pulled in at three o'clock, and he had the wedding dress with him. The sheriff found silk thread from the dress snagged on the canoe seat and some lace from the train snared on a bush at the top of the gorge. Charlie either jumped or fell.*"

"*You're not just saying that so I won't be scared?*"

"*I'm telling you everything I know.*"

"*Do you think Charlie would still have killed himself if you'd told Lulu he wanted to pull out of the wedding?*"

"*God, Chloé, I don't know. I have enough to feel guilty about without that. I mean, if I hadn't run out of gas, or met Lulu, maybe none of this would have happened. I also wouldn't have had you. Lulu introduced me to your father.*"

"*When did that happen?*"

"*At the end of the summer.*"

It was weird thinking you wouldn't exist if someone hadn't run out of gas. I didn't like the idea that my life was as erasable as that. "*Did Lulu have a big funeral for him?*"

"*No. She was in no condition to do that. Especially after she found out . . .*"

"*What?*"

"*Being in love with someone else wasn't the only thing Charlie was doing behind Lulu's back.*"

CHAPTER 14

Five days after Buddy and Evie fished Charlie's body out of the water, they were up at dawn trailering the outboard back to Valhalla to collect the beaver traps. The party tents had vanished and the ropes of gardenias that had garlanded the Great Camp were gone. A platoon of uniformed help was already at work making things look more normal than Evie knew them to be. Doris the maid was on the porch fluffing pillows. Gardeners were mowing the lawns and trimming hedges. Clinger and his son Hank were varnishing the brightwork of a sailboat that didn't need varnish.

The staff nodded and mumbled "Morning" as Buddy and Evie put their boat in the water, but no one said what they were thinking. Not a word was uttered about Charlie.

A few short and surprisingly discreet articles appeared buried in the back pages of the New York papers, all of which included the words *groom . . . Adirondacks . . . drowning . . . tragic . . . accident . . . private lake . . . heiress . . . heartbreaking*, but made no mention of how a wedding dress figured in the sadness.

Buddy said Sheriff Dunn and his deputies had been paid off by Langley to keep their mouths shut about the dress. When a member of the Mohawk Club wanted a favor, the sheriff knew it was a good idea to say yes and not ask any questions. That is, if he wanted to get reelected. Evie told herself it would be easier for Lulu if people didn't know they had found Charlie wearing her wedding gown, but Buddy got it right when he said, "Pretending something bad never happened doesn't change what happened."

A heat wave rolled in that day and it was pushing 90 by noon. Being out on the lake brought no relief. The air was listless, humid, and smelled of the mudflats. The surface of the water flat, glassy, and black threw back the glare of the sun in Evie's eyes. She felt unbalanced and unmoored from herself, as if she were trapped in a fever dream that belonged to somebody else.

A red-and-black seaplane buzzed them and landed at the other end of the lake. Taxiing to the Mannheims' dock, they watched Win Langley get out of the pilot seat wearing a business suit and carrying a briefcase.

The heat and scavengers rendered the pelts of the beavers trapped in the shallows worthless. Crows, crawfish, leeches, and, from the looks of the tracks, a family of skunks had gotten to them. "Everything likes a free meal," Buddy said.

By 3 p.m. that afternoon, Evie and her father had gathered up their traps and the beaver worth skinning out and were back at the boathouse. They were pulling the skiff up onto the trailer when Evie noticed that the mowers had been left out on the lawn and the hedges were still half-clipped. Clinger and his son had deserted the sailboat that didn't really need varnishing and were nowhere to be seen. Cans of varnish were open and brushes left out. Valhalla was deserted.

"Where the hell is everybody?" Evie looked around and saw Lulu in a bathrobe standing up on Valhalla's topmost balcony pouring herself a drink from what looked to be a quart bottle of vodka. When Evie waved, Lulu tossed the now empty bottle over the railing. As it shattered on the stone path below, Lulu turned, disappeared back into the bedroom, and closed the curtains.

Win Langley emerged from the Great Camp and walked slowly toward his floatplane. When he saw Evie and Buddy he stopped to say goodbye. "I wanted to thank you both for bearing up so well through all this." He had a way of shaking your hand, gripping it with his right and clasping it with his left, that made Evie feel special.

"What's going on? Where is everybody?"

"Miss Mannheim let everyone go with a month's pay."

"What? Who's going to take care of everything?" Buddy was putting the lids on the open cans of varnish.

Win shook his head. "To be honest, I don't know."

As the lawyer opened the door to his seaplane, Evie grabbed the sleeve of his seersucker suit. "You can't let her do that!"

"I have no say in the matter . . . Lulu fired me too." Lighting his pipe, he added, "Don't worry, I'll see that you're paid in full for your services." That wasn't what Evie was worried about.

No one knew who'd snapped the photo of Charlie in the wedding dress with Lulu screaming at the sight of him sprawled out dead that appeared in the tabloids the day after Charlie's family had him cremated. But those Lulu fired did not feel sorry for their former employer when the sordidness of her loss finally made headlines.

Evie tried to call Lulu twice at Valhalla. The first time she left a message on the answering service. The second time Lulu didn't pick up, Evie couldn't think of what to say so she just breathed for a minute to let Lulu know she was there before hanging up. There was a rumor a floatplane touched down on the Mannheims' lake and took off thirty minutes later, but nobody knew whether she was on board.

Lulu had not been seen for three weeks when Evie decided to distract herself from the sadness by trying to fly-fish at night. Armed with a nine-foot fly rod and a couple of huge woolly gray flies Buddy had tied to resemble a humungous bug or perhaps a baby mouse, Evie took the Jeep up the old logging road to Sutter's Point where the Mink flowed into the north end of Lake Millicent.

Waders on, up to her chest in the current, she cast her line into the darkness by starlight. All rhythm and wrist, she could not see where her fly landed, only feel it as it drifted across the mouth of the river. Stripping the wet line back with her left hand, feeling it slide between the forefingers of her right while her other three digits gripped the cork handle of her rod, she worked the fly across a pool Buddy called "the canyon." Under its still surface the lake bottom fell to a depth of two hundred feet.

Thinking about how her fly might look to a fish, Evie forgot about Charlie's corpse, Lulu's disappearance, and the fourteen hundred dollars she still needed. She was oblivious to everything but the pull of the river around her until the silence was shattered by a noise that didn't belong on the water. It was a loud, long, groaning crack like the sound a tree makes when it splinters as it falls, followed a few seconds later by the deafening boom of a violent explosion.

As the bang echoed over her and across the lake, she guessed it was Morlocks fishing with dynamite. Scrambling up onto the bank, she ran for the Jeep. Glancing back to see if they were coming after her, she saw someone had driven a boat up on the rocks in the middle of the river. Not a rowboat like the one she and Buddy used, it was twenty-five feet long at least. The boom was its gas tank exploding. As the flames spewed across the water, Evie could see that it was the Mann-heims' twenty-six-foot Chris-Craft, the *Aloha*, and Lulu was floating facedown with the current.

Running out into the river, knowing she'd drown herself if she fell in with her waders on, Evie used the reel end of her fly rod to snag Lulu's body just before her eyes lost sight of it in the darkness of the lake.

When Evie dragged her up onto the riverbank, Lulu gagged up a lungful of water and vomited. Her puke smelled of vodka and her scalp was bleeding. Lulu's body had been thrown through the *Aloha*'s windshield; bits of glass glistened in her hair. When Lulu finally sat up, she started to laugh.

Evie wrestled her into the Jeep, sure that Lulu had a concussion at the very least. Shifting gears, she double-clutched the Willys up the logging road back to Rangeley. When she turned onto the county road, Lulu suddenly sobered up. "Where are you taking me?"

"To the hospital."

"No way. I don't want my picture in the paper again."

"Then stop doing crazy shit."

"You don't take me back to Valhalla, I'll jump out of this car." The car was a Jeep that lacked doors and seat belts and Lulu was crazy— Evie did as she was told.

When they got to Valhalla, it was two in the morning and Lulu was snoring. Except for the light up in Lulu's bedroom, the Great Camp was dark. When shaking Lulu didn't wake her, Evie slapped her. When that didn't open Lulu's eyes, Evie got nervous. Putting her ear to Lulu's bony chest, she heard a heart beating fast and fluttery, as if a bird were trapped inside her rib cage.

The back door was wide open. Evie carried her up the back steps. The weight of the size 2 heiress reminded her of a gutted doe. She couldn't find the light in the mudroom, but as soon as she stepped into the kitchen, she knew there was someone else in the house. Evie jumped as a pair of raccoons that had been stealing Oreos bolted across the room and out the back door.

When she turned on the light she saw the kitchen wasn't just a mess. The counters and floor were littered with mouse shit and raccoon scat, but most of the chaos had been rendered by Lulu. Empty vodka bottles rolled underfoot; half-finished cups of ramen noodles grew mold so nasty even the raccoons wouldn't eat it; dirty dishes and stagnant water clogged both sinks of the gourmet kitchen; and shards of crystal goblets and Wedgwood china crunched beneath the soles of her boots. Purple stains on the wainscoting told Evie that Lulu had thrown more than one bottle of red wine against the wall in rage.

Lulu's bedroom was carpeted with dirty clothes, mildewed towels, and crumpled tissues crusty with snot and tears. The sheets were torn off the bed, drawers were pulled out and upturned, closets ransacked, clean clothes thrown down with the dirty. Evie didn't know what Lulu thought she was searching for during the month she had been holed up in Valhalla by herself. But whatever it was, it wasn't her drugs.

An arsenal of addictive substances was neatly laid out on a mirrored vanity table. There was a prescription bottle that didn't come from a drugstore containing 325-milligram tabs of oxycodone, inch-long glassine envelopes of heroin, a ziplock bag of rock cocaine, and a glass crack pipe. No question, the seaplane that had taken off shortly after landing on the Mannheims' lake carried at least one passenger who was a drug dealer.

Evie dropped her on the bed and rolled her onto her side so she couldn't choke on her own vomit if she got sick again. Lulu opened her eyes just long enough to mumble, "Good to be home," then fell back asleep.

It wasn't until then that Evie realized how angry she was at the woman whose life she had saved. Buddy was right. Lulu was nothing but a spoiled rich bitch.

Hurrying down the back stairs, remembering the kitchen floor was a minefield of broken glass and raccoon shit, she took the servants' hall that led to the library in search of a phone. She wanted to call Buddy and Flo, to hear their voices and be told to come home. Longing to be a kid again, she hoped it might change the way she felt about life if she said, "I was wrong. You were right. Next time I'll listen."

Something was wedged against the library door. She got the light on and saw that the marble bust of Adolphus Mannheim had been knocked off the mantel. His white head with its neat stone mustache and pointed beard lay on a Persian carpet a foot away from his neck. When she got down on her knees and began to pick up the pieces, she realized Adolphus wasn't the only thing Lulu had smashed. There were shards of milky white porcelain and under the couch she found the remains of a Chinese maiden with downcast eyes.

Picking up the pieces, she laid them out on the desk. Evie was wondering if the same guy who had fixed the stone girl that had captured her imagination could repair the carnage when she saw a crumpled note from Win Langley.

> *Dear Miss Mannheim,*
> *I know the last thing you need is more distressing news. Regrettably, your accountants at the firm of Lieber, Sloan & Weiss have informed me that shortly before you were to be married, Charles forged your signature as guarantor of a $5 million loan from a bank in Moscow. We have*

*not as of this writing been able to locate those
funds in any of Charles's accounts that we have
knowledge of.*

*As you know, my legal specialty is estate
planning. I strongly suggest we alert the proper
authorities and seek the counsel of a firm that
specializes in criminal law.*

Suddenly, Evie felt sorry for Lulu again. Not knowing what else
she could do to help, she went into the kitchen, put on a pair of rubber
gloves, and began to clean. Two hours later, it wasn't what Flo would
have called "clean," but at least the dishes had been washed, the sinks
unclogged, the floor mopped, and the raccoon scat was gone.

It was morning now. Evie sat on the steps of the main staircase
and waited for Lulu to regain consciousness. When she looked up,
the broken girl on the pedestal greeted her like an old friend, and she
wondered what it was about that statue that made her think anything
was possible.

"WHERE ARE MY FUCKING DRUGS!" Evie heard Lulu
shouting before she saw her.

"I flushed them down the toilet."

"I can buy more." Lulu was naked, except for a cigarette lighter
and a pack of Marlboro Lights. She did have red pubic hair.

"You can also die, it's up to you."

"What have you been doing?"

"Cleaning your kitchen."

"Why'd you do that?"

"Because if people saw how you've been living here for the last
month, they wouldn't work for you, no matter how much you paid
them, because you're crazy!"

"You want Harvey's job?" Lulu walked down the stairs as if she
had clothes on.

"No thanks." Evie found the offer insulting.

"What are you going to do?" Lulu's hand shook as she lit a cigarette.

"Save up and go to a school where they can teach me how to fix things. Like her." She pointed to the statue. Evie wasn't sure where the notion came from, but saying it out loud solidified the idea and suddenly made it seem as if that was the only thing in the world she had ever wanted to do.

"You want to be a restorer?" Lulu was on the landing, standing next to the statue now.

"Yeah, if that's what you call it."

"You really think you'd be good at it, I mean, that's really what you dream of doing?"

"Yes." Evie was more certain of it than she was of anything in her life.

"Okay. I'll give you a job." Before Evie could stop her, Lulu had pushed the statue off its pedestal.

Shards of marble and chips of the plaster that had been used to hide the cracks scattered around Lulu's bare feet. A chunk of stone that until a few seconds ago had been a dimpled thigh clattered down the grand staircase. Lulu stood next to the empty pedestal naked and forlornly defiant. Taking a long drag on the cigarette smoldering in the corner of her mouth like a lit fuse, Lulu exhaled. "It's not like she wasn't already broken."

The torso was split in three pieces, revealing the rusted iron pins that had been used to hold it together. The raised leg that gave no hint of what the marble girl was running from or toward was severed at the knee; the outstretched arm torn from her shoulder.

Evie was on her feet now, fists clenched. "Why the fuck did you do that?"

"Because I'm angry and because I can." Lulu's voice was calm and steely as she slowly headed back up the stairs. "And because I'm a rich bitch and because worse has been done to me." Every few steps, she added to the reasons why. "And because everything I touch turns to shit and I was stupid enough to fall in love with a thief who would rather be dead than marry me." She wasn't making excuses, just stating facts.

When Lulu got to the top of the stairs, she called out, "So Evie, are you going to put the pieces of her back together again or am I going to throw her in the garbage?"

Lulu looked down for an answer, but Evie was gone.

CHAPTER 15

I hadn't been out of the apartment in three days. My mother said we both needed fresh air. My legs were shaky and my step uncertain as we walked to Parc Montsouris. Taking in the sunlight on my face, I could feel my mother's story illuminating my own.

I remembered her taking me and the shotgun that slept in her bedroom to an apple orchard in the Dordogne. I could still hear her saying, "Squeeze the trigger. Don't jerk it." Then, after I'd fired both barrels, cautioning, "Never point a gun at someone unless they want to hurt you. And then make sure you don't miss."

Ignoring the chirp of an incoming text on my cell phone, I asked, "Is Scout the reason you taught me to shoot a gun when I was nine?"

"Yes . . . I guess. I didn't think anything was going to happen, but . . . Christ, I must've traumatized you."

"I thought it was cool. Bragged about it to the boys at school."

Now I realized it wasn't an accident that we had an eighty-pound pit bull that went ballistic every time a stranger came to the door. "And when I wanted ballet lessons, you made me take that karate self-defense class."

My mother smiled. "Every girl knows how to dance. I wanted you to be able to protect yourself."

I had liked calling my karate teacher "sensei" and earning different-colored belts. Sitting on the park bench, we reminisced about how, whenever I wanted to make my mother laugh, I would bow and say, "Oui, sensei," and "Non, sensei," and "Sacrebleu, sensei." The Japanese word for teacher in karate means "the one who has gone before you."

CHAPTER 16

Four days after Lulu pushed the statue down the stairs, Evie started work as a shelver at Bargain-Mart. As she made sure the four-packs of bum wad didn't get mixed up with the jumbo twelve-rollers, she considered how many trees got cut down each year to wipe the world's ass. It was her way of avoiding thinking about all that had happened at Valhalla. The assistant manager's voice crackled over the PA, "SPILT MILK IN AISLE THREE." Evie didn't know what that meant until the PA system boomed, "IN CASE YOU DON'T UNDERSTAND ENGLISH, EVIE, THAT MEANS GET YOUR FANNY OVER TO DAIRY AND CLEAN IT UP."

Buddy had warned her she wouldn't like the job. "Being ordinary is no fun," was how he put it. But ordinary was precisely what Evie wanted after the events at Valhalla. She had told her parents about pulling Lulu out of the river after she drove the Chris-Craft up on the rocks, but said nothing to anyone about Lulu pushing the statue off its pedestal.

As she sliced boiled ham for a rush order of twelve subs, it occurred to Evie that Valhalla was a beautiful trap. Once it closed on you, the only way to escape was to leave a part of you behind. Trappers called it *ringing off*. If you were a muskrat, that meant you had to leave your foot in the trap. Evie didn't have a name for the part of herself she left behind in the jaws of Valhalla.

When the lunch-hour rush slowed, Evie noticed locals were giving her the eyeball and whispering. She wasn't sure whether it was her disfigurement, the fact that her Bargain-Mart T-shirt was too tight across her breasts, or perhaps because, as Buddy had put it with backwoods snobbery, "Quimbys don't work by the hour." Then Morris Clinger, the ex-boatman at Valhalla, came over with a wad of Red Man in his cheek. "Just wanted to shake your hand and say much obliged." But before she could ask what he was thanking her for, the PA interrupted. "YOU GOT AN OVERFLOW IN THE LADIES', EVIE."

At the end of her eight-hour shift, the only positive thing Evie could think of having to do with working at Bargain-Mart was that it ended at 5 p.m.

Evie found the day so brain-numbingly boring she decided to try smoking so she'd have something to do during her cigarette breaks. Sitting on the bench across the street from the beauty parlor, she was just lighting up when a red Mohawk Club Land Rover pulled up in front of the pharmacy. The top was down and Win Langley was at the wheel. When he got out of the Land Rover, she noticed he had an aluminum brace on his left knee. He was wearing shorts, a necktie, knee-socks, and the same kind of hiking boots the guy on the Swiss cocoa box wore. Going round to the back of the Jeep, Langley lifted up a long, narrow mahogany case with brass fittings and smiled like a kid.

She was thinking about how even though Langley felt the need to dress up like he was on the Matterhorn and he belonged to the Mohawk Club, he still came across as a pretty likable guy, especially when he called out to her from across the street, "Goldilocks! Aren't you a sight for sore eyes."

Formal as ever, he took her hand in his two-handed shake and did his little bow. The leg with the brace was zippered with scars and the flesh rippled from a skin graft. Knowing how much she didn't appreciate people taking notice of her disfigurement, she felt guilty for staring at his, especially when he caught her. "Climbing accident . . . long time ago in Europe."

"What's in the box?"

"It's a present from an old friend." He lifted the lid. Nestled in maroon velvet was the most beautiful rifle Evie had ever seen. Its stock was made of burled walnut and ran the length of the barrel. The curve of its raised Monte Carlo cheekpiece made Evie think of a violin.

Even more unusual, there was no knob on the arm of the bolt action, instead just an elegantly tapered finger of steel not unlike the handle of a silver spoon.

"Wow, that's some gun!" Inlaid and engraved, it was so pretty you forgot it was lethal.

"It's a Mannlicher-Schönauer. 6.5 millimeter. Made for the king of Romania in 1936—always wanted one. First day of deer season, this rifle and I will be stalking Flathead Mountain." He smiled as he showed her the gun and took aim at the plateau atop the summit that gave Flathead Mountain its name. "Here, hold it. See how it feels." Evie wasn't expecting him to hand her the rifle.

Opening the bolt, she noted the magazine had been altered. "Why's it only take two cartridges?"

"If you can't put an animal down in two shots, you don't deserve the kill."

Evie brought the elegant rifle to her shoulder. It was light and satiny against her cheek. "So how in the world did you do it?" the lawyer asked.

"Do what?" Evie handed him back the rifle.

"Get Lulu under control. She said you talked her into hiring back the staff at Valhalla."

"I didn't tell her to do that." Evie suddenly understood why Clinger had thanked her.

Langley smiled at her. "Very discreet of you to keep it to yourself. Being able to hold on to a secret is a rare attribute in this day and age. Shows character."

"Since I didn't tell her anything and she doesn't listen to anybody anyway, I don't know what it shows, but whatever. Did she rehire you?"

"Did you tell her to do that too?" Evie could see how Langley would be good in a courtroom.

"I don't know what you're talking about."

"That's right, I forgot. Yes, she offered me my old position, but at this point in my life, when people fire me, I stay fired. It's a question of trust. I guess she hurt my feelings." Langley put the rifle back in its case.

"Who's going to look after her?"

"I thought that was your job, Evie?"

"No thanks, I got my own fish to fry."

At that moment, the sleigh bell attached to the door of the pharmacy jingled and a silver-haired man sporting a better tan than George Hamilton emerged. White teeth, bright blue eyes, he wore a safari jacket, and as he walked down the sidewalk he whistled a samba while shaking a pair of prescription bottles of pills in either hand as if they were maracas. Fifty? Sixty? It was hard to tell how old he was, but Evie could see that when he was young, he must have looked a lot like Matthew McConaughey. Evie could tell he wasn't a local even before he called out, "Μήπως η μικρή φίλη σου με τα μεγάλα στήθη ξέρει ότι μιλάει με έναν βρώμικο γέρο?"

Evie smiled and asked, "What language is that?"

"Greek. If Andy hadn't been there when I fell, I would not be standing here now." Langley introduced them.

Evie didn't know if she was more surprised by the fact that Andy kissed her hand or that he had a southern accent when he said, "Pleasure to meet you, Miss Quimby."

"If you have a southern accent, how can you be Greek?"

Langley answered for him. "Andy's wife has a beautiful house in Greece."

Evie couldn't tell if he was making fun of her when he winked and added, "And I miss her so much I'm forced to flirt with every pretty girl I see."

~ ~ ~

Dill was in the middle of giving Scrotum's mother highlights when Evie entered the beauty parlor. She buried her face in the glossy magazine Dill had left open on a chair and waited. Thinking the perfume sampler in the latest edition of *Vogue* smelled like snake, she switched to an old issue of *Vanity Fair*.

Evie opened to an article about a glamorous middle-aged Italian lady named Ida, who had a freak accident early in her marriage that put her in a wheelchair. There were photographs of her on board the 220-foot yacht her husband had named after her. It was just as Evie got to the part about the yacht being called the *Idonia*, which means *Ida and me*, that she realized the woman's handsome husband was the same guy who had just kissed her hand.

Evie was thinking about all the different ways you could interpret him saying, *And I miss her so much I'm forced to flirt with every pretty girl I see*, especially when she knew herself not to be pretty, when Buddy rapped on the window and motioned for her to get in the truck. She could tell he was in a bad mood from the way he was puffing on his cigar.

Evie was surprised when her father took the turnoff into Valhalla. The maid showed them into the dining room. As Evie stepped in out of the sunlight, it took her eyes a moment to penetrate the darkened room. Her mother, clutching a long, gnarled hickory walking stick, looked like a witch about to cast a spell.

There was something under a white sheet on the table that at first glance looked so much like a body Evie flashed on the thought that Lulu had finally succeeded in killing herself. But Lulu was very much alive, sitting in a corner of the room, pale, remote, and looking guilty. An ashtray filled with half-smoked cigarettes was propped on her knee. They had clearly been talking for some time. From the look on Lulu's face, Evie could tell Flo had told her things she had not enjoyed hearing.

"What's going on, Mom?"

"Lulu came by the cabin this morning and told me you want to be an art restorer. Is that true?"

Evie looked around the room nervously. "It's an idea that has occurred to me."

Flo ignored Buddy and his stogie and focused on her daughter. "Why didn't you mention it?"

"It's harder to pretend I'd ever have the chance to do something like that if I say it out loud. And because Buddy would have told me what the hell did I know about restoring or who the hell was going to hire me for something like that, and I would have had to answer nothing and nobody."

Flo pulled the sheet off the table. The broken pieces of the statue Lulu had pushed down the stairs were neatly laid out. Buddy blew a smoke ring. "There's no fixing that."

Flo gave Buddy a look that said *Shut up* and asked, "Evie, tell me the truth. Do you think you could put her back together again?" Evie walked slowly around the table. Picturing the statue as she was when she had first seen her on the pedestal; holding on to what the marble girl had once been, her mind began to pick up the pieces, turning them over in her imagination, her brain reassembled the parts, first slow, then fast.

Evie took a deep breath. "I can fix it. But not her."

Lulu licked her finger to remove a smudge of mud on the tip of her velvet slipper and clarified, "I'm not part of the job. You won't even have to talk to me if you don't want to. I've got all the tools and things you'll need and books to help you."

Evie checked out a crate containing boxes of chisels, cans of epoxy, clamps, drill bits, and stainless steel pins. "How did you know what to get?"

For the first time Lulu looked Evie in the eye. "I've broken things before. I called a restorer who's done work for me."

"Why did you say to people I told you to rehire everybody?"

"Because I wouldn't have done it if it weren't for you."

"I never said anything like that."

"It's the way you looked at me when I pushed the statue over. Like I was a monster."

"You are."

"Luckily I'm not hiring you to be polite."

"So why are you doing this for me?"

"You cleaned my kitchen."

Buddy had heard enough. "This is crazy. We're out of here—"

Flo cut him off. "What's crazy is our daughter wasting her time shelving at Bargain-Mart and rebuilding outboard motors."

Buddy's cigar ashed on the carpet. "Where in the hell is Evie ever going to get a job restoring things like that around here?"

Evie could tell Flo had thought this through. "She could work for a museum or go to New York."

Lulu didn't help the situation when she offered, "Berlin's cool."

Buddy was shaking his head *no*. "She doesn't want to live in a city."

"Yes I do!" Buddy looked at his daughter like she'd just slapped him in the face.

"I'll pay you the same hourly rate that you get at that Bargain-Mart." Lulu held out her hand to shake on it.

Before they did, Flo stepped between them and nailed Lulu with an arctic stare. "I warn you, if anything bad happens to my daughter, you will answer to me. Are we clear?"

Lulu nodded and smiled. "I always wondered what it would be like to be part of a real family."

~ ~ ~

Evie did not bill Lulu for the hours she spent studying the stack of books on art restoration that she took back to the cabin. She read them slowly and aloud at the kitchen table just as she had done with *Pride and Prejudice*. Contrary to Flo's maxim on the wisdom of keeping thoughts and feelings separate, Evie realized straightaway that to reclaim the wonder of something beautiful that had been damaged, she would have to think and feel at the same time.

When she came across technical terms that were foreign to her, words and expressions she was uncertain of, she heard Flo's voice inside her head saying "Look it up" and she would reach for the hard-back *Webster's* by the salt and pepper shakers. That restorers always refer to the left hand of the statue they're working on as the "sinister hand" was one of the less useful things she learned.

Surfing "restoration" on the Internet, she scrutinized all kinds of video clips and documentaries showing restorers practicing their craft. Ignorant of the value of the marble girl, unaware that a conservatory-trained restorer would have spent a decade apprenticing to a master before taking on the challenge of a job like the one she was about to embark on, Evie didn't know enough to be nervous. At least at first.

Having used epoxy to patch holes in all kinds of fiberglass boats, she reasoned that working with the resins used to cement fragments of stone and fabricate facsimiles of parts too damaged to repair would not be beyond her. What worried her was drilling out the rusty hundred-year-old iron rods that held together the three large chunks of marble that composed the torso and connected the arms and legs. The Internet said she should replace them with stainless steel pins, but that seemed like asking for disaster. Evie was sure she'd end up doing more damage than good until she found out that the pressure produced by the buildup of corrosion and rust around those iron bones would eventually have caused the statue to explode. Evie told herself she and the stone girl were lucky to have met.

To practice drilling into marble without cracking the stone, she and Buddy drove up to the cemetery in Lumberton and purchased the remnants of an old white marble headstone that had once belonged to *Agatha L. Huddlestone—Beloved Mother and Wife*. The cemetery keeper told her the Morlocks had taken a sledgehammer to it on Mischief Night back in October, then snuck in the next night and set fire to a mausoleum just to show there was no stopping them.

~ ~ ~

A week later, Evie pulled through the gates of Valhalla nervous and impatient to find out if she had any talent for the vocation she had pulled out of thin air and set her heart on. Clinger was sitting on the steps of Valhalla waiting for her. The wad of tobacco stuffed in his cheek created the impression that he was speaking in tongues. After he said it twice, Evie figured out he was telling her, "Miss Mannheim's down in New York City. Doin' what, I have no idea. But she told me to tell you if you need any more tools and such, you can order 'em up, special delivery." He handed her a credit card. Following him up onto the porch, he spit and said, "I gotcha everything set and ready best I could." Then he led her into the dining room, which was no longer a dining room.

The thirty-foot-long banquet table was gone, as were the chairs, sideboard, paintings, and carpets. Drop cloths had been tacked to the floor. The shattered remains of the statue were now laid out on a stainless steel table that looked as if it belonged in an operating room. A massive workbench was placed in front of the picture window. Tools, clamps, bottles and cans of solvents, polymers, and epoxies particular to restoring marble were neatly organized on metal shelves. The chandelier had been removed and work lights strung from the rafters. As Clinger closed the door behind him he said, "Good luck." Evie knew she was going to need it.

There were twice as many pieces to be glued together as she remembered. Suddenly all the fragments looked the same. She had no idea where fist-size chunks of marble, smooth on one side and jagged on the other, belonged. Were they part of the statue's arms, legs, stomach, back? More intimidating was the round oatmeal container half-full with unidentifiable pinkie-size shards of stone that had once been flesh.

Evie wasn't daunted, she was paralyzed. She stood there staring at the stone puzzle for almost two hours. Then, slowly, as shafts of sunlight made visible by dust fell across the fragments of broken marble, the memory of how the statue first looked when she mistook it for a naked ghost materialized in the forefront of Evie's mind. She began to see how each part was different from the one next to it and the key to making her whole was recognizing what was unique and special about each one.

Clearing the workbench, she slowly began to group the fragments of stone by body part—left arm, right arm, right leg, left leg, torso. She placed four-by-fours between the sections so there would be no confusion. The fewer pieces there were on the steel table, the clearer it became.

Moving calmly and carefully, but excited inside, Evie turned the pieces over in her hands, memorizing the sharp edges by touch. Her focus was so single-minded, it wasn't until she carried the largest section of torso across the room and gently placed the 120-pound chunk of marble snug against the other two pieces of the stone girl's abdomen, that Evie realized her palms were bleeding. She asked Clinger if he could lend her a pair of gloves.

Evie had never seen the back of the faceless marble girl—the angle of her shoulder blades, the shape of her buttocks and how they were in turn tethered to the stone girl's thighs, were all a mystery to her. Feeling defeated before she had even begun, all Evie had to say when Lulu's seaplane landed just after 4 p.m. was, "I need photographs of your fucking statue."

"Nice to see you too, dear. I don't have any photos of the statue."

"You have to. I need to see what her back looks like."

"Maybe there's something in the attic."

A tall, leanly muscled man in a tracksuit was getting out of the seaplane carrying glossy bags from shops Evie had never heard of. "Who's he?"

"My new trainer. I needed something to cheer myself up." It was what Lulu's mother said when she bought herself presents at Tiffany.

"Does something have a name?"

Lulu smiled and turned to the trainer. "Slavo, Daisy will show you your room. I've got to help Miss Quimby."

~ ~ ~

Following Lulu up the steps to the Great Camp, Evie noticed she was dressed differently. The hoodie and warm-up pants of her posse days were gone. Lulu was wearing a gray dress that made her look like a matron in an Eastern European prison circa 1966. Evie did not know its plainness made it chic or that it was Prada, but she was right to sense something had shifted. No longer able to pretend she was a teenager at thirty-plus, Lulu had decided to impersonate an adult.

As Evie trailed her through Valhalla and up the grand staircase toward the attic, Lulu found fault wherever she looked, calling out to the servants, "There's dust on top of the picture frames. . . . The flowers should have been changed two days ago. . . . How many times do I have to tell you the Tiffany lamp gets forty-watt bulbs." Having never seen or heard her take the slightest interest in the housekeeping of the Great Camp, Evie wondered what was going on when the sight of a spiderweb overlooked by a maid prompted her to bark, "Am I the only person who cares about any of this?"

Suddenly hearing the echo of her voice in the staircase, Lulu froze. From the look of shock on her face, you would have thought she had put her finger in a light socket. Shaking her head, Lulu muttered, "Christ, I'm turning into her."

"Turning into who?"

"My mother. I sound just like her. It's what she used to walk around saying."

Evie half recalled Buddy saying Mrs. Mannheim had smoked herself to death when Lulu was a teenager. "What was your mother like?"

Lulu thought about it for a long moment. "Bitter."

"About what?"

"Everything money couldn't buy. . . . But in particular the fact that my father had girlfriends . . . and boyfriends."

All Evie could think to say was, "Wow." She felt sorry for Lulu, but still had not forgiven her for the statue. As they headed up the back stairs to the attic, Evie asked, "Did your mother have a Slavo?"

"Several." Lulu looked at her sideways and added, "You're good at putting things together, aren't you, Evie?"

The attic ran the length of the Great Camp—long and narrow as a bowling alley, it was a jumble of dead persons' things, neatly arranged

and layered in dust. Steamer trunks, covered with stickers of desti-
nations Evie had never heard of; a dozen pairs of riding boots for a
woman with a long, narrow foot; a Victorian birdcage big enough
to imprison a flock of chickens; racks of out-of-fashion ball gowns;
wooden skis with bear-trap bindings; a baby crib filled with broken
dolls; they found the photo albums Lulu was looking for piled under a
rug that had once been worn by a polar bear.

The albums were bound in green leather and dated in gold. Evie
started in 1913. As she flipped through the albums, Lulu stood behind
her, stopping Evie every few pages to tell her more than she wanted
to know about Mannheims who had died young, drank themselves
to death, been addicted to morphine, been driven mad by syphilis,
impregnated showgirls, or were secretly gay.

Evie wasn't sure whether Lulu was bragging about how fucked
up her family was or making excuses for how fucked up she was. Still
waiting for Lulu to apologize for pushing the statue down the stairs,
Evie found Lulu's running commentary on the many skeletons in the
Mannheim family closet more and more irritating.

There was a definite frostiness between the two women by the
time Lulu mentioned, "I'm thinking about adopting a child. Maybe
from Africa or Cambodia. Since you were adopted I wanted to know
what you thought of the idea?"

"I think you should start with a dog." Evie wasn't trying to be
funny, but Lulu laughed and started to act more like herself.

An hour and a half later, Evie found a manila envelope tucked in
the back of 1939 that contained a series of sepia-tone eight-by-ten por-
traits of a pair of debutantes in ball gowns posed on either side of the
marble girl. In one of them the photographer had turned the pedestal
around, and posed the society girls hiking their gowns up and looking
back over their shoulder as if they were running up the stairs after the
statue. What made the hair on Evie's arms stand up was that in those
photos the stone girl had a face. The expression on it was wide-eyed
and urgent and Evie could see she was running from something, not

toward it. Looking closer, she saw the eyes and mouth were rendered full of fear as if the stone girl knew there was no escaping from what was chasing her.

"What happened to her?"

Lulu thought she was talking about the blonder of the two women in the photograph. "My great-aunt married a—"

Evie cut her off. "I'm talking about the statue. How'd she lose her face?"

Lulu raised up her hands and said, "Not guilty."

Evie had what she wanted and was on her way to the stairs when Lulu pulled a pink backpack out of a jumble of old luggage and muttered, "What a sick puppy." Evie looked back and saw the book bag contained a stack of old porno magazines.

"Whose are those?"

"Mine."

Evie was stunned. "Why would you want them?"

"Somebody gave them to me to show me what men want."

"How old were you?"

"Nine."

"That's disgusting."

"Yeah. That's one word for it. He was a friend of my father's. I called him Uncle Fred. He gave me a kitten."

"What do men want?"

"Normal men or freaks? Not that there's always a difference."

"Normal."

"Sex is about power for men."

"What's it about for women?"

"Deciding how they feel about that."

CHAPTER 17

While Evie struggled to make the stone girl whole, Lulu embarked on a different kind of restoration project. Driving through the gates at 8:30 every morning, Evie heard Slavo encouraging Lulu by shouting, "You're slow and you're lazy," as he led her back from their two-mile run.

Then, two or three hours later, when Evie would look up from her workbench, she'd see Lulu out on the porch, strapped into the belts and pulleys of a machine Slavo called "the Reformer." Pilates was a word Evie hadn't heard before. Lulu said it was good for her core.

The new and improved version of Lulu didn't stop there. The cook complained it was impossible to make anything worth eating now that Miss Mannheim had cut out gluten, sugar, dairy, meat, salt, and starch.

In the afternoon, Lulu would be out on the lawn, drenched in sweat, practicing kickboxing, which mostly consisted of Lulu punching and kicking the Serbian Adonis and him shouting, "Harder. . . . You hit like a girl."

Curious, Evie wandered down and asked, "Why kickboxing?"

Breathless, Lulu paused to answer, "My shrink says I need to learn how to protect myself."

It was Evie's turn to regret sounding like her mother when she replied, "In real life, Slavo would hit you back." The next day, Lulu was wearing boxer's headgear and Slavo was hitting her with a closed fist.

When Evie said good night to the shattered statue at 6 p.m., Lulu was under a sheet on the massage table out on the screened-in porch, grunting as Slavo's oiled hands worked out her kinks, a glass of white wine waiting as a reward.

What Evie liked most about restoring the statue was that as she was working on it her mind didn't have to worry about Lulu or anything else. When she came back to the cabin and her parents at night, the broken girl was with her. While she was sitting at the kitchen table eating dinner with Buddy and Flo, her mind would tinker with the fragments of marble that still lay scattered in her head. After she went to bed, more than once, she dreamed of herself at the workbench just about to cement the last missing piece into place only to discover that she had made a mistake that was impossible to fix. And then there was the dream that the missing pieces of the statue's head were found and Evie was able to give the stone girl back her eyes, face, and the pleated braid she had once worn like a crown, and make her whole.

Twenty-one days after she started, Evie had all the pieces of the statue epoxied and pinned together. Clinger and Slavo helped her lift it up and slip the steel rod that ran through its torso into a stand that put her at eye height and allowed Evie to turn her around and examine her from all sides. The muscles matched up, the geometry of her limbs in connection to the body was correct. Her legs were raised at the angle a woman's legs would assume if she were running for her life, and her right hand reached out for something to save her with appropriate urgency. Evie had got all that right, but her triumph was short-lived. Now when she looked at it, all she saw were the cracks between the pieces of stone she had assembled and which still had to be filled in. As Clinger put it, "You got some caulking to do."

Experimenting on the fractures and gaps that scarred the stone girl's right breast, Evie tried to fill in the fissures with pigmented epoxy. The color was right, but the filler seemed to eat the light rather than capture it, and the cracks she had filled made the stone girl's breast look like dead flesh.

She tried grinding up the shards of marble that were left over in the oatmeal box, mixing their dust with plasticine and filling in the gaps with a palette knife. But when it dried, Evie realized all she'd done was give the marble girl stretch marks. She tested every technique the books recommended only to find the cracks less visible but some-how more distracting, which meant the following day would have to be spent painstakingly picking out the filler that did not do justice to the rest of the statue. Evie did not want to make the marble girl look brand-new, just to erase any indication that she had been pushed down a flight of stairs.

A week of trying and failing and trying and failing left Evie feel-ing stupid and angry at herself. In the middle of dinner, she burst into tears. Buddy's advice was simple. "You can't unbreak something." Flo told her, "If it was easy, everyone would be able to do it."

Neither made Evie feel any better. In fact, there was no distract-ing her from her misery until Buddy tried to open a stuck door to an overhead cabinet Flo had been asking him to fix for months. Yanking with all his might, the cabinet door flew back and struck Buddy square in the face, cracking his two front teeth in half. Her father had always prided himself on his pearly smile. Holding his two front teeth in his cupped hand, blood streaming down his chin, he began to curse. His teeth broken at an angle, Buddy looked like he had fangs. Evie forgot about the stone girl long enough to laugh.

The next morning, Buddy dropped Evie off at Valhalla and drove on to Speculator to see the dentist. By then Evie had faced up to the fact that she needed to talk to someone who had actually restored a statue. The return address on the crate the restoration materials Lulu had ordered from New York read "Jacques Clément—Fine Art Restoration—4 Staple Street, New York, NY." Evie dragged the hall phone into the dining room, closed the door, and cold-called Jacques Clément.

His voice was gruff; a French accent and static on the line made communication difficult. As Evie tried to explain who she was and what she wanted, he interrupted her twice to yell at his assistant.

"Could you please repeat that, I was distracted."

"Lulu Mannheim ordered some supplies from you about a month ago."

"Right. You're the friend who's trying to repair something." She heard him pause to strike a match and take a long drag on a cigarette. "What is it exactly you want from me?"

"Well, the statue's made of white marble. Really old marble. And I've epoxied it together, but . . . how do you make the cracks not show?"

Pencil and pad in hand, she was waiting to write down his instructions when after a moment of silence he sighed. "That is easy . . . you put it in a box and send it to me with a check." Her face flushed at the boredom and arrogance in his voice.

"I want to do it myself." She heard him sucking on his cigarette.

"How old is the marble?"

"Two thousand years."

Jacques laughed. "Says who?"

"Says me." Evie glared at the phone and mouthed the word *asshole*.

"Fax me a photograph of it and I'll get back to you."

He rattled off a number; before she could say *thank you* or *goodbye* he hung up. Faxing him photos of the statue both front and back, Evie waited by the phone for his call. Through the window she could see Lulu out on the lawn playing with the twelve-week-old Irish setter puppy she had bought instead of adopting a third-world child. Watching the way Lulu tried to teach the dog to sit, Evie realized a more appropriate starter pet for Lulu would have been a goldfish.

There was no phone call from *Jacques Clément, Fine Art Restoration*, that day. Once she looked him up on the Internet and saw the list of museums he worked for, she was not surprised he couldn't be bothered. Knowing how ignorant she must have sounded made Evie feel all the more stupid for not being able to figure out a way to fill the cracks with something that looked and felt real enough to bring the stone girl back to life.

Evie was relieved when Buddy, fresh from the dentist, picked her up early. As she climbed into the pickup, Buddy gave her a look he called his *smolder* and smiled big. "What do you think?"

Evie peered at the new front teeth that replaced the two that had broken in half the night before. "Wow . . . they look real."

"They are. Dentist glued them back on."

"Who is this dentist?"

"You got something wrong with your teeth?"

"No."

Evie was late getting to Valhalla the next morning. Lulu had finished with the Reformer and was calling for someone named Ivan. Distracted and lugging a knapsack over her shoulder, it took Evie a moment to figure out Ivan was the name of the new dog.

"I'm selling Ivan."

"Why?"

The dog was up on the porch following the maid around. "The ungrateful little bastard likes her more than me."

"Who gives the dog his food?"

"The maid."

"A dog belongs to whoever feeds it."

"Just like with men." Slavo didn't think that was funny, but Evie did. As she headed up onto the porch, Lulu called out, "Flo rang me and said you're having trouble with the statue."

Evie froze halfway up the stairs. "I'll let you know when I'm ready to quit. And next time my mother calls . . . tell her if it was easy everybody would do it." She stayed locked in the dining room with the broken girl for the rest of the day, refusing to come out even for lunch.

Evie did not see the dusty black panel van barrel down the drive and pull up behind the main house, but Clinger did. Recognizing neither the vehicle nor the man who got out of it, the boatman walked quickly up from the dock to ask him his business.

Clinger didn't like the look of the driver. Scruffy beard, silk scarf knotted around his neck, skinny with a paunch, wraparound sunglasses, gray skin and sweating, the guy reminded Clinger of a snail out of its shell. Most of all, Clinger did not like the stranger dropping his cigarette on the gravel instead of putting it out in his own goddamn ashtray. Figuring him for either lost or selling something Miss Mannheim didn't want, Clinger was about to tell him to pick up his butt, get back in his van, and turn his ass around when Lulu and Slavo came out for kickboxing.

"It really was unnecessary you driving all the way up here, Jacques." The restorer had called Lulu after he heard from Evie.

"Your little friend sent me a photograph of the statue—Greek, second century BC."

"It's third century, actually, but what's your point?"

"She doesn't have a clue what she's doing. I have to stop this before she fucks it up beyond repair. That statue belongs in a museum. You want her to fucking destroy it?"

Slavo gave Lulu a look that said, *Do you want me to hit him now?* Lulu waved him off. She looked up and saw Evie standing on the porch.

"Did you send for him?"

"No."

"Show me what you've done to the statue and I'll salvage what I can." Lulu looked back to Evie, not sure what to say.

"You're going to see it eventually, so it's not like putting it off is going to make any difference."

The restorer pushed ahead of Evie as they entered the dining room. The statue was upright on its stand and a sheet was draped over it. When he pulled it off, his body blocked Lulu's view. The Frenchman muttered, "Fuck."

Clinger and Slavo were in the room now too. Lulu started to make excuses for Evie. "She's not finished yet, it's not fair to judge." When the restorer stepped away from the statue, Lulu stopped talking.

The cracks and gouges were gone, and the luster of whatever Evie had filled them with had the same milky luminescence as the marble quarried in antiquity.

The restorer touched the stone girl's breast as if he was planning to go to bed with her. Bringing his face close, he sniffed the surface of the marble as if he were an animal. Drawing a line with his fingertip across her torso, he asked, "She was broken here and here?"

Evie nodded and watched him lick the tip of his finger with a surprisingly pointed tongue, touch the smoothness of the flesh rendered in stone, and then taste the residue of Evie's handiwork.

"What did you use?"

"Dental cement."

Lulu cackled and clapped. Jacques Clément, nodding in bemused agreement, stepped forward, took hold of Evie's shoulders, and kissed both sides of her face. It was after he let go of her and said, "Very beautiful, I'm impressed," that Evie realized she had just let a man kiss her disfigurement.

Lulu shouted for Daisy to get glasses and a bottle of champagne. Evie was still thinking about what it felt like to have the restorer's lips brush against her port-wine stain birthmark when there was a knock on the door.

"What are we celebrating?" It was Win Langley.

In the excitement of Evie's triumph, Lulu had forgotten she had invited Langley to dinner. Win wanted her to sign on to an environmental project he and the Mohawk Club were sponsoring. It involved reintroducing animals once native to the Adirondacks that had been hunted and trapped out of existence. Lulu was big on anything environmental. Plus, as she had admitted to Evie, she felt bad about firing the lawyer for doing his job and telling her Charlie was a thief. The restorer, having already driven eight hours that day, was relieved when Lulu asked him to spend the night.

Evie was packed up and heading for the Jeep when Lulu ran after her. "You've got to stay for dinner. It's your night."

Evie shook her head *no*; ratty coveralls, Metabond dental cement stuck in her hair, and having not bothered to take a shower that morning, Evie said, "Thanks, but I'm not exactly dressed right."

Evie was still shaking her head *no* as Lulu pulled her back into the house, insisting, "You can shower here. I'll lend you some clothes and call your mother and tell her you'll be home by eleven."

In the end, Evie had to cut the dental cement out of her hair. After shampooing and showering with soap that made her smell like a lemon, she came out of the bathroom and found clean underwear and a dress already laid out for her on the bed. The bra was lacy and the matching panties were a thong. Evie had always laughed at women who went in for stuff like that, but knowing that her own underwear smelled like turpentine and sweat and not wanting to seem ungrateful or funk up the dress, she put them on.

The dress was sheer and white and came from a store called Calypso. As she twirled around in front of the mirror, she saw Lulu standing in the doorway watching her. "Do you ever wonder who your real parents are?" Lulu lit a cigarette.

"No."

"You might have a brother or a sister for all you know."

"I know what I need to know about them."

"What's that?"

"They took one look at my face and didn't want me."

Lulu blew a smoke ring. "Fuck 'em. They're not good enough to kiss your feet." Evie liked her for saying that.

At Lulu's urging Evie left the John Deere hat behind and pushed her hair back out of her face with a velvet headband. Feeling a bit like a doll, she even let Lulu talk her into putting on red lipstick. Her feet being two sizes larger than her hostess's, Evie came down to dinner barefoot. It might not have been the first time men had looked twice at Evie Quimby for reasons other than her disfigurement, but it was the first time Evie noticed it.

Since the dining room had been taken over by the restoration of the statue, dinner was served in the library. Although the days were still hot, now that August was drawing to a close the night had a chill to it and a fire had been lit.

Lulu relaxed her dietary rules for the evening and there was cream in the lobster bisque, bacon in the salad, bread, and everybody had red wine with their lamb chops except for Evie. When she asked for a Dr Pepper, the restorer called her a barbarian, but said it in a nice way. All the silver knives and forks and spoons, flickering candles, freshly pressed linen napkins, a hand-embroidered tablecloth, and Jacques Clément and Win Langley taking turns monopolizing the conversation and complimenting Lulu on the meal she didn't cook—Evie felt like she was channeling *Pride and Prejudice*.

Jacques told a funny story about having to repair a statue of a Venus Aristotle Onassis bought because it reminded him of the first woman he ever saw naked.

Lulu asked, "Who was that?"

Everybody laughed when Jacques answered, "His mother."

Not to be outdone, Win got everybody's attention when he revealed that the extinct species he wanted to see roaming the local woods again were "top-of-the-food-chain predators. We'll start with gray wolves, then mountain lions."

"What if they eat the tourists?" Lulu wasn't trying to be funny.

"They'll probably get indigestion." Win knew how to make people laugh without seeming to be a show-off.

Jacques was just starting to tell another story when Evie volunteered, "I saw a catamount once."

The restorer looked puzzled, "What is this catamount?"

Win answered for her. "It's what people in the Adirondacks used to call mountain lions, cougars." He turned to Evie skeptically. "You are aware, according to the forestry service, the last mountain lion was shot over a hundred years ago?"

"I know what they say and I know what I saw. My father and I were out hunting last winter up near Kettle Mountain and saw a female, a hundred and fifty pounds at least, pull down a deer in the snow."

Lulu was skeptical. "Are you sure it wasn't a bobcat?"

"The deer was a stag. The cat was big. We found fang marks on the stag's neck, nine inches apart."

"Why didn't you shoot it?"

"For one thing, we would have been arrested for poaching, but mostly because it was too beautiful."

Jacques winked at Lulu. "This woman can do anything. If she can cook, I'm marrying her."

Win was more interested in the predator. "How did you know she was a female?"

"She had two cubs with her."

Win raised his glass to Evie. "Goldilocks, you are full of surprises." Lulu, suddenly looking sad at the mention of the nickname Charlie had given Evie, rang a silver bell and told the maid it was time for dessert.

Lulu lingered at the table over brandy and told Win she was okay with reintroducing wolves, but couldn't get behind importing mountain lions. Evie followed Jacques out onto the porch for a cigarette as he bragged about the eight-foot bronze sixteenth-century statue of Shiva he had saved from "catastrophe" for the Metropolitan Museum of Art.

There was no moon, but the Milky Way was bright and the air smelled like citronella and woodsmoke. By the time the restorer had tossed his cigarette down into the damp grass, his arm was casually draped around her shoulder.

Though Evie did not find him remotely handsome, she liked the way he looked at her through his pale blue eyes. She liked it even more that instead of wandering to her birthmark, those eyes seemed to be focused on something inside of her that she herself could not see.

Though no boy had ever put his arm around her shoulder like that, much less a man, as he leaned in closer she knew he was going to try to kiss her. And that knowledge made her smile, in part because in her mind forty-one-year-old Jacques Clément was absurdly old, but also because she knew exactly what he was going to do before he did it. Evie remembered what Lulu had said about sex being all about power for men, but sensed there was something potent and empowering in letting a man do something to you that you wanted done.

Even though the restorer's beard was flecked with gray and he smelled of cigarettes, Evie wanted to know what it would be like to be kissed on the mouth. It was just about to happen when she saw Win Langley in the doorway watching. Suddenly embarrassed, she held up her hand to stop the restorer's advances. Jacques Clément shrugged and smiled. Pulling out a pen, he wrote his cell phone number on a matchbook. "I'm moving my studio back to Paris. If you want a job, call me. I'll pay you in room and board and what I teach you."

Evie was still trying to figure out if he was serious or not when Lulu and Win came out onto the porch. The lawyer lit his pipe and said, "Sorry to interrupt. But if Lulu will let me borrow you, Evie, I think we might have a job for you."

"Who's we?"

"The Mohawk Club. There's a statue . . . well actually there are two of them. They're part of a wonderful stone fireplace that was done by Karl Bitter, the same fellow who did the statue in the Pulitzer Fountain in New York. Come by with Lulu tomorrow and I'll show you."

Evie drove home slowly that night, still wearing the white dress and the velvet headband. Her coveralls, JCPenney underwear, dirty socks, and John Deere hat sat beside her in a paper bag. Top down, a chill in the air, but feeling warm, she did not turn on the radio for fear that the sound of the outside world would break the spell of what she felt happening inside of her.

Though the compliments she had received in the white dress, the feel of Jacques Clément's lips, and the job offer from Langley were nice and totally unexpected, what made the day special was there was no longer any doubt in her head or her heart that she was a restorer. The stone girl testified to that. As Evie drove into the fog that swirled out of the forest, she felt as if she could fix anything.

CHAPTER 18

It was strange hearing my mother describe how my father hit on her that night. When I was little and asked her about how they met, she had left that part of the story out. Mothers often do.

"So it wasn't love at first sight."

"No. That took a while."

"When did you know you were in love with him?"

My mother didn't have to think about it. "It was the night he got out of bed in the middle of winter, went outside naked, and inscribed my name onto the brass plaque outside the door."

"Did you tell my father about Scout?"

"No. Never."

"Why?"

"What I loved most about your father was that he never felt sorry for me. I wasn't going to let Scout take that away from me."

CHAPTER 19

Lulu drove over to the Mohawk Club with Evie the next day to check out the job. The entrance was marked by a pair of massive stone pillars made of river rock, topped by a beam that displayed the club insignia—a Mohawk in profile with bristling black hair. Just in case you missed the "No Trespassing" postings that ringed the property line of their forty-seven thousand acres, there was a five-foot-wide sign with white lettering that glowed even in the darkness of a shady day announcing ALL FISHING, SHOOTING, HUNTING, TRAPPING, CUTTING OF WOOD, CAMPING, AND ALL TRESPASSING HEREIN IS HEREBY FORBIDDEN UNDER PENALTY OF LAW.

A half mile down a gravel road, one of the club's red Land Rovers suddenly pulled out of nowhere and motioned for them to follow. Passing vast netted pens where flocks of game birds were being bred, hatched, and fattened to be shot in the fall, Evie asked Lulu, "Have you been here before?"

"Once, when I was eleven, right before my father died. He brought me to watch a pigeon-shooting contest."

"How's that work?"

"There's an eighteen-inch wall around a field the size of a baseball diamond. A guy with a short-barreled shotgun stands in the middle and another guy squats in a box behind him and throws pigeons up in the air with his bare hands. If the guy with the gun kills the pigeon before it flies away, he gets a point and spectators clap."

"What's the eighteen-inch wall for?"

"If you wing a pigeon and it lands inside the wall and it flops over, you don't get a point . . . so a lot of pigeons get shot on the ground."

"Real sportsmen."

"My father sent me home before it was over."

"How come?"

"I watched him shoot like forty pigeons, then this one gets thrown up, and he fires both barrels. . . . When my father missed and the pigeon flew free, I clapped."

"That's great." The Mohawk Club Land Rover led them past a semicircle of guest camps that looked like a WWI army installation.

"Trouble was when my father got home he told me the pigeons that the men missed didn't fly away and live happily ever after, they just flew back to the club coop and got thrown up and blasted the next week. The message being, I guess, homing instincts are a killer."

Win was standing outside the turreted clubhouse smoking his pipe when they pulled up. Forest-green Bavarian jacket with horn buttons, he bowed like a diplomat, then salted them with compliments. It seemed to Evie that she had entered a foreign country.

Following him into the fortress of masculinity, Evie was surprised and a little disappointed. The ceilings were low and the furnishings both spartan and threadbare. Glancing in the dining room where tables were being set, she saw that the only women on the premises other than herself and Lulu were servants. When Evie and Lulu stepped into the lounge, the men stopped talking and looked up from their papers.

His fellow members weren't exactly unfriendly—a few smiled nervously. After a beat of silence, conversations started back up and laughter could be heard again. But Evie couldn't shake the feeling that the membership of the Mohawk Club was embarrassed by the presence of women who were not obliged to fetch them coffee or bring them a fresh bowl of nuts.

The walls were adorned with the expected menagerie of antlered and fanged heads of animals and stuffed game fish of epic length. More transfixing and disturbing were the hundreds of framed photographs of members in the moment just after the kill. Their arms draped lovingly around the carcasses of caribou, water buffalo, moose, elephant, polar bear, mountain goat, antelope, tiger, rhino, lion; there was even a photo of a guy proudly shaking the hand of the gorilla he had just shot with a revolver. The expression on the faces of the men with their trophy kills, smiling, sweaty, and glassy-eyed with testosterone, reminded Evie of the way the Morlocks had looked at her when they pulled her into the truck.

As the members came in from fishing and left with shotguns and scoped rifles to practice their aim in anticipation of the opening day of hunting season a few weeks away, Evie reached a dark conclusion. If Lulu was right about sex being all about power, then hunting had something to do with sex. Not particularly liking that thought and the questions it raised, Evie was relieved when Lulu said, "Win, when is this place going to join the twenty-first century and let women in?"

Win laughed. "I couldn't but agree. Every year I bring it up at the board of governors meeting, and every year they tell me the same thing."

"What's that?"

"If we accepted women, it wouldn't be a men's club."

When Evie and Lulu didn't laugh, he added, "You know how it is. . . . Older members are worried they'd have to watch what they say. Then there are those that come here to escape their wives."

"So why do you belong, Win?" Lulu enjoyed needling him.

"I'm not as rich as you are, Lulu. I'm forced to make do."

"Where's the Karl Bitter sculpture?" Evie had looked him up that morning.

"Oh, it's not here in the main clubhouse, it's in the playhouse up at the top of the lake by the gorge. We'll go by boat."

"The playhouse?" Lulu had never heard of it.

"It's a little theater really. In the old days the club went in for amateur theatrics, sing-alongs, and sketches." Win opened the door and they headed down to the dock and got in the club launch.

They tied up at the bottom of the gorge where it opened up into Lake Constance. A set of recently repaired wooden stairs zigzagged up to the bluff. Hidden behind a wall of fifty-foot hemlocks, there was a barn-size building constructed to resemble a Swiss chalet.

Two workmen were eating lunch outside when they arrived. As they approached, Win explained, "Before we got cable TV, members used to screen movies here on Saturday nights. There's a bowling alley downstairs. We thought it would be fun to get it back into shape for the Club's hundred and twenty-fifth anniversary coming up. We were hoping to hold the opening-night cocktail party here, but three days ago a bunch of kids broke in and vandalized the place."

As soon as Evie stepped inside she knew it was the Morlocks. In addition to the generic *fuck you* and *eat shit* spray-painted on the walls, she spotted a Day-Glo orange cock and balls identical to the one Scrotum and Otto had tagged on the side of the bridge coming into Rangeley.

At one end of the room was a raised stage, at the other a fire-place large enough to roast an ox. Evie could see right away what Win wanted her to restore. On either side of the hearth stood a pair of seven-foot limestone giants. One was a leering, horned, cloven-hoofed satyr, the other a Mohawk maiden about to take a bite out of an apple; she wore nothing but a feathered headdress. Politically incorrect, but anatomically exact.

Win leaned over Evie's shoulder as she assessed the damage. "It appears they shot them with a .30-30." He picked up a shell casing off the floor and handed it to her. "They kept the satyr's horn as a souvenir." Chunks of a thigh, two pieces of a shoulder, and a chin lay scattered on the floor.

Win lit his pipe. "So, Evie, is the damage reparable?"

Evie found the subject matter of the sculpture vaguely offensive. But it was beautifully carved and she was still five hundred dollars shy of the cost of laser surgery. She said, "I'll need photographs to work from."

"No problem. Now what do you think will be a fair price for your labors?" Evie could tell Win was enjoying this part. Evie was about to say two hundred dollars when Lulu jumped off the stage.

"Evie's going rate is a thousand dollars per week."

"Fantastic. Just one thing. Our hundred and twenty-fifth is next weekend, can you do it in a week?"

"I don't know if that's enough time. I mean, just getting here takes me over an hour each way, then there's the boat ride on top of that."

Lulu already had it all figured out. "You can stay at our old guide camp on the other side of the gorge and borrow a boat from us to get back and forth. Ten-minute commute. Clinger can help you, he's running out of things to varnish anyway."

Win shook her hand and said, "Done!" As he wrote out a check for half, he added, "I'll get the photographs and have a boxed lunch dropped off for you first thing each morning."

When they got back to the Quimby cabin, Lulu waited by the Range Rover while Evie ran inside to pack a bag and break the news to her parents that she'd need to sleep over at the Mannheim guide camp in order to get the mantel repaired in time. As Evie had predicted, Flo said, "Yes," and Buddy shouted, "No way in hell." Leaning against the fender looking up at a sky that promised rain, Lulu listened to Buddy and Flo arguing inside about what was and wasn't best for Evie.

If Lulu knew the Quimbys better, she would have realized that Flo had won the battle when the screen door slammed and Buddy stomped out onto the porch and lit a cigar. He came right to the point. "Why are you doing all this for my daughter? And don't tell me it's 'cause she cleaned your goddamn kitchen."

Lulu pushed her sunglasses up and was about to repeat the mantra that had gotten her to this point in her life—*because I'm rich, because I can, and because it's what I want*—but stopped herself and replied, "Because I'm tired of being a selfish shit." Lulu paused to light a cigarette. "And because I like to think that if I had had someone looking out for me when I was Evie's age who didn't want to just fuck me or take my money—usually both—I might have had a chance of turning out to be a different kind of person."

Buddy was still taking that in when Evie burst out of the cabin, backpack slung over her shoulder. Evie was in the Range Rover and Lulu was turning around to head down the drive when Flo suddenly threw her hands up and called out, "Wait! Evie, you forgot the cookies." Then, turning to her husband, "Buddy, run in and get them, will you?"

When Buddy came out a few minutes later and handed Evie a cookie tin with a Santa Claus on the lid, he winked and whispered, "In case you run into a bear."

As the Range Rover bounced down the rutted drive, Lulu asked, "What was that about?"

"My dad's paranoid." Evie opened the tin. Beneath a dozen oatmeal cookies lay a loaded snub-nosed .38-caliber revolver and Buddy's night-vision glasses.

Lulu bitched for the tenth time that day about the lack of cell phone reception in Townsend County and stopped at a pay phone in Rangeley to call Clinger and tell him to get the guide camp ready for Evie and arrange to have the tools and restoration supplies trucked down to the Mohawk Club. Evie ran to the hardware store to buy a gallon of turpentine and a wire brush she hoped she could use to stipple the epoxy just before it fully hardened to give the repairs the same granular texture as the rest of the limestone mantel.

She had purchased what she needed and was on her way back to the car when she spotted the Morlocks coming out of the liquor store with a case of beer. Hoping she could make it back to the Range Rover before they saw her, she quickened her pace. Kevin's red pickup had a pair of mud-splattered Kawasaki dirt bikes in the back. Patching out of the parking lot, he screeched to a stop. "Hey Giblet, without your hat I hardly recognize you." Evie ignored him and kept on walking. The truck moved slowly, keeping pace beside her. "I like the new headband look."

Scrotum volunteered, "Shows off your best feature," and they all laughed.

"We hear you've gone lesbo with Lulu Mannheim." That was Otto.

Kevin pulled at the wispy blond beard he was trying to grow. "Maybe we'll stop by for a visit one night and we can all party together."

Otto reached out a paw to slap her ass, and Evie jumped out of the way, dropping the can of turpentine she was holding.

"Be seeing you soon, Giblet." Kevin blew her a kiss as he drove off.

The floatplane was waiting when they got to Valhalla. As she got out of the Range Rover, Lulu shouted, "Ivan!" The setter puppy bolted down from the porch. Picking the dog up in her arms, Lulu baby-talked him. "How's my handsome man?"

Evie could see Slavo was sitting on his suitcase by the plane. "Where's your trainer going?"

"I'm returning him."

"How come?"

"I like steak, but I don't like to eat steak every night. . . . I was thinking about flying someone in to give me piano lessons."

"You have a type in mind?"

"Sensitive . . . long fingers, tight butt." Clearly Lulu had decided sex was simpler if she talked, and maybe behaved, like a man.

Evie got in the boat Clinger had put out for her to take down-lake to the guide camp. "Thanks for everything."

Lulu handed her the tin that contained more than cookies. "When you finish, you can finally teach me to fly-fish."

Evie called out, "For sure," and pushed off from the dock.

She ran the skiff flat out down the glassy water. An hour later, Evie was tying up next to Clinger's boat at the Mannheims' side of the gorge. She had driven past that spot a dozen times over the frozen channel on the back of Buddy's skimobile during the winter, but because of the snow she had never noticed the steps that were cut in the rocky path up to the top.

The guide camp was set back from the lip of the gorge and was not visible from the water below. More of a shack than a proper cabin, it had a tin roof, and just like all the other buildings at Valhalla that housed servants, it was painted butter yellow with dark green trim. There was nothing special about it, except the weather vane attached to the roof was shaped like a trout.

Clinger called out from inside the cabin, "I got you set up best I could it being short notice." The camp was one room, ten-by-fifteen at most, bunk beds, potbelly stove, a table by the window that offered a glimpse of the Mohawk Club's playhouse through a break in the wall of hemlocks on the other side of the gorge. The calendar on the wall was from 1957, but all the other amenities were strictly nineteenth-century. No electricity, no running water, the toilet was an outhouse back in the woods. Drinking water was supplied by a five-gallon jug turned upside down on an old-fashioned dispenser with a spigot. Clinger lifted the lid of a cooler packed with ice and perishables. "I got you a cold chicken for tonight, tomatoes from the garden, eggs, milk, pickles, and such." Bread, cold cereal, and a bag of potato chips were in a wooden box lined with tin to keep the mice out. Two-burner alcohol stove, two plates, two cups, two chairs, two knives, two forks—except for the fact that Evie was staying there alone, it was sort of romantic.

Evie ate two drumsticks and a tomato for dinner. Turning out the kerosene lantern, she climbed into the bottom bunk and fell asleep thinking about how, for the first time in her life, she actually felt lucky.

Evie was up at first light. Motoring across the gorge in the skiff, she watched an otter surface and breakfast on trout. She took the stairs up the club side of the gorge two at a time and was ready to start work before 7 a.m.

The workmen had finished painting over the obscenities. As promised, there was a box lunch and a stack of close-up photos of the mantel taken when it was first installed in the spring of 1904.

Studying the photos through a magnifying glass, the longer she looked at the statues, the less she liked what was being depicted. The naked Mohawk girl's expression irked her. Lips parted seductively, the tip of her tongue just touching the apple she was about to take a bite of. Yet, the rest of her expression said she was terrified: eyebrows raised in alarm and one hand outstretched as if to fend off the satyr on the other side of the hearth. Evie wondered whether the sculptor wanted you to think she was horny and scared or horny because she was scared.

Imagining how a real Mohawk woman might have slit the satyr's throat and skinned his hide before eating him, she reeled in her very mixed feelings and reminded herself she had already deposited the check.

The female figure had been shot three times, the satyr twice. Examining the bullet wounds, she was relieved to see she wouldn't have to take apart the whole mantel to repair them. Sorting through the chunks of limestone that had splintered off during the attack, Evie determined what could be epoxied back into place and what she would have to sculpt herself. The satyr's missing left horn would be easier than it looked. She would make a mold of the right, cast it in resin, then rework it. The chin could be glued back, but her neck would have to be re-created. The old photographs helped, but it wasn't until Evie stripped off her coveralls and pulled off her T-shirt to look at herself topless in the bathroom mirror that she figured out how to address the problem. It took running her fingers round her own neck, feeling the way the muscles and tendons of her throat connected to her chest, for Evie to understand all that goes into holding your head up.

Evie worked until after 7 p.m., took the boat across the gorge in the gloaming, ate the rest of the chicken, and fell asleep. Next day, she did it all over again. With no stones to be pinned, the work went faster than it did on the marble girl.

Three days into the job, Langley brought over five of his fellow club members to inspect Evie's handiwork. Even though it wasn't finished, they all clapped. Evie felt like she was onstage. Langley bragged for her, "Evie's self-taught. Local prodigy." She wasn't used to getting compliments from men. It made her feel breathless and tipsy, like she'd just chugged a twelve-ounce can of Colt 45.

Langley took her aside as the other club members talked about whether it was worth it to install a new bathroom. He was excited for her and patted Evie on the back. "I can't tell you how proud I am of you, Evie. You have real talent." Langley called out to an older man in a tweed jacket and matching knickers. "Walter, come over here for a minute."

Evie recognized him as the man with three fingers she saw getting out of the seaplane at the dock the day they found Charlie's body. "Walt here is on the board of trustees of a university in Boston that just so happens to have a fine arts department where you can major in art restoration."

Walter shook her hand just the way Langley did. "I see now why Win's been singing your praises. I'd be happy to write a letter of recommendation for you."

Evie didn't understand what was happening until Langley said, "I'll fly us over to Boston in the fall and see about getting you a scholarship. I can't promise, of course, but I do have some influence, and with Walter on board I don't see how they can say no."

It was so unexpected, so exactly what Evie longed to hear, she began to cry. Langley offered her his handkerchief and said, "It's a pleasure to help a girl with so much potential."

The next day it rained nonstop. The humidity fogged the goggles of her gas mask. When she took them off to work on the satyr's horn, the fumes from the resin made her feel like her brainpan had a flame under it and her eyes burn.

The fact that the water in the playhouse was turned off and there was only one eight-ounce bottle of Poland Spring left her dehydrated and feeling dizzy. Still, at the end of the day, she felt good about the job and left a note for Win saying she would have to wait for it to stop raining before she came back to touch up the pigment of the caulking and make sure that it dried true to color. She added a P.S. "Even if I don't get a scholarship, I will always be grateful for your help."

When Evie got back to the guide camp that night, the rain pinged metallic and nonstop on the tin roof. Chugging two big glasses of water from the dispenser, she popped an aspirin and decided to make herself a sandwich. She got the ham and cheese on the bread, but when she reached for the pickle jar her hands did not cooperate. Suddenly feeling numb and dizzy, bordering on vertigo, it was all she could do to sit down on the bed. With each breath, Evie found it harder to focus. As the room blurred, she imagined she was being wrapped in cotton gauze and then . . . nothing.

~ ~ ~

When Evie woke up, she was lying facedown on the bottom bunk, her clothes and boots on. The shades were pulled down, and from the milky gray light pouring around their edges, she guessed it was dawn. It had stopped raining. Standing now, but still feeling like she was in the grip of a bad dream she couldn't remember, she sprung the shades and was startled to see the sun was setting, not rising.

Unnerved that she had slept through an entire day, Evie wondered what was wrong with her. As the numbness in her limbs began to fade, she realized that her hips ached and her mouth tasted foul and suddenly that she had to go to the bathroom.

Staggering out the back door, she pulled down her jeans and underwear and squatted. It burned when she peed, and when she looked down she was stunned to see that her pubic hair had been shaved. And she then knew something worse than bad had happened. That she could not remember it made it all the more terrifying. Horrified by the realization that someone had taken a razor to her crotch while she was passed out, Evie started to run. Panic propelled her into the forest, crying out as if the jaws of a trap had just closed on her. Pine boughs slapping at her face, she scrambled up a game trail slick with mud on all fours, falling more than once. In the end, she was so turned around inside her head that when she stumbled through the pines and found herself back at the guide camp, she was more lost than ever.

Head spinning round to see if whoever had done this was still out there in the darkness, Evie darted back into the cabin. As she turned the cookie tin upside down, the revolver clattered to the floor. Snatching it up, holding it with both hands, she was ready to fire. It was then she saw that the lipstick Lulu had given her had been used to scrawl a cock and balls on the mirror. The head of the penis had a smiley face. The Morlocks.

Seeing the half-made sandwich on the table, she retraced the events of the previous evening. The sound of the rain tap-dancing on the tin roof as she came home, the glug of the five-gallon jar on the water dispenser as she filled her glass, drinking it in one gulp because she had been thirsty all day, then pouring herself another glass of water, and then starting to make a sandwich that she never ate. Evie knew with grim certainty that the water in the jug had been spiked.

She found a razor and a can of Gillette shaving foam in the trash. Her backpack had been upended on the floor. Her wallet was there, the eight dollars she had still in it, but the pink Swiss Army knife with all of her keys on it was gone. Still sobbing, anger cresting fear, she dragged the bunk beds away from the wall to block the back door. Armed and loaded in a corner, she stared out the front window thinking about how she would make them pay for what they had done.

It was almost 11 p.m. when a flicker of light across the gorge caught her eye. Someone had turned the lights on in the playhouse. The cemetery keeper had told her that the night after the Morlocks toppled Agatha L. Huddlestone's headstone, they returned to set fire to a mausoleum. And when they burned the float dock in town, as soon as it was rebuilt, they came back to torch it again.

Grabbing Buddy's night-vision goggles, gun in hand, she scrambled down to the skiff and cast off. She took the stairs up the Mohawk Club's side of the gorge at a run and was drenched in sweat by the time she got to the top. Slipping through the curtain of hemlock, she heard someone laughing. Gun held high, clicking back the hammer of the revolver, she thought through what she'd do when she burst through the door. One shot in the air to scare the shit out of them, she'd order Kevin and Otto to lie flat on their faces and get Scrotum to tie them up. Then she'd pistol-whip him down to the floor and hog-tie him herself with an extension cord. After that . . . she'd improvise.

But when Evie flattened herself against the side of the playhouse and peered through the window, it was not the Morlocks she saw. It was Win Langley. His back to her, he had his laptop open. On the screen, she could see a man doing shadowy things to a girl's body. Win called out, "You gotta see this." A beat later, she saw Andy, the silver-haired man who looked like a wrinkly Matthew McConaughey and spoke Greek with a southern accent. He shouted, "Do you fucking realize the trouble this could cause the rest of us? This isn't a game. When you joined this peculiar institution of ours, my friend, you knew what would be expected of you."

"No harm, no foul."

"You fucking never learn, do you, Scout?" It was at that moment, the girl in the sex video's face came into view and Evie saw that she had a port-wine stain birthmark across the side of her face.

The two men argued for a few minutes. Evie's mind was so fractured by then, she couldn't make sense of what they were saying. When they came out, she was standing in the shadows less than four feet away. The muzzle of the revolver was aimed just below Langley's belt. At that range, she couldn't miss.

CHAPTER 20

My mother's voice was flat and her eyes were dry as she recounted this nightmare. She told me that part of her story as if it had happened to somebody else, somebody she had lost touch with long ago and wished she had treated with more understanding when it would have made a difference.

I tried to imagine the horror of what it must have been like, but the one thing cancer had taught me was, when the worst things you can imagine actually happen to you, it's never how you imagined it would be; it's worse, because you're the person who has to live with it.

It was almost midnight by then. The moon had come and gone. We were in my room, me under the covers, my mother sitting on the edge of my bed, staring at the map of Parts but little known. Whatever words I could have chosen would have been inadequate, so I just hugged her. "So what happened after you shot him outside the playhouse?"

"It didn't happen there. I couldn't pull the trigger that night. I was too ashamed to say a word; just let him walk away."

"You had nothing to be ashamed of. He raped you!"

"What I was ashamed of was that I was so flattered that a rich man with a seaplane who belonged to the fucking Mohawk Club took an interest in me, so desperate for praise I let my own self-doubt blind me. That I'd actually thought he cared about me made it worse. What I'm still ashamed of is that I was so needy of a man telling me I had potential. Talent."

"Who did you tell?"

"No one."

"Jesus. Why not?"

"2001 in the Sister Lakes was like 1951 everywhere else. Women, girls didn't report things like that." My mother finally started to cry. "I felt like I'd done it to myself. I still feel that way."

"I wish you'd blown him off the face of the earth."

"Me too."

My mother turned out the light and got under the covers with me. It was a long time before either of us fell asleep.

After I took my meds in the morning, she picked up where she'd left off. I thought I already knew how her story ended, but there was more to cry about.

PART IV

CONSOLIDATION OF LOSS

B y the time she climbed back up to the guide camp, Evie had made up her mind not to tell Flo or Dill or Lulu or anyone else what happened. To repeat it, share it with another person, would only make the damage Langley had done to her harder to repair. She thought of herself like the stone girl. To restore what Langley had shattered, what was left of Evie Quimby, she would have to reclaim dominion over her life and body. To do that, Win Langley had to feel as violated as she did. Shooting him would not be enough.

Evie forced herself to go back to the playhouse the next day to finish repairing the statues. For what she was planning to work, Langley had to think he had gotten away with it; that she was too stupid, powerless, and humiliated to report it to the police. Her hands shook as she mixed pigment and grit to hide the damage. Still able to taste the stink of him in the back of her throat, she dropped her palette knife and ran to the toilet to vomit.

At the end of the day, one of the caretakers handed her an envelope. Inside was a five-hundred-dollar check for the balance and an invitation to the club's upcoming 125th-anniversary cocktail party to be held at the newly restored playhouse. Evie left a note saying she had other plans.

On the day of the party, Evie drove to the women's clinic in Lake Placid and had herself tested for sexually transmitted diseases. The results came back negative, and she wasn't pregnant. These facts offered only minor reassurance.

When Lulu tried to treat her to a trip to New York in her floatplane and arrange for Evie to get a personal tour of the antiquities department from the curator of the Metropolitan Museum of Art, Evie thanked her and said, "I'm not ready." At any rate it wasn't hard for Lulu to talk herself out of flying into Manhattan. It was September 2001, and their days were spent glued to the television watching jumbo jets fly into the Twin Towers. The whole world seemed to have crashed and burned. Flo sensed a change in her daughter but thought the sudden onslaught of melancholia was a side effect of 9/11.

Dill threw a baby shower for Connie in the beauty parlor the week the maples turned scarlet and orange. Evie called at the last minute to say she was sick, which Dill knew was a lie because his mother saw Evie through the window of Gibbon's Sporting Goods, browsing the gun department. Even Buddy knew his daughter was acting strange. Why did she suddenly feel the need to buy a secondhand scoped Savage deer rifle when there were already twelve firearms squirreled away in the Quimby household? "What's wrong with the guns we got?" Buddy asked.

"They're not registered or licensed."

"So what?"

"I don't want to break any laws." Collecting her gun registration, gun license, hunting license, and all the other things no Quimby had every bothered with, Evie went into her bedroom, closed the door, and studied the vascular diagrams in the copy of *Gray's Anatomy* she had purchased the day she got tested for AIDS, syphilis, gonorrhea, and various other STDs.

Flo did not know that when Evie went to talk to Jimmy the crow, she cawed with tears in her eyes. But she sensed her daughter was closing the shutters on her life at age seventeen, and that bothered her profoundly. When she asked Evie what was wrong, her daughter only said, "I'm scared of having my disfigurement removed."

Flo had told her not to call her birthmark that a thousand times.

"Well, maybe now that you have the money for the operation, we should call the doctor, make an appointment at the hospital, set a date for the surgery. You've waited so long, worked so hard, it's understandable you'd be nervous."

But every time the subject came up, Evie ended the conversation the same way: "I'll decide everything after deer season."

Flo had no idea what was going on in her daughter's mind until she came out of the woods with a basket full of mushrooms and saw Evie chopping wood. Hearing the way she screamed "Fuck him!" each time she brought down her ax, Flo understood. Evie didn't hear her mother the first time she said, "We need to talk."

"I don't feel like talking." Evie brought down the ax.

"There's something you need to know."

The log split in two. "What?"

"When I was thirty-five years old, I was raped."

Evie stopped chopping. "Why are you telling me this now?"

"Did something like that happen to you?" Evie went back to chopping and said nothing. "Evie, listen to me. Instead of telling anyone or going to the police, I kept it to myself. Silenced myself. And I've been paying for it ever since."

Evie thought of the stone girl and said, "Going to the sheriff would just make things worse."

"Why would you think that?"

"Because I can't prove it. And because Buddy would find out, and no matter what he said or promised us, he wouldn't be satisfied until somebody put a bullet in the man."

"You let me handle your father. Who was it?"

"I didn't see him." The ax came down again.

"You're lying. You know who did it, and we're going to the sheriff to get that dirtbag arrested."

"The sheriff won't do anything."

"Why not?"

"The man who did it belongs to the Mohawk Club. My word against his. You know how it works. All the sheriff can do is get me some money."

Knowing her daughter was right, Flo went inside, lay on her bed, and wept. As she listened to the sound of Evie's ax echoing in the autumn air, she remembered the night she watched Buddy bury a man who deserved to die in the forest.

CHAPTER 22

W in Langley's eyes opened at 4:30 a.m. on the first morning of
deer season. Lying in the very same Mohawk Club cabin that
Teddy Roosevelt favored, he glanced out the window and smiled. Five
inches of snow had fallen on Townsend County during the night. The
hike up Flathead Mountain would be difficult, but the twelve-point
buck he had seen there over the summer would be easier to track in the
snow. Legally, you couldn't kill anything until after sunrise. Believing
certain rules were important, Win would wait until first light before
he loaded his rifle.

He had flown up the day before. Knowing a storm was predicted,
he stopped work at noon. His firm, W. H. Langley & Associates,
occupied the entire twenty-third floor of 400 Park Ave and specialized, not surprisingly, in providing financial and legal advice to families with multigenerational wealth. Which basically boiled down to
helping them navigate the gray areas that allowed them to avoid lawsuits and paying taxes. Curiously, four of his five junior partners were
women. When asked why, he always smiled and said, "They work
hard and they're loyal."

Boarding his seaplane at the 23rd Street Marine Air Terminal, he
was airborne by one, and with the help of a tailwind landed in front of
the Mohawk Club just as the first flurries of snow began to fall.

As Win swung his legs out of bed and strapped the aluminum
brace on his left knee, he paused as he did most mornings to think
about his late wife Margot and the fall that had nearly killed him along
with her. Once he had the brace on, his limp was imperceptible, but
Win knew that his God-given athletic grace had been taken from
him the day of the accident. Unable to run, he missed his tennis and

squash. Some mornings—usually around Easter, Christmastime, and on his birthday—he missed other things as well, occasionally even his dead wife, Margot.

Being a forty-year-old widower had certain social advantages, however. There was an acute shortage of men who had gone to all the right schools, knew all the right people, and, rarest of all, worked at something that made money for his friends. As Porter Moran put it when he first came to the city, "In New York, if you're straight, single, solvent, and you've got all your fingers and toes, you're a catch."

Win was dressed now and in the Mohawk Club's dining room. The kitchen girls came in extra early the first day of deer season and laid out a buffet—scrambled eggs, sausages, and oatmeal. Win had all three. There were eleven other members who made it up for opening day. Most liked to go out in pairs or groups of three for the camaraderie of the kill, but Win preferred to hunt alone. Thermos of coffee and a turkey sandwich in his backpack, he went to the gun room and took out the Mannlicher that had once belonged to the king of Romania.

It was still dark when he headed out to Flathead Mountain in one of the club's Land Rovers, chains on all four tires. The club owned all of Flathead, except for a finger of state forest on the western slope. When members hunted there, they always took the public roads around the lake, then turned up onto the fire road to get back onto club land. The top of the mountain was a two-hundred-acre plain of balsam, flat and green as a billiard table. It was dotted with meadows cleared by a forest fire in the summer of '69 rumored to have been deliberately set by the club to give its members a clear shot at the game.

Win was not the only hunter out that morning. When he turned out of the club entrance, he saw an old pickup, headlights on, parked a couple hundred yards back down the road. He was about to turn around and tell them in the nicest possible way that if they tried to hunt on club property they would be arrested and their truck impounded, but when he glanced back in his rearview mirror, the pickup moved on and followed him slowly out onto Route 7.

There was more snow than he thought and the roads were slick and cocooned in fog. When he got to the turnoff, he smiled at the sight of the sheriff placing a stuffed antlered deer head in the snow-crusted brambles, just off the county road to tempt hunters lazy enough to shoot from a moving vehicle. The sheriff set his trap in the same place every year. Five-hundred-dollar fine plus court costs, deer season was a boon to the local economy.

It was snowing again now, and as the Land Rover disappeared up the fire road, Sheriff Dunn waved over the pickup that had been following Win through the predawn fog. When the window came down, he was surprised to see Evie was alone.

"Where's your father?"

"You know Buddy, Uncle Billy, he thinks every day is open season on deer."

The sheriff laughed. He saw the sled Buddy used to haul game out next to the snowmobile in the back of the truck. Pointing to the rifle in the gun rack behind her head, Uncle Billy put on his cop voice. "You got a hunting license?"

Evie showed it to him. She knew he was teasing when he said, "Not signed . . . hundred-dollar fine."

"Haven't started hunting yet." Sheriff Dunn handed her a pen. It wasn't until he watched her sign the license that he noticed her hands were shaking.

She off-loaded the skimobile on state forest land. Sled tethered behind her, her new lever-action .243 Savage slung over her shoulder; snow billowed up in her face as she headed up the western slope of Flathead Mountain at full throttle. A family of hares scurried to get out of her way and a mink leapt back into its hole. Ducking low under a length of barbed wire stretched across a game trail, Evie passed unnoticed onto Mohawk Club property.

Win kept the Land Rover in low as he followed the rutted switchbacks of the fire road up the south side of the mountain. Falling snow made it hard to see, but the pinewoods dusted in white reminded him of Christmases in the Upper Peninsula. Aside from the fact that he never got what he wanted, those were happy times.

Even with four-wheel drive and chains, the Land Rover slithered sideways and more than once nearly slid off the track. He couldn't see more than twenty feet ahead of him, but he knew he was near the top when his cell phone rang. You couldn't get reception in Townsend County until you were over four thousand feet up. The call was from his office and he did not answer it.

With the snow, the last quarter of a mile was too steep for the four-wheel drive. Taking the folding walking stick he used to keep his balance out of his backpack, he shouldered his rifle and slowly began to climb. Pain grabbed at his left knee, but the stick helped, and once he got above the ridge it was easier going.

The sun was just coming up over Saddlers Mountain twenty miles to the east. Loading the two 6.55-millimeter bullets he had allotted himself into the magazine of the rifle, he chambered the first round and was just releasing the safety when he heard the whine of a skimobile in the distance. Making a mental note to write a letter to the sheriff about poachers, he headed to the big meadow on the western end of the plateau where he had seen the buck over the summer. The club's gamekeeper had put out corn and salt licks to lure deer out of the woods. Win was careful to stay downwind. The air was heavy and damp as he crept toward the edge of that meadow, and in the cold his excitement turned to vapor.

Still as a lizard, he waited, binoculars around his neck, crouched among the trees. Experiencing the same tingly feeling he felt when he waited for Evie to come back to the guide camp and take a big drink of water—it was the foreplay of the hunt Win liked best.

Letting his mind wander as he waited for the animal he'd come to kill, he remembered that after he had blinded his mother, she would read to him from the Braille edition of his favorite book, *The Count of Monte Cristo*. If he nestled too close to her, snuggled his head against her breast, she would say, "That's enough. Time to sleep." Then the door would close and he would be left alone in the dark. She never said she was scared of him, but he could tell.

The buck he had claimed as his the summer before stepped out into the meadow and nibbled at the corn around 10 a.m. It was bigger than he remembered, three hundred and fifty pounds at least. Counting the points through his binoculars, he came to thirteen. Flattening himself out, he inched forward so only his face and the barrel of his rifle protruded from the wall of green that encircled the meadow. Three hundred yards away, the buck had his tongue on the salt lick, and his harem of does were timidly stepping out of the woods to join him. Eye to the scope, finger on the trigger, he centered the crosshairs just behind the stag's shoulders for a clear shot to the heart.

Raising his barrel two inches high and to the right to account for distance and wind, he was a heartbeat away from pulling the trigger when the crack of a gunshot echoed through the forest. The buck's ears twitched at the sound and in one stride was at a full run. Struggling to keep the animal in his sights, unsure of the distance now, Win led him by a foot and fired. His shot was high. When he got to the salt lick, he found one of the thirteen antler points lying in the snow. Pocketing it, he smiled at the thought of asking Evie to glue it back on once he had the head mounted. Following the deer tracks into the far side of the woods, he heard the skimobile again.

The buck's hoofprints were bigger than his fist. He glimpsed the does clustered out of the wind just below the lip of the western slope. He was on state parkland now. There were hardwoods scattered among the pines there, and as he walked the only sound was the crunch of fallen leaves beneath the snow. It had stopped snowing and the sun was behind him. Pausing to catch his breath, he heard the sound of some other animal walking ever so slowly through the snow-crusted deadfall.

He scanned the forest for the buck, saw nothing, and moved on. He knew something was out there. Stopping suddenly to examine a bit of fur and a bloody spot of snow where a hawk had disemboweled a rabbit, he heard the crunch behind him again. Taking two more steps and then stopping abruptly, he heard it again.

The thought that he was being stalked made him smile. It was a boyish thought. In the Adirondacks, man is at the top of the food chain, unless that story Evie Quimby had told over dinner at Valhalla about the catamount and her cubs was really true. The fantasy of encountering something that could fight back with claws and teeth while he was out deer hunting was too much fun to let go of. Spinning round, rifle to his shoulder, knowing it was nothing . . . he was startled to see Evie Quimby twenty feet away.

Lowering his gun, Win chuckled. "Sneaking up on someone in the woods on the first day of deer season is a good way to get shot, Goldilocks."

As Win stepped toward her, she raised her rifle and pointed it to his head. "I know what you did to me." Her voice cracked and she sounded like she was about to cry. She had rehearsed this moment a hundred times, but the one thing Evie hadn't expected was that Win Langley would be glad to see her.

"What on earth are you talking about? Stop pointing that gun at me and tell me what's wrong." His tone was scolding and made her feel like a child.

"You drugged and raped me!" She was shouting and tears were streaming down her face.

"Evie, you're talking crazy. I would never . . ." His voice was as gentle, just, and fatherly as Atticus Finch's. "If someone did those things to you, I'll help you. We'll go to the police and find out who was responsible and see that they're punished." Win knew what to say. It wasn't the first time he had been in a situation like this, but it was the first time a woman had confronted him with a gun in her hand. It raised the stakes.

"I saw you watching the movie you made of me. Your friend was there."

"That's a very serious and false accusation." He knew she wasn't going to shoot him. "I don't know what you think you saw, Evie, but I guarantee you the gentleman who was in the playhouse that evening, my old friend Andy, will put his hand on a Bible and swear that what you claim happened never occurred. Look, what you went through is terrible, but you said yourself you were drugged. You're hardly a reliable witness."

"Drop your rifle in the snow." His gun was pointed toward the ground, and when he raised the tip of his barrel, Evie surprised him by firing a shot just above his head. He could tell from the way she ejected the spent cartridge and levered in a live round that she knew her way around guns.

"You realize you just committed a felony? You go to prison for assault with a deadly weapon. I'm serious, if you don't turn around and walk out of these woods now, I will see that you are punished to the fullest extent of the law." Evie just stared at him. She was aiming at his head. Knowing she couldn't miss at such close range, he tried to distract her. "How did you know I was here, Goldilocks?"

Win studied her face in the hope of picking up a hint of what she would do next. The blood-red birthmark he found both repulsive and beautiful made her hard to read. He knew by now he could not just let her walk away, he had to break her before she left, reduce her to a scared, ugly girl.

"You told me last summer when you showed me the king of Romania's rifle."

"If you're thinking about repeating this twisted fantasy of yours to anyone, they won't believe you. They'll just write you off as a slut, out to shake down a rich man who made the mistake of trying to be nice to you. The whole thing is absurd. Why would I want to rape someone who looks like you?"

Evie began to back away. When she let out a sob, Langley was sure he had cracked the girl's resolve. But the insult just made Evie see him as nothing more than a high-class Morlock. "I don't know, why would you, Scout?"

At the mention of his nickname, Win knew he had to stop this before it went any further. Eyes on him, Evie didn't see the snow-covered log behind her. When she stumbled back, rifle across her chest, he shouldered his Mannlicher and fired. He was already thinking how he'd explain it all to the sheriff: *terrible accident . . . she came out of nowhere . . . such a great girl . . . so much potential.* He knew he had hit her square in the middle of the chest. What he hadn't counted on was his bullet striking the heavy steel side plate of the old lever-action rifle she was holding.

Evie scrambled to her feet, stunned that he had actually tried to kill her. As Win frantically worked the bolt action of his rifle to reload, Evie reminded him with eerie calm, "If you can't do it with two shots . . . you don't deserve the kill, isn't that what you say, Win?" Evie kept him in her sights as she backed further and further away.

"Evie, listen to me very carefully. I know something that can change your life."

"I'm going to change yours."

He thought about running, then remembered he couldn't run. "I can help you. There's a woman in New York who . . ." He was shouting, but Evie was over a hundred yards away now. She was no longer pointing her gun at his head. The crosshairs of her rifle scope targeted a spot just above his right knee, well to the left of the femoral artery she'd seen diagrammed in *Gray's Anatomy.* And then she did the last thing Win Langley thought she would do—she pulled the trigger.

The bullet knocked his right leg out from under him, sprawling him back, spread-eagle and belly-up in the snow. Shock, pain, and adrenaline electrified his nervous system. When he looked up and saw her pulling off the leather belt that cinched her parka as she ran toward him, the thought occurred to Win that she was going to strangle him.

Staring down at his leg, he saw blood and splintered bone and tendons that could never be repaired. Screaming as the pain burned through him, he knew Evie Quimby had aimed to cripple him for life.

Evie stood over him belt in hand and pulled out the forty-nine-dollar tape recorder she'd bought at Walmart the day before. She pressed the record button as Win gasped, "You fucking shot me!"

"Admit what you did to me and I won't let you bleed to death."

Win gagged and threw his head back and growled, "I drugged and raped you."

"Say my name and where it happened."

"I drugged and raped Evie Quimby in the . . . fuck, it hurts."

"Where did you rape me?"

"In the fucking guide camp, goddamnit. Put the tourniquet on." A circle of blood was spreading out around him.

"How did you drug me?"

"Animal tranquilizers in the water jug. . . . Help me!" She could see Scout was terrified, and she was surprised that she felt guilty for taking pleasure in his fear.

"I'm not the first, am I? What are the names of the other women you hurt?" Langley passed out before that question was answered. Looping the leather belt around his right thigh just above the shattered kneecap, she applied the tourniquet just the way they told her to at the first aid class she had taken at the Y in preparation for this moment.

The bleeding slowed to a trickle and she ran to the skimobile and pulled the sled around. Packing snow around his leg, she took out the cell phone she'd also purchased at Walmart. Knowing that Flathead was one of two mountains in the county high enough to get a signal, she dialed the number she had written on the back of her hand. "Hello, sheriff's office? This is Evie Quimby. There's been a hunting accident." When she hung up, she slipped the tape recorder into a ziplock plastic bag and hid it in the snow under the bottom boughs of a blue spruce that stood out among the pines.

The accident report was relayed. The sheriff was already at the top of the fire road checking out the Mohawk Club Land Rover when Evie roared down off the mountain splattered with blood, pulling the man she'd shot behind her. Tears were streaming down her face. She did not regret shooting Langley or think she had done something wrong. Her sadness came from the realization that like the shadowy things he had done to her body, the blood on her hands marked her more permanently than a birthmark that could be removed with twenty-five thousand dollars of laser surgery.

All the sheriff knew was she had shot a member of the Mohawk Club. Though more than a few locals, especially after a few beers, had voiced a desire to put a bullet in one of the hoity-toity sportsmen that had them arrested for setting foot on club land, this was the first time a member had actually been shot . . . at least by a local. But given that this shooter was Buddy's daughter and his own niece and the club notoriously litigious, Sheriff Billy Dunn knew that no matter how he handled the investigation, he would be held accountable. Rather than wait for an ambulance to make it over from Speculator First Aid, the sheriff called in the state police medevac helicopter.

Snow whirled up and bit at their faces as the chopper landed. Evie said nothing as the medical team jumped down and tended to Langley. His clothes were cut away, a clotting pack was applied to the wound, and an IV stabbed into his forearm. The sheriff, seeing gristle and bone, asked, "How bad?"

"Fifty-fifty. If she hadn't put a tourniquet on him and packed him in snow, the guy would have bled out for sure."

The sheriff took that in and muttered, "Fuck." He turned to Evie and asked, "How'd it happen?"

"He stepped out just as I was firing at a buck." She had stopped crying. Dunn figured she was in shock.

All the sheriff said was, "Show me." The deputy who had been off duty when the call came in pulled up just as he was getting on the back of Evie's snowmobile. The deputy had an elkhound he was training for bear hunting in the back of his patrol car. The sheriff told him not to let the dog out, but it got out anyway, and ran ahead of them into the forest, nose to the ground.

The bloodstain Langley's wound left in the snow looked like a giant red carnation. When they arrived the elkhound was licking at it. Evie had ejected an empty cartridge two hundred yards from the bloodstain, so her story would line up in terms of where she would have had to have been standing to shoot Langley by accident. The sheriff took photographs and seemed satisfied that it was a typical hunting accident. Langley hadn't been wearing a fluorescent vest—no way she could have seen him; no one to blame from a legal standpoint until the elkhound started digging under the blue spruce.

Smelling blood on the ziplock bag, the hound came up with the tape recorder in his mouth. Evie petted the dog as the sheriff played the recording through.

"He did that to you?"

"Yes." Her voice was small and hoarse.

"Doesn't give you the right to shoot him."

"You ever been drugged and raped?"

The sheriff thought about that for a while and said, "No, I haven't." Then Billy Dunn thought about the fact that in nine days the locals in Townsend County would be voting on whether he'd be sheriff for another four years. One question he had to consider was whether the citizenry's dislike of Buddy Quimby outweighed their resentment of the Mohawk Club. Letting Buddy slide about hunting and fishing regulations was one thing, but this was different. He had daughters of his own and he did not like the idea of them having a father who was unemployed.

"Confession at gunpoint is not going to carry any weight. Might not even be admissible. Man who's been shot and bleeding to death will say anything to stay alive."

"You don't believe me?"

"You got any proof other than this recording?"

Evie shook her head *no* and the sheriff said, "Maybe Langley won't want to risk you giving your side in court. Then again maybe he will. People don't like getting shot. He dies and all this tape is going to do is put you in prison for a long time."

"I wanted to hurt him, not kill him."

"Maybe that was a mistake." Then the sheriff read Evie her Miranda rights.

When they got back to the fire road, all the sheriff said to the deputy was, "I'm taking Evie back to the office to make an official statement. And don't ever bring that fucking dog to work again." He made no mention of the bloodstained tape recorder in his pocket and let Evie sit in the front seat of his cherry-topped SUV. The last thing he needed was Buddy hearing his daughter had been arrested for attempted murder from someone other than himself.

Evie told him her parents were up at a cabin on the Mohawk reservation and wouldn't be back until the next day. The sheriff knew that meant Buddy and Flo were on a cigarette run to NYC. Not wanting to further complicate the situation, he made no mention of the fact that Buddy gave him a 20 percent cut to look the other way. As Sheriff Dunn drove them off the mountain, he considered all the different kinds of trouble Buddy could cause him.

He put Evie in the cell he used for drunks and husbands who beat their wives and told his dispatcher he'd fire her ass if she told anybody he had Evie Quimby in custody before he was ready to make an official statement. Then he put a call in to the state police air rescue unit— Langley's heart had stopped twice en route to the hospital in Albany and was now in surgery. Deciding to wait until morning to call the district attorney about what the charges would be, he called out to Evie, "Do you want KFC or a burger for dinner?"

"Don't I get to make a phone call?"

"I'll notify your parents as soon as they get back."

"You're saying I can't make a phone call?"

Given that she was a minor, he could have said no, but then there was the Buddy factor. He handed her the phone and said, "You've got three minutes." He regretted it as soon as he realized who she was calling.

Evie got Lulu's answering service. The message she left contained

the words *Win Langley, drugged, raped, videotaped, hunting accident.*
When Evie handed the phone back, she crumpled to the floor and
began to sob. The sheriff did not make her feel any better when he
removed her bootlaces.

An hour later Sheriff Dunn received a phone call from a New York
City criminal lawyer who informed him that he would be leading the
"team" of attorneys Lulu Mannheim had retained to represent Miss
Quimby. There was no bright side to that day for Evie, except that
now that she had shot Langley, her father would not feel obliged to put
a bullet in the man who had raped his daughter.

Win Langley was wheeled out of surgery at 7 p.m. and regained
consciousness just after ten. The ventilator was still in his throat when
he remembered Evie standing over him in the snow, tape recorder in
hand. When he screamed, the nurse thought he was gagging on his
own vomit. The surgeon who performed the operation burst into the
recovery room and pulled out the ventilator. Win whispered, "How
ruined am I?" The surgeon thought he was talking about his leg, not
the tape recording of his confession.

The next morning, Langley resisted the urge to retreat into his
morphine drip and demanded a phone and a fax machine. Once they
were in place and the nurse had left the room, he called Tom Reynolds
in New York and dictated three documents. Reynolds wasn't a lawyer,
he was an investment banker who specialized in real estate. Win had
introduced him to a rich girl from Greenwich and served as best man
at their wedding. When Win did that, you owed him. Reynolds had
good reasons to be discreet and do exactly as asked.

Win was not surprised when Lulu Mannheim, accompanied by
one of Evie's lawyers, showed up at his hospital room around midday. As soon as they walked in, Win said, "Before anyone says anything they regret, read this." It was a letter addressed to the sheriff of
Townsend County and read as follows:

This letter is to certify that I, W. H. Langley, in
no way blame or hold Miss Eve Quimby legally
or criminally culpable in any way whatsoever for
the accidental gunshot wound I received on the
morning of October 27th on Flathead Mountain.
It was a hunting accident pure and simple, and if
anyone was to blame, it is myself. When I walked
into the woods on the western slope of Flathead
Mountain, I heard a gunshot and knew another
hunter was close by. Not announcing myself or in
any way signaling my presence, I can only fault
myself for being shot. Miss Quimby was in no
position to see me and I suddenly stepped into her
line of fire just as she was about to shoot a buck.
Furthermore, I wish to establish that if it were
not for Miss Quimby's on-site first aid and heroic
effort to get me immediate medical attention, I
would not have survived.

Lulu stopped reading. "What about the rape and the video and the drugs?"

"I think someone did all that to her, but you don't honestly believe I'm the kind of man who could ever—"

"It's been my experience that men are capable of anything."

"Evie was drugged up and didn't know what she was seeing."

Having had more than a few hallucinatory experiences involving drugs, Lulu knew about seeing things that weren't there. Likewise, she found it hard to believe Win was a rapist until she looked at the bottom of the page and saw that the place for him to sign the letter and the notary to attach their signature and stamp were blank.

"Why haven't you signed it yet?"

"Because I'm willing to report what your friend did to me as a hunting accident if, and only if, this deeply disturbed girl agrees in writing to stop making up grotesquely false stories about me." Langley groaned in pain as he handed the lawyer two more documents. The first contained a blank space for Evie's signature. It boiled down to Evie swearing that Win never drugged, sexually assaulted, or filmed her, and that in return for the "good and valuable" sum of one dollar she agreed never to repeat such allegations or make any attempt to take legal action against him in regard to this matter for the rest of her life. The penalty for reneging on the agreement had seven zeros after it.

The third document was an ironclad confidentiality agreement between Lulu and Win which stipulated that if Lulu ever repeated Eve Quimby's false allegations to anyone or in any way made public statements of a derogatory nature about Mr. Langley's character or professional conduct, she would be legally obliged to relinquish ownership of her eighteen-thousand-acre property and house known as Valhalla to Mr. Langley.

Lulu's lawyer said, "You can't sign this."

Langley growled, "If you don't, I will make sure Evie Quimby spends the next twenty years of her life in prison."

Evie's freedom in exchange for Langley walking free and continuing to be the most charming rapist in New York. Lulu lit a cigarette and stared at the documents that would silence them.

Langley told her, "It's against the law to smoke in a hospital."

Lulu replied, "Go fuck yourself."

Langley's triumphant grimace reminded her of the smile on Uncle Fred's face when he showed her dirty pictures of the things he wanted her to do for him. He had threatened to take away the kitten he had given her if she told anyone about their secret game. Knowing that's what this was for Langley, a sick game, she told him, "I hope they have to amputate. Get the fucking notary in here before I change my mind."

Lulu and Langley signed simultaneously. A notary made the lie legal.

As Lulu's lawyer put copies of both agreements into his briefcase, Langley called Sheriff Dunn and said, "She can sign it now." They had talked earlier in the day and come to an understanding of how appreciative Langley would be for the sheriff's cooperation.

Lulu watched it go down. "You've got it all worked out, haven't you, Win?"

"Given that I'm the injured party, I think I'm being more than magnanimous, protecting myself in this way." What shocked Lulu most of all was the way he said it. She knew people would believe it.

Sheriff Dunn brought Evie out of her cell and into his office. He pulled down the shades so the dispatcher couldn't observe, then handed her a pen and the confidentiality agreement Langley had faxed. "Write your name here and you can go home, Evie."

Evie read it through twice. Each time her mind snagged on the phrase "for the good and valuable sum of one dollar." A dollar was what Kevin had offered to pay her for letting him touch her disfigurement. As she put pen to paper, she could hear Scrotum jeering, "Five bucks for all four of us!"

Evie was about to sign when she suddenly shook her head no and told the sheriff, "I want to talk to Lulu first."

"Just sign it, Evie. Langley's written up a statement calling it a hunting accident." He handed Evie a copy.

She read the last sentence aloud. " 'I wish to establish that if it were not for Miss Quimby's on-site first aid and heroic effort to get me immediate medical attention, I would not have survived.' I'm a hero?"

"As soon as you sign it."

"Langley tried to shoot me. I don't trust him. I want to talk to Lulu, make sure he signed it."

Dunn saw her point. Langley hadn't mentioned he'd taken a shot at the girl. "Make it quick." Handcuffing her to the chair, he put the phone in front of her and left the room.

Langley's doctor came in with the nurse to check his dressing, and Lulu and her lawyer went out into the hall just as her cell phone rang.

Evie's voice was small. "I can't do it."

"Why?"

"Because I want to tell a judge what he did to me. You'll back me up."

"Evie, you don't understand. To get you out of this, I just signed an agreement. I say one word about what Langley did to you, slander him in any way, he gets Valhalla."

"You promised him I'd sign?"

Lulu's lawyer got on the line. "No, Miss Mannheim doesn't have the legal power to guarantee your cooperation or force you to sign anything, but if this goes to court, she will have to deny any knowledge of the rape or she'll lose Valhalla."

"I don't want her to lose anything, I just want to hold on to my pride."

Lulu was back on the phone. "Evie. There's no fucking justice with shit like this. I know it sucks, but you gotta sign it. Langley is a lawyer. They'll believe him and you'll go to jail."

Evie's eyes darted around the sheriff's office, desperate for a way out. Glimpsing a framed newspaper clipping from the *Lake Placid News* of Dunn and a woman he had saved from drowning in Lake Millicent, Evie saw a way for her to escape Langley's trap, damaged but whole.

The last thing Evie said to Lulu was, "I want Langley to be as scared of me as I am of him."

When the doctor finished rebandaging Langley's leg, Lulu walked back into the hospital room alone.

"Where's your lawyer?"

"I don't need him for this part. It's between you and Evie."

"I'm glad you understand that, Lulu. Believe it or not, I'm sorry for the awkward position her false accusations put you in." Langley eyed his fax machine impatiently and called the sheriff again. "Where's Evie's agreement?"

Sheriff Dunn had put Evie back in her cell by then. "She refuses to sign it."

Langley took a deep breath. "I want her charged with attempted murder and no bail. I'll call the district attorney soon as we get off."

Lulu waited until he hung up to ask, "How are you going to explain your statement?"

Langley ripped it in half. "Now that I have your nondisclosure agreement, Lulu, if it goes to court, you won't be able to say a word in her defense."

"If I were you, I'd call the sheriff back and say you changed your mind."

"Why the hell would I do that?"

"Because a few minutes ago my attorneys faxed your notarized statement exonerating Evie of any responsibility for the 'hunting accident' and praising her for her 'heroic effort' that saved your life to the *Lake Placid News, New York Times, New York Post* . . ."

Langley's eyes went blank and his face trembled with rage. Turning on his morphine drip, he called Dunn back and said, "Let her go."

Just to let Win Langley know how she felt about him, Lulu spat in his face before she left the room.

Sheriff Dunn drove Evie home. Halfway across the Mink River Bridge, he stopped the patrol car and told Evie to get out. The snow had melted off and it was suddenly unseasonably warm. A pair of fish hawks circled overhead and Evie could see a shadow that looked like a trout twenty feet below. Sheriff Dunn lit a cigarette as he leaned against the railing. "You care about Buddy, don't tell him about the rape."

"I'm not stupid."

Then the sheriff took out the bloodstained ziplock bag with the recorder inside and tossed it in the river. "Just so you know . . . it's over."

The sheriff waited with Evie at the cabin until Buddy and Flo got back. She let her uncle tell most of the lie about the shooting. Flo knew the truth as soon as she heard Evie had been involved in a "hunting accident." When the sheriff showed her a copy of Langley's statement, all she had to say was, "I'm so sorry you had to go through that, Evie."

Buddy was more interested in the trajectory of the story. "If the buck was on a rise and Langley was in between Evie and the deer, and she was aiming for the buck's head, how the hell did she hit Langley in the knee?"

The sheriff knew Buddy would ask that, and he and Evie had agreed the answer would be, "She sneezed."

And then there was Buddy's next question, "If it was an accident, why did my daughter spend the night in your jail?"

Billy Dunn satisfied his cousin's curiosity on that one with, "Your daughter was upset and I was on duty—what was I going to do? You don't let a child spend the night alone thinking she might have killed a man."

CHAPTER 23

For three days and nights I lost myself in the forest of my mother's past. She was still my mother and I would always be her child, yet her telling and me listening to her story changed each of us in ways large and small. Neither one of us had any idea where the truth would take us, but we both knew there was no turning back.

It was Monday now, May 7th, 2018. Our flight to New York was scheduled to take off from Charles de Gaulle at 9 a.m. When I opened my eyes that morning, dawn hadn't broken yet. My mother was standing at the foot of my bed, folding my underwear in the darkness. Stacking them like pastel pancakes, she tucked them neatly into my suitcase next to the socks she had already rolled into pairs.

"I can pack my own bag, Mom."

"I know. But I like doing it, reminds me of when you were little." My mother was already showered and dressed for the trip. I could see my meds carefully labeled in ziplock bags in the living room, ready to go into her carry-on. As my mother made room in my bag for my blue jean jacket, she reached into my pockets and pulled out a condom.

She laughed when I said, "Wishful thinking," and tucked the condom into my suitcase next to the socks.

In a week I would find out if I had a shot at living through summer. As I brushed my teeth, I tried to prepare myself for the worst by imagining what it would be like if I didn't find a blood relative in the Adirondacks willing to give me a bone marrow transplant. How would it feel to hear my doctor say, "I'm sorry, but there's nothing more we can do"? I suddenly felt a rush of such pure panic that I had to hold onto the sink to keep from falling down.

Closing my eyes, I tried to think positive thoughts, but all I could see was Langley smiling at the foot of my bed as he handed me a fucking bouquet.

When I came out of the bathroom, I asked my mother, "Do you think Langley came to Paris because you didn't sign that nondisclosure agreement and he wanted to scare you to keep you from telling Radetzky you were raped?" Thinking about Langley kept my mind off cancer.

"Langley had no reason to think I'd tell Radetzky that. Getting raped had nothing to do with Charlie's suicide. Radetzky never even mentioned Langley's name."

"You think it was just a coincidence Langley shows up in my hospital room and two days later Radetzky Skypes you?"

"I don't know what to think except it's time to leave."

Our plane was an hour late taking off from Charles de Gaulle. I sat in the window seat, my mother was next to me on the aisle. Turbulence hit as drinks were being served, and the captain told us to fasten our seat belts. The plane shuddered and dipped. My mother said, "I fucking hate flying," but what she really fucking hated was going home. I took my meds and washed them down with a swig of Pepto-Bismol to keep from vomiting them up.

As I ate my peanuts, I looked out the window and watched England appear thirty thousand feet below us only to see it vanish in a swirl of clouds so white and cottony they looked like special effects. A few minutes later, Ireland came and went the same way. After that, as far as I could see there was nothing but the pale blue where sea and sky were one.

"What happened to her?"

"Who?"

"The marble statue of the girl?"

"I have no idea—sold, given to a museum, for all I know Lulu pushed her down the stairs again." Seeing I'd finished my peanuts, my mother gave me hers. "I had no business trying to save her. No idea what I was doing."

"Do you ever hear from Lulu?"

The mention of her name made my mother smile. "No. . . . I read about her once and a while. Something about saving the elephants. I think she's big on Buddhism now."

"Why didn't you two stay in touch?"

Turbulence shook the plane and the seat belt light came on. "We were bad luck for each other."

"Is that the same reason you don't talk to Flo anymore?"

"No . . . my mother and I just kept having the same conversation over and over again, and since it always made each of us sad—" *The plane shuddered again, more violently this time. Drinks spilled and somebody's carry-on bag fell out of the overhead luggage compartment. My mother's hand gripped mine.*

"Am I going to meet Flo and Buddy?"

"Yes . . . if you'd like." *I looked at my watch and thought 12:30 p.m. Paris time meant the sun was just rising over the Sister Lakes.*

"Do they still live in the cabin on the mountain?" *I was trying to ask a neutral question.*

"Flo does."

"Where's Buddy?"

My mother closed her eyes and took a deep breath before she told me. "Buddy's in prison." *Suddenly I understood why my mother made all those excuses for my grandparents never coming to visit us in Paris.*

"When were you planning on getting around to telling me that?"

"I'm telling you now." *Hearing the sharpness in her voice, she added,* "I'm sorry. And I'm sorry I can't think of anything better to say other than I'm sorry about a lot of things."

"What did he go to prison for?" *In my head I heard the clattering chink and clink of quarters being fed into a jail pay phone.*

"Arson. . . . A man burned to death in the fire."

"Was Buddy guilty?"

"Not in his mind."

CHAPTER 24

The first week of November 2001, Flo and Buddy stood on the dock at Valhalla and watched a floatplane take off with their daughter and Lulu inside. Evie told them that Lulu was taking her to New York to look at colleges and go to museums and that she would return in a week; ten days max. As the plane arced south against a cold slate-blue sky, Buddy wept because he sensed Evie wouldn't be coming home anytime soon. Flo cried because she knew it for a fact.

Lulu said something, but the engine of the floatplane was too loud for Evie to understand what she was being told. Shaking her head *no* and pointing to her ears, she shouted, "I can't hear a word you're saying." Lulu plugged in a pair of mic'd headsets. Earphones on, they spoke as if separated by a distance far greater than the cramped width of the cabin.

"I set up an appointment for you at NewYork-Presbyterian Hospital with a plastic surgeon who specializes in removing birthmarks."

Evie sounded far away when she answered, "I decided I'm better off the way I am." She had left both her John Deere hat and the velvet headband behind. Her hair was tied back off her face with a red scrunchie.

Lulu didn't get it. "What are you talking about?"

"Seems like asking for trouble, making yourself more attractive to men."

When Buddy and Flo got back to the cabin, they found a cookie tin on their bed. Inside was twenty-five thousand dollars in hundred-dollar bills and a handwritten note that said, "I love you."

By that spring, Win Langley had exhausted the surgical options that were currently available to improve the strength and functionality of his right leg. What had been his bad leg was now his good leg. Physical therapy could do no more. He needed a cane to walk across a room, and there were days when each step he took reminded him of Evie Quimby.

In the city, a forest-green Bentley and chauffeur made sure he arrived in style and never had to walk further than from the curb to the front door of wherever he was going. The hunting accident and the stoic forgiveness he had shown the young woman who had accidentally shot him; his refusal to press charges against a fellow hunter, had made Langley more popular and welcome than ever. Christian groups, veterans, and the NRA often asked him to speak on the importance of character and spiritual generosity.

To navigate the steep and uneven trails around the Mohawk Club, he had a custom four-wheel-drive, fat-tired electric wheelchair made for himself. He could still fish from the bank, but no longer cast a fly from mid-stream. Similarly, he was able to hunt birds from a duck blind or at a standing shoot with a loader behind him, but his stalking days were over. In short, it wasn't the same.

From the start, Buddy had his doubts about his cousin the sheriff's explanation of events surrounding the "hunting accident." He was not alone in that. Given that Evie had won the county shooting contest for children under the age of sixteen when she was ten, everybody in Rangeley had questions about how Evie could have fired four feet low at a distance of two hundred yards.

When the sheriff took a vacation in Hawaii he couldn't afford and came home talking about running for the State Senate, Buddy grew even more suspicious.

As he was getting out of his patrol car one starry evening to investigate a call that came in about a bunch of kids dynamiting fish ten miles up lake from Rangeley, a burlap sack was placed over the sheriff's head and a revolver cocked next to his ear. Buddy came straight to the point. "What happened to my daughter?"

Buddy only had to punch Sheriff Dunn once in the gut to get him to confess that the fishing trip to Hawaii and the State Senate run were Win's way of saying thank you for throwing the tape recording of his confession into the river. His cousin shat himself as he sobbed out the specifics of what Win Langley had done. Buddy considered the idea of burying his cousin in the same part of the forest where he disposed of the man who raped Flo, but decided the worst thing he could do to Sheriff Dunn was let him live out his miserable life looking over his shoulder.

After he let the sheriff go, Buddy sat alone on the lakeshore and opened a door inside his head to bad thoughts. He had seen Langley crab-walking with his canes into Harlan's Tackle Shop. His daughter had settled her score and done it Quimby-style, but Buddy felt a loss of something more heartfelt than pride that demanded he take action.

It was not macho honor that prompted him to resort to violence. It was the unbearable emptiness he felt whenever he thought of his daughter. He missed Evie in ways he did not have words for. More importantly, he knew his daughter would never come back to the Sister Lakes, not even for a visit, as long as Langley was alive.

Flo having had her reasons for thinking it best to keep what Langley had done to their daughter a secret from him, Buddy felt it was within his rights not to share his plan with his wife.

Ignoring his traplines after ice-out, Buddy spent most of that spring forty feet up a spruce tree on the far shore of the Mohawk Club's lake watching club members come and go in their floatplanes through a spotter scope.

First Friday in May, four seaplanes landed within an hour of one another. For the last of the arrivals, a fancy electric wheelchair was rolled out on the dock and he saw Win Langley hobble out of the cockpit, followed by a white-haired man who looked like a polar bear in a three-piece suit. Buddy watched as Win handed the old man his cane and wheeled himself up to the Roosevelt cabin.

Evie's father did not know that the club's "Game Committee" had convened that weekend to witness the illegal release of a mating pair of mountain lions. Captured in the Sierra Madre, the cats had been driven cross-country from New Mexico hidden in a cattle truck. The only predator Buddy was interested in was Win Langley.

That night, Buddy paid a visit to Clinger. When he wasn't working at Valhalla, the old boatman took care of the Mohawk Club's collection of vintage wooden lake boats. He was fond of Evie and had shown Buddy a postcard she'd sent him of the Eiffel Tower. Clinger understood what was being asked. The next day, the boatman put five pounds of sugar in the fuel tank of the club's emergency generator.

Just after 7 p.m., Buddy killed the power line leading into the club off the county road with two blasts of oo buckshot and slipped past the pens where flocks of birds were being bred to be shot. While members ate elk steaks by candlelight in the clubhouse, Buddy waited in the shadows for Win Langley to come back to the Roosevelt cabin.

Watching the way the wheelchair swerved recklessly across the lawn, Buddy figured Langley was drunk. A shadow staggered up onto the cabin's porch and went inside. Buddy shoved wedges under the doors, front and back, so they couldn't be opened from the inside. As a meteor pierced the moonless night, Buddy doused the porch with gasoline and tossed a match. The cabin exploded into flames, crackling like kindling. A man screamed inside and Buddy felt he had done what he had to do.

It wasn't until the next day when the sheriff paid an unofficial visit that Buddy found out that the man he burned to death at the Mohawk Club was a seventy-three-year-old investment banker who had borrowed Win's electric wheelchair without permission because he was too drunk to walk. The sheriff knew Buddy had set the fire, but out of a mix of shame, fear, and blood loyalty said nothing.

Buddy regretted throwing the empty five-gallon plastic gas can into the lake when it floated up in Rangeley with his and Flo's fingerprints on it. She had nothing to do with it. As the sheriff argued in Buddy's defense, the gas can was at best circumstantial evidence. What convicted him was the caretaker finding a set of keys to

Buddy's front door, truck, and Willys Jeep attached to a pink Swiss Army knife in the woods a hundred yards from the torched cabin, which was strange because the state police had scoured the area twice and found no such thing. It was Win Langley's way of letting Evie know he hadn't forgotten about her.

Lulu hired Buddy a lawyer. If Evie had reported the keys stolen the night of the rape, a different judgment might have been passed down. In return for Flo getting off with a suspended sentence as an accessory after the fact, Buddy pleaded guilty and would not be eligible for parole for fifteen years.

Evie was in Paris by then, living with Jacques Clément. She wanted to come home, but Flo told her there was no more home to come home to. Evie said she didn't care and was coming back anyway. Flo whispered into the phone, "If you love me, stay away."

Evie didn't understand until Flo said, "If you come back here, that bastard Langley will figure out a way to hurt you again."

CHAPTER 25

O*ur plane had to circle New York for more than an hour waiting for a freak weather system to pass. When we finally landed at JFK, the passengers applauded and the pilot told us a tornado had touched down in Brooklyn earlier that day. As we shouldered our carry-ons, a woman in the row ahead of us turned on her smartphone and relayed a news report. A girl out walking her dog during the storm in Prospect Park had been killed by a falling tree branch. As we shuffled toward the exit, the passengers around us muttered, "Horrible. . . . Poor girl. . . . What was she thinking going out in weather like that?" But I remember thinking that girl was lucky, not because she got killed by a falling branch, but because she didn't know death was coming until it hit her. Cancer wasn't like that. I knew what was hanging over my head.*

Alternating with each breath between hoping for a miracle and preparing for the worst, I felt like I was haunted by my own ghost.

My mother and I had dual citizenship—French and US passports. We entered the country as Americans because the line was shorter. Our plan was to spend the night at the airport and then drive up to Rangeley in the morning. When my mother turned on her iPhone, five messages popped up. She deleted them before I could see who they were from. When I asked her who was trying to get in touch, all she said was, "Nobody I want to talk to."

I could tell whoever nobody was rattled her. When customs asked her, "Anything to declare?"—my mother just stared at him. He repeated the question twice before she nervously blurted out, "My daughter's got drugs."

I knew what she meant, but customs didn't. Even after we showed him that the pill bottles in my backpack all had labels from a hospital in Paris and my mother pulled out the bulging folder of my medical records that she kept ever ready in her purse, they still felt obliged to bring out a German shepherd to sniff our bags. When I tried to pet the dog, the customs agent told me to keep my hands to myself. My mother whispered, "Welcome to America." It was funny, sort of.

By the time we got out of the arrivals building with our suitcases it was 6 p.m. in NYC and midnight in Paris. Having been awake for seventeen hours, we were jet-lagged and cranky. My mother had just gotten her period; I'd stopped menstruating after chemo. As the shuttle bus took us to the car rental, I heckled her into agreeing to teach me to drive on the back roads of Rangeley. When I urged her to rent a convertible so we could be like Thelma and Louise, my mother reminded me the movie ended with the women driving off a cliff. We opted for a white Jeep Cherokee.

When another text came in, and then another, I finally asked, "Who are you avoiding?"

My mother showed me her phone. The texts were from Charlie's brother. The latest read, "I know you're in New York. I need to talk to you. It's urgent. Please."

I was surprised when my mother texted him back, "Meet me tomorrow, 7 a.m., in the lobby of the JFK Holiday Inn. I'll give you thirty minutes."

I was even more surprised when I asked her what changed her mind about talking to him and she answered, "Talking to you."

That night we shared a double room with a view of the parking lot. For the first time in weeks I actually felt hungry. My mother wanted to go out and find an organic restaurant. She had this idea that drinking kale smoothies was going to make me less appetizing to cancer. In the end, she gave in and let me order a burger and fries from room service. The burger was bad bordering on inedible and the fries soggy, but I liked watching American TV. As my mother picked at her food, she got on her computer. I was watching a rerun of an episode of 30 Rock that I had never seen before, laughing at something Tina Fey said to Alec Baldwin, when my mother suddenly shouted, "What a fucking sick monster!"

"Langley?"

"Radetzky. He was arrested yesterday."

My mother had googled Radetzky in preparation for the meeting. A newspaper article popped up headlined NYU PSYCHIATRIST ARRESTED

FOR CHILD PORNOGRAPHY. *I echoed the sentiment as I read the sordid details of the story over her shoulder. "Over a thousand images . . . children as young as three . . . anonymous tip."*

Peering at the shrink's photograph, I said, "He doesn't look like a monster." My mother answered, "Monsters never do." We chain-locked the door and set the alarm for 5:30 a.m. My mother wanted to be certain we were checked out and long gone by the time the monster showed.

I woke up at 3 a.m., nauseous and sweaty. Barely able to make it to the bathroom; vomiting and diarrhea followed. Before I knew what it was to be really sick, when I threw up or got the runs, I used to moan, "I wish I was dead." I was careful not to say things like that anymore.

Cancer had made me superstitious. Omens and fate and the alchemy of luck loomed large in my imagination. Was it a bad burger seasoned with E. coli, or had cancer decided to take another bite out of me? I had come to think of my disease as a creature—twisted, cruel, sadistic, perverse, and soul-killing as a man who preys on children.

My mother got panicky at the sound of me retching in the bathroom. Taking my temperature and seeing it was 101 F, she called my doctor in Paris. When I heard them talking about checking me into a hospital in New York, I lied and told her I felt better.

Dawn checkout took forever. Then my mother realized she had left our passports back in the room. Then we couldn't find them because they were in the medical folder. We were dragging our suitcases toward the parking lot when a yellow taxi pulled up. Dr. Radetzky jumped out wild-eyed and looking like someone who had been pushed down a flight of stairs. He shouted, "Where are you going? You agreed to talk to me."

"That was before I found out what you are. Leave us alone or I swear I'll call the police." My mother was yelling and people were looking.

He ran toward us. My mother was throwing our suitcases in the back of the rented Cherokee and I thought I was going to throw up again.

As we jumped into the car, my mother hissed, "Lock the doors."

Radetzky grabbed hold of my mother's door before she could slam it closed, bellowing, "I'm innocent, goddamnit!"

Suddenly hearing the violence in his own voice, the psychiatrist let go of the car door and held up his hands in surrender. My mother had the car started and was backing up. He pounded on the side windows, pleading, "Win Langley planted those photographs on my computer."

My mother slammed on the brakes at the mention of Langley's name. She kept the doors locked and cracked her window just enough to demand, "Why would he do that?"

"To stop me from asking questions about Charlie. My brother interned for Langley's firm the same summer he got all that money from the bank in Cyprus." The jets flying low overhead made it hard to hear what Radetzky was saying. "I told Langley I was tracking down you and all the people mentioned in the sheriff's report."

"When did you tell him that?"

"Twelve days ago." My mother and I didn't need a calendar to figure out Langley showed up in my hospital room two days after that.

Radetzky's face was pressed close to the window of the rental car. His breath fogged the glass as he pleaded his case. I can't remember exactly what Radetzky said, but it went something like this: "When I called Langley, he couldn't have been nicer. He told me the bank loan was news to him, but he had always wondered how Charlie had been able to afford a BMW and go to expensive restaurants. He said he remembered Charlie mentioning he had a rich aunt, which sounded like the kind of lie my brother liked to tell about himself. When I told Langley there was no rich aunt, he seemed genuinely hurt. He talked about the personal sense of loss he felt when my brother killed himself, and how he still felt guilty for not realizing how troubled Charlie was; 'sexually confused,' is what Langley called it. My brother was many things, but he wasn't——"

My mother interrupted, "Why did he put on the wedding dress?"

"Maybe he didn't. Maybe somebody put it on him after he died. My brother was too selfish to kill himself."

"Selfish how?"

"He didn't care about people. He was charming, good-looking, and totally lacking in empathy. Charlie had a gift for making people fall in love

with him. He called it 'making them believers.' He got a thrill out of using people, particularly women."

As Dr. Radetzky calmed down, he started to sound more and more like a shrink. "When Langley invited me for lunch to talk about my brother and give me the names of people who might know something about Charlie's private business dealings, I took him up on the offer. He took me to his club, the Racquet Club. Takes up a whole block on Park Ave. Ultra-WASPy, sort of place Charlie would have loved. When we got there, just as promised, Langley hands me a list of names, phone numbers, copies of pages from his personal diary noting events and parties he went to with Charlie. I pull my computer out of my backpack so I can take notes at lunch, and the maître d' tells me, 'It's against club rules to bring business materials or computers into the dining room.' Langley apologizes for not warning me, hands my computer with his briefcase over to the coat check, and we go into the dining room. When we come out after lunch, Langley's chauffeur is waiting and says he's already put our things in the car. It was the only time my computer was out of my sight. Two days later, I was arrested."

"How did you know I was coming to America?"

"Langley told me."

My mother took that in and put the car in gear. "I can't help you."

"Have you been listening to me? I've lost my job, my reputation. My ex-wife won't let me see my own son. Langley's destroying my life."

My mother stepped on the gas. We were three hundred miles from Rangeley, but we were already in parts but little known.

CHAPTER 26

Evie was so disoriented by the connection between Radetzky and Langley, she got lost trying to escape the maze of service roads surrounding JFK. Driving fast but not knowing where she was going, she ended up in long-term parking twice.

Evie told herself she was a different person from the scared teenager who had run away from Rangeley in a floatplane seventeen years ago; reminded herself she was a grown woman, a widow who had a life, a career, and a sick daughter. The birthmark was gone, but she still felt like damaged goods.

Chloé waited until they were on the Grand Central Parkway to say, "I think Langley put kiddie porn on Radetzky's computer to make it so no one would believe him. Discredit him before he found something that would get Langley in trouble."

"We can't risk that. We don't know what kind of man we're dealing with. He could be like Langley. You never fucking know, that's the problem."

Cars honked and brakes screeched as she cut across three lanes of the parkway to get onto I-278. Crossing the Hudson on the Tappan Zee Bridge, just before they got on the New York State Thruway, Evie stopped at a T-Mobile store and bought a new SIM card for her iPhone. She wanted no more calls from Dr. Radetzky.

As Evie tried to figure out how to get back on the thruway, Chloé fiddled with the old SIM card. "I think Radetzky's telling the truth. He has no reason to lie."

"What if he's just using us? Trying to get us to buy into some conspiracy to make it seem like he's innocent? I don't want to talk to the creep, okay?"

"What if the creep is innocent and you're being paranoid?"

Evie kept her eyes on the road. Her past wasn't just chasing them, it was sitting in the backseat of the car, breathing down her neck.

"Langley is Radetzky's problem, not ours."

"He came to my hospital room! Langley's like cancer: you ignore the problem, it just gets worse."

Evie slammed on the brakes. "I don't want anything to do with Win Langley, okay? After everything I've told you about what he did to me, is that so fucking hard to understand?"

"I get it. It was terrible, he fucked up your whole life."

"No you don't get it." My mother was shouting.

"Okay. I don't get it. I wasn't raped. I never shot anybody. But I have fucking leukemia, and if someone I have never met, who I don't even know—someone who has problems of their own and for sure doesn't want a needle stuck in their pelvic bone—doesn't put their own problems aside and help me . . . I'm screwed."

Evie was not a believer in ethical karma, but she was too exhausted to fight. Pulling over to the side of the road, she turned off the car. "We're running out of time. I'm just trying to keep you from . . ."

When Evie choked on the word, Chloé said it for her. "Dying."

Her voice was suddenly so small and distant it seemed to Evie as if her daughter were already gone. Shutting her eyes to that thought, shaking her head *no* to that possibility, Evie took her daughter's face in her hands and said, "He didn't fuck up my whole life . . . I had you."

Pulling her daughter close, feeling the thinness of her child's ravaged body, the bones beneath her flesh, Evie thought of what the stone girl had taught her. *You put the broken pieces back together as best you can and move on.*

CHAPTER 27

F rom the front seat of the Cherokee, doing 70 mph up the New York State Thruway, America was a blur of things to worry about. It had been ten days since Evie had first told her daughter about shooting Langley. So many lies had to be explained. So many truths uncaged. Mother and daughter felt stalked by something they didn't understand. The present, past, and future all seemed as dark and cancerous as Chloé's white blood cell count.

Few words were exchanged between them as they headed north. Silence seemed the safest and most eloquent way to communicate their growing anxiety. Minute by minute, they were getting closer to finding out whether they had traveled 3,482 miles to have their hearts broken.

They got off the thruway just past Albany and took county roads from there. The towns grew smaller and grimmer and the farms more ramshackle as they proceeded north. Then the forest laid claim to the land, and wooded mountains rose up around them greener and denser and more unwelcoming than Chloé had imagined or her mother had remembered.

They crossed over into Townsend County just after 4 p.m. Evie began to hum a tune and, realizing it was "Touch of Grey," said, "We're getting close." It began to drizzle, and a half hour later as they came down off the back side of Saddlers Mountain on Route 7, the Sister Lakes showed themselves, misty, blue-gray, and mysterious as the day.

Crossing the Mink River Bridge, they saw a moose on the far bank. Chloé thought it a good omen. All Evie saw was that the "Welcome to Rangeley" sign was riddled with bullet holes and had a cock and balls spray-painted on it. There were still Morlocks in the woods.

Evie pulled the car over in front of the town hall. It was in better repair than she remembered. The two-story clapboard barn of a building with a cupola on top had recently been repainted white with green trim. In the old days it had been used for town dances, Grange meetings, and the occasional speech by a politician in search of votes. Mary Lou's convenience store was across the street. Through the window they could see Scrotum and his mother working the counter. Evie walked around to the back of the hall, praying they would find the adoption records.

Chloé tried the back door; it was locked. "Where do we go to to get the key?"

"The sheriff has the key."

It had been a cold winter. There was ice in the lake well into April and spring was late. It was the second week of May, the buds of the sugar maples had only just burst, the forsythia yet to bloom, and the shops still boarded up. Besides Mary Lou's, the Rangeley Inn was the only establishment open for business.

Evie had reserved a room with twin beds under her married name. She had no desire for anyone but the sheriff to know she had come to town. After she found what she needed, she'd call Flo and arrange to visit Buddy in prison. Right now all she wanted from Rangeley was the birth certificate that would provide the names of the mother who had given her away and the man listed as father.

The Rangeley Inn was just down the street from the public dock. It was a long low building that started out life as a dormitory for the employees of the sawmill that had eaten the parts of the forest that were easy to cut. Unlike the mill, it had refused to fall down and had been converted into a motel that catered to hunters and fishermen on a budget. It featured a deserted six-booth café that was mostly bar called On the Rocks. A chubby teenager who introduced herself as Dot checked them in.

The beds squeaked, the tub was stained, the water from the faucet was brown, and the pull chain that hung from the light fixture in the bathroom was tied into a hangman's noose. In addition to being assistant manager of the Rangeley Inn and the maid, Dot was their waitress that night. They both ordered the trout, which was fresh and cooked in bacon grease. The smoky fat taste made her think of Flo frying up the brookies Buddy would catch in the dawn before breakfast. Chloé ate two bites and said she was full. They talked in French.

Dot stopped at their table. "Are you from Montreal?"

"We're from Paris." Chloé took note of the fact that her mother didn't mention she had grown up in Rangeley.

Dot said, "Wow. That's so cool."

Chloé waited until her mother went to the ladies' room to ask Dot, "Do you ever hear of a family called Quimby?"

Dot made a face. "God, how do you know them?"

"I don't, I just heard about them."

"Not surprised. Scary, weird, and crazy. Father's in prison. Mother lives up on the mountain. When I was a kid we called her the Witch Lady."

"What about the daughter?"

"She left town before I was born, but my mom said she had this awful big red thing on her face. Everybody called her Giblet-Face." Her mother had not told Chloé about the nickname.

Dot looked up as Evie came out of the ladies'. "Your mom's beautiful."

"Yes, she is."

As Evie sat down at the table, she could tell Chloé was upset. "What's wrong?"

"I'm just starting to get what it must have been like for you to grow up here."

"It wasn't all bad . . . there were nice parts."

Evie ordered blueberry pie for dessert. As Dot disappeared into the kitchen to get it, the door to the café burst open and a dozen ten-year-olds wearing Little League uniforms swarmed in, followed by their parents. The kids were shouting, "We won!" and "Kicked Lake Placid's ass!" Evie had forgotten how rough, ragged, and loud the locals were. Women aged fast in Rangeley. There only seemed to be two choices—after you got knocked up, you either got fat or skinny; there was no middle road for girls who stayed in Rangeley. The men smelled of sweat and beer and looked as if they wished they were somewhere else.

Evie's eye was drawn to a woman with pale blue eyes who must have been pretty twenty years ago. Her hair was dyed the color of a Cheez Doodle, caked makeup hid a black eye, and when she smiled you could see somebody had knocked out her front tooth while they were at it. It wasn't until Blue Eyes tilted her head back to down the last of what was not her first beer of the night, that Evie realized it was Connie. Dot was the baby she was carrying that summer Dill dyed her hair green. The big guy with the greasy ponytail in the Harley-Davidson sweatshirt who was handing out beers was Otto—the Morlock who had tried to pull her into the truck. Connie looked over at their table. Otto was staring right at them. Neither one of them recognized her without the birthmark that had defined her.

As Dot came out of the kitchen with their pie, Evie handed her daughter her wallet and whispered in French, "You pay for it. I'm going back to the room."

Evie was halfway to the door when Dot called out to Connie, "Hey Mom, they were asking about your friend Evie Quimby."

Otto tilted his head like a dog who can't figure out where his chew toy went. Connie got off her barstool and eyed Evie's face suspiciously. "What happened to you?"

"I got married and, as you can see, had a daughter."

Evie was about to introduce Chloé when Connie blurted out, "I mean what happened to your face?"

"I had laser surgery."

Connie hugged her and added, "I'm back with Kevin, can you believe it?"

CHAPTER 28

The Townsend County Sheriff's Department had changed since Evie had spent the night there. The folksy tin-roofed cabin with two-barred rooms out back was gone. In its place was a redbrick municipal building with a flagpole, paved parking lot, and a twenty-cell jail that was called the Sister Lakes Correctional Facility.

Stopping for gas on the way to see the sheriff the following morning, Evie asked, "What's the new sheriff like?" The woman who worked the pump called him a "cocksucker," and the mechanic volunteered, "He likes to write tickets. Cost me a hundred dollars to take a piss in the parking lot, back of the liquor store." When Evie asked why they elected a ticket-writing cocksucker, she was told, "After Sheriff Dunn got caught with his hand in the cookie jar, we were stupid enough to think we'd be better off with somebody honest." Evie knew it was going to be more difficult than she thought to get the new sheriff to break the law for her.

When they got there, Evie told her daughter to wait in the car while she talked to the sheriff. Chloé ignored her and got out of the car anyway. "I'm bored. . . . I want to come."

Evie snapped. "Christ, can't you just do as I ask for once."

Chloé took a step back. "You don't have this worked out, do you?"

"No."

If Chloé had gotten angry or called her a liar, it would have been less painful for Evie. Instead, her daughter forced a smile. "What happens happens. You're doing the best you can, Mom." The fact that her sick daughter was trying to make her feel better made Evie feel worse. Chloé sat on the hood of the Cherokee and plugged in her earbuds.

There was a line at the front desk. A woman had lost her dog and feared it had been eaten by a bobcat. A deputy brought in a teen-age mother who had been arrested for shoplifting a twelve-pack of chicken thighs from the Bargain-Mart. Sheriff Colson was in the back doing paperwork on a stolen truck. He wore a Stetson on his shaved head, and his wire-thin frame was bulked up with the muscle mass you get from pumping iron. Crisp black uniform, yellow patch pockets, and a matching canary stripe down his pant leg, he looked like a hornet. Evie waited until the sheriff glanced up from his paperwork to say, "Hi Dill."

He did not seem like the kind of guy who once dreamed of cutting Madonna's hair. When he came out and hugged her, his hat fell off and they both laughed.

"Connie called me last night and said you were back in town." The sheriff's badge seemed to have dropped Dill's voice an octave.

"What'd she tell you?"

"That you'd changed." He was staring at her face. "And that you looked French."

He told the deputy to hold all calls unless an emergency came in, and took her into his office and closed the door. He was still staring at her face. "I always said you were gorgeous." When he said the word "gorgeous," he suddenly sounded like the teenager who worked at his mother's beauty parlor.

"How did you end up sheriff?" The only thing left from Sheriff Dunn's reign was the bullet-riddled stuffed deer head they still used to bait hunters into firing from a moving vehicle.

"Well, I was deputy for ten years."

"You know what I mean."

Dill took a deep breath. "I made a friend the summer after you left. We would meet at that pool at the base of the falls down on Cold Brook." Evie nodded. She knew the place. "I was late one day and the Morlocks found him naked and beat him up so bad he lost a kidney. When nobody did anything, I decided there was more to life than doing Madonna's hair." He was still Dill under all that muscle. He was also a cop.

"Look, Evie . . . I know why you left Rangeley." Evie wasn't expecting that.

"How did you find out?"

"Your uncle, Sheriff Dunn, told me. You were drugged and raped at the Mannheims' old guide camp. It must have been horrible for you."

"It was."

"If it's any consolation, I arrested Otto, Kevin, and Scrotum for sexual assault shortly after I joined the force. They did two years in prison. They were the ones who beat up my friend."

"It wasn't the Morlocks."

"Who the hell was it?"

Knowing that telling Dill the truth would bring Langley back to her daughter's bedside, all Evie had to say was, "That's not why I'm here."

"Evie, if a predator is still out there, I should know. I might be able to prevent him from doing the same thing to some other girl."

"I *need* your help with something else." Evie pointed out the window. Chloé, sitting on the hood of the Cherokee, earphones on, eyes closed, was singing along to a French rap song. "My daughter has leukemia. . . ."

Dill listened stone-faced as she explained why she needed to see the sealed court records that were locked in Rangeley Town Hall. When she finished, he nodded *yes* but said, "I'm sorry, Evie, but I can't break the law for you. There has to be some other way."

"There isn't, goddamnit!" When she started shouting, Dill stood up and put his cop hat back on.

Desperate, Evie reached out to stop him from leaving, knocking a framed photograph off his desk. As Dill picked it up, she saw it was a photo of him standing with his arm around a man in medical scrubs. "I'm married. He's a veterinarian. I'd like you to meet him."

"I don't want to meet anybody. All I want is to save my daughter's life."

"I've got to go back to work now, Evie. Let me know if there's anything I can legally do to help you."

Evie whimpered, "Please."

"You're welcome to take a few minutes and pull yourself together in my office. Your girl shouldn't see you like this."

Evie collapsed back in her chair and wondered how she would tell her daughter that they had run out of hope. She watched helplessly as Dill left the building. He stopped at the Cherokee and said something to Chloé. Her daughter called out to the sheriff as he got into his patrol car, but he ignored her and drove off.

Evie went into the ladies' room, rinsed her face with cold water, then walked out into the parking lot like a zombie. She had no idea what to do next until Chloé told her, "Your friend the sheriff dropped this." She held up two keys attached to a tag that said "Rangeley Town Hall" with the alarm code written beneath.

CHAPTER 29

The sheriff was gone before I could thank him. Bone ache and nausea made it hard to be hopeful. We pulled into a diner and I felt better after I ate half an egg sandwich and washed down my daily dose of mercaptopurine and my weekly hit of methotrexate with a chocolate milk. After that we stopped at a hardware store and bought flashlights and a Coleman lantern.

Turning up a deserted dirt road, we stopped the car and my mother handed me a pair of her coveralls. When I asked her why we were changing clothes, she told me, "If Mary Lou or Scrotum looks up from the cash register and sees a pair of tourists sneakin' round town hall, they're likely as not to dial up the law." Twenty-four hours in the Adirondacks and my mother was suddenly talking North Country.

"How long do you get for stealing court records?" My mother saw fresh bruises on my legs as I pulled off my jeans and stepped into the coveralls.

"Maybe this is too much for you. I'll drop you back at the inn and do this part by myself." My mother put the flat of her palm on my forehead to see if I was running a temperature.

"No way! Breaking and entering with your mother is a once-in-a-lifetime opportunity." She laughed at that, but when I added, "Something I can tell my grandchildren about," her smile evaporated. The key the sheriff dropped wasn't magical, and odds were that all we would unlock was disappointment. I don't think either one of us really believed I was going to live past summer; pretending just kept us going.

An hour later we were huddled at the back door of Rangeley Town Hall. We had the alarm off and the lock turned. Pushing open the door, we were confronted by a maze of cardboard boxes stacked eye-high wall-to-wall. A sign read "Maximum Legal Capacity: 400 Persons." There had to be *a thousand boxes. A century's worth of court records, once neatly cross-indexed for easy access, had hastily been packed up when the courthouse flooded and were now filed in the order they were off-loaded from the truck.*

Our plan was simple, but tedious. Go through every box that bore the year of my mother's birth and look for court-sealed adoption records of a girl born with my mother's birth date—June 21, 1984. She did the heavy lifting. Pulling out boxes magic-markered '84 while I used her Buck knife to slit them open, we rummaged through judgments, testimonies, indictments, settlements, sentences, lawsuits, and liens by lantern light, looking for the name "Quimby."

We found most of the records from my mother's birth year up in the attic. The sealed records were in red folders. With the sharply angled roof just above our heads, the chatter of bats waiting to come out at sunset was louder there. I was not reassured when my mother told me that stories about bats getting caught in your hair were greatly exaggerated.

We had been at it five hours straight. I was yawning when I slit open the top of a mildewed cardboard carton and saw a red folder with the word "ADOPTION" neatly typed out on a gummed label. There were more than fifty adoption folders in that box. Not knowing the name of my mother's birth mother, we had to go through the contents of each file page by page.

Sitting side by side, my mother and I flipped through the broken lives of women. Most were unwed teenage mothers; a few were women deemed unfit for parenting due to diminished mental facilities and/or thought to be a danger to the welfare of the child.

When I saw a thick folder dated two days before my mother was born, I tossed it back in the box. I missed. Papers spilled out onto the floor. Hurriedly stuffing documents back into the red binder of heartache, I was about to tell my mother I was too tired to go on when I caught sight of a photostat of a birth certificate with the name "Eve Quimby" on it. It was paper-clipped to another photostat of my mother's original birth certificate. She was born just before noon and weighed seven pounds six ounces. Her name on the original was listed as "Baby A." I had no idea why the adoption was dated two days after her birth, all I cared about was that her mother's and father's names, followed by their Social Security numbers, were neatly printed in the box provided. Whoever filled it out noted, "baby girl, born with large PWS birthmark on face."

"I think this is you." I handed her the birth certificate. She read the names of her parents aloud like a judge passing sentence. "Mother—Christine Stone—age eighteen. Father—Arthur Solange—twenty." She did the math in her head. "She'd be fifty-two now. He'd be fifty-four. They'll still be alive, we'll find them." She didn't refer to them as her parents.

"What if they won't help me?"

"I'll persuade them." The way she said it both scared me and made me feel safe. Then she told me she was going to go outside to call the lawyer in Albany to get him to start tracking down Christine and Arthur. Halfway down the stairs, my mother began to weep out of sadness and relief.

I found a police report mixed in with her adoption papers. Her birth parents were wanted in the Commonwealth of Massachusetts for the manufacture and distribution of methamphetamine and credit card fraud. At the time of the birth, Christine was incarcerated at the Essex County Jail. Before I could read more about them, a bat dropped from the ceiling. Swooping down, its leathery wings fluttered against the papers in my hand. I shrieked, stuffed the folder in my coveralls, and ran.

CHAPTER 30

Chloé brought the scavenged folder of her mother's adoption paperwork to dinner, but Evie didn't have it in her to look any further into her past that night. She had unearthed the names of the parents who had betrayed her at birth for her daughter, not herself. Morbid curiosity could wait until tomorrow. She had already called the lawyer and told him that Christine and Arthur had police records. He said that would make them easier to locate. Probation officers would have addresses, names of past employers. He promised to call her as soon as he had any news.

Neither mother nor daughter wanted to say what they were thinking as they faced one another in the back booth of the Rangeley Inn. The math was simple, the laws of genetics clear. There was a fifty-fifty chance that one of her grandparents' marrow could save her life. The unknown variable in the equation of survival was the human element.

They ordered the trout again and said little; in part because they were exhausted, but mostly because they feared that if they voiced the possibility that their luck might have changed, they would jinx it.

They slept in the same bed that night. Chloé's bare feet were like ice. As her mother rolled a pair of socks down over her toes, Chloé smiled at the memory of Evie dressing her for kindergarten and wished she were six again. Evie waited until her daughter was asleep to whisper, "We're going to get through this."

Sheriff Colson was just getting into his cruiser when Evie pulled in the next morning and called out, "I found your keys." She had gotten up early, dressed in silence, and left her daughter sleeping back at the inn.

"I knew I dropped them somewhere." A stiff wind had blown

up. Dill used one hand to keep his hat on his head and caught the keys midair.

"I'm sorry about yesterday. When this is over, I'd like to meet your partner and . . ." Evie knew that sounded gratuitous and lame. "What can I say, I'm a fucking mess."

"Whenever you're ready, the invitation stands. Did you find what you needed?"

"I'm one step closer."

"Were your birth parents locals?"

"I don't know yet. I'd never heard of them."

"You know the brother of that guy who drowned in a wedding dress was up here the other day asking questions about you and Buddy and Win Langley. You know anything about that?"

"No." She didn't like lying to her friend, but she didn't want to complicate things. Dill seemed disappointed.

"That's weird, because he told me he had just talked to you on the phone when you were in Paris."

"You asked me if I knew anything about that, not if I talked to him."

"You sound just like Buddy."

"Maybe I'm more like him than I realized."

"That's what I'm afraid of."

As Sheriff Colson watched Evie pull out of the parking lot, he found himself thinking about the night the Morlocks had chased him and Evie into the ruins of the abandoned sawmill at the end of town. They hid in the darkness of one of the old cast-iron kilns used to dry lumber after it had just been cut. Pressed close, ankle-deep in stagnant slime, water rats scurrying around their feet, they heard Otto shout, "I'm going to get you faggots," and bang a length of rebar against the sides of the kilns as he and Scrotum and Kevin hunted for them. When Otto peered into the kiln they were hiding in, Dill looked over at Evie just as she was unclasping the blade of her Buck knife.

Eventually, the Morlocks got bored and went down to the lake to gig frogs. Dill still wasn't sure whether it was the thought of what Otto would have done if he had found them or the possibility that Evie had it in her to stop Otto with her knife that made him piss himself that night.

Evie drove back to Rangeley in a haze. The temperature had dropped ten degrees and storm clouds were blowing in. Fog drifted out of the forest. She had driven down Route 3 thousands of times. She knew every curve by heart, but suddenly felt as if she didn't recognize the road she was on.

Driving fast, not watching the blacktop, she had her cell phone in her lap. She was impatient for the lawyer to call to tell her where to find her parents. Her eyes darted down, checking to make sure she hadn't gotten an email while she was talking to Dill, and when she looked back at the road, she glimpsed something she had only seen once before in her life.

Fifty feet ahead of her, straddling the white line and staring her down, was a catamount: unblinking, tawny gold, its tail half as long as its body. Slamming on her brakes and spinning the steering wheel, her Cherokee three-sixtied and skidded straight for the mountain lion. The cat did not move.

Evie closed her eyes and braced herself for the sickening thud of death. When the car finally came to a lurching stop and she opened her eyes, the catamount was gone. Scrambling out of the car, she scanned the forest, but there was no sign of it anywhere and she was not at all sure she had not made it up.

Hands shaking, she lit a cigarette. She heard a whine in the distance and looked up to see the blur of a motorcycle screaming down the mountain toward her. A hundred yards away, it started to slow down.

The helmeted driver was bent low over the cowl and wore a second skin of red leather. The engine had to be a 1,000 cc. Downshifting, the motorcycle approached slowly. The biker lifted the visor and said, "I was just coming to visit you." It was Lulu.

~ ~ ~

Chloé didn't wake up until after 10 a.m. Her mother left a twenty-dollar bill and a note by her pillow reminding her to eat breakfast. Hoping to raise her blood sugar enough to concentrate, she took a bite of a power bar and reached for her mother's adoption file.

Fifteen minutes later she found a neatly typed note on the letterhead of a New York City lawyer addressed to the Honorable Frederick C. Simmons, Townsend County Judge:

> *Dear Fred,*
>   *I know what we had agreed upon, but given the circumstances, my clients hope Your Honor will understand why they are no longer interested in adopting Baby A—after some soul-searching, they do not feel equipped to raise a child with a disfigurement of that magnitude.*

~ ~ ~

Evie wasn't surprised to find Lulu at age fifty zippered into red motorcycle leathers riding a Ducati capable of reaching speeds in excess of 170 mph. Restoring things for rich people had taught Evie that a woman with Lulu's wealth and temperament was always looking for a new thrill to straddle. What surprised Evie was finding Lulu looking for it off-season in the Adirondacks. She would have expected her to be rocketing down the back roads of Tierra del Fuego or Tasmania or . . .

After all that had gone wrong at Valhalla, Evie always imagined Lulu moving on, shuttering the log palace, and leaving it up to future generations of Mannheims to try to find happiness in the Sister Lakes. Flashing back on the day they first met at the side of the road down by Cold Brook, Evie menaced by Morlocks, Lulu unable to find her way home, Evie guessed everything and nothing changes. But she knew with certainty, she did not want the drama of her own life to become Lulu's next thrill.

Her Cherokee was still blocking the road, door open, engine running. Lulu, helmet on, the beast of a motorcycle idling between her legs; Evie standing in the middle of the road befuddled by an apparition, they were spared the awkwardness of having to hug and exchange insincere pleasantries. The decision to cut contact with one another seventeen years ago had been unspoken.

"How did you find out I was back?"

"Dill called and told me everything."

"When did you and Dill become friends?"

"He did my hair after you left. I was a little surprised when he became a deputy, but when he ran for sheriff, I decided why not and helped get him elected."

Evie glanced over at her car. "I better get going."

"I'm sorry about your daughter."

"Me too . . . you have any kids?"

"I'm my own child." Lulu pointed to the skid marks. "What did you brake for?"

"Believe it or not, I thought I saw a mountain lion."

"You probably did. I heard a rumor the Game Committee at the Mohawk Club secretly released a pair that had been trapped out west." Evie remembered Win Langley talking about reintroducing "top-of-the-food-chain predators" to the forest the night she met her husband.

Lulu took off her helmet. Her hair was hennaed an unnatural shade of red. A face-lift or two, plus Botox, made her look like a distant relative of her old self.

"I need to talk to you, Evie."

"Can we catch up another time? My daughter's back at the inn and I need to check on her."

"The Rangeley Inn's a dump. Stay at Valhalla."

"I appreciate the invitation, but there are things we need to take care of by ourselves."

"I can help you and your daughter."

"If I need to borrow money I'll let you know."

"You don't make it easy to be a friend."

"I didn't mean that the way it sounded."

"Just have a cup of coffee with me. Hear what I have to say, and if you never want to talk to me again, fine . . . please." Mostly because "please" wasn't a word she ever remembered Lulu saying, Evie agreed.

Lulu trailed her back down Route 3 into town. When Evie pulled into the parking lot just up the street from the Rangeley Inn, she saw Chloé standing by herself out on the end of the public dock. Her daughter waved and hurried toward her. She was shouting something, but the fog on the lake swallowed up her words. Evie couldn't hear what she was saying.

Lulu was off her motorcycle and in the midst of reminding her of a conversation they had had when they first met. Evie stopped listening when her cell phone rang. It was the lawyer in Albany who was tracking down her parents. Reception was spotty. Static made it hard to hear. Evie shouted into her cell phone, "What did you just say?"

The lawyer repeated himself, "I'm sorry to have to tell you that both of your parents are dead." Evie dropped the phone. Chloé started to run to her, but halfway down the catwalk of the dock, she had to stop to catch her breath. Evie could see she was getting weaker. Certain that the death of her parents killed any chance of a bone marrow transplant, knowing that there was nothing to look forward to now but watching her daughter waste away, Evie bit her knuckle to keep herself from screaming.

"Mom, you're not going to believe it." Chloé was smiling.

"I'm ready to believe anything." Evie's voice was barely audible.

"You have a sister. I found it in your adoption records. She's your twin." Evie staggered and Lulu grabbed hold of her hand. "That's what I came here to tell you. Her name is Clare Loughton. She lives in New York." Evie flashed on Win Langley standing in the snow, just before she shot him, shouting, *I know something that can change your life.*

Dazed and numb, Evie struggled to put together the pieces. She turned to Lulu. "How do you know her?"

"She's rich." Lulu said it as if it explained everything, and in a way it did.

Lulu and Chloé were talking to each other now, introducing themselves, saying how much they'd heard about the other. Chloé was excited. "We know where she lives, we don't need to track down your parents. It's great news, no?" It had been so long since her daughter had anything to be happy about, Evie did not want to spoil it by mentioning the fact that she had just found out that the parents whom she had never met were dead.

"It is great news, honey. I'm just in shock . . . to find out I had a sister all these years . . . and never knew it." In her mind, Evie was remembering the day she met Lulu, how Lulu had stared at her face and said, *You remind me of somebody I know.* Evie let go of Lulu's hand. "Somebody should have told me."

Lulu nervously lit a cigarette. "Maybe they were trying to protect you." Then, glancing at Chloé, added, "And maybe this is something we should talk about later."

"My daughter and I don't have any secrets . . . at least, not anymore."

"Remember when I told you about the friend of my father's who I called Uncle Fred, but who wasn't my uncle, who taught me what men liked when I was nine? He and his wife adopted your sister."

Chloé broke the silence. "Why do men do shit like that?"

Lulu blew a smoke ring and put a finger through it. "Entitlement, *droit du seigneur*, and because most women, with the exception of your mother, don't have the balls to shoot men for doing shit to them."

Evie leaned back against the hood of her car to keep from falling down. "Christ, what's my sister like?"

"I don't really know her. I see her at things, a couple of times a year. She was really fucked up as a kid. Bulimic, pills, loved acid, did a couple of semesters at McLean. She went through a bad time, I'll fill you in later. . . . I mean, she's still kind of drifty, but she's pulled herself together. I think she'll help you."

Chloé asked, "What's McLean?"

"Psychiatric hospital in Boston."

Evie took a deep breath. "I think I need a couple of minutes by myself. Chloé, ask Lulu if she'll help you pack up our suitcases."

"Where are we going?"

"Lulu invited us to Valhalla."

"Can I ride there on the back of her motorcycle?"

"No." Evie and Lulu both said it at the same time.

Evie picked up her cell phone out of the mud and walked slowly out to the end of the public dock. She was tired of being at the mercy of people she had never met and events she had no idea had occurred until it was too late to change them. Every time she thought she knew where she stood in the universe, the universe had moved on and the readings of her compass changed.

The fog that rolled in off the lake was so thick that when she looked back, she could no longer see the shore. Evie called the lawyer to see if he had learned anything about the strangers who conceived her that was worth holding on to. She discovered that in a failed attempt to outrun the police on the New York State Thruway, her father had been killed in a car crash two weeks after her birth. Her mother served two years at the women's correctional facility in Framingham, Massachusetts, then worked her way through UMass. Shortly after graduating with honors, her mother overdosed on oxycodone.

Evie was surprised to find herself mourning the fact that she did not have the chance to tell them she forgave them. Reaching out for her own absolution, she called Flo.

CHAPTER 31

The fog never burned off that day. Following the motorcycle through the front gates of Valhalla, Evie knew Lulu had put her own stamp on Adolphus Mannheim's Norse fantasy when she spotted a fifteen-foot-tall chrome Easter bunny, sculpted by Jeff Koons, on the lawn in front of the Great Camp.

The man who took their bags up to their rooms was the new camp superintendent Hank, Clinger's son. A maid Evie would later discover was Doris's daughter and second cousin to Scrotum came out to say lunch would be ready in ten minutes. Everybody was tied to the place by blood.

Chloé's head swiveled as she took in the log palace's vast porch. Its railings were still bent into the shapes of animals, the boathouse still looked like a Japanese shrine, and the alpine guesthouses still made mother, and now daughter, think of *Heidi*.

When they stepped through the front door, Evie was surprised to see that the stuffed trout and mounted heads were all gone. The dark paneling had been pickled white, and all that was left from the past was the marble statue of the faceless girl on the landing.

After chicken salad sandwiches and tomato bisque, Lulu gave them what she called "the fifty-cent tour." Two holes of the golf course has been commandeered for a solar-heated greenhouse that could grow vegetables right through the winter. When Lulu took them into the old gristmill to show them her "office," Evie was shocked to find a real office where real work was being done.

Evie watched as Lulu rattled off instructions to a pair of assistants about futures she wanted traded on the Hong Kong market while marking up a deal memo regarding the forty-story tower she was building in Houston.

"When did you become a businesswoman, Lulu?"

"When I realized I wanted to spend more money than I had."

Lulu seemed more like her old self when she took them into the recently renovated stables. The horses in the stalls were called Danish Warmbloods, and the blond twenty-two-year-old horse trainer was called Sven. He wore jodhpurs, riding boots, and a T-shirt that said "Swedes Do It Better." Lulu laughed like a teenager when she heard Chloé whisper to her mother, "I wonder if he does it better than Slavo." Lulu was touched that even though she and Evie had not talked, Evie had cared enough to talk about her.

On their way down to the dairy barn, the tour was cut short by a sudden blast of bone ache that made Chloé gasp. As they hurried back to the Great Camp, it began to rain. There was a fireplace in Chloé's bathroom. Kindling was lit. As Evie dried her daughter's hair, Lulu filled the tub with bubble bath. Having never known the luxury of taking a soak in a room warmed by a log fire, Chloé half smiled. "I could get used to this." It was obvious she was in pain.

Once Chloé was out of the bath and tucked up on a couch in the living room dreamily watching reruns of *30 Rock* with a Percocet drifting through her bloodstream, Evie and Lulu retreated into the library.

Pulling up her unknown twin's Facebook page, Evie stared at pixelated snapshots of a woman who looked just like her, except for the fact that her hair was three shades blonder and there was a husband in every picture. Checking out pics of Clare Loughton, she saw a life that seemed to consist of nothing but attending charity benefits, opening nights, walking pugs, blowing out candles on birthday cakes, all always with a husband by her side. If his hand wasn't holding hers, his arm was sure to be draped protectively around her shoulder as he kissed a cheekbone identical to her own. Evie found herself feeling oddly jealous of her twin's life, husband, and, yes, if she were being honest, the diamond studs that sparkled in the lobes of her sister's ears.

As Evie scrolled through her twin's alternate universe, Lulu fleshed out the pictures, "She grew up in a fantastic apartment on 72nd and Fifth, great terrace. . . . Went to Spence with my loathsome cousin. . . . Her mother died of an aneurysm when she was ten or eleven. . . . Did a lot of acid. . . . Clare was in college when her perv father had a massive coronary. . . . She inherited a real estate portfolio worth four hundred million dollars, probably more than twice that now." Then Lulu added with a smirk, "You have a better nose and longer legs."

Evie closed the lid of the computer. "Why are you so sure she'll help us?"

"She feels guilty." Lulu poured herself a glass of white wine.

"For what?"

"Being alive."

"What does that mean?"

"After her father died, she married this asshole so-called movie director from LA. He was one of those guys who make you feel shitty for inheriting money except when you're spending it on them. Anyway, she got pregnant and had a baby and, of course, gave him the money to make a film that was unbearable. Like watching a night-light. He started cheating on her. Worse, he didn't even try to hide it. One night, up at her place up on the Hudson, she was high and a-half-bottle-of-wine tipsy and they got in a fight and she decided she had had enough. Put the baby in a bassinet, got in her car, and stepped on the gas. Five miles later, she realized she had left the bassinet on top of the car."

"Jesus Christ!"

"She had a complete breakdown. Spent almost a year in a mental hospital. Stopped doing drugs. She got remarried a few years ago. From what I hear, the worst you can say about the guy is that he's boring."

"Will you call her for me?"

"What do you want me to say?"

"You have a friend who needs to talk to her."

Lulu thought about that. "Do I mention you're her long-lost twin?" It was raining harder now. Lulu put another log on the fire.

"No. Just say she and I have something in common."

Lulu laughed. "If I say that, she'll think you're having an affair with her husband."

Evie thought about it for a while. "Tell her you have a friend who knew her when she was little."

Lulu left the room to make the call. The log in the fire spat embers onto the carpet. Evie kicked the glowing coals back into the hearth and opened the red folder that contained the legal papers pertaining to her birth.

The adoption was arranged several weeks before she was born. Christine Stone had known she was having twins. She wanted them to go to the same family. She also wanted twenty-five thousand dollars. Fred and Liz Loughton agreed. A contract was signed and witnessed. Money was placed in escrow. They might have been buying a pair of adjoining lots. The Loughtons ceased to be interested in the twofer when they heard about Baby A's face. Evie had always known Buddy and Flo were allowed to adopt her because no one else wanted a child masked by a birthmark. It wasn't until now that Evie realized how lucky she was.

Lulu burst into the room. "It's all set. She's coming to my apartment in the city the day after tomorrow for tea."

"You didn't give her any hint that I was her—"

"No, not a clue. But I did mention that if she helped you out I would be eternally grateful and send a large check to the charity of her choice."

"Money is always involved, isn't it?" Evie was thinking about the $25K.

"Except between us. You know, you're the only person who has never asked me for a favor with a dollar sign attached to it."

It wasn't until they had finished dinner and Chloé had gone to bed and Lulu had opened a second bottle of Meursault that Evie thought to ask, "How did Clare Loughton's parents hear about a pregnant girl in Townsend County?" In the adoption records there was no mention of any adoption agency being involved.

"Loughtons had a big camp up on Racquet Lake. I remember hearing my mother once say his banker set it up."

"Do bankers do that sort of thing often?"

"If the client's big enough. Private Wealth guys are basically high-class fixers. Loughton and his wife wanted a kid, couldn't have a kid, banker found one."

"Who was the banker?"

Lulu bit her lip. "Porter Moran."

"How do I know that name?"

"He's the guy Buddy burned to death when he set fire to Langley's cabin at the Mohawk Club. Porter sponsored him for membership in the club, gave him his first job in Private Wealth." It took a few heartbeats for Evie to realize that Porter Moran was the same P. Moran who snapped the photograph of Langley and the two other men fishing on the Mink that captured her, aged twelve, hiding in the forest, watching something she didn't understand.

"You know Charlie's brother called me?"

"He spoke to me too."

"Do you think Langley had anything to do with Charlie's death?"

Lulu looked into the fire. "I wanted to think so. Besides hating Langley for what he did to you, part of me is still looking for someone to blame for Charlie other than Charlie, which is a roundabout way of saying there's some part of me that's still in love with the bastard. Weird how feelings work."

Lulu jabbed a glowing log with a poker. The flames rose and the heat roiled over them. "It was the way he looked at me when we had sex that I miss." Lulu was as blunt as ever. "Like I was the first woman he had ever seen naked. Who knows, maybe I was." Suddenly they were both envisaging Charlie's corpse in a silk chiffon wedding dress appliquéd with pearls.

"We don't have to talk about this, Lulu."

"I'm okay. I mean, I'm not okay, but it happened and we move on." Lulu lit a cigarette. "Anyway, back to fucking Win Langley. When Charles's brother first got in touch with me last month, I hired somebody to check it out. The night Charlie drowned, Langley was at a party at a client's house on Fishers Island."

"Where's that?"

"Long Island Sound, near Connecticut. Langley took off in his seaplane that morning. He had Ian Conklin with him and some older banker, I can't remember his name. They were Charlie's groomsmen." Evie remembered the creepy way Ian smiled at her breasts as he reached out and zipped up her coveralls that first day at Valhalla. The banker Lulu couldn't recall was Walt, the three-fingered asshole who was going to help Langley get Evie a scholarship. "The guy with the house on Fishers Island had a distinct memory of their floatplane taking off just before he left for church, ten o'clock service. Four hours later, Langley landed at the lake. Flight records check out. Langley was still on Fishers Island when Charlie jumped off the gorge."

"Radetzky showed up at our hotel at JFK yesterday morning. Told me some freaky story about Langley putting kiddie porn on his computer to shut him up."

"It wasn't Langley who did it."

"How can you be sure?"

"The charges against him were dropped yesterday afternoon. It was in this morning's paper. Charlie's brother called me just before I got on my bike to find you. It turned out a psychiatric patient hacked into his computer, put the shit there. Dill checked it out with the New York police; it's true."

Evie bummed a cigarette. "That doesn't explain how Charlie got some bank in Cyprus to lend him $250,000 when he was twenty-one years old. What's Radetzky going to do now?"

"He told me his brother has caused all of us enough misery. Says he's done with it."

"Are you?"

"No, but since there's nothing we can do about Charlie or Langley, I'm going to focus my attention on helping your daughter get well . . . if that's okay with you?"

Evie nodded. "Thank you, but . . . there's something you should know before you get involved in my mess. Langley showed up in Chloé's hospital room in Paris."

CHAPTER 32

That first morning at Valhalla, I woke up feeling better than I had in weeks. No bone ache, no new bruises, temperature normal. I wasn't any less sick than I had been the day before. The disease was just playing with me, but I was happy that cancer had decided to take the day off.

Lulu had told me that the room I was sleeping in had been her old bedroom. The mattress was king-size and canopied. The walls covered in a shade of pink silk I associated with lingerie. Having woken early and numb to hunger, I snooped.

The closets were full of old clothes circa 2001: Prada she never got around to taking the tags off of, party shoes that looked like they had only been worn once. Next to the fireplace was a wall of books. The only title I recognized was Infinite Jest. I knew it because it had been open on the bedside table of the boy from the debating team the night we undressed one another.

He had written me an email when I was in the hospital that I had read as a love letter. Late the previous night, a girlfriend of mine had texted that he had hooked up with a girl who I thought was my best friend. I told myself, what's a broken heart compared to mutant white cells and discovering you have an aunt who can save your life? But that morning in the softness of Lulu's old bedroom, I felt well enough to be hurt.

Feeling sentimental, remembering my debater told me I would adore the novel, and wondering if he said the same thing to every girl he undressed, I took Infinite Jest out onto the balcony and sat on an old-fashioned wicker lounge chair that offered a panoramic view of the lake and the forest beyond.

I liked the book until I got to page 17. There I found a neatly folded newspaper clipping from the New York Times, dated March 13, 2001.

The Style section had done a spread on a Moroccan-themed party in Palm Beach that had been given to celebrate the engagement of Lulu Mannheim and Charles Radetzky. There was a photo of them on the dance floor looking impossibly young and in love. Even in black and white, Charlie's smile was so bright and handsome, it made me want to squint.

I studied his face for some sign of insincerity, thievery, madness that could have made him put on a wedding dress and jump off a cliff three months later, but I found none. I didn't pay much attention to the quartet of tuxedoed men posed around Charlie, all of them wearing tasseled maroon fezzes that had been given out as party hats, until I realized the man on the far right was Win Langley.

The party had been thrown for Lulu by a couple called Tatiana and Dexter Greuen. Given that they were both under thirty and had a twenty-six-room house on the beach, it was obvious they were super rich. The article mentioned that Tatiana's grandfather was a "former ambassador, world-class yachtsman, and celebrated philanthropist," i.e., Tatiana had the money. It was also clear that Tatiana was decidedly less photogenic than her husband. In the text of the article, Langley was credited with introducing the recently married host and hostess as well as Lulu and Charlie. The newspaper quoted him, "What can I say . . . I'm an incredible romantic. When I see two people who are right for each other, I love to play Cupid."

When I finally went downstairs for breakfast, I heard my mother laughing in the way she used to before I got sick: playful and reckless. She and Lulu were trading war stories about their love lives. Lulu was laughing so hard she had tears in her eyes. My mother was in the midst of telling her about Dr. Bliss, the French gynecologist who had asked her out on a date in the middle of a pelvic exam. I had heard the story before, but not in such graphic detail.

Listening to them, I was startled by the way they talked about men, not exactly as if they were the enemy, more like they were immovable objects. I didn't know a lot about men, not much more about boys, but I wanted to believe it could be different for me.

My mother and Lulu took such obvious pleasure in each other's company, I had to ask, "You two have so much fun together, why didn't you ever see each other all those years?" They stopped laughing. My question was taken more seriously than I expected.

The women eyed each other warily, not sure how honest they wanted the other to be. My mother spoke first, not to me, but to Lulu. "I apologize for running away to Paris without saying goodbye or telling you where I was going—"

Lulu interrupted. "Actually you left a note that said, 'Thanks for everything.'"

My mother winced at that. "I didn't want to have to explain myself."

Lulu wasn't expecting that. "After all the crazy shit I've done, why would you think you had to?"

"Explain myself to me. I mean, flying to Paris with fifty bucks to my name to ask a horndog like Jacques Clément for a job? Yeah, it sounds romantic, but I knew when I went there that he was going to hit on me. And if I wanted it to work out, I'd probably have to . . ." My mother suddenly remembered I was sitting at the table.

I finished the sentence for her. "Sleep with him?"

"Well at least put up with it. But I got lucky. I liked him. And we ended up falling in love. For the record, in the end I was the one that seduced your father." My mother turned to Lulu. "I also knew that if I told you what I was going to do, admitted it out loud, I would have heard how crazy it was and never had the courage to go through with it." My mother poured herself another cup of coffee. "The longer I put off calling you, Lulu, telling you what I had done to myself, the harder it was to pick up the phone."

Being fourteen, I didn't think it rude to turn the tables and ask Lulu, "What's your excuse?" Lulu stepped out onto the porch so I wouldn't inhale the Marlboro she was putting a match to, and answered through the wire mesh of the screen door, "I didn't call your mother because I envied her."

"For what?" It was my mother's turn to be surprised.

"Having a career, being able to fix things, a husband, a baby, a fresh start." The way she rattled off her reasons made it clear this wasn't the first

time Lulu had thought about the question. Exhaling a plume of smoke out of the corner of her mouth, she added, "And . . . I guess I felt guilty for introducing you to fucking Win Langley." Putting her cigarette out against the screen, Lulu turned and headed off to the gristmill, calling out over her shoulder, "We should have killed the bastard!"

CHAPTER 33

By noon, Lulu had made all the arrangements. The next morning a floatplane would pick them up at Valhalla at 9 a.m. Weather permitting, in three hours and fifteen minutes they would land on the East River and a town car would take them to Lulu's triplex loft in Tribeca. At 5:30 p.m., Clare Loughton would come to tea and discover she had a twin sister who needed help involving a needle being stabbed into her pelvic bone. What happened after that was pure speculation.

Would Clare Loughton help? Could she help? Evie knew there were all manner of medical conditions that would rule out her twin as a viable donor. She second- and third-guessed every decision she made. Should she have written Clare Loughton first? Sent her copies of the adoption records? Given the woman time to get used to having a twin before asking her for help? The only certainty was that they would soon find out what kind of person Clare Loughton, a.k.a. Baby B, had grown up to become.

There was nothing left for Evie to do in Rangeley but take Chloé up the mountain to meet Flo. Eighteen miles as the crow flies, thirty-two by road; having not seen her mother face-to-face since 2001, it was a bigger journey than that for Evie.

The dirt track up to the cabin was steeper than Evie remembered. It was cratered with potholes and slick with mud from a brief but hard rain that fell on the ride over. The Cherokee bottomed out and slithered sideways as she spun her wheels up the incline.

When they got out of the car, Evie could tell by the expression on her daughter's face that the Quimbys' mountainside retreat was not the Disney set she had fantasized. The skinning shed slouched off one corner of its foundation and was tilted at such a precarious angle it looked as if it were about to tumble down the mountainside. A clan of calico cats who lived beneath eyed mother and daughter suspiciously as they got out of the rental car. Two shades of purple lilacs were coming into bloom, but corroded machine parts and outboard motors rusted beyond repair blighted the meadow. A six-foot sapling had sprouted through the rot in the floorboards of the broken-down Willys.

But time had only made the cabin with its log walls more silvery. The sugar maple that provided it with shade had just blossomed yellow-green. Snowdrops flowered around the porch where a half cord of split kindling was neatly stacked. The plank table Evie had helped Buddy hammer together when she was seven was still there, and on it a bowl of fiddlehead ferns that had been picked that morning.

A pickup truck that had been purchased since her departure was parked behind the skinning shed, but there was no sign of Flo. Evie called out, "Mom?" The only reply she got was the echo of her own voice. When she tried the front door, she was surprised to find it locked.

Going around to the back, Evie saw that Flo had doubled the size of the garden. Old window screens had been salvaged from the dump and repurposed into a chest-high fence to keep out deer and rabbits. Evie cupped her hands and again shouted, "Mama? We're here!" but there was still no response.

The back door was locked as well. Not wanting to worry Chloé, Evie didn't say what she was thinking as she peered through curtained windows. Broken hip? Stroke? Heart attack? The only indication her mother was alive was a half-finished picture puzzle on the dining room table and a freshly scrubbed floor.

The forest was closer, less scenic, and more impenetrable on the Quimbys' mountainside than it was at Valhalla. Pointing to the wall of two-hundred-foot spruces that loomed up around the homestead, Chloé asked, "Why are the trees so much bigger here?"

"Because they've never been cut. There's spruces back in those woods that are two hundred and fifty years old, maybe more."

"Does your mother know we're coming?"

"When I called her yesterday, I told her we'd be here at three thirty p.m." It was past four. Evie eyed the tree line. Something was moving in the big spruce whose topmost branches had been blackened by a bolt of lightning.

At the sound of a caw, Chloé pointed—"Jimmy the crow!"

Evie laughed and stepped up onto the stump where she had once charmed crows with a pair of dimes. "More like his granddaughter. Crows only live eight or nine years." They were searching their pockets for coins when Flo appeared out of the tree lines.

She had an old-fashioned picnic basket in one hand and a double-barreled shotgun in the other. Colored beads and the wing feather of a blackbird were woven into the white of her braid. Her mother was both smaller and larger than Evie remembered.

She had imagined their reunion countless times, longed for it, but now that it was upon her Evie felt like the moment was a weight pressing down on her chest. Breathing became hard. She did not know what to say, or rather, she knew what she was supposed to say, but resented having to say it.

Before the reunion could be ruined with words, Chloé ran to Flo. The witch-like granny dropped her basket and gun and threw her arms open wide. Though Chloé was half a foot taller, Flo lifted her off the ground and spun her around in the air, announcing to the forest and to the lost daughter she had not birthed, "Aren't we a wonder."

Flo's face was wrinkled and shrunken as if mummification had already begun, and long silky hairs bristled out of a mole on her cheek. She looked shyly up at Chloé and, her voice trembling with heartbreak and age, whispered, "You're as beautiful as your mother."

Eyes got sparkly with tears and Flo and Evie said the things they were expected to say: *I've missed you, I love you, I love you too.* Chloé chimed in, "Mom talks about you all the time," which wasn't true, but made Flo feel good.

The conversation stalled. Flo reached out and touched the right side of Evie's face and flattened her palm on features no longer obscured by disfigurement. "When did you—"

"A few years ago."

Flo studied her the way she would a flowering plant or mushroom she had never seen before in the woods. "Why did you wait so long?"

Evie shrugged. "I was busy being a single mother." Wanting to be more honest with herself and Flo, she added, "I needed to learn more about what men wanted from me."

"Well . . . when you figure that one out, explain it to me."

Chloé pointed to the gun. "What's the shotgun for?"

"We've got copperheads up in the rocks where I pick my green dragon leaf." The picnic basket was filled to the brim.

"Snakes?" Chloé looked down into the knee-high grass they were standing in. "Around here?"

"Not today, but you never know with snakes." Flo picked up the shotgun and the basket, and they followed her to the skinning shed. The shed, like the cabin, was locked. Her mother wore her keys around her neck on a lanyard with an evil eye attached to it.

"When did you start locking everything up?"

"After Buddy went to prison. Let's just say some of the locals felt free to settle old debts."

At the mention of Buddy's name, Evie and her mother exchanged a look. They had not talked about him yet and they were both wary of what the other would have to say on the subject. Evie would have brought it up then, but when Flo handed the shotgun to Chloé, she got distracted.

Chloé remembered the shooting lesson her mother had given her in the Dordogne apple orchard and kept the barrel pointed to the ground, then opened its breech with a snap to see if it was loaded. It was.

"I see you taught her about guns."

"Among other things."

"Spoken like a Quimby." When they went back to the cabin,

Flo brewed a broth of nettle tea, which she said boosted the immune system and Chloé said tasted like dust bunnies. Then they looked at a photo album filled with snapshots of Flo and Buddy when Evie was young.

By way of small talk, Flo mentioned she drove over to the prison three counties away in Malone every other Saturday to see Buddy and they exchanged weekly letters. She kept them wrapped in bundles tied with a different-colored ribbon for each of the sixteen years he'd been in prison. "What does he write about?"

"Mostly we argue about books."

"Buddy? Books?"

Untying a packet that contained correspondence from her father's first year in the slammer, Flo said, "You'll like this one," then cleared her throat and read aloud. "Dear Flo, *Pride and Prejudice* pissed me off. Most of all I can't believe my daughter thought I was anything like that asshole Darcy. . . ."

Evie was still trying to imagine Buddy reading Jane Austen in prison when Flo stepped out onto the porch and lit a cheap cigar, the same brand and size Buddy smoked, explaining, "I light them when I miss your father."

"You hated the smell of them."

Flo looked sad when she said, "I still do, but it's something."

Chloé was in the kitchen putting a paste made of orangeroot on what looked to be poison ivy. Realizing this was as alone as she was going to get with Flo, Evie blurted out, "Do you blame me for Buddy going to prison?"

"I blame Buddy for being Buddy, which isn't fair given who Buddy is and always will be." Flo let the cigar smolder.

PART V

TO HOLD
AND TO HAVE

CHAPTER 34

I t was almost three in the morning in New York City and a woman
who looked just like Evie Quimby was being rescued from a bad
dream by the sound of her own voice shouting, "No!"

Clare Loughton wakes like this often. Sometimes, the nightmare
involves her dead father Fred and the bedroom door that didn't have
a lock on it. But tonight, it was the other nightmare. The one where
she's the monster there's no escaping from.

It always starts the same way. She walks into the laundry room and
finds her husband fucking the nanny. She thinks, but isn't sure, he's
fucking her in the ass. Clare won't let him do that, and it is something
he says she would let him do if she really loved him. They argue, she
takes the baby and gets in her Audi station wagon. She's tipsy from red
wine, Percocet, and anger. U2's "With or Without You" is playing on
the car's stereo. She drives for almost a mile, then looks back to make
sure her daughter's all right and sees the car seat empty.

Because this is just how it happened, her nightmare is so real that
even after she opens her eyes and sits up in bed, it takes her a moment
to realize she's not running down the road, looking for a bassinet with
a dead baby in it. She's in the new life she has made for herself in the
bedroom of the twelfth-floor duplex at 800 Park Ave. Peter Shandley, the man she married three summers ago, is lying next her. He has
never tried to fuck her in the ass, and her mind is such that she sometimes wonders what that means.

Even though he has to leave for work in three hours, he wakes with
her and rolls out of bed to get an Ambien to help her get back to sleep.
Because she still does not trust her own judgment when it comes to
pills and a great many other things, Peter's in charge of doling out her
meds as well as the megadoses of vitamin supplements, probiotics, and

metabolic repair capsules his nutritionist in Switzerland said would make them look like they were fifty at age seventy. All of which tells Clare, Peter is smart and cares about their future.

Clare sticks out her tongue, Peter places an Ambien on it. Holding the glass of water he's brought her with two hands like a child, she washes it down.

He's tall, long-armed, and naked. He has silky black hair on his chest and back, so much of it that her nickname for him is "the Beast." As he gets back in her bed, he tells her in a voice that's as soft and comforting as a baby pillow, "It's just a dream. Nothing to worry about."

Nestling close to him, she sees him watching her in the darkness like a sentinel. Falling back to sleep, she murmurs, "I'm lucky to have you." He whispers, "We're both lucky." If her eyes hadn't been closed, she might have noticed Peter didn't look like a man who felt lucky.

Clare had trouble waking up when the alarm went off at 8 a.m. Unable to find her glasses, the world was a blur as she slipped on her robe and headed downstairs. She was surprised to see her husband still sitting at the breakfast table in his suit and tie. Normally Peter would have done forty-five minutes on the rowing machine, downed a power shake spiked with brewer's yeast, and been on his way to his office by now.

She found him bantering with their cook about the Mets' pitching rotation. Peter didn't just talk to servants, he was genuinely interested in the things they had to say. That was another of the many things she liked about him.

"What are you still doing here, Beast?" He said he liked the nickname, but never why.

"I canceled my morning appointments so we could talk. I'm worried about you."

"I'm fine." Kissing his cheek, she came away smelling of aftershave and sweat. As she sliced a banana over a bowl of gluten-free granola, Peter gave the cook a look that told her to go out on the terrace and water the plants.

"Last night you weren't fine. You have to slow down, Clare. I've been telling you for weeks you're trying to grow your foundation too fast. But I'm serious now, it's time to hit pause." Five years ago she had put $15 million into a charitable trust she had named after her dead daughter—the Grace Loughton Foundation. "This plan of yours to dump half your real estate assets into Grace is . . ." As they each took their megavitamins, he searched for the right word. "Irresponsible bordering on crazy. It's your money, Clare, but I think you're getting in way over your head."

"It's our money."

"No it's not. It's your money, and it's entirely your decision how it's spent." Peter wasn't like her ex-husband. He never asked her to invest in business schemes or pretended to her friends that he was richer than he was. A moderately successful stockbroker, Peter made somewhere in the neighborhood of $1 million a year. By Park Avenue standards, he was poor. The apartment, the house in Nantucket, the villa in St. Barts, the lodge in Aspen, the jet, and all the rest of it were in Clare's name. Peter made that clear to anyone who asked, and sometimes to those who didn't. Clare saw that as proof positive he was different from all the other men she had known.

He left the management of Clare's fortune to the trustees and lawyer who had come to her rescue after her nervous breakdown. He looked at papers they gave her to sign, helped her understand why her real estate portfolio sometimes earned a 6.5 percent profit versus 9 percent and occasionally as much as 11 percent, but outside of checking to make sure everything added up, he stayed out of it. Because of that, Clare was surprised when Peter added, "But if it was my money, if half of all that real estate was mine and we really were equal partners, I wouldn't let you give away my half. It's crazy." He had a gentle way of making her feel stupid.

"Why? We'd still be rich."

"It's not the money. It's that you don't know anything about running a big foundation. Right now you give away, what? About a million bucks a year to women's causes. You know what you're doing, you know where your money's going. You start giving away forty million a year, your foundation turns into a company. You're going to be buried in grant requests, people hustling you, hitting you up twenty-four hours a day."

"That's why I'm hiring Susan. She's worked at the Rockefeller Foundation for six years. If I don't firm this up, I'm going to lose her."

"Just wait a year. If you still want to do this, I'll be behind you one hundred percent."

Clare swallowed the last of her pills. "What difference is a year going to make?"

Peter looked hurt. "When we got married, you said you wanted to have a child with me."

"I know. I'm just not sure I'm ready for that yet." Clare played with her iPhone.

Peter held her hand. "You're thirty-three. I'm thirty-two. My clock's ticking." Clare got up to get more orange juice. Peter pulled her back into his arms. "Once we have a kid, I don't care what you do. You can give it all away if that's what you want. We can move to New Jersey and live off my salary for all I care."

"I'll think about it." When Clare said that, Peter knew he was ninety-nine percent of the way to yes.

"Well, while you're thinking about it . . ." Peter slipped his hands inside her robe. "Why don't we go upstairs and . . ." The Beast whispered his desires as matter-of-factly as if he were placing an order at Starbucks.

Pushing him away playfully, Clare smiled. "You think I'm easy, don't you?"

"Yes and that's one of the many things I love about you." He smiled gleefully. He made her feel just foolish and safe enough to do whatever he asked.

They each made a quick phone call before they went back upstairs to the bedroom. Tossing their iPhones onto the chair nobody ever sat in, the Beast bent her over the bed and she forgot about the foundation for a little while.

After they were finished Clare drifted off to sleep. Not for long, twenty minutes at most. Sex had a calming effect on her, not unlike a Nembutal. When she opened her eyes, she felt refreshed and the world was in focus, in part because she found her glasses. Peter's side of the bed was empty, but seeing the depression his body had left in the mattress made her appreciate him. It was not every husband who, three years into a marriage, felt the urge to blow off a morning's worth of appointments to make love to his wife.

Glancing out the window to see if it looked like rain, she saw him down on the terrace talking on the phone. Wanting him to know how much she cared about him, she tiptoed down the stairs to surprise him. The Beast had his cell phone to his ear. She was about to say, "I just want to remind you how much I love you," when she realized her husband was talking to her lawyer.

"Everybody can relax. I'll talk to her trustees today. Once I get her pregnant, she'll realize the kid will hate her if she gives away half its money to a fucking charity." If the Beast had said "our kid" instead of "the kid," she wouldn't have been so offended. Without a word, Clare silently retreated and went back upstairs. As she filled the bidet, she reminded herself, *It is my fucking money.*

The foundation's office was in Dumbo. It was a long commute, but Brooklyn, like the Beast, felt like a fresh start. As she walked through the door that morning, her assistant told her the dentist could only see her at 5 p.m. and she'd have to reschedule Lulu Mannheim. She had a cavity that was bothering her and had put off having it filled for a long time. Clare would have canceled tea if she hadn't known seeing Lulu would annoy her husband. Peter and his friends didn't care for Lulu Mannheim. As Peter put it, "She acts like a guy."

Sitting at her desk, she called Susan Rosen at the Rockefeller Foundation. "I need a good lawyer."

"You have one."

"He listens too much to my husband. The same goes for my trustees. How hard would it be to replace them all?" As with all large inheritances, Clare's assets were managed by a group of trustees, and their approval was necessary for any large expenditure or bequest.

"That's a serious move. What's wrong? Do you think they're mishandling your money?"

"No, they know how to make money, they just don't know how to let me give it away. They're deliberately dragging their feet on our plans to expand the foundation. And my Neanderthal husband thinks if he gets me pregnant, I'll change my mind."

CHAPTER 35

The last time Evie set foot in Lulu's Tribeca loft, the ruins of the Twin Towers were still smoldering. The World Trade Center had been rebuilt, but her life still felt on the verge of collapse.

Stepping out of the elevator with Lulu, Chloé trailing, Evie remembered herself at seventeen. Staring out the loft's wall of arched windows, watching the smoke rise from the carnage of 9/11, Evie was so desperate and unsure of how to repair the damage that had been done to her, she flipped the same coin she used to charm Jimmy the crow to decide whether to run away to Paris. She could not recall whether it was heads she goes and tails she stays or the other way around, but she knew that if she had called it wrong that day, she never would have had a daughter to save or lose.

In a little less than three hours her unknown twin would ring the doorbell. Her fear of all that could go wrong was spiked with existential curiosity. In the womb, they had started as one—a single zygote that was split into two. What would happen when they tried to reunite?

Since October 2001, the 6,000-square-foot loft had changed more than Lulu. The white leather Italian sofas were gone; the look was Scandinavian now. A Basquiat skull presided over the living room, a Louise Bourgeois spider clung to the wall, and a curving staircase that appeared to float in midair now rose up through the roof to a glass and steel double-cube penthouse that boasted a shallow infinity pool.

The excitement of the trip to New York distracted Chloé from the fresh bruises that had sprouted like blue mold on her thighs overnight and a headache she hoped wasn't a symptom of leukemic cells marching into her brain.

When she got to the loft she went up to the terrace, plopped in a poolside chair, and Instagrammed snaps to her friends in Paris—her in the copilot seat of the floatplane as they took off from the lake; a bird's-eye view of the city skyline as they dropped out of the clouds to land in the East River; the chauffeured Mercedes that picked them up from the Marine Air Terminal; and now last but not least a selfie of her wearing Lulu's sunglasses posed next to the pool with the city at her feet.

Chloé knew her mother had brought her along to meet Clare Loughton to play on her twin's sympathies, to make it harder for the woman to say "No." The idea that she was auditioning for her life, that some rich woman who was coming to tea at five would decide whether she had a future on the planet, seemed both absurd and unfair. She went back downstairs where Evie was in the midst of rehearsing with Lulu what she planned to say to her twin.

When Chloé heard her mother say, "I can't save my daughter's life, but you can," she interrupted, "Maybe we should get a wheelchair for me to sit in so she gets it that I'm dying."

Lulu lit a stick of incense in front of a life-size Buddha and retreated to the kitchen. "Anyone else want a Diet Coke?"

Evie reached out to take her daughter's face in her hands. "Chloé, we're almost there."

"No we're not." Chloé knocked away her mother's outstretched arms. "There are a million things that can go wrong; that with my fucking luck undoubtedly will go wrong. You can bullshit yourself, but don't do it to me!" Chloé was shouting now.

"There's a difference between bullshit and hope."

"Yeah . . . and what's that?"

"Faith. For lack of a better word."

"Faith in what? Don't tell me you're suddenly getting religious?"

Evie looked at her watch. "Why don't you go upstairs and put on your blue dress?"

"I forgot it. Left it at Valhalla." Evie had asked her daughter twice if she had remembered to pack it. "I never wear a dress. Who are you trying to impress?"

Evie was about to lose her temper when Lulu stepped in. "She can borrow one of mine."

Being fourteen, Chloé had to have the last word. "You really think she won't give me a bone marrow transplant if I wear jeans?"

Lulu took her upstairs, opened her closet, and handed her a dress. When Chloé tried it on she said it made her look fat. Having lost twenty pounds in the last month, Chloé looked like a skeleton over-dressed in Chanel. When Lulu looked at her critically and quipped, "I wasn't going to say anything, dear, but you could afford to lose a few pounds." Chloé laughed darkly and felt better.

At ten minutes to five, Lulu's phone rang. Clare Loughton was running late. Tea was pushed back to drinks at six. Evie told Lulu not to have a second glass of white wine, and Lulu was about to tell her to fuck off when the doorman called to say, "Lady named Loughton's here."

Evie stared at the fish-eye view provided by the video monitor of Lulu's security system and watched another version of herself step into the elevator. The similarities were as superficial as they were profound. Evie had a purse identical to the one slung over her twin's shoulder; the only difference was that Clare's was purchased at Hermès for twelve thousand dollars, whereas Evie had bought hers from a Nigerian street vendor outside the Paris Métro for sixty euros.

Stranger still, as Clare Loughton checked out her reflection in the mirrored walls of the elevator, Evie saw her twin make the exact same *I don't really like what I see, but what can I do* face that she made when she looked in the mirror. Evie had always thought that look was due to the years she had spent seeing disfigurement reflected back at herself. Now observing her blemish-free twin dismissing herself with the same grimace, Evie had to wonder, *Where does all the doubt come from?*

As the elevator approached their floor, Lulu shooed Evie and Chloé into the library just off the living room. They had it all planned out; Lulu would break the news to Clare that she had a twin, then Evie would come out and introduce herself and find out whether hope was bullshit.

Clare came into the loft reading a text from her husband. He had canceled a business dinner, sent the cook home, and was volunteering to make dinner for them. It was hard to stay mad at a man who offered to make spaghetti carbonara for you. After exchanging a perfunctory air kiss with Lulu, she texted back, "Yum! Yum!" and wondered what Peter would say when she told him about her decision to eighty-six her lawyer and trustees.

The library door ajar, Chloé peeking over her shoulder, Evie watched as Lulu made nervous small talk. She and her twin had the same walk, but her restorer's eye picked up small differences. Clare's nose was smaller and more turned up; her neck longer and enviably swan-like. Whereas Clare's accent, honed by twelve years at Spence, was brittle with sophistication, Evie's voice was lower and inflected with a North Country cadence. The biggest difference was in their eyes. Clare's were a paler shade of blue, more ocean than lake.

"So where's this mysterious person who knew me when I was little?" A glass of white wine was offered and accepted.

"She'll be out in a minute." Lulu's hands trembled as she lit a cigarette. "Look, Clare, you know you were adopted."

"Where's that coming from?" Lulu was about to tell her when Clare's phone chirped another text. "Sorry, it's Peter again. He's making dinner to get out of the doghouse . . ." Clare texted back that she'd be home by 8 p.m. "What were you saying?"

Lulu got to the point. "I don't know how else to break this to you, but you have a twin sister."

Clare had trouble processing the words she had just heard. "What? . . . Is this some kind of joke?"

"No." Lulu handed her the folder that contained the adoption records.

As she flipped through it, the blush of white wine faded from her cheeks. Turning chalky, Clare muttered, "This is fucking nuts. Why didn't this person come to me herself? Where did you get these records?"

"Your sister gave them to me."

"Where the hell did she get them? Lawyers told me it was impossible, that the records were sealed. How do you know they're even real?" Clare eyed the papers suspiciously. "What does this woman want from me?"

Evie could see it was going south. She was about to step forward and explain when Chloé pushed past her. "My mother doesn't want anything from you, but I do." The door was wide open now.

"Chloé, let me explain to Clare why we're here." Clare's head jerked back at the sight of her twin. Evie reached out to stop her daughter from making it worse, but Chloé shrugged her off.

"It's my life. I can speak for myself." Chloé walked toward her, fists clenched and voice raised, as if she were going to hit her. Clare looked frightened and stood up suddenly, her chair falling back. There was no stopping Chloé. "I have leukemia, and I need a bone marrow transplant, which my mother can't give me because she had hepatitis!" She was shouting between sobs. "So you are my last fucking hope and I am scared."

In that instant, Clare Loughton was once again running down a dark road looking for a bassinet. Dropping the adoption papers, she backed away from the memory and shook her head *no*. Lulu and Evie looked on helplessly; it could not have been going any worse.

Evie watched in disbelief as Clare suddenly stepped forward, folded Chloé into her arms, and in a maternal voice Evie recognized as both universal and her own whispered, "Everything's going to be okay, baby. Yes, of course I'll help you."

Lulu took Chloé upstairs to her bedroom and distracted her from the harshness of reality by getting under the covers, eating popcorn, and watching one of Lulu's old Fred Astaire and Ginger Rogers movies. Sitting in the dark watching dancers glide across the ballroom of a black-and-white world, Lulu confided, "I got into Fred Astaire when I was kicking heroin. It's impossible to be sad watching tap dancing."

Clare and Evie sat in the kitchen and tried to have a normal conversation, awkwardly blurting out questions and answering with fragments of their lives. At first, it seemed they had nothing in common except loss, an allergy to strawberries, and DNA.

Evie explained the HLA blood test Clare would have to take to make sure she was a viable donor, then showed her diagrams the doctor in Paris had given her illustrating how the bone marrow would be extracted from the back of her pelvis, processed, and frozen at 4 degrees Celsius. Clare was visibly relieved to hear that she would be given a light general anesthetic before being stabbed with a six-inch needle and that it would be over in two hours.

Watching Clare work her cell phone as she tracked down doctors was an education in how things worked if there was a hospital wing with your last name on it. Exceptions were made, appointments with less wealthy patients bumped. She heard her twin say, "That's not good enough," more than once. What the physician she spoke to said was impossible, quickly became possible. Clare would have her HLA test at 8:30 a.m. the next morning and the lab would send the results to both Clare and Evie by 3 p.m. at the latest. When Clare finally hung up, she grinned sheepishly. "I must have sounded like a rich bitch."

"No. Not at all."

"Yes I did."

"Okay, a little."

They laughed, then Clare asked, "What's the next step for Chloé?"

"Once we have your marrow, she'll spend a week in a hospital and have chemo and radiation. . . ." Evie dreaded the prospect of watching her daughter be clinically poisoned again. "It's horrible to watch your child suffer, not being able to do anything. As a mother you somehow feel like it's your fault." Lost in her own worries, she had forgotten how her twin's daughter had died until she saw the way Clare was looking at her. "I'm sorry. That was a stupid thing for me to say."

Clare sounded hollow when she replied, "Sometimes, it is the mother's fault."

As they walked toward the elevator, Clare surprised Evie. "If it's all right with you, and Chloé of course, I'd like to go to the hospital when they do it, be there for you both." When Evie explained that the procedure would be done in Paris, Clare smiled. "I'd still like to be there." The last thing Clare said before she stepped into the elevator was, "Thank you."

"For what? You're the one who's helping us."

The doors were closing when Clare called out, "I always wanted a sister."

Clare gave her address to the driver of the taxi, but she was not at all sure where the trip she was on would take her. As she sat in the back of the cab clutching a folder full of adoption papers gifted by a stranger who shared her face, the reality of what she could still not quite believe had happened washed over her in waves: warm, surreal, and more than a little disorienting.

Heading home that evening, Clare felt as if a door had been opened that offered a whole new perspective on her world and who she was. The rush that accompanied its unlocking was not unlike the sensation she remembered experiencing the first time she took acid in eighth grade. Though she could hear her shrink cautioning her about the implications of that analogy, Clare knew the sea change she felt taking place inside herself was real; not merely wishful thinking.

The wonderment of suddenly finding out she had a twin sister was tempered only by the discovery that she also had a niece who was dying of cancer. Because Clare had made so many mistakes in her life, she was careful not to delude herself about what this doorway might open her up to. Her newfound sister could turn out to be a total asshole, and even with a bone marrow transplant, her niece might not live long enough to become a friend. But then again, maybe it might just all work out.

She had woken up that morning an orphan with only a husband

to keep her from drifting back to the sadness of the night she left the bassinet on top of the car. Her future seemed to have expanded by a multiple of three. Evie, Chloé, and Lulu, who brought them together—the three women made her feel anchored to something larger than herself.

When Clare got home, her husband was out on the terrace manning the grill. Spaghetti carbonara had turned into his favorite meal rather than hers. Steaks were ready to go on the grill, a béarnaise sauce had been whipped, the table set and candles lit. He had made an effort, but she wondered, for whom? Clare had not forgotten how angry she was at the Beast for the way he had talked about her on the phone that morning.

The Beast watched her standing up on the step stool she used to trim what was out of reach and smell the white blossoms that had sprouted from the topmost branches of an eight-foot apple tree that grew out of the planter next to the railing. The Beast cautioned her, "It's a long way down if you slip."

Clare stepped down and announced, "I just had the best day of my life."

"I thought the day we met held that distinction."

"This is a different kind of best."

"Are you going to tell me or do I have to guess?" He brushed the vegetables with olive oil and turned them on the grill.

"You know I was adopted."

The Beast smiled. "You're thinking maybe we should just jump-start our family and adopt a kid?" Peter was good at telling her what she was thinking.

"Actually I wasn't thinking that at all."

"Not a bad idea, though."

"What I was going to say, I mean, the reason I brought up being adopted is . . . I just found out I have a sister."

As the steaks sizzled, Clare told him about Evie and Chloé and the bone marrow transplant and the HLA test she would take in the morning. When she finished, the Beast turned the meat over and poured himself a glass of red wine. "I don't want to rain on your parade, but something about all this seems fishy. You don't know anything about this woman."

"Lulu's known her for years."

"Then why did she wait until now to contact you? How do you know this Evie Quimby person is who she says she is?"

"She's my identical twin. She looks just like me." In her excitement, Clare had left that part out of the story.

The steaks were done and waiting to be cut. Peter was leafing through the adoption papers. "Have you told your lawyer about this?"

"No, but I will once I find a new attorney."

The Beast began to cut up the meat. "What's wrong with the lawyer you have? Ken Strauss has been a good friend to you and the foundation. He's worked for the foundation for free; you can't beat that."

Feeling a chill in the air, Clare stepped back into the living room to get her sweater. She called back over her shoulder, "I just think it's time for a change. New lawyer, new trustees."

Glancing in the mirror as she put it on, Clare caught the way the Beast stared at her as he told her, "Whatever makes you happy makes me happy." The expression on his face didn't match the reassuring words coming out of his mouth.

Frightened by the thought that the calm, accommodating voice she had been listening to for the last three years was a lie, Clare kept her back to her husband and pretended she couldn't see his face when she asked, "Are you hiding something from me?"

The Beast mouthed the word *bitch* and asked innocently, "Why would you think that, Clare?"

"It's what my instincts tell me." She was facing the Beast now.

"Well your instincts are wrong."

"No they're not. I just stopped listening to them until today."

After they ate the steak, the Beast wanted to have sex. Clare lied and said she had gotten her period. As the Beast turned out the light, he sighed, "That explains everything."

"What's that mean?"

"Whenever you get your period you act weird."

Clare waited until she was sure her husband was asleep before she left their bed, went into the guest room, and locked the door.

The next morning she was in her doctor's office at 8:30 a.m. Blood was drawn and her physician promised to have the results of the HLA compatibility test completed by midday. She texted the news to Evie and they made a plan to meet the next day in Brooklyn to discuss the logistics; when and where the marrow would be taken.

Clare was coming out of the medical center when she bumped into a white-haired septuagenarian in a three-piece suit fumbling with a prescription bottle. Pills scattered across the pavement. Bending down to help the old man pick up his pills, she was surprised to find herself face-to-face with the most senior of her trustees, Walter Morrissey.

"Dropped the damn pills my doctor just gave me." With only three fingers on his left hand, he was always dropping things. He seemed frailer than she remembered.

"Is everything okay, Walter?" She liked the aging financier, in part because he always remembered to send her flowers on her birthday. She was dreading telling Walter she had decided to replace him.

"As okay as it can be when one gets to my age. Doctor says I need a bypass."

"I'm so sorry to hear that."

"Well they say getting old isn't for sissies. But it's serendipitous meeting you like this."

"How so?"

"I've been putting off telling you, but I'm going to have to step down as your trustee. My health just isn't up to it."

Clare was relieved but tried not to show it. "I'll miss you. It won't be the same."

"If you have time for a cup of coffee with an old man, I'll share some of my concerns about my replacement and your future."

"Is there something wrong?"

"No, I just want you to know how proud I am of how you're growing your foundation, and how important it is that you pick a trustee who'll help you get the others to move faster."

"I'm so glad to hear you say that." The old banker took her arm as they headed down Madison Avenue. They stopped in a café two blocks down and took a table outside. Walter gallantly insisted on going in and getting their lattes himself. When he got back, he watched her sip her coffee as he suggested a series of names to replace him. The names meant nothing to her, but when Clare finished her coffee, he said something that meant a great deal to her.

"Whoever you pick to take my place, it should be your choice. Have confidence in your own judgment. You've had some hard times in your life, but you've come through them stronger. It's your money. Not your husband's, not your financial adviser's. Believe in yourself, and you'll do fine."

Clare walked away from that cup of coffee feeling better than she had in years. The old man's words echoed inside her head: *You'll do fine.*

It wasn't until thirty minutes later that she began to hear other voices inside her head. They were the same ones that whispered in her ear when she was sent to the psychiatric ward at McLean Hospital. It would be twenty-four hours before Clare realized who put the snakes inside her head.

CHAPTER 36

We were in the middle of making tuna salad for lunch when the medical lab emailed the results of Clare's HLA test to my mother. The A, BC, DRB1, and DQ genetic keys of Clare Loughton's blood matched mine. Our doctor in Paris called it "very, very promising." I didn't quite believe him and made him say it twice. I tried not to get too excited, but I was more than that.

We had planned to go to the Met that afternoon. Two years ago my mother had repaired the halo of a Buddha that was on loan to the museum. But when she heard me sneeze she called it off.

By sunset, my nose was running, I had a temperature of 102 and my lymph nodes were so swollen it felt like I had unripe plums stuck in my armpits. The throb of mutant white blood cells barreling through the corridors of my bones made it hard to go to sleep that night.

The next morning, most but not all of my symptoms were gone. My head cold vanished, my temperature cooled, and a Tylenol with codeine kept the bone ache at bay. My mother was just heading off to meet Clare Loughton—when and where Clare's marrow would be extracted still had to be worked out. Lulu was doing Pilates with her instructor in the gym downstairs. As the elevator closed behind my mother, she told me to put on a sweater and remember to take my meds.

When I saw she had forgotten her cell phone, I ran out onto the balcony and shouted down to her as she came out onto the sidewalk.

Worried I was going to overexert myself, she wanted to come up and get it, but I insisted on bringing it down to her. I was tired of being cooped up in Lulu's loft. Scurrying to find my shoes, I was breathless and dizzy by the time I got to the lobby.

When I came out of the building, my mother was staring up at the sun with her eyes closed and there was a smile on her face I hadn't seen in a long time. She called it taking a "Sonnenbad," which is sunbath in German. I don't know if it was the sunlight on her hair or my infusion of hope, but I remember being struck by how beautiful and young she was at thirty-three. It's hard for a daughter to see her mother as anything but old. I felt guilty for not realizing until then that my cancer was eating up her life as it devoured my own. But what preserved that moment in my memory was not the way I suddenly saw her, but the way a man across the street was staring at her. The truth is I wouldn't have noticed him if he weren't the second most handsome man I had seen in all my life. Numero uno being Alain Delon in Plein Soleil.

The man watching my mother was forty at most and had long, wavy blond hair. He wore a pale gray suit and laced-up shoes without socks as if to show he was hipper than his suit. But it was the look in his eye I remember most—unblinking and wolfishly curious. If my romantic experiences with men had not been limited to my one-night stand with a sixteen-year-old boy on my debating team, I might have realized that the way this elegant stranger gazed at my mother had nothing to do with sexual attraction.

As I handed my mother her cell phone, I whispered in French, "You have an admirer."

My mother laughed. "What are you talking about?"

"There's this incredibly handsome guy over there checking you out." But when we looked over, he was gone and all she saw was a homeless man fishing empty bottles out of the trash.

My mother thought I was playing a joke on her and called out, "Very funny," as she headed off to the subway.

Though I promised I would go straight back upstairs and rest, as soon as my mother was out of sight I went around the corner to see if I could find a magazine I hadn't read at the newsstand. Looking up as I paid for a French Vogue and a bar of German chocolate, the second most handsome man I had ever seen was back, only now he was eyeing me with the same look he had given my mother. The embarrassing thing was I was stupid enough to be flattered.

CHAPTER 37

The oncologist in Paris called again just as Evie was heading down into the subway to take the 3 train to Brooklyn.

"Have you decided where the harvesting will be done?" His French accent made the extraction of bone marrow sound like picking apples in Normandy.

Evie shouted into her cell phone to make herself heard over the din of gridlock, "I'm on my way to my sister's now to figure all that out." It was strange to refer to a woman she had known for all of thirty-six hours as her sister.

The doctor began to go over the procedure for Chloé. All she could make out was, "I have a team in place." Evie ducked into a Starbucks for quiet just as the French oncologist was saying, "Your sister's stem cells will be delivered through a central venous catheter. As they traverse through Chloé's bloodstream, they will be absorbed into the marrow of her bones. Your sister's stem cells will start making healthy blood for your daughter." Evie had not fully realized until then that for the rest of Chloé's life, her daughter's heart would be pumping her sister's blood.

She and her twin lived in different countries, different worlds. It was unlikely they would stay in contact, but no matter what happened, the bond between herself, her daughter, and Clare Loughton would be forever more intimate and profound than simply close. The expression *your own flesh and blood* had taken on new meaning.

Evie got off the subway in Brooklyn at Clark Street and walked downhill toward Clare's office in Dumbo. Evie liked the neighborhood—the park with its carousel along the riverbank, the nineteenth-century warehouse repurposed for twenty-first-century life.

May feeling like July, the air tasting like the sea, Evie indulged the fantasy that after Chloé got well she could move her studio to a street like this in Brooklyn and that she and her new sister could meet for lunch and coffee and be what she imagined sisters were to one another. Passing a florist shop, she bought a dozen pink peonies, hoping twinship applied to taste in flowers.

Clare's building was in the midst of renovation. Scaffolding made it hard for her to find the front door, and when she did it was unlocked. Workmen were monopolizing the elevator, so she took the stairs to the third floor. Knocking on a door marked "The Grace Loughton Foundation" but getting no answer, she pushed it open. Clare had said she had two women working for her full-time, but they were not to be seen. Instead she found herself facing three men in business suits. She recognized the tallest from Clare's Facebook page as her husband, Peter Shandley. He stared at her blankly, which surprised Evie. She would have expected him to have been more startled by the resemblance between herself and his wife. Evie smiled and reached out to shake his hand. "I'm Evie Quimby, your wife's—"

The husband cut her off. "I know who you are."

The shortest of the three stepped forward. "I'm Clare Loughton's attorney." He handed her papers that bore an official seal. "This is a restraining order."

There was pounding in the building and Evie thought she had heard him wrong. "I'm sorry, could you repeat that?"

"This is a protective order issued by the court of the City of New York. You are not permitted to contact my client either in person or by phone, email, or through a third party in any way whatsoever. Nor are you allowed to come closer than a hundred feet to any of Clare Loughton's residences or places of work, all of which means you are now in violation of this court order, and having entered these offices without permission, you are also guilty of trespassing and breaking and entering."

Evie felt like the world had turned into a toilet and she was being flushed. "What are you talking about? Your wife asked me to come here. She agreed to give my daughter—"

The husband took over. "My wife has been mentally unstable ever since the death of her daughter. The way you ambushed her . . . pressured her and played on her guilt pushed her off the goddamn edge."

Evie was frantic. "This is a mistake. Your wife went to her doctor yesterday morning and took a blood test. They told her she was a match."

"And then she went out and took God knows what and was found naked, hallucinating, screaming at traffic in the middle of Park Avenue. Did you give her LSD, mescaline, what?"

"This is insane. I've got to talk to Clare. Where is she?"

"She's in a psychiatric hospital . . . happy?"

Evie's voice broke. "She promised to help us."

The husband wasn't finished. "How much money were you trying to shake my wife down for? Is your daughter even sick?"

Evie had no memory of leaving that office. She must have walked down the three flights of stairs because thirty minutes later she was collapsed on the curb between two parked trucks, weeping.

A meter maid with dreadlocks was bent over her asking, "Do you need help?" Evie was blind to the green Bentley that pulled up in front of Clare's building across the street. A chauffeur opened the back door and helped a dapper man get out of the backseat. It wasn't until she saw the cane that she realized it was Win Langley.

Her twin's words echoed inside her head: *Sometimes, it is the mother's fault.*

~ ~ ~

Evie sounded far away when Lulu picked up her cell phone and heard, "Is Chloé in the room with you?" Evie was calling from the street. An ambulance wailed, a dog barked.

"No, she's upstairs watching another Fred Astaire movie." Lulu was in the library about to jump on a conference call with her partners on the real estate deal in Texas. "How did it go with Clare?" When she got no answer, she asked, "What's wrong?"

Evie's voice was a hoarse rant broken by sobs. "LSD . . . psychiatric hospital . . . restraining order." The specifics tumbled out of her, messy, dark, and jumbled. It made even less sense to Lulu when she heard Evie say, "And then fucking Win Langley showed up."

"What was Langley doing there?"

"I don't know. We've got to find Clare. We have to make her understand that if she doesn't do this for Chloé . . ." Evie's voice trailed off in a whimper.

"Look, they probably took her to Bellevue and pumped her full of benzos. They'll hold her seventy-two hours for observation, then she can check herself out." Lulu was trying to calm her down.

"How do you know that?"

"I tried to kill myself once. Overdosed a couple of times before I met you." Lulu lit a cigarette and flashed on the memory of Win Langley visiting her in the psychiatric ward with a bouquet of calla lilies. He introduced her to Charlie shortly after that. He called it his "get well" present. "What did Langley say to you?"

"Nothing. He didn't see me. I was across the street. I saw that fucker go into the building." Rage momentarily stemmed the flow of Evie's tears.

"It's a big building." Lulu had invested in a tobacco warehouse on the same street. "That doesn't necessarily mean Langley has anything to do with this."

"I waited. An hour later I watched him come out with Clare's husband and drive off with him. They were smiling." Suddenly her voice was ominously flat. "I took a picture. There were two guys with them. I want to know who they are. The short one said he was Clare's lawyer. I need to find out how they're connected to Langley."

"Evie, we've got to concentrate on getting in touch with Clare, getting her to go through with this transplant. What matters is your daughter, not settling a score with Langley."

"Just do it. Please. I'll meet you in that bar around the corner from your loft in an hour."

"Evie, get in a cab. Come back to my loft. We'll talk here."

"I don't want Chloé to see me like this." She was crying again. "And could you bring me some clean clothes? I was in the gutter. I'm a mess."

Lulu and Langley had been avoiding each other for seventeen years. When they did find themselves in the same room at a party or event, Langley would always smile and nod and give her an insincere bow. She would turn her back or, if she had had a glass of wine or two, mouth the words *fuck you* and walk away. The confidentiality agreement she had signed to keep Evie out of prison for shooting Langley had bought her silence. To breach it would have cost her Valhalla and, worse still, put it in Langley's hands.

She had no proof, heard no rumor, but she was certain that Langley had drugged and raped other women in the intervening years. The look he gave her when their eyes locked across a room sent the message: *I can touch you, but you can't touch me.* She felt guilty and ashamed that she had not called Langley out as a predator. Saying nothing didn't just make her complicit, she was his accomplice. She was angry at herself for doing nothing and angry at Clare for fucking up at the worst possible moment.

Lulu's cell phone chirped the arrival of the photographs. She didn't recognize the two men who were with Langley and Clare's husband. The tall one was carrying a suitcase and she could see a town car waiting for them. Langley's chauffeur was holding open the door of the green Bentley for Langley and the husband. Enlarging the pics, she saw that Clare's husband wasn't so much smiling as smirking at a private joke. The expression on his face was eerily familiar. It took her a moment to remember she had seen the exact same look on Charlie's face when he headed off fishing with Langley.

Lulu emailed the photographs of the men leaving Clare's building to her lawyer, accountant, money manager, and the two trustees of her trust fund with the instructions, "Tell me what I'm looking at and keep my interest to yourself." Then she called the number of a firm that provided services not entirely within the letter of the law.

Lulu was late getting to the bar. She found Evie sitting at a booth in the back looking like she had just been mugged. Dazed by disappointment, anger, and regret, Evie had fallen while walking back to Tribeca across the Brooklyn Bridge. Both her knees and one elbow were skinned raw. The walk hadn't cleared her head, but the fall had.

"Sorry I took so long getting here. I had to wait for Ortley Security to send me a contract to sign. They're all ex-cops. They're good; helped me track down what was left of the money Charlie embezzled."

"What do we need them for?"

"To find Clare. Her husband could have stashed her in some cushy hospital out of state, but most likely he took her to Bellevue. If she's got a psychiatrist, he'll try to talk her into checking herself straight into rehab. We have to get to her before that happens." Lulu paused to order a gimlet.

"What about the photograph I sent you?"

"The short one is Ken Strauss. He's a partner in a white-shoe law firm. After her baby died, he helped Clare with the divorce, kept her shit-heel husband from ripping her off. He's Clare's personal attorney and provides legal counsel for her foundation pro bono."

"And the one with the suitcase?"

"Tom Reynolds, investment banker. Specializes in commercial real estate. Puts deals together. No connection to Clare except that he and his wife play tennis with Clare and her husband on weekends."

"You don't find it strange Langley was there?"

"Look, Evie, you hate Win Langley, I hate him, but everyone else in a certain tax bracket in New York thinks he's a great guy. I'm not surprised Peter Shandley calls Win when his wife has a bad acid trip and gets carted off to the ninth floor of Bellevue. Making embarrassing problems go away for rich people is what Langley does for a living. Plus, the husband worked for Langley after he got out of college, before he went to business school. I know what you're thinking." Lulu pulled up the picture on her cell phone. "Except for Langley there's nothing sketchy about any of these guys, aside from the fact that they're all really handsome and know it . . . and that they all belong to the Mohawk Club."

Evie didn't seem to hear what Lulu was saying. "In the last three hours, I've called Clare forty-seven times and left literally forty-seven messages."

"They take away your cell phone when you check into Bellevue."

"I get that, but the point is her mailbox is still taking messages."

Lulu told the waiter she wanted another gimlet, then said, "So?"

"Cell phones only takes forty voicemails. Somebody is checking her messages and erasing them. . . ."

"Her husband was a dick for saying what he said to you, but he's just trying to protect her."

"Protect her from what?"

"Maybe he thought you were after her money. You don't realize how druggy Clare used to be. She used to drop acid on the way to school. And then the way her baby died. Maybe having Chloé's life in her hands, having all of us depending on her, freaked her out. I mean, Christ, she was always fragile."

"I heard Langley say the exact same thing to Charlie about you."

"He wasn't wrong about that."

Evie shook her head *no*. "Helping Chloé was Clare's chance to make up for what happened to her baby. I could see it in her face."

Lulu was nettled by the mention of Charlie's name. "Then why the fuck did she take acid? She knew you and Chloé were counting on her." The second gimlet was going to work on her.

"Win Langley drugged me so he could fuck me without my knowing it was happening. Maybe he or someone else drugged Clare to get something without her consent."

Evie went into the ladies' room and washed her face. Picking dirt out of her skinned knee, she put on the clean clothes Lulu had brought for her. The women agreed not to say anything to Chloé about the setback.

As soon as they stepped out of the elevator, Chloé knew. "I'm not going to get a transplant from her, am I?"

"It's going to take longer than we hoped."

"You once told me the hardest part of being a mother comes when your child asks you questions you think you have to answer with lies."

"I remember."

"I'm not a child."

~ ~ ~

Ortley Security reported back to Lulu twenty-four hours later. Evie and Chloé watched her take the call. When she hung up, they had no clue whether it was good news or bad.

"Is she at Bellevue?"

"She was."

"Where'd she go?"

"She got out somehow."

"You mean she escaped?" Chloé imagined Clare running down a psychiatric ward in a straitjacket.

"Her husband notified the police and is threatening to sue the hospital. We need to find her before he does."

"How did she break out?" Chloé was stuck on the idea.

"The Ortley guy heard that one of the orderlies went home wearing a pair of diamond studs."

Evie tried calling Clare's cell phone again. The number had been disconnected. It didn't mean anything, but it did.

The next morning when the doorman brought up the papers, Evie opened the *New York Post* and screamed, "No!" The headline read PARK AVE HEIRESS JUMPS.

CHAPTER 38

I was sitting next to my mother at the breakfast table when she opened the paper. Beneath the headline there was a photograph of a stretch of Park Avenue curb—police tape demarked the spot where Clare's body hit the pavement. Inserted on the front page was a smaller photo of Clare in a ball gown at a charity gala. In that moment, I felt as if my mother's twin had taken me with her when she leapt off the twelfth floor; I just hadn't hit the ground yet.

The onslaught of hopelessness had a violence and thrust that created an emptiness so vast it sucked the air first out of my lungs, then out of the room, and then out of my world. There's no getting bone marrow from a corpse. When Clare killed herself, she killed any chance I had of surviving cancer.

My mother reached out to hug me. Her embrace only made it harder to breathe.

Pushing her away, I ran to my bedroom and locked the door behind me. I didn't know how long I had. One month, two. Perhaps through summer. The weirdest part was that there was something about dying I found profoundly embarrassing. My instinct was to run but the cancer was in me. I felt stupid for having given in to the fantasy that we had found salvation in the attic of a town hall in the back of beyond.

Eventually, I unlocked the door and let my mother in. Lulu followed a few minutes later and the three of us got under the covers. I'm not proud of the fact that the only thing I can remember about the conversation was that not one word of sympathy was uttered nor a tear shed for Clare Loughton. When I muttered, "I hate her," my mother replied, "So do I."

Lulu was frantic to start flying us around to private clinics in Mexico and Switzerland that offered experimental cures involving extracts of bitter almond and oncological witchcraft that was illegal to practice in America.

My mother made desperate calls to HLA-matching centers and cancer help-lines in the hope that somebody somewhere had donated marrow that was a genetic match to mine—they hadn't.

By lunch I had backslid to anger. When asked what I wanted to eat, I snarled, "What the fuck difference does it make?" Lulu was ordering take-out from Nobu when a hospital my mother had never heard of in Brooklyn called. The medical technician on the line had a thick Jamaican accent that my mother found difficult to decipher. The technician had to repeat herself twice before my mother began to understand. "What I'm saying, ma'am, is Miss Loughton was here yesterday having her bone marrow harvested and she told us to call you to get the exact address of the hospital in France where it was going."

The three of us began jumping up and down and laughing. It was beyond great news until I remembered how much I had hated Clare Lough-ton until five minutes ago. We had misjudged my mother's twin. Each of us was ashamed that we had given no thought to the private demons that drove her to suicide, had shown no pity for the desperation she must have felt as she plummeted twelve stories down to the sidewalk below. We did not mourn her passing until we discovered that she had spent the last afternoon of her life making good on her promise to me.

It wasn't until then that I felt obliged to read the newspaper's version of my benefactress's death. There were few details. A psychiatric nurse reported Clare missing from the ward at approximately 10 a.m. Cameras picked her up passing through security wearing a lab coat with a stethoscope around her neck. Guards at the desk mistook her for staff sneaking out for a cigarette break. At approximately 7:30 p.m. that evening, the doorman of her building saw her get out of a yellow cab. She asked if her husband was home from work yet, he said, "No." The elevator operator remembered, "She seemed nervous, like she was in a hurry." There was no one in her apartment when she jumped. The police were already there when her hus-band came home that night.

After that, life moved on with brutal velocity. Chemo and radiation were scheduled to begin in Paris in less than forty-eight hours. My bone ache seemed to get worse by the hour and night sweats poured off of me during the day. My mother was in the midst of booking our flights back to Paris on her computer when Lulu shut the lid of the laptop. "I chartered a jet so Chloé could lie down."

"I can't let you do that."

"You can't stop me."

Lulu's jet took off from Teterboro Airport just before 9 p.m. that night. It had a bar and a stewardess just for us. I took a selfie of me smiling, holding up a champagne glass to text my friends, but my heart wasn't in it.

After takeoff, I got under a blanket on the couch on the back of the plane and closed my eyes, hoping for a dreamless sleep. My mother and Lulu sat facing one another in the front of the plane. I was just drifting off when Lulu asked the question we'd all been thinking about. "What makes a woman donate her bone marrow to save a child's life and then kill herself? I can understand her committing suicide after her baby died, but why the fuck do it now?"

My mother thought I was asleep when she said, "Maybe she didn't."

"What?"

"Kill herself."

I kept my eyes closed so I could hear the rest of what they were thinking and didn't want me to hear.

CHAPTER 39

The plane landed at Charles de Gaulle at 10 a.m. Paris time. They were through customs and on their way to the hospital in less than an hour. It was Lulu's idea to stop at Angelina on Rue de Rivoli for hot chocolate before checking into the oncology ward.

Chloé received her first hit of chemo that afternoon. The doctors called that first day of treatment "day minus-eight." Tomorrow was "day minus-seven," like the countdown for a rocket launch. Chemo was followed by a blast of radiation. The idea was to kill enough of the cancer cells for the transplant to take without killing her. As her immune system died, the danger of infection escalated. Evie and Lulu had to wear face masks and paper sleeves over their shoes. They slept at the hospital and took turns going back to the studio with its dead plants to shower and change clothes.

The day of the transplant was "day zero." By then Chloé looked simultaneously swollen and starved. The chemo had left the inside of her mouth cratered with open sores that looked as if someone had used her soft palate as an ashtray.

Evie watched helplessly as a central venous catheter was inserted into her daughter's jugular. The infusion of the dead twin's live stem cells was about to begin. The doctor told Evie it was time to leave.

As Evie gave Chloé a final kiss goodbye, Chloé reached out and grabbed her hand. The sores in her mouth made her voice sound like a death rattle. "No matter how this turns out for me, swear you'll find out what happened to Clare."

Evie bit down so hard on her lip she tasted blood. "I promise."

Five minutes later an alarm went off—Chloé's heart had stopped beating. Nurses and doctors burst into the room. Evie tried to get to her child's bedside, but they pushed her back into the hall. The alarm was still ringing. Putting her head to the wall, Evie closed her eyes and made a bargain with God.

The medical team put paddles to her daughter's chest—once, twice, three times. Chloé's arms and legs jerked in an imitation of life. Time slowed and much was said inside Evie's head during the two long minutes that passed before her daughter's heart began to beat again. The Almighty had kept its end of the bargain, Evie would keep hers. Staggering down the corridor, she pulled out her cell phone and dialed quickly. "Mama . . . I need you to come to Paris."

Flo arrived on the morning of June 1—"day plus-four." Chloé began to vomit blood that afternoon. Transfusions were required and her temperature rose to 103 degrees. Doctors were unable to pinpoint the source of the infection; a new course of antibiotics was administered via the catheter in her jugular and Chloé was put in an isolation room with positive air pressure, clean air pumped in 24/7. Between vomiting and diarrhea, it didn't stay clean for long. That afternoon, her heart stopped beating again. It took almost three minutes to bring her back this time.

Flo went to a church across the street from the hospital. Trying and failing to remember how to say the Lord's Prayer in Mohawk, she lit a candle. Lulu shook the oncologist by his lapels and told him she'd give him a Porsche if Chloé didn't die. Evie punched the wall so hard she cracked a knuckle. They each did what they could, but knew it wasn't going to help.

PART VI

ENTRAPMENT

F or Sheriff Colson, a.k.a. Dill, June 1 was the morning a fly fisherman from Brooklyn Heights tried to take a phone call from his wife while fishing a pool in the Mink River known as Indian Rock. The phone was dropped. What exactly happened after that was open to speculation.

As best Dill could put it together, when the New York angler reached into the water to retrieve his iPhone, he slipped, stumbled back, and hit his head on the rock that gave the pool its name. Stunned but not knocked out, the fisherman would have gotten away with a concussion if he'd just had it in him to take two more steps to shore before he passed out; or if he had landed faceup instead of facedown in the shallows; or if the bait fisherman who found him hadn't lingered over a second cup of coffee that morning and had arrived at Indian Rock five minutes earlier; or if a thousand other things had happened differently, the fly fisherman would not have drowned in six inches of water.

Dealing with the dead was part of Sheriff Colson's job; thinking about all the little things that could have prevented a body from turning into a corpse helped him keep death at arm's length. As he and his deputy dragged the angler out of the shallows and carried him up through the woods, Dill was struck as always by the weight of the departed. A hundred-and-eighty-pound man weighs a hundred and eighty pounds whether he ceases to exist or not, but the dead always felt like a heavier burden than the living to Dill.

What made a bad day worse for Sheriff Colson was the hour he had to kill at the deceased's A-frame cabin on the lake, waiting for the wife and children to get home. A neighbor told him the family was grocery shopping at Bargain-Mart.

Knocking on the kitchen door just in case the neighbor got it wrong, he peered through the window. A child's drawing was attached to the refrigerator with a magnetized ladybug; a smiling stick figure held a fishing rod and, at the top of the page, "Daddy" was spelled out with a backwards *D*.

Dill sat down on the porch and tried to think of words he could utter to explain the unexplainable to a woman who had become a widow between breakfast and lunch. The boy who had pissed himself the night the Morlocks chased him and Evie into the abandoned sawmill felt like weeping.

Desperate to distract himself from the grief at hand, he glanced down at the stack of old newspapers tied up for recycling. The sight of a front-page photograph of a dead woman beneath two-week-old headlines in a New York paper got Sheriff Colson thinking like a cop again. It bothered Dill that all the while he was telling the mother of the two small children that her husband had drowned, his mind was on Evie Quimby and why she had lied to him.

When Dill had called Evie the week before and asked if she had found a donor for her daughter, Evie had said yes, but not gone into specifics other than that she had discovered that she had a sister living in New York and that the transplant was being done in Paris. There was no mention of the fact that the donor was her identical twin, or that the twin was worth close to a billion dollars, or, most importantly of all, that the twin had decided to jump off the top of a building.

Being a sheriff, Dill was used to people leaving out parts of the truth that were difficult to explain. He understood that Evie was worried sick about her daughter, but he had risked his job and broken more than one law to help her steal the court records that led Evie to the now deceased heiress. Dill thought that cancer or not, Evie owed him the truth or at least an explanation.

Feeling used, impatient to find out what Evie had entangled him in, he pulled his cruiser over and called her cell phone. As was his practice with witnesses who were less than forthcoming with the facts, he baited her with concern that was both genuine and calculated, and started the phone conversation with, "How are you and Chloé holding up?"

"Touch and go. We won't know if they got all the cancer until . . ." Evie finished the sentence with a wail. Feeling like a ghoul, Dill decided to put off his cop questions until her daughter was out of the woods. He was in the midst of saying the usual things about cancer being "terrible" and "thinking positive thoughts" and "my prayers are with you" when Evie suddenly asked, "Have you seen Win Langley?"

Having never heard Evie say a bad word about Langley, it never occurred to Dill that Langley could have been the one who raped her. The sheriff made the mistake of presuming that Evie was feeling guilty about the karmic connection between the hunting accident and her daughter's misfortune when she asked about the man she shot all those years ago.

"Oh yeah, he's all good. He's got a new knee. Still limps, but he's walking around without a cane now and flying his own floatplane again." The sheriff had run into Langley at Harlan's Tackle Shop and Langley had explained that the surgical procedure involved borrowing ligaments from a cadaver. Like everyone else in Rangeley, Dill liked Win Langley, simply because he was the least snobby of the Mohawk Club crowd. "He asked about your daughter. Wanted to know what hospital Chloé was at in Paris so he could send flowers. He told me to tell you he's thinking about both of you."

"You see Langley again, you tell him we're thinking about him too." Later Sheriff Colson would ruminate on the way she said those words.

CHAPTER 41

Valhalla had no visitors the summer of 2018. Beds stayed stripped, curtains drawn, boats pulled out of the lake. The staff at the Great Camp was aware Lulu Mannheim was in Paris, but had heard nothing about what she was doing. All Rangeley knew was that Evie Quimby had shown up out of the blue back in May, no longer looking like "Giblet-Face," and talking French to a sickly daughter. Then, without explanation, seventy-two hours later, Lulu, Evie, and the girl had flown off in a floatplane and not returned.

Lulu's absence was a blow to the local economy. Merchants and tradespeople missed her extravagances and shopping sprees. Like the black bears that rummaged the town dump, Lulu Mannheim was an attractive nuisance. Townspeople liked pointing her out to tourists and, as with the bears, warned visitors not to get too close.

Part of the fun of summer was complaining about how Lulu ran stop signs on her motorcycles, backed up traffic with her goddamn horse-drawn carriage, and kicked up a wake that tipped canoes coming into town at full throttle at the wheel of the twenty-six-foot *Aloha II*. Denied the pleasure of being able to bitch about her presence, the locals came up with explanations of her absence that grew more and more far-fetched.

A realtor in Speculator claimed he knew for a fact that Lulu was selling Valhalla to a Chinese billionaire banking on a water shortage in the twenty-second century. The town clerk, who was a bigwig in the local Republican Party, insisted that Lulu had secret plans to turn Valhalla into a camp for Syrian war refugees. When Flo sent a postcard of Notre-Dame to the girl who was taking care of her chickens and minding her garden, Mary Lou and her son, Scrotum, told any and everyone who came into their convenience store that Lulu Mannheim and Evie Quimby had gotten married and that Flo had flown to France for their lesbian wedding.

Sheriff Colson was the only one in Rangeley who was aware that Evie's daughter was battling cancer. Revealing the girl had leukemia would only have given the county another thing to gossip about, so Dill said nothing. Similarly, he did not discuss the fact that Evie had had a rich twin sister who killed herself with anyone other than his husband, Jan, the veterinarian he lived with out on Route 3.

Dill heard nothing from Lulu or Evie that summer. Though neither woman was legally obliged to tell him the truth, he felt their silence was vaguely conspiratorial; that they didn't trust him was obvious, and their secrecy made him increasingly uneasy. So much so that in mid-July Dill called up a New York City detective, who fished the Mink for two weeks every fall, to find out if Clare Loughton's suicide was as straightforward as the newspapers reported it to be. The fly-fishing detective checked it out and relayed that there was nothing suspicious about the heiress's death. The husband was at work when she jumped, and the police found the apartment littered with photographs of the baby she had left on top of the car. Dill couldn't argue when the detective opined, "Too much money makes people crazy," yet he could not shake the feeling that there was something untoward in the confluence of misfortune in the lives of Lulu, Evie, and the unknown twin.

More than once that summer, Sheriff Colson closed the door to his office and started to dial Evie and Lulu only to stop himself because he knew it would be easier for them to lie long-distance.

Each time he did not make that call, Dill would stare at the empty chair across from his desk and wonder why Evie had sat there and refused to tell him who had drugged and raped her seventeen years ago. Her uncle was the sheriff—why didn't she press charges then? And why did Sheriff Dunn tell him that the Morlocks had molested Evie if that was not the case? Was he protecting Evie or someone else? Most of all, Dill wondered why he was sure it wasn't over.

CHAPTER 42

The last day of August, a flatbed truck barreled through the gates of Valhalla. Lulu was driving, Evie rode shotgun, and there was a ten-foot slab of Adirondack bluestone tied down in the back with chains. The women had flown in from Paris the night before. That morning, they had watched the rock they were carrying being cut out of a quarry in a neighboring county.

Lulu had given Clinger's son, Hank, less than twenty-four hours' notice of her arrival. A cryptic email sent from a mobile phone indicated that only two bedrooms would need to be made up. In addition, Lulu instructed him to purchase a public-address system specifying only, "I want it to be loud," and a generator to power it. Hank was to deliver and set up both in front of the old guide camp above the gorge. No explanation was given, and no mention was made of the two-thousand-pound stone on the back of the flatbed.

When the women pulled up in front of the Great Camp, Evie got out of the truck carrying a canvas satchel that jingled with tools brought from France. Without saying a word, she walked down to the dock. Hair cut short, she had lost weight. A housemaid was later overheard commenting that Evie looked "sad as a sweater left out in the rain." When one of the staff asked, "How's your daughter doing?" Evie acted as if she didn't hear the question and got in an outboard, pulled the starter cord, and set out down the lake.

Thirty minutes later, a shadow that looked like a giant locust was seen moving across the seven holes that were left of Adolphus's old golf course. Subsequently, a deafening metallic whoosh and clatter descended in the form of a Sikorsky S-58T heavy-lift helicopter, which circled once, then landed on the lawn. Hank, shouting above the racket of rotating blades, asked, "Are you going to tell me what's happening here, Miss Mannheim?" To which Lulu responded, "No."

The men who jumped out of the helicopter attached cables to the stone, and the Sikorsky slowly lifted the monolith into the air. As the helicopter headed out over the water, the stone, dangling by a thread of steel, swung back and forth like the pendulum of a giant clock.

By then, Evie was standing on top of the gorge. When the helicopter arrived, she guided it in and the stone was set down in front of the guide camp where she had been drugged and raped. Stood on end directly across the gorge from the Mohawk Club's playhouse, it was meant to be seen.

News of Lulu and Evie's return, accompanied by boozy eyewitness accounts of the chopper airlifting a two-thousand-plus-pound slab of rock down to a camp no one had set foot in for seventeen years, reached Dill when he stopped at the Rangeley Inn to break up a bar fight. Kevin and the now middle-aged Morlocks had started it and seemed to have won until Scrotum made the mistake of calling the sheriff a faggot. Dill regretted pulling out his billy club and hitting Scrotum in the kidneys and Kevin in the knees . . . sort of.

The stone was still a mystery, but the purpose of the sound system became clear to Dill when the Mohawk Club called the next morning to file a noise complaint. Evie had pumped up the volume at 7 a.m. through a pair of six-foot speakers. When the club manager crossed the gorge and asked her to turn it off, all Evie said was, "You're trespassing."

Dill didn't know if Evie was in violation of local ordinance, but there was no question she wanted it known that she had returned. Putting that rock in front of the guide camp, blasting oldies from the exact same spot where she had been sexually assaulted, Evie was sending a message to someone, and Sheriff Colson wanted to know who the hell that someone was.

Colson called Valhalla. A maid picked up and informed him that Miss Mannheim and Miss Quimby were "unavailable." The sheriff told the maid, "You tell them, I'm running out of patience, and if they don't contact me in person before end of day tomorrow, I'll shut down whatever the hell it is they're doing down in the gorge."

He was sorry Evie's kid was sick, but he was tired of waiting for her to tell him the truth. She and Lulu were hiding something they knew he would have felt obliged to prevent. If Evie wasn't going to treat him like a friend, Dill was going to start treating her like a suspect. Feeling the same kind of pissed off he had when he pulled out his billy club the night before, Dill was fed up with their bullshit.

Twenty-four hours later, having still not heard back from the women, Sheriff Colson got in his cruiser, turned on the flashing red light, and paid an official visit to Valhalla.

He could hear the Grateful Dead echoing across the lake before he even got out of the car. The water and an overcast sky made the music sound spooky and dirge-like. Dill could not recall the name of the tune, but he remembered Buddy would often sing a verse or two of the Dead to a man just to give him fair warning he was about to kick the shit out of him. Whatever Evie was up to, she was doing it Quimby-style.

When a maid told him that Lulu and Evie had gone down to the gorge, the sheriff borrowed a boat without asking. One hand on his hat, the other on the throttle, he headed down-lake to have it out with the women. Staying close to shore, he watched a pair of finches chase a red-tailed hawk from their nest; what annoyed him most was that the women did not think they needed his help.

The paranoid side of the sheriff imagined that Evie and Lulu didn't confide in him because in spite of the muscle mass he had added to his frame, they still thought of him as an ex-hairdresser with a badge. But maybe they simply thought that with Evie's balls and Lulu's money, they could take the law into their own hands.

It was three o'clock by the time Dill tied up the boat and climbed the Mannheims' side of the gorge. Evie was standing on a scaffold in front of the stone, rough and blue-gray as the lake on a cold and windy day. She had tapered the stone into an obelisk by then and was in the midst of using a tungsten-tipped chisel to cut something into the rock. Lulu was on her phone, texting. The music was so loud they did not hear him approach. When he saw the letters Evie had cut into the rock, Dill backed away from the stone and took off his hat. "I'm so sorry, Evie."

~ ~ ~

Forty-eight hours later, Evie was having trouble with the letter *D*. Whetting the stone, she told the chisel what to do with her left hand and imposed her will with three sharp blows of her mallet. Lulu had ridden down through the woods on an electric motorcycle—silent and frighteningly fast—and brought lunch in her backpack. They had finished eating and Dorothy Dandridge was on the sound system now.

Climbing back on the scaffold, Evie picked up a brass letter she had forged in Paris and tapped it into the notches for the *D* she had just cut. The brass capitals glistened in the glare of the sun, making the inscription seem written in fire.

As she admired her handiwork, a floatplane—red fuselage, black wings, and pontoons painted like trout—came in low overhead. Lulu made a gun out of her hand and pulled an imaginary trigger as if to shoot it out of the sky. "Win Langley's new plane. He's flying again."

"So Dill told me. Says the fucker can walk without a cane now too." The women watched Langley's floatplane circle back. They expected it to follow the gorge and land on Lake Constance in front of the Mohawk Club, but instead Langley banked sharply behind them, angling down into a heavily forested narrow cleft in the mountains two miles back of the guide camp.

Lulu shielded her eyes with the flat of her hand. "What the fuck's he doing? There's nowhere to land a plane back there."

"There's Dog Pond." Evie flashed on the day she and Buddy nearly drowned taking a canoe over the falls at the back end of the pond.

"No one ever lands on Dog Pond—it's not long enough." Lulu, in one of her incarnations of daredevildom, had taken up piloting. "He tries to put down there, he'll either hit the trees going in or crash into the rocks at the far end." As Langley's plane dropped down into the basin just beyond Kettle Mountain and disappeared from view, Evie asked God to make it crash.

CHAPTER 43

Win Langley was in the pilot seat. Clare Loughton's widower, Peter Shandley, sat next to him, looking sweaty and grim. Langley could not tell whether Shandley was suffering from a sudden attack of grief, guilt, or airsickness.

Ken Strauss and Tom Reynolds, the other two men who had been at the foundation that day, were buckled in the back. It was a reunion of sorts. The four men had not seen one another since Clare's memorial service at St. Bartholomew's. Tom, who played football, piano, and cello with equal dexterity while at Yale, had picked out the hymns.

They were flying up for the Mohawk Club's annual meeting. Knocking off from work in the city before lunch, they were airborne by noon. Looking forward to the club's three-day celebration of the joys of hunting and fishing. There were cocktail parties scheduled to celebrate both the opening and the closing of the festivities. In between a formal dinner, a pigeon shoot, and a barbecue on the lake, it was the only weekend of the year when wives were welcomed into the Mohawk Club. Ken's and Tom's spouses were driving down from a horse show where they were competing in Lake Placid.

Langley's new knee, like his new floatplane, made him feel young; or at least younger than he had felt for a long time. He was free from the embarrassment of scooting around the club like an invalid in a four-wheel-drive wheelchair. He couldn't run, but he was able to manage a crab-like, lopsided jog, and his footing was sure enough for him to wade into a trout stream without risk of drowning. He was not completely emancipated from the pain of his past injuries, but enough so that he was no longer reminded with every step that a teenage girl had gotten away with shooting him. Though he did not discuss it with the men in the plane, news of Evie Quimby's miseries made him feel not just like he'd won, but as if he'd gotten to fuck her all over again.

At the start of the flight Langley was all business, checking his gauges and keeping a watchful eye out for commercial air traffic. But the plane was on autopilot now. Jackets were off, ties loosened, headphones on. The men were mic'd into the same channel and beers were being handed out. Langley opted for a Red Bull and asked, "So how are my fellow Lost Boys doing?" It was how Langley referred to the men closest to him; what they called themselves in private.

Tom Reynolds yawned, which is what the laconic Texan always did before he said something he knew present company would find amusing. "My wife, God bless her soul, gave me seven days of salmon fishing in Iceland for my birthday under the condition I wouldn't make her come along." Reynolds's wife, Helen, hated fishing.

Ken piped in, "And then his good friend Ken, whom he now seriously owes, was kind enough to help her book the fishing camp." Langley had introduced Ken to Tom Reynolds when they got their MBAs at Harvard.

Reynolds crowed, "A full week of the deluxe wilderness package at Ingersal." Ken and Reynolds high-fived.

Langley barked a laugh. "What a wonderfully stupid woman you married."

Having never fished for salmon in Iceland, much less experienced Ingersal's deluxe package, Shandley didn't get why the men were laughing. "What's so funny about her giving you a fishing trip?"

Reynolds explained, "Ingersal has all of these gorgeous Icelandic girls working for them. We're talking guides, drivers, even the cooks are tens. Best part is Ingersal doesn't tell you which one of the chicks is a pro, so when you get there and a twenty-year-old Viking goddess starts flirting with you and laughing at all your jokes and then sneaks into your tent and fucks your teeth loose, you not only get to catch a thirty-pound salmon, you go home thinking you're the stud of the Western world. It's the third time I've been there."

Shandley still didn't get it. "But if you've been there twice before, you knew she was a hooker. It's no surprise that she fucks you. What's so special about that? That's what hookers do."

Reynolds gave the bereaved younger man a hopeless look. Ken, who had twice been to Ingersal himself, stepped in. "Ingersal gets a new girl every year. It's special, because the hooker doesn't know you know she's a hooker. So when you ask her to do nasty shit, she has to act shy and pretend she's never done it before and that she's doing it because she's in love with you. You know she's lying, and yet, paradoxically, it's romantic."

The men thought that was hysterical, until Shandley announced, "I miss my wife."

The men got quiet then. After an awkward moment of silence, Reynolds volunteered, "We all miss her, Peter."

Ken added solemnly, "Tragic . . . beyond words."

Langley took Shandley's hand in his. "It takes time, but you will get over it." Then added, "Trust me on this. I've been there." They all knew about the climbing accident. Langley wanted to get off the subject of dead wives. Calling back to Ken, who had been out to Silicon Valley the week before on business, "Did you get a chance to talk to Dolenz when you were in San Francisco?" Dolenz was the newest addition to Langley's fraternity of Lost Boys. Win had taught him to fly-fish, and in return, his protégé had got them in ahead of the pack on a couple of start-ups that had taken off.

Ken filled him in, "I had dinner with him and his wife. Father-in-law bought them an amazing house in Pacific Heights. Cute baby. He's all good, but it can't be easy being married to a woman who's blind."

Langley smiled. "Well, it certainly makes it easy for him to keep her in the dark."

There was laughter in the cockpit until Shandley suddenly began to weep. The man's tears made the others nervous. Reynolds and Ken shot Langley panicked glances. From the look on their faces, one would have thought the plane had just been struck by lightning when

Shandley suddenly sobbed, "I'm sorry, I just can't get used to the idea Clare is dead."

Shandley's blubbering filled Langley with a contempt bordering on revulsion. His first instinct was to slap the man and tell him, "Fucking pull yourself together," but as the Sister Lakes appeared below them, he thought of a better way to shut Shandley up.

Langley's voice was calm, patient, and full of avuncular compassion as he told he weeping Lost Boy, "The important thing for you to do now, Peter, is focus on your future. Take pleasure in the things that bring your joy. Which is why we are going to sneak in a couple hours of dry-fly fishing on the Cascades this afternoon."

Shandley shook his head no. "Don't you hear what I'm saying?"

Langley smiled, but there was an edge to his voice as he said, "Oh I hear you . . . but you'll feel different once we get there."

Reynolds looked at his watch. "Love to, Win, but the cocktail party starts at six thirty p.m. My wife will kill me if she drives all the way down from that horse show and I'm not there."

Strauss concurred. "It would take too long to four-wheel up the fire road and then hike down. Not enough time."

Langley checked his altimeter. "There is if we put down on Dog Pond. It's just after three. We've got all our gear on board. We'll be on the stream by four. Sneak in an hour and a half of fishing, get back on the plane, take off, I'll have you back at the club dock six o'clock sharp."

Neither Langley nor his passengers saw Evie and Lulu staring up at them as they passed low overhead.

Langley suddenly banked the plane sharp and hard down to the right. The sudden descent jerked the men back in their seats, and for a moment it felt as if the plane were falling, not flying.

Reynolds peered out the window at the puddle of blue that was Dog Pond. "That's not a very big pond. You ever land there before?"

"Once. A long time ago." As Langley leveled off, a pocket of turbulence dropped them three hundred feet.

Shandley tasted vomit in the back of his throat and stopped crying. "What the fuck are you doing?" The pond looked smaller the closer they got to it.

"This is too risky for me. Pull up." That was Ken. The right wing cleared a rock ledge known as the Cat's Tongue by less than ten feet. Their descent grew steeper.

"Anybody who is uncomfortable with the pilot can get out now." Langley had decided they all needed a wake-up call. He was the only one who was still smiling when the pontoons hit the tops of the spruce trees that surrounded Dog Pond.

Evie and Lulu saw Langley's plane in the distance clip the tree line, then drop from view. Listening intently, each hoped for the sound of impact, the bang of a fuel tank exploding. All they heard was the shrill call of a cardinal feasting on pokeberries at the edge of the woods.

"You think they crashed?"

Lulu was looking through binoculars now. "We would have heard it."

"Not if they hit water."

Evie climbed behind Lulu on the electric motorcycle and together they flew into the forest. Disappearing down a game trail, silent as witches on a broom, they hoped for the worst.

Langley pulled back on the stick, revved the engine as the float-plane plunged, and finally got the nose up just enough to keep the Cessna from cartwheeling across the glassy surface of the pond. The floatplane landed on one pontoon and bounced. Langley reversed the prop, the plane keened sideways, and the tip of the left wing dipped into the water. The floatplane spun three-sixty. Yanking the rudder hard to the right, Langley caught just enough air to avoid a head-on with the small rock island in the middle of Dog Pond, and the seaplane slowly came to rest on the far shore.

Reynolds broke the silence. "You could've fucking killed us! What were you thinking?"

Langley lit his pipe. "I wanted to remind Brother Shandley how much better it feels to be alive than dead." As he blew out his match, he stared at Shandley. "Have I made myself clear?"

His passengers let Langley walk ahead and took their time getting into their waders, lingering so they could talk behind his back. Slowly assembling their fly rods, the men watched Langley—fly rod in one hand, walking stick in the other—make his way down the pebbled shoreline, testing his knee as he walked.

His Lost Boys eyed one another as black flies swirled around them. Reynolds was the first to speak. "It wasn't like this when Porter ran the show."

Without looking back, Langley suddenly called out, "I heard that," and laughed as he disappeared into the woods.

Climbing down the narrow path among mammoth slabs of rock dragged down from Canada a hundred thousand years ago by the glacier that once blanketed the forest with a mile-deep river of ice, Langley claimed the fourth and best of the pools for himself. All moss, ferns, and pine; the milky wings of a butterfly danced above a riffle that hid the shadow of a trout.

The bank, thick with conifers, deadfall, and bramble, left no room for a back cast. Langley deftly rolled his fly out across the surface of the pool, careful not to spook the shadow he was after. He hadn't fished the Cascades since his *hunting accident*, and he was pleased that his sense of balance had returned. Waist-deep in the current, he felt more sure-footed than he had in years. Still as a snake on a cold day, Langley watched as his dry fly drifted above the trout and thought of all the fun he had missed hobbling about on a cane, confined to the riverbank in his electric wheelchair. Smiling at all the ways he would make up for lost time, he saw the shadow move, surging just beneath the surface of the stream, shark-like, toward his fly.

Licking his lips with the tip of his tongue, Langley could taste the tingly *I won* feeling that told him he was alive. A heartbeat away from the tug that would signal him to set his hook, a rock suddenly plummeted into the pool and the shadow of the fish he thought he had already caught vanished.

The sight of Evie and Lulu standing up on the boulders that formed the waterfall so startled him that he fell back into the stream. Evie had hoped Langley had crashed and burned, but the sight of him scrambling to regain his footing as water poured into the top of his waders gave her a taste of the satisfaction she was looking for.

Langley demanded, "What do you two want?"

Evie answered by throwing a rock the size of a baseball at his head and Lulu laughed. The women said nothing.

Determined to get a response, Langley shouted up over the babble of water rushing past him, "How's your daughter doing, Evie? I've been thinking about going to Paris and checking in on her again." Evie threw a second stone straight at this head. Ducking, he dropped his rod. Lunging into the stream, he grabbed it just before the current swept it over the next set of falls. When he looked back, the women were gone. Composing himself, Langley called out, "My friends showed me the photos you took of us outside poor Clare's office. Very becoming."

Langley was the only one of the foursome who didn't pull a trout from the Cascades that afternoon. When the floatplane took off from Dog Pond and cleared the tree line with twenty feet to spare, everyone on board thought there was nothing to worry about. Langley did not feel the need to mention running into Evie and Lulu. The women could not hurt him.

Evie Quimby wouldn't risk doing anything that would give him reason to pay a second visit to her daughter, and the nondisparagement clause in the confidentiality agreement Lulu signed made him safe from her. Having always coveted Valhalla, Langley almost wished Lulu would get caught up in the fervor of the #MeToo movement and say something scurrilous about him. As he gained altitude and circled south, he took pleasure in imagining all the ways he could eviscerate Lulu Mannheim's credibility in a court of law. Drug arrests, suicide attempts, month in a mental hospital, the fact that she had tried to rehire him. Langley had an email she sent him apologizing for her "insanity" and begging him to work for her again. And then there was the sex tape of her threesome that was still available online.

As promised, Langley got the Lost Boys back to the clubhouse at six sharp. Quickly showering, he put on a seersucker suit nearly identical to the one he wore thirty-six years ago when Porter Moran invited him up to his town house to discuss his future. Win personally chauffeured Ken's and Tom's wives in an ATV up to the cocktail party in the playhouse so the ladies' shoes would not get muddy.

It was a warm evening. A bar had been set up on the lawn in front of the playhouse so that the members and their wives could enjoy the sunset. The weather obliged and the sky blushed coral and fleshy pink. It wasn't until his second sip of champagne that Langley noticed the obelisk standing tall on the Mannheims' side of the gorge. In the last light of day, something glistened on the face of the stone that had no business being there. As Langley moved to get a better look, he heard the club manager grumbling about Sheriff Colson not responding to the club's noise complaint. Wives were pointing at the marker, wondering aloud what purpose it served. Too far away to read what the capitals of brightly polished brass set into the rock spelled out, Langley borrowed a pair of binoculars that were being passed around.

CHLOÉ QUIMBY CLÉMENT
JULY 1, 2003–AUGUST 18, 2018

The inscription wasn't finished, but as soon as Langley realized it was the daughter's tombstone, he knew there was no telling what Evie would do now.

CHAPTER 44

The stone, like Evie Quimby, was a bafflement to Langley. Why erect a two-thousand-pound, ten-foot-tall memorial to a daughter who died of cancer in front of the cabin where you were drugged, stripped naked, shaved, and . . . More than once during the course of the Mohawk's Club's festivities that weekend, Langley slipped away to the gorge by himself to reminisce about what he thought of as "the intimacies" he had shared with young Evie, and to contemplate the significance of the stone and the message she was sending him by placing it there.

As locals said, Evie Quimby always was "batshit crazy." The fact that she had merely shot him when she had the chance to get away with killing him seventeen years ago proved that to Win Langley. But there was also a cunning to her madness. No question crippling him had been an inspired revenge. He took Evie Quimby seriously.

While the daughter was alive and vulnerable, Evie was controllable. The daughter was leverage, insurance; now that she was dead, Langley regarded Evie as a gutshot animal bleeding in the forest. Like any wounded beast, she was dangerous, but only if you got too close. There was no need to go after her unless . . .

Langley realized the women recognized him as a predator, but they were blind to the peculiar institution he served and the role he played in its machinations. The men who referred to one another as Lost Boys considered themselves businessmen, venture capitalists who exploited commodities, resources, assets that without their husbandry would be wasted. But in Langley's mind, he was a hunter; the others mere harvesters. He stalked the game and let his friends do the skinning. Win Langley found it exciting that Evie was out there in the woods wanting to do her worst and unable to hurt him.

But Evie was not finished with the tombstone. The next day, when Lulu Mannheim's name was suddenly chiseled into the stone, Langley was forced to reevaluate what was happening on the other side of the gorge. Lulu was the one who had paid for the stone and hired the helicopter that had ferried it down-lake. Given that it was on Mannheim property, he puzzled over its placement. It occurred to him that it was in part simply the women's way of saying *fuck you* to the patriarchy of the Mohawk Club, but it also occurred to Langley that the giant tombstone was placed in almost the exact spot where misguided Charlie had fallen to his death in bridal white. Naturally, Win Langley kept to himself all of the different thoughts the stone conjured.

Langley and his Lost Boys didn't feel the full weight of the stone until the third and final day of the annual meeting. In the morning there was a pigeon-shooting competition. The members and their wives sat in gilded party chairs behind the shooters. Knowing that throwing live birds into the air for target practice was illegal and that a less esteemed club would have been shut down for such an offense, there was a sense of forbidden fun to the contest. When it was over, Tom Reynolds was given a silver loving cup for killing fifty out of fifty, and the dead birds were collected and strewn among a stand of oak in the forest as a treat for the wild boar that would be hunted with dogs when the season opened in November.

Lunch was an old-fashioned picnic by the lake. To make the one weekend a year where wives were invited to the club fun for the ladies, everyone was instructed to dress up as if it were 1897. The women wore long skirts and frilly high-neck blouses, and the ones who really liked to dress up accessorized with parasols and white kid gloves. The men all sported knickers and straw boaters except for Ken Strauss, who came as a city slicker and looked the part with a derby and spats. Old photographs were consulted and everything was just as it was in the first annual meeting back in 1897, even the menu, which featured potted turtle.

When Ken sighed, "Ah, the good old days. No income tax and women can't vote," his wife Bissie threw a roll at him. Langley applauded and announced, "I want it on record that I for one am embarrassed to belong to the last club in America that doesn't allow women to join."

His fellow members took exception and began to toss out the names of other clubs where men reigned alone and supreme. Long Pole Country Club, Bohemian Grove, etc. One wife who was on her third glass of wine interrupted, "I think we should start a hunting and fishing club for women only. Make all the men who work there wear tight shorts and shave their legs."

"You'd get sued for sexual harassment." Langley was relieved everyone had stopped talking about the tombstone across from the playhouse, and was enjoying the banter when Tom whispered in his ear, "We need to talk."

Ken and Peter Shandley had gone out on the float dock. Even at a distance, Langley could tell that Shandley was agitated. Strauss looked grim. The conversation turned to a discussion about the difference between flirting, making a pass, and harassment. When one woman volunteered that she put a can of mace in her thirteen-year-old daughter's Christmas stocking, Langley excused himself and followed Tom out onto the long, narrow wooden catwalk that led out to the float dock where the seaplanes were moored and the other two Lost Boys were waiting.

As soon as Langley got there, Shandley blurted out, "What the fuck is my wife's name doing there?"

"I don't know what you're talking about, but let's remember voices carry on the water." Dessert was just being served a hundred yards away. Shandley pulled out his cell phone and showed him a photograph he'd taken less than an hour ago. The final inscription on the tombstone read:

CHLOÉ QUIMBY CLÉMENT
JULY 1, 2003–AUGUST 18, 2018

BELOVED DAUGHTER OF EVIE QUIMBY
GRANDDAUGHTER OF FLO QUIMBY
FRIEND OF LULU MANNHEIM
NIECE OF CLARE LOUGHTON

Just below Clare's name in slightly larger letters, Evie had chiseled out the words GONE BUT NOT FORGOTTEN. The last line read like a threat.

CHAPTER 45

The giant tombstone for Evie's daughter up on top of the gorge was the subject of much debate in Rangeley. Some thought it a touching gesture by a bereaved mother with deep roots in the Sister Lakes. Others saw it as just another example of the Quimbys' need to do things differently than normal people. Who the hell Clare Loughton was was a mystery to everyone but Sheriff Dill Colson.

Flo stayed on in Europe after Evie and Lulu. When she finally returned, her absence was explained by a walking cast on her right foot. Spotting her limping up Main Street, walking stick in hand, Dill pulled his cruiser over and got out to offer his condolences. "I'm sorry for your loss, Flo."

"Being sorry for the way things are won't change them." A yellow-and-red parrot feather found in the Jardin du Luxembourg was woven into her hair.

"Well, if there's anything I can do to help."

"How about you getting my husband out of prison?"

"He'll be home soon."

" 'Soon' is a word like 'sorry,' and I'm running out of time to make a difference." As Flo continued on down the street, Dill called after her. "What have you done to your foot?"

Flo's expression softened. "When I was in Paris, I felt the need to get falling-down drunk in the hope that I'd feel better about life in the morning. It didn't work." Having known the Quimbys his whole life, it all made sense to Dill . . . sort of.

That night, when Dill's shift was over, he stopped at Mary Lou's to get a cup of coffee for the ride home. Kevin, the Morlock, who much to everyone's surprise now had a job at the Mohawk Club, was holding forth as he brown-bagged a beer. The sheriff came in just in time to hear Kevin tell Scrotum that he'd seen Hank Clinger busting a nut carrying "old Pocahontas with her busted foot" up to the top of the gorge and then watched Flo, Lulu, and Evie scatter an urnful of ashes. Kevin laughed as he described the scene. "It was hilarious. The wind blew the shit right back in the bitches' faces." The sheriff went outside and wrote Kevin's truck a ticket for a broken taillight that wasn't broken until Dill hit it with his billy club. As he drove home, the sheriff considered the possibility that everyone in Rangeley was part Morlock, himself and Evie included.

Two days after they scattered the ashes, a hard rain fell at dawn and didn't let up. By then, Lulu and Evie had talked Flo into staying at Valhalla until the cast came off. As Flo and Lulu lingered over coffee that a.m. in the kitchen, Evie went out onto the porch and sat on a cushioned bench where the Wi-Fi was strong. Rain pelted the lake, fog moved down through the pines, and the far shore disappeared.

Evie opened her laptop to check her emails and began to weep.

> Dear Mama,
> I want you to know that being dead isn't
> as scary as you'd think . . .

Evie remembered the night in the hospital back in Paris when her daughter had woken from a nightmare drenched in sweat and had promised to send an email if she found out there was something "after all this." Knowing the message had been written months ago and sent via a preprogrammed email scheduler called Boomerang did not make the communiqué any less miraculous or ghostly to Evie. Tears streaming down her face, she closed her eyes and smiled. The last line of this message from the dead read:

> I know reading this is making you cry, so
> listen to what I'm telling you. I am your

sensei now and sensei says when you think
of me, I want you to smile.

When Flo and Lulu came out onto the porch and read the email,
they too began to weep. Catching a glimpse of one another trying to
smile through their tears, the women began to laugh. Mascara running down her cheeks, Lulu asked, "What's a sensei?"

"It's what Chloé called her karate teacher. When she was little she
used to say, 'Mais non, sensei,' to make me laugh when I told her to
clean up her bedroom. Sensei means *the one who has gone before you.*"

The women had stopped crying now and were sharing funny stories about Chloé when Lulu looked up and saw Dill's cruiser coming
down the driveway. "What the hell is he doing here?"

Evie closed her laptop. "I invited him."

"What for?" Flo was just lighting up one of Buddy's cigars.

"He called and said he had some questions to ask me when I felt up
to it. He sent me a condolence card. I wanted to get it over with."

"You're not thinking about telling him?" Lulu watched as Dill got
out of the cruiser.

Evie shook her head *no.* "Like Buddy used to say, 'Putting off
answering a sheriff's questions just gives the law more time to realize
they're not asking the right questions.' "

Dill came up onto the porch and they went into the library. A maid
took his wet rain slicker and hat and hung them in the front hall. A fire
was lit and another maid brought out coffee and cake. Dill said, "This
isn't a social visit," and pulled out a tape recorder.

"Does that mean I should take away the cake or call my lawyer?"
Lulu said it as if it were a joke, but Dill didn't laugh.

"I just thought I'd tape our conversation so I don't misquote anybody." As Evie waited for Dill to ask his questions, she felt her pulse
rise and her breath quicken. Dill didn't scare her, but his uniform
did. "Evie, when I called you back in May to check on how things
were going for your daughter, why didn't you mention that the sister

you were getting the bone marrow transplant from was your twin. I mean, most people would have said something about discovering something like that. And then you not saying anything about this new sister of yours being worth all that money or the fact that she jumped off a roof?"

"It didn't seem important. All I had time to think about was my daughter."

"Were you included in Clare Loughton's will?"

Evie found the question insulting. "Why would she leave me anything? I barely knew her."

The fire spit a coal out onto the carpet. Flo kicked it back before it could burn a mark. "Why are you so interested in Clare Loughton?"

"I just want to understand why you put her name on your daughter's memorial."

"It was a gesture. I wanted people to remember her."

"People in general, or people belonging to the Mohawk Club?" Dill was better at asking questions than they had expected.

"What's your problem, Dill?" Evie gave Dill the same look she did when they'd hid from the Morlocks and he wet his pants.

Dill cleared his throat. "Could I talk to Evie alone?"

"It's not necessary."

Dill pulled the Mohawk Club directory out of his pocket. "I think one of the people in this book raped you." Evie reached for a piece of cake and chewed slowly, trying to think of what was safe to say. "Knowing you the way I do, I think putting up that marker is your way of saying to that person, 'I've got nothing to lose and I'm coming for you.' "

"If I was coming for somebody, why would I warn them?"

"That's the part I haven't figured out."

Dill pushed on. "I know who it was, Evie." She hadn't expected this.

Flo jumped out of her seat and shouted as if she didn't already know the answer, "Well who the fuck did it?"

"Porter Moran. It's why Buddy set the fire that killed him."

Flo turned her back. "You can't warn the dead."

"Maybe Moran had an accomplice?" Dill studied Evie's face for a reaction. When he didn't get one, he pushed on. "Evie, if there's someone who was involved in your assault who's still alive, why not come forward and press charges?"

"The same reason I didn't seventeen years ago. I was drugged. My testimony wouldn't hold up in court."

"Why are you not telling me the truth, Evie?"

"I haven't said a single thing to you that's a lie."

"That's not the same thing as telling me the truth."

Evie smiled. "Now you're the one who's starting to sound like Buddy."

Dill put away his tape recorder. "I'm trying to help you, Evie."

"And I'm trying to keep you out of trouble."

Dill took a piece of cake after all. "What are your plans?"

"I'm driving up to Canada with Lulu." That was the only falsehood she told him.

"What happens after that?"

"I'll return to Paris. Go back to fixing broken things."

"Well, that's a relief."

"How so?"

"You won't be my problem."

They talked for another ten minutes, then Dill got up and put on his rain slicker and hat. The last thing he said was, "If you're around these parts for hunting season, you be sure to get a license. I don't want to have to arrest you."

They drove up to the Quimby cabin in the rain that afternoon. Flo wanted to check on her garden. She had written Buddy promising to pickle some tomatoes and bring them to him when she drove over to the Franklin Correctional Facility on visiting day. Except for the fact that a family of squirrels had come down the chimney without an exit strategy and expired in the firebox of the woodstove in the kitchen, everything was in order. The squirrels had started to rot. They opened up all the windows to air out the stink and burned sage and sprinkled dry lavender, but Flo couldn't get the smell of dead things out of her nose.

While her mother picked her heirloom tomatoes and Lulu harvested snap peas, Evie wandered over to the skinning shed and thought about the life lessons she had learned there. When she opened the door, a breeze made a wind chime out of the hundred-plus cobwebbed traps that hung from the rafters. All manner of catching devices tinkled overhead: leg traps of assorted gauges, rusty Conibear traps, cable steel snares that garroted creatures who put their noses where they didn't belong. Hunger and curiosity killed most. And then there were those baited by the musk of calling lures who found death in search of sex. Evie remembered Buddy telling her, "You want to catch an animal, you've got to think like that animal. And once you trap it, be damn sure it doesn't bite you."

Lulu ate more snap peas than she put in her basket. Flo was just picking the last of the tomatoes when she looked up and saw Evie checking out the old Willys. Flo called out, "Battery's dead and the oil pan cracked going over a rock." Flo knew Evie wasn't interested in going anywhere in the rusted-out Jeep when she saw her daughter reach in under the front seat and pull out something small, wrapped up in oilcloth, that Buddy had hidden there a long time ago. Watching the way Evie palmed the .32-caliber pistol into her pocket, it scared Flo how much of Buddy had rubbed off on her daughter.

Cupping her hand as she lit up a cigarillo, Flo inhaled the smell that clung to her husband when he climbed into bed after they had had an argument; it was Flo's turn to recall one of Buddy's favorite axioms: *If you don't have the grit to finish a job, don't start it.*

~ ~ ~

The next morning, Lulu assembled the entire staff of the Great Camp, gardeners and gamekeepers included, on the front porch and made an announcement. "I'm going away for two weeks. Mrs. Quimby will be staying here and in my absence you should treat any and all of her requests as though they were mine." The kitchen staff in particular didn't like the idea of being bossed around by Flo.

Among the other things pertaining to the care and maintenance of Valhalla that were discussed that morning was the fact that kids had been buzzing the house with remote-controlled toy drones. *Lulu* instructed the gamekeepers to shoot them down. It was all very North Country *Downton Abbey*, especially when Lulu finished up by informing her employees, "You will all be amused to know that I'm finally going to learn how to fly-fish. Evie and I are going to the Gaspé Peninsula in Canada where she will be teaching me how to catch a salmon in the Grande-Cascapédia." Wild, cold, remote; located on the south shore of the Saint Lawrence River where it meets the Atlantic, the Gaspé made Rangeley seem cosmopolitan.

The Cascapédia was not a river to learn how to fly-fish on. Given that Lulu Mannheim had never been seen with a rod in her hand, her head caretaker, Hank Clinger, was surprised by the announcement. More out of character, Lulu was journeying up to the Saint Lawrence by car rather than floatplane—it was a ten-hour drive. When Hank suggested his employer might want to consider mastering the basics of fly-fishing in her own lake, Lulu smiled. "Have the Range Rover serviced by tomorrow." Grand and imperious, it was as if Lulu was deliberately giving her staff reason to trash her at the bar in town after work.

That afternoon the women went into Harlan's Tackle Shop on Main Street and Evie helped Lulu pick out a ten-foot graphite rod, two titanium reels, lines, leaders, chest-high waders, and a fluorescent life vest inflated by a small canister of compressed air, plus four dozen flies with names like *Lady Amherst*, *Silver Doctor*, *Curry's Red*, and *Munro's Killer*.

The bill came to over four thousand dollars. Old Man Harlan was overjoyed. When he found out Lulu was going to wade out into the Grande-Cascapédia—which means strong current in Mi'kmaq—for her first fly-fishing lesson, he thought but did not say, *That's as good a way as any to drown.*

Harlan delighted in telling anyone and everyone who came into his shop in the days to come about the jaw-dropping amount of money Lulu had spent on fishing equipment. Laughter was shared at the arrogance and stupidity of the rich woman thinking that buying a lot of expensive gear would catch her a salmon.

Kinder souls in Rangeley assumed going fishing up in Canada was Lulu's way of taking Evie's mind off the grief of losing her daughter. Others took it as proof that Scrotum was right about the women being lesbian. He and the Morlocks made more than a few crude jokes at the bar about what the women would get up to with their fishing poles in their tent at night. Lulu and Evie were counting on the loose talk. They didn't want Langley or his friends to know they were going to New York City on a very different kind of fishing expedition.

The day of their departure broke blue-skied and Indian-summer warm. It had been a long time since Evie had seen an Adirondack summer take its final bow. The leaves of the hardwoods the original Adolphus had planted were so green it was hard to imagine that in two weeks they'd start to turn color and fall. She had forgotten how quickly the end comes. Hank Clinger loaded their luggage into the Range Rover. As they got ready to go, Flo limped down off the porch and stuck a plastic Virgin Mary on the dashboard. Lulu thought it was funny. Evie asked her mother, "What's that for?"

"Luck." Hank thought they were talking about fishing. A drone buzzed overhead. One of the gamekeepers pulled a shotgun out of the back of his pickup and fired off two shots. The drone crashed into the lake fifty yards offshore and sank. If it had come down on dry land, they would have seen that it contained a video camera and asked why.

Evie got behind the wheel, and as they headed out the drive Lulu thoughtfully lit a Marlboro Light, put her feet up on the dashboard, and addressed the plastic Virgin. "I know, I shouldn't be doing this, but . . . what the fuck."

Evie had given her friend more than one opportunity to pull out. "If you've changed your mind, don't want to go to New York, I understand."

"I'm talking about this." Lulu held up her cigarette. "Smoking." Lulu had quit in Paris. It was her first cigarette since.

"I mean, I'm not a moron. I can read the warning on the box. I know it's hazardous to my health." Lulu exhaled a ring of smoke. "Yet, every time I swear off them, tell myself, *Never again will my lips touch one of these fuckers*, something in me can't resist." Waxing philosophical, Lulu asked, "Did it ever occur to you that cigarettes and men are similar vices?" Lulu talked about men the way men talked about football or golf. They were a pastime to her, a hobby, escape.

Evie was focused on one particular man—Win Langley. Having no idea where the journey she was setting off on would take her or end, she felt obliged to say, "What I'm saying, Lulu, is you don't have to be part of this."

"I do, actually. When we spooked Langley up at the Cascades, he shouted, 'My friends showed me the photos you took of us,' not *friend*, *friends* plural. I gave those photographs you took of them leaving Clare's office to six men—my banker, my attorney, my money manager, my accountant, and the two old farts who have been the trustees of my inheritance since 2001. Men I pay a great deal of money to to be loyal to me. Men I thought were *my* friends, and since it appears at least two of these fuckers feel more indebted to Langley than they do to me, I'm going to find out who they are, fire their asses, and sue the shit out them." Lulu talked like it was all about money, but Evie knew that wasn't what bothered her friend the most. Late at night, when they shared a bedroom in Paris, she had heard Lulu sigh in her sleep with longing and bitterness, "Fucking Charlie."

At Valhalla's front gate, Evie turned left and took the county road east. Google Maps told them that their real destination, NYC, was seven hours and thirty-seven minutes away. Twenty minutes later, just as they were coming out of a slow turn that cut through a stretch of state forest thick with the white trunks of aspens, Evie saw a man kneeling on the side of the road by the limp body of a large pale yellow Lab with a bandanna tied around its neck. The women could tell by the way the man cradled the animal's head that he was on a first-name basis with the injured dog.

The size and coloring of the animal made Evie think of Clovis, which in turn made her think of Chloé sobbing at age twelve when distemper turned Clovis mean and they had to put him down. Evie slammed on the brakes and jumped out of the Range Rover, calling out, "Your dog get hit by a car?"

There was a frantic helplessness in the man's voice when he responded, "No. I don't know what's wrong with her." When she first saw him she thought he was younger, but as she ran toward him, she noticed there was gray in the blond of his beard. Stanford T-shirt, a Tibetan mala bracelet around his wrist told Evie he wasn't a local.

Evie put her hand on the dog and was relieved to discover it was still breathing. The man explained, "I was getting ready to go kayaking down Cold Brook and she jumped out the window of my camper to chase deer." Cold Brook was a mile and a half back in the woods. He wore hiking shorts and his bare legs were scratched raw and bleeding from running through the brambles and deadfall after the dog. "When I found her she was going into convulsions." It sounded to Evie like the dog had gotten into a trap, baited with poisoned meat. Her dog Homer died that way, but she didn't want to say that to the man.

Lulu was behind the wheel of the Range Rover now. Shouting, "Get the dog in the car and we'll drive you to a vet," Lulu pulled a U-turn. The driver of the oncoming car stood on his horn and shouted, "Asshole." Lulu called back, "Fuck off," and put the pedal to the metal.

Passing a logging truck on a blind curve, it occurred to Evie that they and the dog might die before they got to the vet. The stranger in the backseat talked soothingly to the dog as though it were a sick child. "You're going to be okay, Biscuit."

Somewhere en route Lulu said, "I'm Lulu by the way. That's Evie." It wasn't until Biscuit's owner introduced himself as Marcus that Evie noticed he had green eyes. As Evie remembered it, the nearest vet was an hour away in Speculator. She wasn't optimistic Biscuit would survive the journey; Homer hadn't. Just outside Rangeley, Lulu swerved into the parking lot of the old Evinrude dealership, which was now the Sister Lakes Animal Hospital.

The waiting room was crowded: a woman with a sick parakeet, an old man with a mutt that needed shots: and a mother and child holding a toy poodle, all three suffering from ringworm. Marcus had the unconscious Lab in his arms when they burst through the door. The receptionist heard the word "poison" and hurried them into the back of the clinic. Marcus reappeared a moment later, looking grim. "They're going to pump her stomach." Looking away as if he were about to tear up, he forced a smile. "I don't know how to thank you for all your help. There's no need you waiting around. I'll call a taxi when I'm finished here."

The parakeet lady laughed at the mention of the word "taxi." Lulu explained, "There's no taxis in Rangeley, we'll wait for you." Evie assumed Lulu was being nice because Marcus had good legs and green eyes. Not wanting to catch ringworm from the poodle family, they went outside and avoided small talk by gazing at their smartphones. Evie was sure the dog wasn't going to make it.

When the vet appeared a half hour later with Biscuit alive, well, and wagging her tail, Evie was surprised and Marcus was overjoyed. The vet was tall, stoop-shouldered, freckled, and had a foreign accent Evie couldn't place. "As soon as I pumped her stomach she woke up. No sign of poison, which is curious. Could be neurological—the X-rays did not reveal anything, again curious. So, it's good news, but still potentially worrisome." Evie didn't figure out who the vet was until he said, "You must be Evie. Dill talks about you all the time. I'm Jan."

"Who's Dill?" Marcus was scratching Biscuit's stomach.

"Jan's husband is the sheriff. We grew up together here."

Marcus smiled and stared at Evie a moment longer than was necessary before he said, "Must have been idyllic."

Evie let it go with, "Not really." The bill was $211. Marcus took a waterproof wallet out of his back pocket and handed over three one-hundred-dollar bills. When the vet couldn't make change, Marcus told him to donate the difference to the local ASPCA. There was no doubt that he was a genuinely nice guy.

On the ride back, Biscuit panted and Marcus, who didn't mention his last name, grew more talkative. Gesturing to the fly rods and waders in the back of the Range Rover, he asked, "Where are you going fishing?"

Evie and Lulu both said, "Canada," and felt foolish for lying to the stranger.

"Do you live in Rangeley year-round?"

Lulu answered for them. "No, I live in New York, I just come up here for weekends and in the summer. Evie's visiting. She lives in Paris. She's a famous art restorer."

"I'm impressed."

"There's no such thing as a famous art restorer."

Marcus switched gears to French, "Quelle sorte de choses restaurez-vous?" His accent was better than hers.

"Whatever needs fixing. Sculpture mostly."

"Where do you live in Paris?"

"On Rue Daguerre. Near the Montparnasse Cemetery."

"Didn't the mobile guy, Alexander Calder, have a studio on that street?" Clearly Marcus wasn't your average kayaker with a dog.

"Are you in the art world?"

"No, I just appreciate beautiful things I can't afford to possess."

Lulu was planning on driving him down to the stretch on Cold Brook where the kayakers parked, but when they passed the spot where they had first seen him and the sick dog, Marcus spoke up. "You can let me out here. I've put you two to enough trouble. We'll walk back down to the falls." As he got out of the car he told Biscuit to sit, then reached into Evie's car window to shake hands. "It was nice meeting you both. You know, I'm in New York every few weeks for business. You've been so kind. When you get back from Canada, I'd love to take you both out to dinner or lunch in the city to show my appreciation."

Evie started to say, "That's not necessary," when Lulu cut her off. "That would be great, our number is 917-324-5550. He punched it out in his cell phone, shouted thanks, and disappeared into the rustle of aspen leaves in the wind." Lulu had a smirk on her face as she headed down the road.

"Why did you give him my number?"

"Because I saw how he was looking at you. He likes you."

"Don't be ridiculous."

"And I saw how you were looking at him."

"You're projecting."

"He's handsome, he has green eyes, he speaks French, he's a dog lover, and has a black American Express card."

"How do you know that?"

"I saw it when he opened his wallet to pay the vet. He's a catch and you could use some cheering up."

"There's only one thing that will cheer me up." Evie was thinking of the promise she made to her daughter to find out what happened to Clare Loughton.

Lulu wouldn't leave it alone. "Evie, how long has it been since you had sex?"

"None of your business."

"Six months? A year? A year and a half?" Suspecting it had been longer than that, Lulu told her with genuine concern, "That's unhealthy."

PART VII

INADMISSIBLE EVIDENCE

CHAPTER 46

Wanting the world in general and Langley in particular to believe that they had retreated in grief to the Gaspé Peninsula, the women did not stay in Lulu's loft when they finally got to the city that night. They had talked it through and agreed not to set foot in Tribeca and to avoid any of the luxe neighborhoods or trendy restaurants where Lulu might be recognized. Instead, Evie and Lulu camped out in a drab and barren two-bedroom floor-through in the East Village that had been advertised on French Airbnb as "bohemian chic" and featured water bugs the size of mice. Knowing that her accountant could have been one of the "friends" who passed on the photo to Langley, Lulu avoided leaving a trail of credit card receipts by stuffing twenty thousand dollars in cash into her backpack. Tired from the drive, they ordered in sushi that was dubious and Lulu cracked open a bottle of cognac. "I feel like I'm in a Nancy Drew novel written by Patricia Highsmith."

Evie laughed. "It feels more *American Psycho* to me."

As Evie lay in bed that night, she thought about Biscuit and the dog lover with green eyes and wondered aloud, "What the fuck am I doing?" When sleep came, she dreamed she was locked inside a coffin with Chloé.

At the end of that last sad day in Paris, Lulu had called the president of Ortley Security and made an unusual request. Halfway through telling the Mormon former FBI agent, Ogden Ortley, what she wanted, Ortley cut her off. "We're not in the business of committing felonies for our clients." Less than a minute after he hung up on her, Ortley called back on another line and recommended an "independent contractor" who might be helpful in obtaining the kind of information she and Evie desired. Describing him only as "Israeli, ex-Mossad, discreet, and very expensive," Ortley gave her a phone number and a first name—Ephraim. Before he hung up the second time, Ortley, on speakerphone, cautioned, "You know you two are about to cross a line there is no coming back from."

Evie spoke for both of them when she said, "That line was crossed a long time ago."

Since returning to the States they had had two short phone conversations with Ephraim. His voice sounded just like Omar Sharif in *Lawrence of Arabia*. At the end of their last phone call he reminded them, "Ladies, I trust you understand that the documents I am obtaining for you cannot be used in court."

When Evie said, "We just want to know the truth," Ephraim sighed long-distance. "That might come at a price you're not prepared to pay."

Lulu growled, "How much?"

Ephraim laughed. "I was speaking metaphorically."

Other than Flo, Ephraim was the only other person in the world who knew Evie and Lulu's fishing trip to Canada had taken them to an apartment on the top floor of a brownstone between Avenues A and B.

As had been prearranged, the independent contractor came to make a report the next morning at 10 a.m. The women were underimpressed. Ephraim Tenenbaum was an elfin man, less than five feet tall with a clubfoot. His face was all jaw and made Evie think of a nutcracker. Introducing himself, he asked for a cup of hot water and produced his own tea bag. When Lulu lit a cigarette, he smiled impishly. "If you persist in smoking in my presence, we will have to do this over the phone. So if you please, save us the bother." He was politely rude.

Once Lulu had grudgingly put out her cigarette, he handed her a flash drive. "On it you will find Clare Loughton's prenuptial agreement with her husband Peter Shandley and a copy of her will, which the probate judge ruled favorably upon last week."

Lulu flicked her lighter. "Give us the highlights?"

The little man opened his laptop. "The husband inherits twenty million dollars and the apartment on Park Ave. More interesting to you ladies is the fact that if your friend had lived eleven months longer and had been married for a full four years, according to the provisions in the prenuptial the husband would have received an additional ten million dollars, which is to say Mr. Peter Shandley had a great many reasons not to want his wife to jump off the terrace last May."

It wasn't what Evie expected or wanted to learn. "Who gets all Clare's money?"

Lulu chimed in. "She had to be worth seven hundred million dollars, probably more."

Ephraim smiled. "It all goes to the charitable foundation she established prior to her marriage to Shandley. The other men you asked about—Strauss, Langley, and Reynolds—benefited in no way from this woman's death."

Evie felt stupid. Lulu got angry. "Half Clare's fucking assets are in real estate, maybe more. Who's going to liquidate it?"

Ephraim enjoyed watching the women overreact. "Her trustees. One of whom, by the way, is a former judge who was appointed after your father, Mr. Quimby, set fire to a previous trustee."

"Porter Moran was one of Clare's original trustees?"

"I thought you'd find that a curious coincidence. Also interesting is the fact that Mr. Moran's town house was purchased by Mr. Langley."

"Did you find out anything more about Reynolds and Strauss?"

Ephraim hunched over his laptop. "They're middle-class boys who squeaked into the Ivy League playing sports. Strauss—squash, Reynolds—football. Mediocre students until they interned for Langley. Then they buckled down. Harvard Business School, both married very rich women."

Lulu asked, "How rich?"

"Roughly in the four-to-five-hundred-million-dollar range, plus moneys that have been set aside in trusts for future generations.

Within two or three years each husband had made a series of investments that made them wealthy in their own right. Midsize, privately held companies, a shopping mall in California, overseas real estate deals—"

Lulu interrupted, "Which they bought into with their wives' money."

"That's what you'd expect, but I went over their tax returns. Corporate and personal. They raised the money independently—banks, private equity. Neither took a penny from their wives or has ever managed their spouse's money. They are what used to be called Horatio Algers who happened to have the very good fortune to fall in love with rich women." Ephraim laughed to himself as he sat back from the laptop.

"What's so funny?"

"My father always used to say it is as easy to marry a rich woman as a poor woman."

Lulu looked at the little man as if she wanted to shoot him. "Why didn't you, then?"

"I didn't want sex to feel like a job. No offense."

"None taken. Any idea who passed on the photo Evie took of Langley and the others?"

"Your guess is as good as mine, Miss Mannheim."

"I'm not paying you to guess."

"None of the men in your employment who had access to the photograph are close friends with Langley, yet all of them have made his acquaintance. Three belong to the same club here in New York, two serve with Langley on the board of the same environmental organization, and all six of them attended at least one of the same schools Langley went to. My advice is that since you don't know which one of them betrayed you, replace all of them and don't explain your decision."

"Why the hell not?"

"Because all six have sterling reputations, whereas you've lived . . . a colorful life. They can hurt you far more than you can hurt them."

Ephraim closed his laptop. "Do you mind telling me why you're so certain there was something nefarious about your friend's death?"

Evie answered, "Our reasons are personal."

"If you want to share them with me, I'll give you my opinion free of charge."

Lulu was flicking her lighter again. "No thanks."

"Well, for what it's worth, I hope you're wrong about these men."

"Why?"

Ephraim stood up and put his computer in his bag. "Because if you're right about them, you can't win the fight I sense you have already started."

As the Israeli limped out the door and down the hall, Evie called out after him, "How do we know you haven't sold us out to Langley too?"

"You can't, but in my expert opinion, if I had done that, you would have heard from Mr. Langley by now."

Evie double-locked the door; she was only half listening when Lulu, rummaging through her suitcase, muttered, "I can't find my phone charger, can I borrow yours?"

"It's in my backpack." Evie was thinking about her father, missing him and feeling guilty for never visiting him in prison, when Lulu suddenly demanded, "What the fuck is this?" Lulu held up a pistol by two fingers as if she were afraid of leaving her fingerprints on the grip. It was the gun Evie had taken from under the front seat of the Willys. Evie had forgotten it was in her backpack.

"It's a .32-caliber revolver. Be careful, it's loaded." Buddy called it a "jump gun." Until that moment it never occurred to Evie to consider whether her father meant that it was to be used when you got jumped or to jump somebody.

The pistol scared Lulu. "What the hell is a gun doing in your bag? You go to jail for having an unlicensed pistol in New York City. What kind of shit are you getting me into, Evie?"

"You're blaming me for getting you into shit?" They had never had this conversation. "If I hadn't gotten into your car that day down by Cold Brook, Langley wouldn't be my fucking problem! Aren't you tired of being fucked over and not doing anything about it?"

Lulu wasn't used to being shouted at. "That has nothing to do with you bringing a gun on this trip without asking my permission."

"Permission? Do you hear yourself, Your Majesty?" Lulu's cheeks flushed as if she'd just been slapped. Evie went into the bedroom and started stuffing her clothes in her bag. "I get it. You're scared. I can do this by myself."

"You can't. You need me and you know it." Lulu snatched the duffel bag from Evie's hands. "And I'm not talking just about my money." Lulu's lip trembled and her carapace of wealth and privilege cracked. "And I am profoundly sorry for inflicting Langley and all the rest of the shit in my life on you. And I had tried with Clare to make up for it. And now that's turned to shit too, unless . . ."

Evie could see the effort it took for her friend not to be the women who broke precious things. "I do need your help and I don't blame you, okay?" Instead of hugging it out, Evie bummed a Marlboro Light. Lighting up, inhaling the smoke of all the things, good and bad, that bonded them, Evie tried not to think of the promise she made to Chloé that last day in the hospital to stop smoking.

Lulu was still holding the revolver. Except for its weight, it looked like a toy. "What are you planning to do with this gun?"

Evie shrugged. "Better to have it and not need it than need it and not have it." It was another one of Buddy's favorite sayings. Evie watched Lulu primly put the nickel-plated pistol in her Chanel purse. "What are you going to do with the damn gun?"

Lulu shouldered her purse. "I'll give it back to you when and if I think we need to shoot somebody." Evie let out a belly laugh so reckless it sounded like Buddy was in the room with them, and not just his jump gun. They were friends again.

Lulu downloaded the flash drive and spent the next four hours poring over the documents in the hope that Ephraim had missed something: a detail that would make the malfeasance they sensed had occurred become tangible. So far there was nothing. Evie was baffled by the legalese that seemed designed to remind her that she had never graduated from high school. She gave up and googled Charlie's brother, Dr. Nicholas Radetzky.

First she skimmed the tabloid story headlined SHRINK BUSTED FOR KIDDIE PORN. She then read an article that appeared in the *New York Times* three days later chronicling the discovery that Dr. Radetzky was falsely incriminated for possessing child pornography by a former patient with a grudge. "What if it happened the way Charlie's brother first told it?"

Lulu looked up from the computer screen. "What if what happened?"

"What if Langley did put the kiddie porn on Radetzky's computer to discredit him before Radetzy could accuse Langley of having Charlie killed. Somebody like Ephraim could do that easily and then just as easily make it seem, a few days later, as if the porn came from one of Radetzky's patients."

"But if Langley went to the effort of ruining Radetzky's reputation by getting him arrested, why would he want to exonerate him? Doesn't make any fucking sense."

"It does. We just haven't figured it out."

Charlie's brother lived in Red Hook, a half block off the water in a gentrified warehouse. When they rang his bell and got no response, they waited in the Range Rover and Evie listened to Lulu reminisce about Charlie in a way that made it clear he was not dead to her.

Forty minutes later, Dr. Radetzky walked right past them, his arm draped over the shoulder of a ten-year-old boy bouncing a basketball. Evie and Lulu were thinking *perv* until they saw Radetzky's ex-wife pull up and the couple argue about their custody arrangement. The wife was an hour early. When the son came out of the building with his overnight bag, they entered without ringing Radetzky's bell. They were right to think he wouldn't have buzzed them in.

Radetzky was watching a basketball game on TV. When they knocked, he called out, "It's unlocked, Zeke." When he looked up and saw the women standing in his apartment, his smile evaporated. "I have no interest in talking to either one of you. Please leave."

His apartment was all bookshelves, meticulously organized. Research papers neatly stacked and boxed, all carefully labeled and indexed. Evie spoke first. "We need your help."

Charlie's brother put on his shrink voice. "That's interesting, because when I last saw you in the parking lot outside that Holiday Inn at the airport and asked you to help me, begged you, do you remember your response? You locked your car doors and threatened to call the police."

"I'm sorry. I shouldn't have done that. I was scared, my daughter was sick." Evie knew she had no right to ask this man anything. "Just because I was a coward doesn't mean you have to be one."

"I'm asking you again, leave. Our conversation is over."

Lulu blurted out, "I'll pay you to tell us what you found out about Charlie and Langley."

Radetzky looked at her with clinical contempt. "I would have thought your relationship with my brother would have taught you there are some things money can't buy."

Lulu made it worse when she said, "I have a right to know what happened."

"If you don't leave my apartment right now, I'm calling the police." He had his phone out.

"We should go now, Lulu."

Evie was heading toward the door when Lulu shouted, "Put the fucking phone down and tell me the truth." She was pointing the .32-caliber revolver at Dr. Radetzky's head.

"Please put away the gun." His voice was still calm, but his eyes and hands were not.

"Lulu, stop." Evie looked as terrified as Radetzky.

Radetzky backed away. "I'm frightened." He might have been talking to himself.

"A crazy rich bitch with a gun, you should be scared." Lulu suddenly sounded like Buddy.

The temperature in the room cooled when Dr. Radetzky clarified, "I'm frightened of Langley, not the gun, Miss Mannheim." He dropped his cell phone and crumpled onto the couch. Lulu's hands were trembling as she lowered the pistol.

Evie did most of the talking after that. "In the parking lot at the airport that day, you told me Langley put kiddie porn on your computer, got you arrested to stop you, ruin your reputation so no one would believe you."

"I can't prove it and Langley never admitted it, but I am absolutely certain that's what happened."

"You're saying Langley framed your patient?"

"Yes." Radetzky stared out the window at the harbor. In the distance a tugboat was towing a barge of garbage out to sea.

"What did you have to do to get Langley to let you off the hook? He goes to all that effort to incriminate you, then clears your name by pinning the blame on your patient? What did you have to do to get your life back?"

"Nothing. . . . That's what made it so terrifying. If he had threatened me, actually told me to stop asking questions about my brother's death, it would have been frightening, but I would have known what I was dealing with. But Langley never said a word that could be construed as a threat or a demand, and that sent a message that was more terrifying than anything that could have been said out loud."

"What was that?"

"That I was at his mercy; that he could do with me as he liked; that I was powerless to stop him unless . . ."

"What?"

"Unless I killed him. And he and I both knew I wasn't capable of that."

Evie knew she and the physician were different in that regard. It was only then that Evie thought to ask, "What happened to the patient Langley set up to take the fall?"

"He hung himself." When the psychiatrist began to weep, Evie understood what getting his life back had cost Dr. Radetzky. Lulu put the gun back in her purse.

Evie asked, "Did you figure out how Charlie got someone to lend him a quarter of a million dollars when he was a senior in college?"

Dr. Radetzky pulled himself together. "My brother had a pernicious gift for getting people to trust him. He thought less of people for liking him."

Lulu had one more question. "Did you find out anything that could help me understand what I was to him?"

Radetzky unlocked a desk drawer and took out a small, pale blue velvet box. "I found this when I went through my brother's things after he died."

Lulu knew what it was before she opened it. Inside was the canary yellow diamond engagement ring. Evie had forgotten about it, but Lulu hadn't. "He took it back to Tiffany's to get it engraved with my initials. . . ." A tear rolled down her cheek as she stared into the sparkle of its facets. "This is *my* engagement ring. Your brother gave it to *me*, why didn't you give it back?"

The psychiatrist cleared his throat. "If you look inside, I think you'll understand."

Lulu had to put on her reading glasses to make out the initials etched inside the platinum band—*CR ♥NA.*

Lulu put the ring back in the box, snapped the lid closed, and tossed it back to the psychiatrist. "Who is she?"

Radetzky handed her an old modeling card that featured head and body shots of a long-legged, generically gorgeous girl named Nina Apple. Height 5'11", bust 34B, hips 35, glove size 8. She was the "someone" Charlie was referring to when Evie, huddled bare-legged up against the riverbank of the Mink, heard Charlie tell Langley, "I fell in love with someone else."

When they got back to the Range Rover, all Lulu had to say was, "Can we not talk for a while?"

CHAPTER 47

The modeling agency named on the card was still in existence. Nina Apple was easy to track down. She sold high-end real estate on the East End of Long Island, specializing in the towns of Montauk and Amagansett. There was a photo of Nina with her twin nine-year-old sons on the real estate agency's website—it looked like a J. Crew ad. There was just one problem. Lulu refused to speak to her.

Evie knew that if she called the realtor and asked about Charlie, she'd get a hang-up or, at best, "You have a lot of nerve." So she rang up and said she was interested in a nine-million-dollar beach house in Montauk. Not surprisingly, Nina said, "When would you like to meet?"

In an effort to look like a customer who could afford such a home, Evie borrowed Lulu's jewelry and Range Rover. As she headed down the stairs, Lulu was still in her pajamas muttering, "Fucking Charlie."

Evie was just pulling out of the garage down the block when Lulu darted into the street and jumped into the passenger seat. "If you're going to talk to that bitch, I want to hear what she has to say."

"It doesn't have to be weird."

"It already is."

Evie was glad Lulu had given her back the revolver. She had hidden it in the vegetable drawer of the refrigerator, just as Buddy would have.

They got to Montauk just after 2 p.m. The sky was so blue it looked Photoshopped, and the mid-September light made everything appear more perfect than Evie knew it to be. Nina Apple was waiting for them at the end of the driveway paved with crushed oystershells in front of a McMansion that seemed absurdly overpriced given that it wasn't actually on the beach, but on a path leading to the beach. False advertising made Evie feel less guilty about wasting the woman's time.

The realtor noted the brand-new Range Rover, the borrowed jewelry, and judged Evie a serious customer. Lulu introduced herself as "Louise" in the hope that Nina Apple would be more forthcoming about Charlie if she didn't know who she was talking to.

The ladies all shook hands, but it was awkward from the start. Nina was forty-two and looked thirty. She had a surfboard strapped to the roof of her car. Next to her, Lulu at fifty looked and felt short, stout, and middle-aged.

The realtor took them through the house saying all the things realtors say. "Gorgeous view . . . fantastic layout for parties . . . super sexy bedroom." Her voice was perky, enthusiastic, relentlessly positive. Evie was inclined to dislike Nina Apple simply because Charlie had jilted Lulu for her, but by dying Charlie had jilted Nina too. There was enough disappointment to go around. Evie dreaded having to confess the purpose of their visit, and the tears and accusations that would come her way.

Nina had finished showing off the house and the three of them were standing out on the dune that fell sharply down to the beach. Birds were working baitfish just beyond the break; the pounding of the surf provided a backbeat to the tension that was building. Evie began by asking innocently, "You were a model, right?"

"A million years ago." The realtor segued back to the sale. "As you can see, the owner planted Japanese pines to build up your dune." Evie felt like a ghoul when she said, "I used to know a guy who hung out with a lot of models back then, maybe you met him? Charlie Radetzky?" Evie and Lulu exchanged a look. They expected Nina Apple to flush and turn away to hide her tears. Instead she laughed at the mention of Charlie's name. "Christ, I haven't thought of him in years."

"Weird how he died." Evie tried to sound nonchalant.

"Super weird." Nina was perky, even when it came to death, then added, "Just between you and me, off the record . . ." Evie and Lulu braced themselves for a truth they had not considered. "The owner has a serious cash-flow problem. I think you could get this place for eight if you offered cash."

Lulu backed away from the woman in disbelief. Her voice was barely audible above the waves. "Was he going to marry you?"

The realtor didn't seem to hear her. "What did you say?"

"What did Charlie tell you about me?"

"Christ, I thought you looked familiar." It took a moment for Nina to put it together, but she got there. "You're not interested in buying this house, are you?"

Evie shook her head *no*. Lulu just stared at Nina Apple in grim wonderment. "Did you know about me?"

"Not until I read about it in the papers. The weekend it happened I had a shoot in Montreal. He said he was going to drive up to meet me."

"How is that possible?" Lulu was deaf to how arrogant she sounded.

Nina stiffened. "Hello? Men lie. I only went out with him for a couple of months. I mean, to be honest, Charlie was never that big a deal to me. It was mostly . . . a physical thing. You know, sex." Lulu knew. "Charlie putting on a wedding dress and . . . all I can say is that it wasn't the Charlie I knew."

When Lulu didn't say anything, Evie asked, "Who was the Charlie you knew?"

Nina thought about it for a minute, then smiled. "Sweet and full of shit, is how I'd sum Charlie up. I grew up in Oklahoma. Charlie went to Princeton, worked on Wall Street, drove a BMW. I was impressed and flattered, but I didn't believe a word he said. I mean, he told me he was going to charter a private jet and fly me down to this sailboat he claimed to have somewhere in the Caribbean, I can't remember exactly where."

Lulu whispered, "Panama." When Ortley Security was tracking down the $5 million Charlie had embezzled, they discovered he had discretely liquidated assets to purchase a seventy-six-foot ketch registered in Panama. Until that moment Lulu had forgotten the name on the stern of the boat was *Nina*.

Nina was surprised. "Charlie really had a sailboat?" Lulu just stared at her. The realtor felt bad for her. "Look, what I'm saying is that it was fun to listen to Charlie make big promises, but I never took what he said seriously. For me it was just a game; stuff guys say to impress models."

Evie thought but did not say, *It was more than that to Charlie*. "Did Charlie mention how he planned to pay for all this?"

"He kept telling me about these partners he had. Older, rich, preppy guys. Wall Street types. He had a funny name for them." Nina squinted into the sun and tried to remember, but couldn't. "Anyway, Charlie claimed he had it figured out so they'd pay him all this money just to walk away from this deal they were in together. It sounded like some kind of insider trading to me, but Charlie bragged it was all legal."

Evie jumped in. "Did he ever mention someone called Win Langley?"

"Doesn't ring a bell, but my memory's shot. Too much pot."

Hoping the woman would recall something that would help them put the pieces of the puzzle together, Evie asked, "How did you meet Charlie?"

"There was this old Euro guy. Playboy type. Handsome, sort of. I guess he was only in his fifties, but back then he seemed like a fossil. Anyway, when I lived in Paris, he was always hanging out at this nightclub, Les Bains-Douches. He liked to take models out to dinner. Kind of a letch, but you know, free meal, why not. We called him 'the Samba King' because everywhere he went, he'd shake his hands like he was holding maracas and sing these really lame Brazilian songs. So, I'm on a catalog job in Miami and he shows up on the beach and invites me and a bunch of girls to a party on this yacht that's, like, ocean-liner big. And there was Charlie." The three women stood on the crest of the eroding dune and eyed one another. Nina was trying to be nice when she turned to Lulu and said, "You're lucky you didn't marry him."

All Lulu could say was, "I'll wait in the car."

Evie apologized as Nina locked up the house. "I'm sorry for wasting your time. We should have just come out and told you what we wanted to know."

"If you had, I would have told you to fuck off." Nina Apple handed Evie one of her cards and added, "Pass it on if you run into someone looking for a beach house. It's a good deal."

When Evie got into the car, Lulu stared straight ahead and whispered incredulously, "He didn't mean anything to her."

Evie didn't know what to say. She was about to put the car in gear when Nina pulled up next to her and lowered her window. "Lost Boys." Evie didn't know what she was talking about. "The guys who Charlie said were going to pay him to sail around the world. He called them the Lost Boys."

As they headed back to Manhattan, the words "Lost Boys" teased at Evie's memory. She had heard someone called a Lost Boy once, but couldn't remember where or when. "You ever hear of the Lost Boys?"

Lulu stared out the window. "It was a movie. Corey Haim was in it. I hooked up with him once in LA."

Evie shook her head. "No, I heard it in a different context, not out of a movie or *Peter Pan*. It was like a club, a tribe."

The day was worse than a disappointment. All they had discovered was Charlie had plans for a future that didn't include Lulu or jumping off a cliff. He had told Nina Apple he was going to finance his early retirement via his partners, the *Lost Boys*, and boasted, "It's all legal," but in fact had forged Lulu's signature to guarantee a $5 million loan from a bank in Moscow. That Charlie was a liar was not in doubt, but there was nothing to connect Langley to any of it, except that he had urged Lulu in writing to take legal action to recover the money and report the fraud to the proper authorities.

Since the only crime Evie could be certain that Langley had

committed was drugging and raping her seventeen years ago in the guide camp, Evie was left with nothing to hold on to except her rage. That and the nagging suspicion she was overlooking something that, had she been smarter, would have been obvious.

It was dark when they got to Manhattan. They parked the Range Rover on East 10th Street and cut across Tomkins Square Park. Evie walked quickly. There were men in the shadows. Evie just wanted to get home, but no longer knew exactly where that was. Lulu dawdled behind. Evie looked back just in time to see her buying pot from one of the shadows. A cop was writing a ticket under a streetlamp. She was sure he saw the transaction. Evie yanked Lulu's arm and hissed, "You get busted buying pot, it will be in all the papers. Langley will know we're here. What's the fucking point? That's the stupidest thing you could do."

Lulu smiled halfheartedly. "In view of what we learned about Charlie today, I think we've already established that I'm not very smart."

Lulu took a bath and tried to soak the melancholy out of her with half a joint and Epsom salts. When she got out of the tub, she put on a robe, turbaned her hair in a towel, and talked Evie into smoking the other half of the joint with her. A pint of chocolate Häagen-Dazs ice cream later, Lulu went to bed.

The last time Evie had smoked pot, Chloé was in diapers. The joint left her high but feeling low.

Further self-medicating with a box of Pepperidge Farm cookies, Evie found herself binge-watching hunting shows on the Outdoor Channel. A twelve-year-old girl stalked a mule deer with a pink laser-scoped AR-15; commercials hawked insurance policies that paid your legal costs if you got sued for shooting a son of a bitch while defending your home. Evie couldn't decide whether the whole world had gotten as crazy as her childhood or the pot had been laced with angel dust.

She was about to turn off the TV when a show called *Guns of Legend* came on the air. The episode was dedicated to the Mannlicher-

Schönauer. Popping the last of the cookies into her mouth, Evie listened as the host of the show drew the viewer's attention to the features that made the rifle a favorite of Ernest Hemingway and renowned ivory hunter W. D. M. "Karamojo" Bell. The host sang the praises of the gun as if he were talking about the Stations of the Cross. "The smoothness of its action . . . the butter-knife bolt handle . . . the Monte Carlo cheekpiece . . . the burled-walnut stock extending to the muzzle of the barrel . . ."

In Evie's mind, these obscure details were a trail of bread crumbs leading into the dark woods of her past. She remembered coming out of work her first and last day at Bargain-Mart and seeing Win Langley taking a Mannlicher just like the one on TV out of a velvet-lined mahogany case. A second later, she flashed on Langley four months after that, dropping the same rifle into the snow just after she shot him on Flathead Mountain. Then, Evie's brain yanked her back again to the Bargain-Mart afternoon: Langley handing her the rifle, saying, "Here, hold it. See how it feels." And in the corner of her mind's eye, she glimpsed Andy, the elegant, silver-haired man with a George Hamilton tan, coming out of the drugstore whistling "The Girl from Ipanema" and shaking a pair of prescription bottles full of pills she now guessed to be Viagra as if they were maracas. He had kissed her hand.

She remembered Dill giving Scrotum's mom highlights when she picked up a magazine and saw a picture of Andy's wheelchair-bound wife. She could not recall the wife's name, but she remembered a glossy picture of a yacht long enough to qualify as "ocean-liner big."

Most importantly, Evie recalled Andy in the playhouse the night Langley watched the film he'd made of himself pulling her lifeless legs apart as if she were a doll. Ugly, drugged half-memories and panicky imaginings of his assault on her body rushed through her brain with a velocity that snapped her head back. Hearing herself whimper as she tried to wash the lubricant and blood off herself with a cracked bar of ivory soap in the cold, hard water of the lake, anger ignited into calm, thoughtful fury that burned like a kitchen match struck in the dark.

The next morning, Evie woke up with a pot hangover. She was

trying not to think of her daughter when suddenly, out of a fog of sad and fuzzy thoughts, it came to her where she had heard the expression "Lost Boys."

Lulu was taking a shower when Evie burst into the bathroom shouting, "Langley said it to Charlie."

"What?" Lulu pulled back the shower curtain and stuck her head out.

"Lost Boys. Langley told Charlie, 'You're a fucking Lost Boy.' It was like reminding him he was a Boy Scout or a Marine."

"When?"

"That summer, right after I met you. Buddy and I were poaching on the club's stretch of the Mink where the riverbank cuts in under the rocks. We looked up and heard them talking. Charlie told Langley he wanted to call off the wedding because he met someone. . . ."

Lulu stared at her in disbelief. "You knew Charlie was going to leave me and didn't tell me?" Evie had forgotten she'd never gotten around to telling Lulu.

Angry, hurt, and naked, Lulu demanded, "Why the fuck didn't you say anything to me?" The shower was still running.

Evie felt ashamed all over again. "I was hoping Charlie would change his mind. Then you invited me to the wedding and . . . I was a kid. I wanted you two to be happy."

"Me too." Lulu turned off the water and reached for a towel. "Could I have some privacy?"

When she finally emerged, thirty minutes later, Lulu held up her hand for Evie to stop apologizing. "It wouldn't have made any difference if you'd told me. I would've believed any excuse Charlie gave me and gone through with the wedding. I was a goner when it came to Charlie."

Lulu thoughtfully rolled a joint with the last of the pot. "What else did you hear Langley and Charlie say about me?"

Evie was still embarrassed. "Langley tried to talk him into going through with it."

"How?" Lulu lit the joint and took a drag.

Evie hesitated. "You're not going to like hearing it."

"Go on."

"He mentioned all the properties you owned. Valhalla, your loft in Tribeca, something about East Hampton . . ."

"Like they say, what's love got to do with it? What else?"

"Langley said you were fragile and pulling out of the wedding would break your heart, that you were his friend and he cared about you."

"Since we know Langley didn't give a shit about me, and since Charlie knew he didn't give a shit, why did Langley bother saying it to him?"

"I don't follow you."

Between tokes of the joint, Lulu explained. "What if Langley suddenly realized midway through that conversation that you and Buddy were down in the water listening? What if they had been talking about the Lost Boys? What if he thinks you heard more than you did? That you know about the Lost Boys."

Evie followed the logic. "Langley flies to Paris because he knows Charlie's brother is going to call me. He shows up in Chloé's hospital room because he knows it'll scare the shit out of me and keep me from saying anything about him to Radetzky."

"Makes sense to me, but I'm stoned."

"The only trouble is, we don't fucking know what the Lost Boys are or what they want or what any of this means."

Evie did not yet understand how this chain of misogyny and malfeasance was connected, but she was certain Dr. Radetzky got it right when he said Win Langley couldn't have done all this by himself. Evie had never set a trapline for top-of-the-food-chain predators, but she knew who to turn to for advice.

CHAPTER 48

The Franklin Correctional Facility was a medium-security prison, five hours north of New York City. Buddy was one of 1,730 inmates. Its windows were narrow, escape-proof slits, and the chain-link fence that surrounded it was topped with razor wire. Visiting hours started at 2:30 p.m. Evie and Lulu got there an hour early and found twenty people lined up outside Visitation waiting to be processed in. Most were women, a few with babies and small children.

As per instructions on the prison website, Evie left her purse in the car and headed toward the line. Lulu had planned on waiting in the parking lot while Evie visited with her father. A guard coming off duty rapped on the windshield of the Range Rover and told Lulu to move on. Neither people nor animals were allowed to remain in the visitors' cars during visitation.

Lulu called out to Evie, "I'll pick you up in two hours," and drove into a sad, small town called Malone where she killed the time in a coffee shop that advertised free Wi-Fi. Pulling up the ancient issue of *Vanity Fair* she and Evie had perused the day before, Lulu reread the flattering profile of the elegant, aristocratic philanthropist Ida DuBorg and her dashing, half-Belgian, half-American, banker husband, Andy, a.k.a. "the Samba King."

There were pictures of Ida's sprawling stone seaside villa in Crete; a double-page shot of a temple dedicated to the Minoan snake goddess whose excavation and restoration she had personally funded with the 220-foot yacht, *Idonia*, anchored in the background.

The article mentioned that the DuBorgs owned homes in London, New York, Florida. Lulu began to make phone calls to Euro friends in those locales who were likely to have made Andy's acquaintance. The patrons of the coffee shop thought she was a nutcase when they heard her begin each phone call with, "It's Lulu, and if I sound weird it's because I'm salmon fishing in Canada."

By then, Evie was inside the prison. Showing her ID and signing the registry log, she was swiped with an ION scanner, which checked for explosives and/or drugs, as she passed through a metal detector. She got through the scanner without incident, but the wire under the cups of her brassiere set off the alarm of the metal detector. A Latina woman with a toddler told Evie she was lucky she only had to take her bra off, rather than be treated to a full-body cavity search by a rubber-gloved hand.

Prison was a fortress of testosterone. The air was rank with disinfectant and sour with the musk of men. The way the guards and some of the inmates stopped talking at the sudden introduction of women into the equation made Evie think of the reaction she and Lulu had received when they stepped into the exclusively male world of the Mohawk Club.

The visiting room was the size of a basketball court. Evie spotted Buddy sitting at a table in the corner. Her father was forty-five the last time she had seen him. He was sixty-one now. He had put on thirty pounds, most of it muscle in his arms and chest; Flo had mentioned that he had taken up weight lifting. Time in prison had not diminished his body, but his face was ravaged.

The restorer in her appraised the damage that was beyond repair. He was no longer the handsome man she remembered. His nose, once long, straight, and Roman, had been rearranged by blunt force; a wound that had healed badly left a crease in his forehead that made him look perpetually worried; and a scar inflicted by a razor blade embedded in the handle of a toothbrush drew a line that ran from cheek to neck. Clearly he had gotten the worse of more than one beating. Yet, when Buddy saw her, he stood up, slowly raised his clenched fists high over his head, and smiled like a man who had just won a fight.

Printed prison rules permitted "one brief embrace and a kiss on greeting," and were equally stingy with farewells. As she hugged him, an ache rose up in her throat.

Evie, like all visitors, had to call ahead so the prison could make sure Buddy wanted to see her. Now the guard hovered close, eyeballing Evie and eavesdropping as she and her father struggled for words. *I love . . . I miss you . . . I'm sorry.* Buddy stayed dry-eyed, but his hands trembled as he held hers and said, "If I wasn't so handsome, I'd wonder what I did to deserve such a beautiful daughter," which made her cry even harder.

When Buddy whispered, "Your mother told me about Chloé," Evie stopped weeping and began to speak in French. "Papa, comment puis-je être sûr qu'un mec ne s'évanouisse pas pendant que je le tabasse pour lui sortir la vérité?"

More surprising to the guard, Buddy answered back in French, "La clef, c'est de convaincre cette ordure que tu préfèrerais en fait qu'il meurt plutôt que d'entendre sa confession." The tapes Buddy mumbled along to in his bunk after lights-out were language lessons. He had been listening to them for over ten years in the hope of one day being able to speak to his granddaughter in French. Buddy's linguistic skills were being put to less innocent use now.

If the guard who was listening had spoken French, he would have understood that Evie had just asked her father, "Daddy, how do I make sure a man doesn't pass out when I'm beating him into telling me the truth?" and the reunion would have been cut short before Buddy could reply, "The trick is convincing the bastard you'd get more satisfaction out of killing him than hearing his confession." They were able to talk freely for almost seven minutes before the watch commander came over and ordered them to "talk English."

Evie was standing in the shade eating M&M's one by one, thinking about all Buddy had told her in both French and English, when Lulu pulled up with uncertain news. "The Samba King had a heart attack at a wedding in Newport and then a stroke on the way to the hospital."

"Is he dead?"

"He was for a couple of minutes. They say he's recovering."

"Where?"

"North of Palm Beach. A place called Ascension Island."

CHAPTER 49

Lulu fabricated convincing excuses to call her accountant, banker, trustees, and all the rest of her moneymen and truthlessly informed one and all that she was having so much fun pulling salmon out of the Grande-Cascapédia that she and Evie had decided to extend the fishing trip in Canada to explore other streams.

Three days later, Evie and Lulu were doing six knots up Florida's Indian River in a twenty-eight-foot Bertram sportfisherman with a flying bridge and a two-berth cabin and galley below.

Determined not to leave a trail, they put their JetBlue tickets to West Palm on Evie's Visa and paid cash for the bareboat rental of the Bertram they picked up in Jupiter. The DuBorgs' winter home in Florida was located at the southern end of Ascension Island: a thirteen-mile-long finger of pricey tropical greenery surrounding pastel-colored villas. The properties were multi-acre compounds, resplendent with massive banyans, towering royal palm, and colorful jungles of hibiscus and frangipani.

The island had been bought and developed in the thirties by old-money families who had decided that Palm Beach had become common. DuBorg's property cut clear across the island and boasted its own quarter mile of white-sand Atlantic beach. Home was a discreet pale pink stucco compound built around a pool and looking out across the two-mile-wide expanse of Ascension Bay.

It was a different universe from the Franklin Correctional Facility and yet they had one thing in common—both were excessively well guarded. There were only sixteen miles of public road on the island, but the police force numbered eight. If a vehicle that looked unfamiliar to the island's constabulary, i.e., didn't bear an Ascension Club sticker, stopped on the side of the road for more than five minutes, a patrol car would pull up and inquire politely, "Is there a problem?"

DuBorg's compound being set well back from the road, Evie knew she would not be able to familiarize herself with Andy's daily schedule on foot. Hence, they approached by boat. Anchoring the Bertram two hundred yards offshore on the bay side, Evie and Lulu, with the help of a spotting scope with 12-40× magnification on the flying bridge, watched and waited for the Samba King to show them his moves.

Evie was confident that with what Buddy had taught her about the art of persuasion, once she finished talking to Andy DuBorg he would not be inclined to reveal their chat to Langley. Buddy had suggested putting a clear plastic bag over DuBorg's head as a conversation starter. As Buddy put it, "It's important the bag's clear. That way, in case the fucker's hard of hearing, he can read your lips." Evie's problem was figuring out how to arrange being alone in a room with DuBorg and not leave any bruises when she was done.

Life had taught her that men treated women worse than they did men because girls didn't hit back hard enough to hurt them.

Shooting Langley in the knee from two hundred yards away in a snowy wood was quite a different thing from what she had in mind for Andy DuBorg. Once she pulled the trigger, the bullet did the job for her. What she planned for Andy would take time; slow, messy, and conducted in a closed room, it would be as intimate as sex.

Evie didn't go into details, but Lulu knew they were going to a dark place. As they waited out on the water for DuBorg to surface that first day, Lulu volunteered, "Just so you know, I'm game for anything that doesn't cost me more than a year in jail." After Evie finished laughing, Lulu added bitterly, "I don't give a shit about DuBorg. I hate the bastard."

"You don't even know him. How can you hate him?"

"He introduced Charlie to what's-her-name. Then he had the

nerve to come to our fucking engagement party." Lulu hadn't told her that before.

But once she finally caught a glimpse of DuBorg, Evie began to wonder if she had it in herself to go through with what she'd been rehearsing inside her head. The spotting scope brought the man and his infirmities into such close, sharp focus it was as if he were sitting next to her.

The stroke had taken its toll. The left side of his face was still hand-some, but the right side drooped and the corresponding corner of his mouth seeped drool. Paralysis reduced one arm to less than useless and his right foot dragged. He still had a great tan, but now a clear plastic tube coiled up from the canister labeled "Flammable" to his nose, force-feeding pure oxygen to his brain and lungs. Clearly the Samba King wasn't going to be dancing anytime soon.

Heat and humidity hovered in the nineties all day. The women slathered on 50 sunblock, put on bathing suits, made jokes about their cellulite, and occasionally jumped into the water to cool off.

Working in two-hour shifts, they took turns squinting through the eyepiece of the spotting scope. Peering through the picture windows of DuBorg's life, they recorded the times of the comings and goings of Mr. and Mrs. DuBorg and their staff. Boredom and the glare of the sun made small talk seem like work, but at night they grew loqua-cious. As swirls of living luminescence illuminated the darkness of the sea beneath them, they rummaged the corners of their friendship for secrets and stories they had not yet shared.

Downing Coronas wedged with lime, Lulu told Evie about a six-month affair she had in Barcelona with a matador named Juanita. As Lulu put it, "She called me *papi*. I thought it might have been the real thing."

Having contracted hepatitis C, Evie could not imbibe alco-hol, but under the influence of the softness of that first evening, she found herself remembering the night in Paris Lulu had sat at Chloé's bedside until dawn feeding her daughter crushed ice and dirty jokes to keep her mind off the abscesses that cankered the inside of her mouth. Suddenly it seemed important to apologize for something she had said long ago. "Remember when we went up to the attic in Valhalla and you told me you were thinking about adopting an orphan?"

"Vaguely."

"Right. Well, I was an asshole to say you should start with a dog. It was a stupid, smart-alecky thing to say. You'd be a great mother. You should adopt a kid, have a family."

"I have a family . . . it's why I'm here."

They slept out on deck, in part because the cabin reeked of diesel, but mostly because looking up at the starlight made them feel they were part of something larger than themselves.

A thump on the bottom of the boat woke them at dawn. They shivered as they scrambled up to look over the side of the Bertram and saw a trio of manatees passing beneath them with the tide.

The DuBorg household thought their privacy so secure that they didn't bother to close their blinds. Evie and Lulu were surprised that Andy, age seventy, and his sixty-nine-year-old wife, Ida, still slept in the same bed, given that Ida was bound to a wheelchair and Andy to an oxygen tank.

Ida woke at precisely 6:30 a.m. Careful not to disturb her husband, with admirable self-sufficiency, she slid herself into her wheelchair. She rolled into a bathroom tiled in turquoise and emerged thirty minutes later, coral lipstick applied just so and hair perfectly braided in an elegant chignon. Olive skin that had seen too much sun, hair dyed a dozen different shades of blond, she was as leathery and elegant as an alligator clutch. Lulu and Evie agreed that Ida DuBorg was beautiful in a hawkish sort of way.

Her cook, maid, and houseman arrived at 7 a.m. via a service drive and parked behind the garage. An elevator brought Ida downstairs in her wheelchair. She rolled herself through the house so quickly the servants had to trot to keep up. When the wind blew in the right direction, they could hear her chatting in Italian to her parrots inside a screened-in porch. Shaded by awnings and shrouded by flowering vines, even with the help of the spotting scope, for most of the day the wife was just a shadow who talked to birds.

The houseman, who appeared to be Cuban, woke Andy at 8 a.m. and made sure he didn't trip over the oxygen tubes that tethered him to his cylinder of O_2 on his way to the bathroom.

Andy's breakfast was served to him on the terrace at 9 a.m. Ida sat next to him and spoon-fed him his oatmeal, wiping away the slobber from the side of the mouth that had forgotten how to close. At 10:25 a.m., Andy was in the gym that adjoined the pool house, lying faceup on a massage table waiting for his physical therapist. She arrived shortly after 10:30 a.m. Dressed in a white jumpsuit, she was so top-heavy Lulu dubbed her "the Breast." As the therapist stretched out his bad leg, Ida gathered up her yoga mat, got out of her wheelchair, slipped behind the wheel of her golf cart, and headed off to her yoga class at the Ascension Beach Club. Somewhere between ten and fifteen minutes after his wife left, Andy pulled open his robe and displayed an erection. Lulu theorized that DuBorg shot himself up in the penis with Caverject.

Ida rolled back to the house in a golf cart at 12:15 p.m. Lunch was at 1 p.m. Watching Ida cut his food for him through the spotting scope, Evie muttered, "Christ, he's like a giant baby."

Lulu volunteered, "Men start out in diapers and end up in them."

That afternoon Ida lowered herself into the pool and swam laps. Arms doing all the work, her legs trailed, twitching a muscle memory of a scissor kick. Andy waded in the shallow end with a foam ring around his stroke-addled leg and did strengthening exercises; the oxygen tank floated next to him in an inflatable rubber dingy. At 5 p.m., a color-coordinated pair of septuagenarians arrived in a vintage Aston Martin to play bridge. Andy had to pass when it was his turn to shuffle the deck.

Dinner was at 7:30 p.m. and they were in bed by 9 p.m. That first night, Andy opened the fly of his pajamas and proudly exposed the part of his anatomy that didn't seem to have been affected by the stroke. Ida threw a pillow at him and it, refusing to even look, but on the second evening of their watch the women saw Mrs. DuBorg laugh girlishly and grab him with both hands as if she were gripping a golf club.

Four days in, they knew more about Andy DuBorg's routine than they wanted to. The problem was, Andy didn't stray from the property. There was always someone in the house. Evie did not see a way for her to ever be alone with him until the curvaceous physical therapist showed up on Wednesday morning with a T-shirt that identified her as an employee of "SUNSHINE PHYSIOLOGIC, 2001 DIXIE HWY, JUPITER, FLA."

Sunshine received a call later that day from Ida DuBorg requesting that his regular physical therapist come at 3:30 p.m. in the afternoon, rather than in the morning on the following day. Lulu's Italian accent was flawless.

They tied up the Bertram at the public dock in the town of Stuart. Evie got to a medical supply house just before it closed. Crisp white polyester short-sleeved tunic, matching pants, and thick-soled white nurse's shoes, Evie looked the part of a physical therapist; the question was could she play it? That night on the boat, she fell asleep counting all the things that could go wrong.

The next morning on her way into the DuBorg compound, Evie's hands began to shake. She shoved them in her pockets, fingers closing around the clear plastic bag Buddy had said would speed communication. She could see Ida out on the lawn talking to a gardener now. In a few more steps the wife would see her and it would be too late to turn back. Suddenly, all Evie had in her were second thoughts.

Her conscience pecked at the ethics of her rage. The crippled old letch had never done anything to her but kiss her hand; introducing Charlie to a model was hardly a crime. More worrisome, there was the distinct possibility that scaring the bastard would clock out his heart before he had a chance to tell her what she needed to know.

Evie stopped dead in her tracks. *What the fuck am I doing?* was the only thought in her head until she remembered Langley telling her just before she shot him, "my old friend Andy will put his hand on a Bible and swear that what you claim happened never occurred."

Andy DuBorg was part of this. The Samba King had been in the playhouse that night. He knew what Langley had done to her. In her head, she was suddenly peering through the window of the playhouse, listening as Andy shouted, "Do you fucking realize the trouble this could cause the rest of us? This isn't a game. When you joined this peculiar institution of ours, my friend, you knew what would be expected of you."

Seventeen years ago, Evie had thought Andy was talking about what the Mohawk Club expected. Now, listening to the past echo inside her head, she heard it differently. Who was "us," and what if that "peculiar institution" he had joined was the Lost Boys?

Knowing that the answers to those questions were lying on a massage table a hundred yards from her, Evie pulled her hands out of her pockets and opened the gate to the terrace that had to be crossed to get to Andy.

Evie didn't realize that the dry cleaning bag had fallen out of her pocket until a breeze picked it up and sent it airborne. Ida screeched her golf cart to a stop and grabbed it just before it landed in the pool.

"I'm sorry, it must have fallen out of my pocket. I'll throw it in the trash."

Ida DuBorg muttered to herself, "*Porco Dio*, everything I have to do myself," and drove off in her golf cart with the plastic bag.

The Cuban houseman opened the sliding glass door to the gym that adjoined the pool house and handed Evie the pager Andy normally wore around his neck. "I'll be up in the big house. You need anything, you push this."

Evie waited until the Cuban had disappeared into the main house to close the sliding door. DuBorg's eyes were closed. "You know, Susie, your healing hands are the highlight of my day." The stroke had left him with a speech impediment that made him sound like a Eurotrash version of Daffy Duck.

Evie picked up a pillow and was getting ready to use it to silence the old man's screams. "It's not Susie."

DuBorg opened one eye. "What a nice surprise." Andy gave her a smile that was half grimace. He still had good teeth. "Did Susie tell you about the happy ending?"

"Oh yeah." Evie dropped the pillow and eyed the tube clipped to Andy's nose. Closing the valve of the oxygen canister it was connected to suddenly seemed like a more elegant way to start their conversation. "Let me just loosen you up with a massage first." Andy liked the sound of that, and his eyes fluttered closed. Four irregular heartbeats later, he gasped. A bubble of spit slowly formed and popped in the corner of his mouth as he struggled to utter a word that sounded like "Help."

He tried to call out for the Cuban, but there wasn't enough air in his lungs to raise his voice above a whisper. Evie adjusted the valve so just enough O_2 trickled into him to keep him fully conscious of the fact that he was about to die. "Who are you?" he rasped.

Fighting the urge to feel sorry for the man she was asphyxiating, Evie leaned in close as if she was going to kiss him goodbye. Her back was to the door. If anyone passed by, they would think she was massaging his good arm, not pinning it to the table.

"I'm the girl your friend Win Langley drugged and raped. He showed you a video of it at the Mohawk Club." Evie's hand was on the valve. "Just so we're clear, I'll enjoy watching you die if you don't answer my questions."

The Samba King was crying now. Buddy said that would happen. He seemed to be looking past her as he sputtered the word "Please."

Evie put her lips to his ear and shouted, "Who are the Lost Boys?" His eyes widened in terror. He shook his head *no*. Evie closed the valve tight. DuBorg stared right through her. She glanced over her shoulder.

Evie hadn't heard the glass door slide open. Ida was in the doorway. Eyes narrowed, the wife's hands gripped the armrests of her wheelchair as if she were bracing for a head-on collision with something that could not be avoided. Ida's voice sounded exhausted and oddly bored. "The fool would rather have you kill him than tell you about the Lost Boys. Let him breathe and I'll tell you what you want to know." Most surprising of all, there was no trace of anger or outrage at the abuse she had seen Evie inflict on her husband.

"Why should I believe you?" Evie sounded calm, but wasn't.

Ida stared at her as if they had met before. "I know what it feels like to be raped."

Evie opened the valve. The Samba King's lungs filled with O_2 and Ida called for the Cuban houseman, explaining only, "It seems my husband is emotional today."

As Evie followed the wife up to the house, she asked, "What made you come back from yoga early?" She was curious whether it was God or luck that had intervened.

"I wanted to remind my husband I expect a present for our wedding anniversary tomorrow."

Ida led her into the high-ceilinged screened-in porch at the far end of the villa. Filled with orchids and the rustle of feathers, it was a giant cage for her birds. The gaudy macaw and a dour African gray squawked in Italian as a dozen smaller birds, yellow finches and pale blue parakeets, fluttered overhead. The maid didn't have to be told to bring in an unopened bottle of vodka in a silver bucket of ice. Ida filled an eight-ounce crystal beaker to the brim with Stolichnaya and drank half of it in three gulps.

Lighting a cigarette in a blue malachite holder, she explained matter-of-factly, "So . . . as you can see, my husband is one of many bad things I have a weakness for." Evie had spent enough time in Italy to recognize her accent as Milanese. Ida's voice was both grand and full of shame. It was easy for Evie to see how Lulu could have turned out like Ida if she had married Charlie. Ida started to fill a second glass of vodka for her; Evie shook her head *no*. The events of the morning had left her feeling drunk and hungover at the same time.

"The Lost Boys are . . . how shall I say . . ." Ida worked her tongue inside her mouth as if she had a bad tooth in her head. "A mafia of gigolos is what I would call them, except gigolo is much too playful a word. They are serious men. Organized, like a company; but secret, invisible. They make their profit, gain power and influence by recruiting young men—charming, well-educated young men, always handsome—who are more ambitious than scrupulous. These young men, they then marry off to spoiled young women of great wealth who have inherited financial interests, companies, properties, assets they are too ignorant to understand and too lazy to appreciate. In my case, it was textiles and shipping." Ida took another gulp of vodka. "Some of these girls, these women, are of course stupid, but some are simply intelligent women who have been encouraged by men to believe they're stupid."

There was a photograph on a coffee table of Ida and Andy at Studio 54 circa '78. Andy in black tie; Ida, falling out of a dress that could have passed for lingerie, looked beautiful, rich, and as strung-out as Keith Richards on a bad night. Seeing Evie's eyes linger on the photo of her glory days, Ida volunteered, "Andy got me off the heroin." Evie remembered Charlie had been Lulu's detox, until he wasn't.

"Who introduced you to Andy?"

"My father's pederast of a banker. Horrible man. Took pictures of himself and little children. His name was . . ." Ida closed her eyes and tapped her head with her knuckle as if it would jog loose the memory. "Moran. Porter Moran." Evie knew where Langley got the kiddie porn.

"Your common everyday fortune hunter, the playboy who wants to live off a rich woman, you see them coming a hundred kilometers away. But the Lost Boys, they are different. A breed apart. They're clean-cut. Have jobs at banks, investment houses, law firms—respectable establishments where your parents, grandparents, guardians have done business for many, many years. You have to understand that the ugly brilliance of this syndicate of men, these Lost Boys, is that they seem in all ways to be just what you would want your daughter to end up with. Especially if she is a party girl, as I was. What you don't know, what nobody but the Lost Boys know, is they got this impressive job, have the nice apartment, drive the Mercedes, the Porsche, because their mentor, their boss, he is a Lost Boy who once met a rich wife with the same lies his protégé tells you. *'I love you. . . . I want to help you. . . . I'll save you from yourself. . . .'* Stupid girls want to believe such things."

Ida thought about that for a moment, then added, "Then, of course, there is the sex. As much or as little as you want; but always *al dente*! To be a Lost Boy, you must be able to turn it off and on like a faucet; they have special talents in that department."

"But if they steal money from the women they marry, why don't they ever get caught?"

"Because the husband doesn't steal it." The alcohol thickened her accent, but she was clear in what she was saying. "The husband never touches the wife's money. He recommends someone older, someone respected, to handle her finances. A lawyer, a banker, whatever."

"And they're a Lost Boy?" Ida nodded. Evie was starting to understand. "But why don't they get arrested for embezzlement?"

"Let us say you inherited a privately held company estimated to be worth one hundred million dollars; for argument's sake, a company started by your grandfather. The older lawyer, banker, whoever your husband has recommended to safeguard your money and who you do not know is also a Lost Boy, shows you a financial report full of facts and figures that indicate the company you have been left is not really worth as much as you thought. It has hidden problems, challenges, needs to be retooled, but thank heavens, this trusted adviser has found a buyer who will give you ninety million dollars for the company you have been raised to have no interest in and know nothing about and is full of problems. And with that ninety million you can invest in something that will give you a much higher return. Because you trust them and they have impeccable reputations, you say, 'Yes, go ahead, thank you for looking out for my best interests.' And then they sell it to another Lost Boy for ninety million, who then sells it for a hundred, or a hundred and ten, or who knows what. The wife doesn't lose money, the men make sure the women always make a small profit, but the lion's share goes to the Lost Boys."

"But kickbacks would show up on the tax return. They'd get caught for money laundering, and even if they didn't, if they're doing all this to get rich, they'd buy yachts, planes, houses; people would see them spending money they didn't earn."

"The yachts, the planes, and so forth, the wives Lost Boys marry already have all these things."

"But if they don't spend the money, they'd have to put it in banks; there would be records."

"They don't use banks."

"Then how do they——"

"Hawala." It was a word Evie had never heard before. Ida explained. "It's Arabic. It means both 'transfer' and 'trust.' It's an ancient banking system used in the Middle East since the time of the Silk Road that doesn't involve cash. No moneys are exchanged. Instead, it relies on an honor system. With the Lost Boys, it is honor among thieves."

"I don't understand."

Ida leaned in close. The macaw squawked as it swallowed the fly that was buzzing round her head. "When a Lost Boy buys something from another Lost Boy's wife for less than its true value, he guarantees, never in writing but with his word, that the husband will be given a corresponding share in the profit from the manipulation of the assets of yet another Lost Boy's wife. They receive a share in a painting, a percentage of a factory, condos in Trump Tower. And so it goes; year in, year out, one man's hand washing another's. Because your rich wife already has a beautiful house, the villa at the beach, if you're a Lost Boy it is easy to build a fortune quickly, and the wife takes pride in the fantasy that she has married a brilliant businessman who loves her so much he has never once asked to borrow money."

"And after they rip off the wives, they divorce them?"

"No. That would give it away. A new husband would have a new accountant. For the Lost Boys, it's 'Til death do us part."

"How many Lost Boys are there?"

"Hundreds for certain. Perhaps a thousand, but I'm only guessing."

"When did this start?"

Ida's laughter flashed a gold bridge in the back of her mouth. "It has existed since Eve inherited the apple orchard, but it was not organized like it is now, not turned into a business until the First World War. They say it began with a solicitor in London who was a retired colonel or major or whatever in the British army. Before the war he had represented the financial interests of a number of young men who had inherited great fortunes only to die in the trenches. Men who left vast wealth to young windows. This solicitor realized there was no shortage of dashing but penniless young officers who looked smart in their uniforms and who believed the world owed them more than a medal, and did not want to earn money the old-fashioned way. The solicitor had the social connections to introduce these men, vouch for their characters, give them enough pocket money to seem more solvent than they were, and then . . . marry them off to rich war widows. Because a lady never concerns herself with anything as vulgar as money, they were ripe for the plucking. The solicitor would stand up as best man at their weddings, give a speech, make everyone cry happy tears. It was all very proper. It always is with the Lost Boys." The birds screeched and fluttered against the screens as a tomcat sharpened its claws on the wire mesh of the door.

"How did you find all this out?"

"I fell off a mountain a long time ago." Ida gave her a knowing look.

"You lost me."

"My husband and I were mountain climbing in Cortina with Langley and his wife of six months. American girl, very rich. Charming, but a bit mad. Believed in her last life she was Mary, Queen of Scots, I think. Anyway, they were ahead of us. And though I cannot prove it, I am certain Langley either pushed or tripped his bride. When she fell, she pulled him with her. I got tangled in their ropes. She broke her neck, and I was left like this. Let's just say it pleased me to learn that Win Langley had been shot."

"That was me."

"*Brava.*" The old lady paused to applaud before she continued. "In the hospital, I suffered a blood infection. Almost died. When I woke up, Andy was weeping at my bedside; he confessed. Since the heart attack and the stroke, late at night when he thinks about dying, the idiot talks to me like I'm a priest and I'm going to forgive him."

It was only then that Evie noticed on the mantel there was a bare-breasted terra-cotta statue of a Minoan goddess clutching a pair of snakes. "If you know, why are you still with him?"

Ida lifted her skirt and displayed her legs twisted and gnarled as the trunks of the banyan outside. "It is hard to walk away from a husband when you're in a rolling chair. The devil you know is better than the one you don't. At least that's what I thought when I was young and stupid. Now that I'm old and stupid, I wonder . . ."

"Will your husband tell Langley I asked about the Lost Boys?"

"You don't have to worry about my husband. But if Langley and the others find out you know about them? Sooner rather than later you can rely on something very unfortunate happening to you."

"Telling me all this, aren't you scared?"

"You can't kill a corpse." Ida tapped the side of her head with a jeweled finger and added, "Tumor." Then she took a deep breath, wheeled herself abruptly away from the table, and opened the door for Evie to leave. "We are done now. I've got to begin preparations for our wedding anniversary tomorrow."

As Evie walked toward her car, she looked back just in time to see the elegant old woman using a broom to drive the birds out of the room that caged them. Evie wondered how long Ida DuBorg had been thinking about setting them free and tried not to worry about what the woman would do next.

Lulu piloted the rental boat back to Jupiter by herself; Evie took Dixie Highway south and picked her up at the marina. Their flight back to NYC didn't take off until 7 p.m. The women spent the afternoon on a bench in front of a lighthouse that looked like a giant pepper grinder; Lulu stared out to sea as Evie relayed the details of what she had learned. The idea that there was a small army of men like Win Langley operating in the shadows of respectability, helping one another exploit their wives, milking them like a herd of prize dairy cows, left the women feeling profoundly angry, frightened, and alone.

Lulu put a match to her last cigarette. "You think the Lost Boys killed Charlie because he wouldn't marry me?"

"I think it was more than that. Remember what Charlie's girlfriend said about how Charlie told her the men he was working with were going to pay him to walk away from a big deal?"

"Yeah. I was their cash cow."

"I think Charlie tried to shake the Lost Boys down. Tried to blackmail them. Threatened to expose them if they didn't pay him off."

"But why'd they put him in the wedding dress?"

"To make it look like suicide and send a message to the rest of the fucking Lost Boys."

"What message?"

"You're a Lost Boy for life. 'Til death do us part."

"It doesn't explain Clare." The physical resemblance between the twins was so strong it sometimes made it impossible for Lulu to look at Evie without thinking of the dead woman. "Clare didn't act like a wife who thought her husband had married her to steal from her."

"Maybe Clare found out something. Maybe without even knowing it, Clare did something that threatened the Lost Boys." Evie was reminded of Clare every time she looked in the mirror. They were all haunted.

"You're guessing."

Evie didn't argue. "We need proof. To catch them in the act of . . ." Evie thought about it for a moment before she finished the sentence. "Trying to kill somebody who knows about them."

"By 'somebody' do you mean us?"

The weather had shifted. Cold air on top of hot conjured up a pair of waterspouts on the edge of the horizon as Evie told her what Buddy had said when she visited him in prison. "Wolves urinate to mark their territory. Smell of it is a 'Keep Out' sign to other predators. You piss inside a wolf's hunting territory, and the pack will get so distracted with hunting you down, they forget you're laying a trap."

The women had been back in New York for two days when word reached them that on the morning of the DuBorgs' fortieth wedding anniversary, the Cuban houseman entered his employer's bedroom and discovered Andy DuBorg had put himself out of his misery by disconnecting his oxygen tube. It was assumed that he had placed his head in a clear plastic bag that had once held dry cleaning to make sure no one would hear him in case he lost his nerve and cried out for help. Evie wasn't sure it was the same plastic bag that had fallen from her pocket, but she felt certain that Ida DuBorg had given herself an anniversary present she had been thinking about for a very long time.

CHAPTER 50

Langley purchased the palatial brownstone on 73rd Street from Porter Moran's estate back in '02. He used the trove of kiddie porn he knew was hidden in the basement playroom to persuade Moran's children to give him a deal on the Francis Bacon painting that had caught his eye on that first evening Moran invited him over to talk about his future.

Porter's children didn't care about their father's reputation, but feared potential lawsuits from the old man's underage victims. Langley kept the most repellent examples of Porter's fondness for children on the hunch they might come in handy. Dr. Nicholas Radetzky was not the first man he had compromised with Moran's perversion. No one called him Scout anymore, but his motto was still *Be Prepared*.

The Bacon hung in his bedroom now. As he tied the black silk bow tie of his tuxedo, he eyed the reflection of the painting in the mirror he used to groom himself. The mysterious fleshy snarl of the not-quite-human forms savagely intertwined with one another on the canvas never ceased to fascinate him. After all these years of looking, he still could not decide if there were two or three bodies involved, or be sure of just exactly who was being fucked by whom. At age fifty-seven, he found the possibility that there were still intimacies he had not yet experienced inspiring.

The day before he had attended Andy DuBorg's funeral in Florida. The Ascension Island Club had its own chapel, St. Luke's by the Sea, just off the eighteenth hole. The pews were packed and the congregation included nearly two dozen Lost Boys who had flown in on their private jets to say goodbye.

Several gave speeches full of humorous anecdotes and heartfelt condolences to his widow. Langley, drawing on his experience in collegiate theatrics, wept on cue when it was his turn at the pulpit. In private, at the reception at Ida's house after the ceremony, he and the men he did business with agreed that Andy's death was a relief. Over the years, DuBorg had become what Langley called "a weak sister"; which, in Langley's mind, was the worst thing that could be said about a Lost Boy. Ida kept her dark glasses on throughout. Not to hide the tears, but to keep anyone from noticing she didn't have any to shed for her late husband.

Langley tied his bow tie twice that night before he was satisfied with the symmetry of his knot. Slipping on his dinner jacket, he polished his reflection with the additions of a white silk handkerchief in his breast pocket and a rosebud in his lapel. Practicing his most modest smile one last time in the mirror, he headed downstairs.

Langley had all manner of reasons to believe he was getting away with more than his fair share of the good life, the most recent of which was the honorary award he was about to be given that evening at a charity gala to raise money for the Wild Forest Conservancy, a non-profit dedicated to saving the last stretches of primeval woodland left on the planet. Langley with the help of his Lost Boys had raised enough money to purchase one hundred thousand acres of rain forest in Brazil. There was no caveat or catch to his good deed other than that it made Langley seem more charitable than he was. It had been a long time since Langley had thought about his wife, who had died mountain climbing in the Italian Alps with the DuBorgs; longer still since he wished Margot were alive. But that night, as he set off to the WFC gala, he grew sentimental and imagined how nice it would be if he had a Mrs. Langley in the audience to stand up and applaud his lifetime achievement award.

The benefit was being held in the upstairs ballroom of the Carlyle Hotel just around the corner from his lair. Stopping to light his pipe, pausing to glance into the store windows on Madison Avenue, he took his time walking there to make sure the room was full when he arrived.

Nearly three hundred people had subscribed to the event. The best tables went for $150K; cheap seats at the back were three grand apiece. The location, the band playing Cole Porter, the women with their jewels and face-lifts, and the deep-pocketed male scrum at the bar brought back memories of the evening Porter Moran had challenged him to charm the daughter of the third-richest man in Palm Beach with the very same words his hockey coach had used: *Show me I'm right about you.*

Langley got his award at 8:30 p.m. It was a lead-crystal vase in the shape of a tree with his name etched across the base. Ken Strauss and his wife Bissie sat at his table. Tom and Helen Reynolds were at the table next to him, along with fellow Lost Boys Ian Conklin and three-fingered Walter Morrissey, the most senior of the tribe. Morrissey was more hunched and spidery than ever. His health had improved miraculously after Clare's death; in fact, he felt so much better that he had decided to stay on as trustee and supervise the liquidation of poor Clare's estate.

Dessert was being served now and the charity auction had begun. The Brit auctioneer from Christie's who had donated his services was mic'd up at the podium, gavel in hand. The audience enjoyed flaunting their largesse, purchasing items for two to three times what they were worth—a week at an eight-bedroom villa in St. Barts; a portrait by a young woman who had just had a show at Pace Gallery; dinner for ten at a restaurant famous for mac and cheese made with white truffles.

The plummy-voiced auctioneer worked the crowd, cracking jokes, and calling out bidders by their first names. "Now, ladies and gentlemen, I draw your attention to a truly once-in-a-lifetime experience. Three days of fly-fishing at the Mohawk Club's legendary forty-seven-thousand-acre Adirondack preserve with none other than our own Win Langley as your guide. Not only will Mr. Langley fly you up in his private seaplane, he will personally pitch your tent and guarantee that if you do not catch a fish, he will pay for your entire trip himself." Langley offered up his now not-so-boyish grin. The crowd laughed, and bidding started at twenty thousand. At

$26K, Ken's wife, Bissie, called out, "Do we get to sleep in the same tent as Win?"

Langley stood up and raised his hands. "Anything and everything is possible, but it will cost extra."

Laughter, applause, the crowd ate it up. A woman at a table in the back raised a paddle and called out, "Thirty thousand dollars." Langley couldn't see her face, but she had on a green silk dress and he liked the squareness of her shoulders. Wanting to see more of her, he leaned to his right. The bidder was Evie Quimby.

Lulu was sitting next to her. She didn't bother to raise her arm when she shouted, "Thirty-five thousand." The auctioneer recognized Lulu from the art sales. "Lulu Mannheim bids thirty-five." Turning and pointing to Evie, he said, "And now, is the lovely lady to your right willing to make that thirty-seven thousand dollars for Mr. Langley's services?" Evie gave Langley a *fuck you* smile and raised her paddle. Langley kicked Ken Strauss under the table and the lawyer reluctantly raised the bid to thirty-eight thousand. "Ladies, do I have thirty-nine?" The women pushed the bidding to fifty, then dropped out and left the ballroom before the dancing began.

By 10:15 p.m., Evie and Lulu were in a town car heading home. Lulu was high on adrenaline. "I think we can safely say we pissed on Langley's territory." Evie smiled and wondered how Langley and his wolves would come after them.

Rolling down Fifth Avenue, as they passed the Pulitzer Fountain, Evie's cell phone rang. She didn't recognize the number. When she picked up, she heard a man inquire, "How was fishing in Canada, Evie?"

She couldn't place the voice and put the cell phone on speaker. "Who is this?"

"Marcus." The name meant nothing until he added, "And Biscuit." Evie had forgotten there was a world out there populated by people whose biggest worry was a sick dog.

"You don't remember, do you?"

"No . . . of course I do, we took you and your dog to the vet."

"Exactly! I'm going to be in New York next week and I was hoping I could properly thank you for coming to our rescue by taking you both out to lunch."

Evie shook her head *no*. "We're sort of busy."

Lulu jumped in, "I can't go, but Evie can."

~ ~ ~

The next morning, Ken and Bissie Strauss bickered over breakfast about Ken paying $50K to go to a fishing club he already belonged to. Home was a fourteen-room duplex facing the park in the Dakota. Bissie, a six-foot-tall, thick-legged WASP, looked down on Ken's bald spot as they argued. It wasn't the money; it was the principle. In Bissie's opinion, since Ken knew she hated fishing, if he had any remote interest in spending time with her he would have bid on the villa in St. Barts. Ken told her, among other things, that since she was still richer than he was, if she wanted to go to "fucking St. Barts" she should have ponied up for the Caribbean getaway herself. Adding insult to injury, he suggested that perhaps what was really bothering her was the medication she was taking for menopause. It wasn't like Ken to speak to his wife like that; usually when they disagreed he simply said what Bissie wanted to hear and quietly did exactly as he pleased. The women bidding on Langley had rattled Ken's cage.

Bissie Strauss spent the better part of that day calling her friends and complaining about Ken. It was after 3 p.m. now and she was running late. She had promised her fifteen-year-old son she would watch his soccer game that afternoon. She was a helicopter parent who actually had a helicopter.

The elevator stopped at every floor on its way down to the lobby. She was teetering through the gates in backless heels when the doorman at reception called out, "A friend just left this for you, Mrs. Strauss." She took the manila envelope, jumped in the waiting limo, and looked for a return address. There was nothing, just her name.

Inside was a photograph taken twenty-two years ago at her wedding reception. Because she wasn't wearing her glasses, the image was blurry, but she knew the photo. She and Ken were taking their first dance. Her husband still had a full head of hair and she looked fat and white in part because she was four months pregnant with her daughter, who was now a junior at Brown.

Bissie assumed a friend must have found it cleaning out an old album and passed it on. Thinking, *What a thoughtful gesture*, she looked for a note, but there wasn't one. It wasn't until Bissie got stuck in traffic and bothered to put on her reading glasses that she saw the picture clearly. The heads of several of the men in the background of the photo watching as they took those first steps in the long waltz of their marriage were circled in red and numbered. On the back of the photo there were names: (1) Porter Moran, (2) Win Langley, (3) Tom Reynolds, (4) Andy DuBorg, (5) Charlie Radetzky.

Below in block letters someone had written:

ASK YOUR HUSBAND WHY HE NEVER TOLD
YOU ABOUT THE LOST BOYS?

An hour later Evie was across town on foot, heading north up Park Ave with a similar envelope for Tom Reynolds's wife. Her wedding pic showed just-married Helen and Tom Reynolds dodging rice as they left the tent on the lawn of Helen's grandmother's forty-two-room summer cottage in Newport. The faces of the Lost Boys were again circled and the same question asked.

Evie was twenty feet away from handing the photo to the Reynoldses' doorman at 800 Park Ave when Helen and Tom emerged from the building with overnight bags in hand. Their seventeen-year-old daughter followed with a taffy-and-white English setter. Evie ducked into the shadow cast by the awning of the neighboring building and watched as the doorman scurried to help them load a blue Mercedes station wagon.

As the Reynolds family pulled into traffic, Evie was suddenly over-come by a sensation more chilling than déjà vu. She had never set foot on the corner of 74th Street and Park Ave in her life, and yet there was something eerily familiar about the stretch of sidewalk she was stand-ing on; something that made her feel that she had been there before in a bad dream. It took Evie more than a few heartbeats to realize that this was the same sidewalk she had seen on the front page of the *New York Post* beneath the headline PARK AVE HEIRESS JUMPS. Evie felt a rush of vertigo as she looked up and saw the apple tree hanging over the railing of the terrace from which her twin had fallen.

The doorman was watering the boxwoods on either side of the entrance when Evie held up the envelope and asked, "I have some-thing for Mrs. Tom Reynolds. What floor is she on?"

"They're in the penthouse, but you just missed them." Evie handed him the envelope. "Who shall I say it's from?"

"They'll know." Evie stared up at the building. The newspapers had said security cameras indicated no one had entered the building after Clare came home and that her husband was still at his office when the police called, seemingly ruling out the possibility that she was pushed. But what if there was already somebody inside the building two floors above in the Reynoldses' penthouse?

CHAPTER 51

K en Strauss stopped off at the Yale Club for forty-five minutes of squash before he came home from work that night. He would have liked to have played another game or two, then lingered at the bar, but it was Wednesday—what his wife euphemistically called "family night." The one evening of the week he and Bissie and the two younger children who had yet to leave for college had dinner together. He knew that if he was late, Bissie would start haranguing him about going back to couples therapy. Lost Boys had a problem with marriage counselors. Since menopause, he and Bissie had an arrangement— don't ask, don't tell, don't embarrass me in front of my friends, and don't be late for family night. He kind of liked being a father and thought of being a husband as part of his job.

As he poured himself a glass of Haut-Brion, his cell phone chirped a text from a thirty-two-year-old lawyer in Oslo he had been seeing for over a year. She liked to fish and sent him weekly naked videos of herself making do without him.

Ken was happy with the arrangements in his life and thought his various partners were as well until Bissie came into the living room and asked, "What are the Lost Boys?"

The attorney in Ken took over. He smiled as he polished the lenses of his glasses with his pocket square. It was what he did whenever a judge asked him a question he wanted to think about before answering. "As I recall, the Lost Boys are Peter Pan's posse . . . you doing the crossword?"

Bissie handed him the first dance photo from their wedding with the five men's faces circled in red. "Someone sent me this. Look at the back."

Ken looked at what was written on the back of the picture and shook his head in bafflement. "Who the hell sent this? Was there a note or anything?" Lulu and Evie bidding at the auction the night before; Ken knew it was from the women, but why? *Was it Clare Loughton? Charlie? Or was there something else Langley hadn't told him about?* He'd call Langley after dinner, but right now he was the one on trial. Ken handed the photograph back to her with a shrug. "That is so weird."

His wife glared at him skeptically. "What's weird, Ken? Besides the fact that you're not telling me the truth about the Lost Boys or anything else."

He launched into his defense slowly. "The only person I can think of who could have sent it . . ." The lie came to him from a kernel of the truth. Experience told him it was the most convincing way to fabricate a falsehood. "There was this girl we all knew back in the nineties. Kayla something. Funny, but a real borderline. We all went out with her, one time or another."

"You mean you passed her around?"

"She was one of those girls. I mean, Christ, it was over twenty years ago. Sex was like shaking hands back then. She called us the Lost Boys." They knew girls like that, but there was no Kayla, and no one who knew about the Lost Boys who wasn't one of them; or at least that's what he had thought. Until now.

"Why would your Kayla send me a photograph of us dancing at our wedding?"

"Probably she saw that thing on you in *New York Magazine*." Their apartment had just been featured in the Design issue. "She's probably envious, sour grapes, wishes she had a husband and an apartment in the Dakota. Kayla always thought Win was going to marry her. Call him and ask him if you don't believe me."

"Win, like you, is a professional liar."

Ken looked hurt. "Win, besides being the person who introduced us, is godfather to our son and the most honest man I know."

"Really?"

"Yes. Please, stop being stupid about this."

"You're sure of that?"

"Win's straight with me."

"Did he tell you he slept with me?"

Ken had no idea. A tweak of jealousy was followed by a wave of nausea. The latter stemming not from Langley fucking his wife, but from the thought *What else is Win hiding?* Ken rolled with the punch like a professional boxer and spun round from defense to offense. "As a matter of fact, Win did tell me about that, Bissie."

Ken hit her with the same look he used on juries when he wanted to make them feel ashamed of themselves for even thinking about a guilty verdict. "I knew it was a hard time for you both. Your change of life, and Win . . . well, he's never gotten over his wife's death and he said you reminded him of her."

Desperate for an explanation for why her money had not made her happier, why her life, marriage, and home that looked so perfect in *New York Magazine* felt so hollow, Bissie blamed herself. His wife's voice broke as she asked, "Is that why you stopped being in love with me?"

Ken gave her his honest look, eyes open wide, brow furrowed, a sad half-smile that said *I don't judge you, I feel sorry for you*, and hugged her. "It's over. Done. I forgive you both, and hey, it's family night."

Bissie choked on, "I'm a lucky woman."

"We're both lucky. Let's remember that." It was what Lost Boys said. The maid brought the food out. His son was still wearing his soccer uniform. His younger daughter had just finished with her thousand-dollar-an-hour SAT tutor. When Ken sat down, he asked his family, "So, did anything exciting happen to anybody today?"

~ ~ ~

The women waited a day before they dropped off a letter for Clare Loughton's husband, Peter Shandley. Inside was a photograph they had obtained that appeared in the *New York Times* three and a half years ago. Clare's laughing as she feeds her husband a big slice of wedding cake. There was frosting on the tip of his nose. When Peter flipped over the photo, he read:

THE LOST BOYS KILLED YOUR WIFE—DID YOU HELP THEM?

If they had been there to watch him, they would have known they were correct in guessing that Peter Shandley did not know his wife had been pushed. The photo fell from his fingers as he staggered out onto the terrace. Shandley sobbed and looked down over the railing. The white blossoms Clare used to stand on the step stool to smell had turned into a half dozen green apples. He knew Walter Morrissey had dosed his wife with LSD, understood why it had to be done, but believing that Clare had jumped off the terrace rather than been pushed had made it easier to play the grieving widower.

Shandley looked up at the terrace of Tom and Helen Reynolds's penthouse two floors up. Clare had given the Reynoldses a key because she was always locking herself out. Being a Lost Boy, he quickly stopped crying about poor Clare. Plucking an apple from the tree, he took a bite. Reminding himself he was "the Beast," Peter Shandley focused on what was best for Peter Shandley.

CHAPTER 52

As a thunderstorm rolled down the Hudson, the women sat in the living room of Lulu's Tribeca loft and watched lightning flicker like broken neon. For more than an hour they had been speculating what Win Langley and the Lost Boys would do next. Evie's mind was already on predators when Flo texted a snapshot of the front page of the *Sister Lakes Gazette*. The North Country weekly featured an article Flo thought would interest her daughter, titled WHY ARE CATAMOUNTS CAMERA-SHY?

In the last year, the Sheriff's Department had received twenty-four reports of mountain lion sightings in Townsend County. The author of the piece, a well-known local naysayer, had written the sightings off as overweight house cats, a farsighted lynx, wishful thinking, and/or a side effect of the local citizenry's fondness for alcoholic beverages. The sheriff was quoted as saying, "As long as the cats don't break any laws, I'm happy to have them back." Evie could just imagine the expression on Dill's face as he said it. Evie was still staring at the catamount question when she said, "They'll have to come for us."

Lulu wasn't convinced. "If nothing else, Langley's smart. And the smart thing for them to do is absolutely nothing. They know if we had proof they killed Clare or Charlie or were ripping off their wives, we wouldn't be sending anonymous letters."

Evie didn't seem to hear her. "Langley will make his move soon."

"How can you be so sure?"

"Because given my history with him, he's got to be worried that if I don't find enough evidence to convict him, I might just be crazy enough to kill him." Evie paused to text Flo back "thanks" followed by a heart emoji. "And because we're going to give him an opportunity to get rid of us that he won't be able to resist."

"I don't like the sound of that."

"If we don't set the time and place, they will."

"Even if we get them to come after us, it'll still be our word against theirs."

"I've got that figured out."

"I want to see them arrested, not shot."

Evie said, "Me too." Lulu wasn't convinced about that either, but in the end she said yes.

~ ~ ~

The next morning a topographical map of Townsend County was rolled out across the desk in the library of Lulu's loft. Aerial photos of Valhalla's twenty-eight square miles were up on the computer. Evie had a ruler out and was making a drawing to scale while Lulu Skyped Clinger up in Valhalla. "I want seventy eighteen-foot-long spruce logs, ten to twelve inches in diameter, brought up to the Cat's Tongue."

The superintendent of the Great Camp's eyes widened. Taking a deep breath, Clinger repeated the words his father had told him he would need to remember to say if he wanted to hold on to his job, "You're the boss, Miss Mannheim."

The Cat's Tongue was a long, pointed granite outcrop that jutted out just below the crest of Kettle Mountain. Steep, densely forested, and arduous to access, it lay on the extreme northeastern corner of the Mannheim property. From the tip of the stone tongue to the treetops below was a sixty-foot drop.

Clinger had his map out now too. "You do realize, Miss Mannheim, the nearest road—and I'm talking logging road, overgrown with saplings thick as my wrist—is four miles south, and that's as the crow flies, not even counting the up-and-down."

"Call the guys with the helicopter."

"You mind telling me why you want to bring in all that lumber?"

"We're going to build a cabin." From the way she said *we*, Clinger knew she meant him.

"Why would you want to sleep way the heck out there when you've got Valhalla?"

"We're going to need a base camp."

Clinger took off his hat and scratched his head. "Base camp for what?"

"Evie and I are going to camp out on the Cat's Tongue until we get a photograph of a catamount."

"Is there a specific reason you think you're going to find a mountain lion up there?"

Lulu put on her wacky spoiled rich woman's voice. "Since nobody will be there but us, the animals will sense it's safe to come out." Lulu let the absurdity of her statement sink in for a moment before adding, "Evie's drawing up the plans now. You'll get them this afternoon."

A mile down from the rock ledge where the cabin would be built, the pine forest flattened out around Dog Pond. Beyond that was Mohawk Club land. Pocked with spongy bogs, it was thick with woodcock and grouse. In two weeks, upland game season would open. The birds would give Langley and the Lost Boys an excuse to come for them with guns.

They knew Langley was too clever to do anything as incriminating as shoot them. The shotguns the men would be carrying and perhaps firing would be used to frighten them into becoming unwitting accomplices to whatever form of accidental death the Lost Boys had determined would be easiest to engineer. But from the Cat's Tongue, the women would be able to see them coming. They would have time to prepare for the worst; at least that's what Evie hoped.

As soon as Flo heard about the cabin, she knew Evie and Lulu weren't setting up a camp on the ass end of Valhalla to get a snapshot of a species of cat that was supposed to be extinct. After spending the last sixteen years in prison, Buddy was scheduled for release in less than two months. The prospect of her daughter going to jail just as her husband was getting out made her weep as she talked to Evie on the phone.

"It's time to walk away from this, Evie, and have a life."

"That's what I'm trying to do, Mama."

Unable to talk her daughter out of using herself as bait, Flo asked wearily, "What do you want me to do?"

Late that afternoon, Flo drove into town and took a seat at the bar of the Rangeley Inn. She ordered an old-fashioned; it was what Buddy liked to drink when he felt the need to spread a rumor. As happy hour commenced, she regaled anyone and everyone with her daughter and Lulu's plan to spend the month of October in a cabin on the Cat's Tongue in the hope of capturing a catamount on film. No cell phone reception, no Wi-Fi, a half-day hike to get to the closest road: most thought it the stupidest idea they had ever heard. Flo did not disagree. Then she brought up the fact that Lulu refused to even talk about putting up an antenna so they could be reached by shortwave, adding, "I could die and my own daughter wouldn't even know to come to my funeral."

CHAPTER 53

Win Langley was in the back of his forest-green Bentley on his way to a meeting with Ian Conklin and Walter Morrissey. A client of Win's was interested in acquiring a parcel of industrial buildings in Brooklyn that were being sold to begin the fulfillment of Clare's wish to liquidate her assets so that her entire personal fortune would be at the disposal of the Grace Loughton Foundation. The seven acres bordering the Gowanus Canal were ripe for gentrification. Given that the trustees of the estate and the recently appointed new director of the foundation as well as his client were all Lost Boys, Win felt confident that the sale would be a win-win for all parties involved, except, of course, for the foundation.

None of the men who knew the truth felt good about what happened to Clare, but if she had gone through with her plan to replace her lawyer (Ken Strauss) and her trustees (Conklin and Morrissey) and hired that woman from the Rockefeller Foundation, there would have been a due-diligence accounting. Questions would have been asked about the wisdom of marginally profitable real estate transactions over the years that had reaped windfall resale profits for others. It was regrettable and unavoidable. Things rarely came to that when the Lost Boys were involved; in fact, it had been nearly fifteen years since it had been necessary for a wife to have an "accident." It happened in Australia, skin-diving off the Great Barrier Reef in waters known to be inhabited by great white sharks. Her body was never found.

The meeting was downtown. The FDR was closed, traffic was snarled. The president was attending a ceremony at the UN. A Lost Boy with a day job at the World Bank was giving a speech. Win had been invited, but he always put business first.

Langley was stuck bumper-to-bumper on First Ave when the manager of the Mohawk Club called to complain about Lulu Mannheim and Evie Quimby building a cabin on the Cat's Tongue without a permit. Langley pretended to be surprised, but he had already heard all about the cabin that was being constructed and the women's plan to spend the month of October camped out on the rock. He had reintroduced a pair of Mexican mountain lions into the food chain without the knowledge of Fish and Game; if the women were lucky, they'd get a snapshot before they died. He advised the club manager to let it go, but he had no intention of doing the same.

Reynolds and Strauss had shown him the wedding photographs that had been delivered by hand. No need to look at security footage; Langley knew it was the women's handiwork.

What he wasn't aware of was that Bissie Strauss had revealed he had serviced her a few years back three drinks after she'd confided how unhappy she was with Ken. But if Langley had known, he wouldn't have worried—it was a mercy fuck, designed only to keep Bissie from having an affair with someone who might encourage her to divorce Ken. In Langley's mind, he had done his friend a favor and the Lost Boys a service. Ken seemed oddly distant since the photographs were delivered, but Langley wrote it off to his being distracted by naked videos from his lawyer in Oslo. Ken had shown him one that revealed her to be double-jointed.

Reviewing the situation in the back of his Bentley, Langley came to the conclusion that there was nothing to worry about. Ken would follow Reynolds's lead. Reynolds was solid; dependable, like himself, but not quite. Lost Boys had each other's backs, and as long as they remembered that, nothing could hurt them but death and taxes.

As his driver headed south, cutting through Chinatown and dodging potholes under the Brooklyn Bridge, he considered the meaning, implications, and most importantly the opportunities afforded by the recent chain of events. He had more questions than answers. First and foremost, how did the women find out about the

Lost Boys? How much did they know? Had the women sent Clare's husband a wedding picture too? What was written on the back of his? He, Reynolds, and Strauss had wisely kept the fact that Clare's suicide was assisted to themselves. Could Shandley have told the women about the Lost Boys?

Lulu Mannheim was arrogant, reckless, and rich enough to jerk his chain and think he'd let her walk away, but Evie Quimby knew better than that. Certain that the women were setting a trap with the cabin, he admired the audacity of using themselves as bait. As the Bentley stopped for a red light, the answer to all these questions was suddenly simple. He would come for the women, but never arrive. He would bring Strauss, Reynolds, maybe Shandley with him and make sure the women saw them coming. And while Lulu and Evie were busy getting ready to spring their trap, whatever it was, someone else, someone the women had no idea was a Lost Boy, would appear and a tragic accident would take place. Sadly, Win Langley would arrive too late to help the women.

Langley knew just who to call—Cal Dolenz in Palo Alto, the Lost Boy with the blind wife whose father had left her a mother lode of Apple stock bought in the eighties. Langley had recruited Dolenz because he had skills that the Lost Boys might find useful someday. Dolenz had served four years in Iraq, Special Forces, before Langley brought him on board and sent the ex-officer and gentleman off to business school. Most importantly, Dolenz was already familiar with Langley's version of the Evie Quimby–Lulu Mannheim situation. Cal had reached out when he heard about Clare Loughton's name appearing in stone and asked if there was anything he could do to help. Dolenz could be talked into handling it. He came to New York regularly for work. It would be easy for him to find an excuse to slip up north to do some hunting. The Bentley pulled up in front of the White Stone Trust building. The meeting was in Porter Moran's old office. Being there brought back memories.

The next afternoon at 3:30 p.m. in the Sculpture Garden of the

Museum of Modern Art, Langley and Dolenz simultaneously tilted their heads to the side to get a better view of the naked metal lady suspended over the reflecting pool. As they admired the voluptuousness of the Maillol sculpture, Langley obliquely laid out the scenario he envisioned. He liked that Dolenz interrupted him midway and said, "What's in it for me?" Dolenz was not a weak sister. Langley offered a number of financial options. Dolenz shook his head *no*. "I'll do it in return for my freedom. I want out of the Lost Boys."

Langley wasn't expecting that. "You know our organization doesn't work that way."

"You have friends, influence. An exception could be made."

Langley wondered if Dolenz was testing his loyalty to the brotherhood. "Once a Lost Boy, always a Lost Boy."

"Then I can't help you with your problem." Dolenz started to walk away.

"All right. Do this for me, and I'll get you out." Langley had no intention of doing any such thing, but he wouldn't tell Dolenz that until he had taken care of the women. After they were dead, he would own Dolenz.

As they shook hands, Langley asked, "Do you mind telling me why you want out?"

"I fell in love with my wife." Langley looked at him as if he had caught a disease.

Two hours later, Langley met Reynolds and Strauss on the east side of the Reservoir in Central Park. Rain was predicted. The men all carried umbrellas. Reynolds brought his daughter's dog. Langley looked at his watch and muttered, "I told Shandley to be here at six o'clock sharp."

Strauss looked surprised. "You sure we want him in on this?"

"It's time Peter realizes that being one of us is a test of character." Langley waved as Shandley jogged toward them.

Langley gave them the broad strokes of what he had arranged with Dolenz as he lit his pipe. "We'll fly up in my floatplane, radio in mechanical failure, and say we can't make it to the club and have to do an emergency landing on Dog Pond. We report we landed safely and ask them to call the club and send a boat to pick us up at the gorge. We'll be in contact with the authorities the whole time. Our alibi will all be on tape. Then we see a fire up in the cabin on the Cat's Tongue. We call the sheriff, but he's two hours away, even by helicopter. We try our best, but by the time we get to the cabin, it's too late to do anything but put our jackets over the bodies."

Reynolds didn't like it. "We nearly crashed the last time we tried to put down on that fucking pond."

"Which is exactly why people will believe it's an emergency landing."

Ken Strauss cleaned his glasses. "Why do we even need to be there? I mean, Dolenz was a fucking sniper."

"Because our arrival will distract the women and we need to make sure the problem's resolved to our satisfaction."

It was starting to drizzle. The men were done. As Langley opened his umbrella he asked Shandley, "You have any idea, Peter, why the women didn't send you a wedding picture?"

"The same reason they didn't send you one, Win. Our wives are dead."

It was a good answer. As Win walked away in the rain, he decided it was too good an answer not to have been rehearsed.

CHAPTER 54

A thermal inversion filled the canyons of Lower Manhattan with fog so dense that when Evie got out of bed that morning and looked out of the big arched windows of the loft, she could barely make out the buildings across the street.

Lulu was already on the phone to Valhalla about helicoptering in the logs and men to build the cabin. Evie poured herself a second cup of coffee and tried to wake up. From the half of the conversation she could hear, it appeared Clinger had just pointed out that if Lulu was going to build a cabin she would need a building permit from the county, and had suggested delaying construction until spring. Lulu cradled her cell phone to her ear, lit a cigarette, and exhaled a cloud of exasperation. "I'm not waiting for an f-ing permit and I'm not putting it off. It's my land and I can do what I want. Cabin's not going to have plumbing or electricity or . . . Yeah, I hear you, Clinger, but so what? The worst thing that can happen is they make me tear it down."

Evie knew that wasn't the worst thing that could happen; what troubled her was that she didn't care. Evie had found a part of herself that was as hard, secret, and indifferent as the Lost Boys.

Feeling the need to remind herself why she couldn't walk away from it all, Evie wandered down an empty hallway in the back of the loft and opened the door to the room where Chloé had slept. The maid had mentioned to Lulu that the girl had left some things behind. Evie had not had the courage to look at them until now. The stuffed elephant that Chloé had been embarrassed to admit she still cuddled was nestled between the pillows; threadbare, stained, and missing an ear.

The detritus of the teenager who had passed through littered the bedside table. A Pez dispenser; a velvet headband borrowed without permission; a lipstick, dark as black licorice, which made her look like a vampire; a bracelet made of dice. Opening the closet, Evie found the leather jacket they had bought at a shop in Clignancourt. Taking it from its hanger, Evie held it to her face and inhaled her daughter's smell: tangy like the sea, fresh, alive.

Tears streaming down her face, Evie went through her daughter's pockets, knowing it was a mistake. A stick of gum; a ticket stub to a movie Evie had forgotten they had seen together just before Christmas; and the small red moleskin diary plastered with Manga stickers her daughter used to write in when she was angry or bored or . . .

Evie had promised Chloé she would never read it, knew she shouldn't open it, but the longing she felt for her daughter was too deep to not give in to. Mistakes are what mothers make and pay for when they try to protect their child from the unforeseeable.

As she pulled back the elastic that secured its cover, the diary opened to January 12, 2018. The date held no special meaning except for the fact that another week would pass before they discovered the flu that wouldn't go away was leukemia. The first sentence Evie read was a gutshot. "I hope I don't end up like my mother . . ." Closing the diary, Evie whispered softly to the child who wasn't there. "That's not going to happen."

Evie was still sitting on the bed holding the jacket that smelled like Chloé when Lulu came in. Pretending she hadn't heard her friend explaining herself to an empty room, Lulu said, "You've got to get out of here."

"What?" Embarrassed, Evie stuffed the notebook back in the pocket of her daughter's jacket.

"You agreed to have lunch with the dog lover." That was Lulu's name for the man they drove to the vet.

"Christ!" Evie had forgotten. "I'm not sure I have it in me to pretend that all this shit isn't happening."

Lulu took the coat from her and hung it back in the closet. "It'll be good for you." And much to Evie's surprise, it was.

She met him in a restaurant she had never heard of. Elegant yet cozy, the bar and the banquets, and the Art Nouveau tiles on the walls had all been salvaged from a bistro somewhere in France.

Marcus was waiting in a booth in the back, reading the *New York Review of Books*. He wore a suit; tie ajar. His beard was thicker than she remembered, and Evie imagined he grew it to keep people from being distracted by how handsome he was.

"Quel plaisir de vous revoir, cela m'a fait plaisir que vous acceptiez mon invitation." She had forgotten he spoke French. Smiling as he stood up, he held out his arms and greeted her like an old friend. Holding her shoulders lightly and perhaps a moment longer than was necessary, he kissed her on both cheeks. As his beard brushed the disfigurement that no longer marked her face, she felt a blush rise in its place.

Distracted by the closeness of him, she missed the next thing he said, but caught up to the moment when he announced, "I have a present for you." He handed her a photograph of his yellow Lab. "It was Biscuit's idea." He had drawn a paw print in the corner. Evie wasn't sure whether she had forgotten what it was like to be charmed by a man or was experiencing something new and different.

Evie ordered a salade niçoise; he had the skate with capers. At first they talked mostly about restoration. He was full of questions about how things could be fixed and she liked the way he listened. When he asked her what she liked most about restoring, she answered, "When you find something nobody knew was there," and told him about the time she worked on the beard of a badly restored bust of a Roman senator and discovered the whiskers hid the face of one of Caesar's wives. Suddenly realizing she was doing all the talking, Evie muttered nervously, "God, I must be boring you to death," but he simply smiled and said, "Tell me another story."

He made no effort to impress her and said little about his life other than mentioning he worked in finance and his specialty was calculating risk. He was more forthcoming on the subject of fly-fishing. Evie found it awkward lying about the salmon fishing trip she and Lulu never took to Canada and was relieved when the conversation turned to the Adirondacks. He had been back to Rangeley since their trip to the vet and caught a brook trout in the Cascades. After he showed her a photograph of himself freeing the brookie to be caught by someone else, she excused herself to go to the ladies' room. She didn't need to go to the bathroom, she just wanted a moment to savor the pleasure of the man's company. As she walked back to the table, Evie thought to herself how much better than nice it was not to think about the Lost Boys for a while.

"When do you go back to Paris?" he asked.

"Not until November. Lulu and I are going to camp out in a cabin overlooking Dog Pond for a month, trying to photograph something that's not supposed to exist."

"What's that?"

"A mountain lion in the Adirondacks."

"What an incredibly cool thing to do."

"Let's see how it turns out."

The check came and he said, "I'd love to see you again."

"Well, if you're ever in Paris."

Marcus took out his cell phone and opened his calendar. "Okay, let's say the third Thursday in November. I'll pick you up at seven p.m., Rue Daguerre." She was flattered he remembered her address.

"Isn't that Thanksgiving?"

"They have turkey in Paris."

"All right . . . it's a date." Saying the word made Evie laugh.

"You're not going to write it down?"

"I'll remember." As he put her in a cab, Evie did the thing she'd been thinking about since they sat down, and kissed him quickly on the mouth.

"What's that for?" He put his hand to his lips as if he'd been struck.

"Being normal."

As the cab pulled away, he called out, "Maybe I'll drop in and see you at the cabin."

Knowing that was a bad idea, Evie told the driver to stop and jumped out, not quite sure how she would explain why she didn't want him anywhere near the Cat's Tongue. When Evie got back to where they had been standing when she kissed him, Marcus was gone. She tried his cell phone but it was off. She told herself not to worry. When he said *drop in*, it was just one of those things people say.

She got back to the loft at 4 p.m. The first words out of Lulu's mouth were, "How did it go?"

"Good." Evie didn't want to spoil it by talking about it.

"If you say 'good,' that means it had to have been fantastic."

Evie laughed. "He says he's coming to Paris and he's going to take me out on a date on November 22."

"That's Thanksgiving."

"There's turkey in Paris." Then they started to talk about Chloé.

Marcus was in a rental car a half block away. He had an earpiece on and was listening to their conversation. When Evie had gone to the ladies' room, he had slipped a disposable $1.98 lighter into her purse that contained a listening device capable of picking up anything said within a radius of fifty feet. He heard the clatter of the lighter on a hard surface and figured the women were smoking. It was difficult to follow the conversation. Listening hard, head cocked and eyebrow raised, he struggled to figure out the antecedent of the "she" they were talking about. Suddenly he heard Lulu's voice boom. "That's fucking it! I am never smoking another cigarette for the rest of my life." He heard the sound of her picking up the cigarettes and the lighter and listened as they rattled down the hollow of a garbage chute.

Marcus with the green eyes whose specialty was calculating risk needed to be certain he understood exactly what the women were doing before he decided how to deal with the problem they posed. He went back to his hotel and considered the potential downsides of each of the courses of action that were open to him and what was in both the short- and long-term interests of the Lost Boys and of course himself, Cal Dolenz.

Langley had no idea that a group of concerned Lost Boys had sent Cal to New York to find out if Clare Loughton was going to be a problem two days before she died.

CHAPTER 55

The same twin-rotor Sikorsky that airlifted the gravestone down to the gorge had to make two trips over Kettle Mountain to transport the lumber, supplies, equipment, and men up to the Cat's Tongue. Lulu had demanded that the cabin be completed in a week. Clinger put a ten-man crew on the job. He and the locals he had recruited slept on-site, worked sunup to sundown, then cranked up the generators after dinner and labored under arc lights for another two hours.

Because they were being paid triple-time for the job, no one complained, but more than a few made jokes about the wisdom of building a ten-by-twelve-foot cabin that lacked a toilet, electricity, and would cost north of $100K. All of Rangeley agreed that in the long history of Mannheims coming up with harebrained ways to waste their money, Lulu's folly up on the Cat's Tongue was the most foolhardy.

Naturally, the Morlocks were quick to speculate on the Sapphic pleasures the women would get up to on the Cat's Tongue. But the truth was the closeness of Lulu and Evie's unlikely friendship, the loyalty over the years, and their unexplained bond were a puzzlement to the entire community. To Rangeley, the women were far more mysterious than the catamount.

The logs were notched with chain saws and laid flush on top of one another "full scribe" in the Scandinavian style of log-cabin building so no caulking was necessary. The walls were eye-high. Kettle Mountain being the last place in the county that still lacked a cell phone signal, Clinger was out of touch with the women and frustrated by the vagaries of the plans for the cabin Evie had penciled out.

The ridge beam was already in place and the last of the rafters was going up when the women finally rolled out of the forest on electric motorcycles, quiet as deer. Both were dressed in Carhartt camo coveralls and steel-toed boots.

Lulu arrived with two cases of beer for the men and gave a short speech thanking them for all their work. Clinger brought up the idea of putting up a radio antenna again, but Lulu made a point of dressing him down in front of the whole crew, saying the whole point of the cabin was to spend the next month not having to listen to the sound of his voice. Amid the laughter, Evie rolled out a map indicating where she wanted them to place the motion-activated infrared cameras. "If anything comes up this mountain, I want a picture of it." The men thought she was talking about mountain lions.

When the beer was finished, four men climbed up on the roof to mount the stupidest-looking lightning rod anyone had ever seen on top of the chimney. It was shaped like a pitchfork, and as Lulu explained, "The Welsh claim it keeps the devil away." Clinger and the rest of the crew went to work mounting game cameras on the deer trails that squirreled down through the pines and thickets of poison ivy between the Cat's Tongue and Dog Pond.

That afternoon a smaller helicopter arrived carrying the club-footed Israeli. He neither introduced himself nor said a word to any of the men as he set up the electronics for the wireless surveillance system. When the motion detectors were activated, whatever the game cameras picked up would be recorded and relayed directly to the women's smartphones.

While all that was going on, Evie slowly climbed down the densely forested incline just to the left of the Cat's Tongue. Using a can of spray paint to indicate the trees she wanted cut, Evie marked a trail straight down the mountainside to the pond below. Since the men were being paid triple-time, they felt no obligation to point out the fact that Evie had selected the steepest and most treacherous route she could have picked to get from the pond up to the cabin.

When the trail was chain-sawed out, a shirtless worker with a red beard and a quivering beer belly asked the women, "Why no cameras on this trail?"

Lulu smiled coquettishly. "Because we'd set them off when we go down to the pond in the morning to bathe," then added with a wink, "I have enough naked pictures of myself floating around on the Internet."

The men's job was over then, and when the crew got back to town that night, they celebrated their week of triple pay at the bar of the Rangeley Inn. The men laughed as the belly with the red beard regaled them for the third time with what Lulu had said to him about bathing naked in Dog Pond. When Scrotum called out, "Fucking dykes are what's wrong with this country," the belly informed him, "My mother's a dyke," just before he broke a beer bottle over Scrotum's head. When the sheriff was called, Dill heard all about the peculiarities of the women and their cabin and asked, "Evie and Lulu have guns up there?"

Clinger, who was more than a little tipsy by then, told him, "No guns. Miss Mannheim thinks her catamount can sense the presence of firearms." Relieved to hear the women were unarmed, Dill told himself to stop worrying about Evie Quimby.

The women moved into the cabin thirty-six hours later, October 11. They came from Valhalla around the south side of the mountain on the mechanical hiss of their electric motocross bikes. Evie had an old duffel bag slung across her back. She had told Clinger it contained books.

Food, spare clothes, a fifty-gallon drum of drinking water, and the rest of the supplies had already been dropped off. They hid their bikes off the trail in a clump of pines with fifty miles' worth of charge still left in their batteries. In case of "emergency" they told Clinger to leave a pickup truck under a tarp off the logging road four miles south, but did not say what that emergency might involve.

The cabin had four small windows, one on each wall, and heavy wooden shutters. By design it was both fort and prison. The interior of the cabin was spartan and had the clean smell of fresh-cut lumber. Two bunks, two chairs, a table hinged to fold up flat against the wall. When the women walked through the door for the first time, one of the four TV monitors sprang to life and they watched a raccoon pass through a thicket with a crawfish in its mouth.

Evie was counting on Rangeley hearing that there were no game cameras on the new trail they had cut down to the pond. The women spent the next two hours extending the surveillance system down its length in the hope that Langley and whoever came with him would say enough about how they intended to dispose of the women to incriminate themselves.

Twenty feet out from the water where the path cut through a narrow gap between shoulder-high slabs of granite, blue with lichen and green with moss, the women began to dig. Even though they were wearing gloves, their hands were blistered by the time they were done with the hole.

After that they waded into the shallows and cut down cattails and laid them across the narrow pit they had dug. Hoping a nasty fall would get their uninvited guests talking about their true intentions, Evie opened her backpack and took out the last of the game cameras. It was identical to the others except she had painted its case to look like stone. Artfully trompe-l'oeiled with flecks of blue, gray, and moss-like green, it was invisible when she attached it to the larger of the two slabs of granite.

Six o'clock, the women sat on the tip of the Cat's Tongue and watched the sunlight die. In the distance, Evie could see the arc of the far shore of the Mannheims' lake, and at the other end of the gorge, five miles back, the darker blue velvet triangle that was Lake Constance, and beyond it the Mohawk Club. Further to the south, flaming more red than blue in the last light of day, was Lake Millicent and the village of Rangeley just visible on the horizon.

Putting binoculars to her eyes for a closer examination of her realm, Evie glimpsed what appeared to be a fish in the treetops that obscured the gorge. It took her a moment to realize it was the trout-shaped weather vane atop the guide camp. Drawing a line in her imagination from Dog Pond, now in the shadow of the mountain, to the copper fish pointing due north, Evie began to understand something that had been bothering her for a long time. "Langley landed here."

Lulu dangled her feet over the drop. "Yeah, we saw him. The day we threw rocks at him in the pool he was fishing down on the Cascades."

"No, I'm talking he landed here the night Charlie died. Look at it! It's less than two miles from Dog Pond down to the gorge. Langley had Charlie's groomsmen with him. I saw them get out of the plane. Ian and what's-his-name, the older guy with three fingers. He put down here so they could meet Charlie that night without anyone knowing they'd come back. They knew Charlie was threatening to expose the Lost Boys. Langley brought the other two with him to confront Charlie."

"You're guessing."

"What if Charlie drove up from New York thinking he was going to get paid off? His BMW was four-wheel-drive. He could've come in the back way, taking the logging road that cuts just west of the gorge, and met Langley and the other two at the guide camp. Charlie tells them he's not only not going to marry you, he's going to tell you about the Lost Boys unless . . ."

Reluctantly, Lulu began to see it. "The model said Charlie was going to meet her in Montreal. It's a three-hour drive."

Evie's voice flattened as she reimagined the night in question. "Charlie and Langley argued, fought? Or maybe the three of them just snuck up behind him and broke his neck. Then he drives Charlie's BMW back to Valhalla. The caretaker sees Charlie's car pull in, naturally figures it's Charlie getting out and going in to sleep in the boathouse so as not to wake the house, but it's Langley. He takes the wedding dress, gets in a canoe, and paddles down to the guide camp. He meets up with Ian and Walter, they put Charlie's body in the dress and push him off the edge. Then they walk back to Dog Pond, take off in the morning, fly around for a couple hours, and land on your lake in front of everybody at Valhalla."

Lulu crawled back from the edge and stood up. "But what about the guy from Fishers Island who said Langley took off that morning?"

"What if he's a Lost Boy?"

The sun was gone now. Evie lit a lantern and they walked back to the cabin. Lulu's hand shook as she struck a match to light the propane stove. Waiting for water to boil, she tried to imagine what Charlie was thinking after his neck was broken and he realized Langley was putting him in her wedding dress. Evie unzipped the duffel bag that didn't hold books and handed her a 12-gauge Remington pump.

The second shotgun was a trombone-action Winchester with the barrel hacksawed off at twenty inches. Evie loaded the Remington for Lulu, explaining, "First cartridge bird shot, second buck, third and fourth rounds are slugs. We don't fire unless we have to."

"I don't want to kill anybody." Lulu had said it before, but was now no longer sure she meant it.

"We stick to the plan, we won't have to."

Lulu watched as Evie begin to assemble a long black sniper rifle that fired .50-caliber bullets. "What's that for, then?"

"To get them talking about how they're going to kill us."

In the bottom of the bag was the shortwave radio they had made sure everybody in Rangeley knew they intended to do without. The pitchfork-shaped lightning rod atop the chimney was the antenna they told Clinger they didn't want.

When they finished dinner and washed the dishes, they dug a hole deeper and wider than the one down by the pond just inside the front door of the cabin and covered it with a drop cloth. Exhausted, Evie and Lulu picked up the sleeping bags and shotguns and climbed out the window. Sleeping in the forest was part of the plan. The cabin was part of the trap.

PART VIII

BURDEN OF PROOF

CHAPTER 56

If I had been out there on the Cat's Tongue when my mother loaded that shotgun, I would have screamed, "It's not worth it!" Told her to stop; made her stop; ripped the gun from her hands and drowned it in Dog Pond. But that would have just been a different kind of mistake. I didn't know about the Lost Boys or the guns or the cabin or the bargain she made with God that first time my heart stopped beating.

She didn't ever tell me the terms of the deal she struck with the unknowable when she stood in the hallway outside my hospital room and watched them try to shock me back to life. I imagine it was the usual "Take me, not my child . . . let her live and I'll do whatever is asked." I had my own promises to keep, and I had made mine to Clare Loughton's ghost. It was that promise that put my name on a tombstone, not complications from acute lymphatic leukemia.

July 1, I was still so sick I forgot it was my birthday until Flo showed up with a cake. When I tried to eat a slice, I vomited, but was happy to see fifteen. A month later, my cancer was in remission and my hair was starting to grow back. I wasn't well, but I could finally walk to the vending machine at the end of the hall without getting dizzy.

Old friends from my lycée began to stop and visit; even the boy from my debating team who slept with the girl who used to be my best friend came to see me. So did the girl. Thankfully, not on the same day. I told them separately that I didn't blame them and that I was over it. I wasn't, but trying to become a better person was one of the things I promised Clare I would try to do if I got a second chance.

I had been dying for so long it was hard to get used to the sensation of being alive. Perhaps because Clare's marrow was making my blood, I felt like a ghost of the girl I used to be.

My oncologist went from guardedly optimistic to optimistic, but contin-
ued to worry about the twenty kilos I lost and wasn't putting back on. The
smell of food still made me nauseous and chewing seemed like work. Since
Lulu had told my doctor on more than one occasion, "I don't care what the
fuck it costs," he suggested I go to the Rothman Clinic in Switzerland and
spend the next three months focusing on just getting strong. My meds could
be monitored and tweaked, the necessary biopsies performed, physical reha-
bilitation provided involving swimming and walking in mountain air, and
tutors could be arranged from the local university to help me catch up on all
the school I had missed. My doctor had sent patients there before. Having
spent ninety-nine percent of the last six months in the same room as my
mother, I liked the idea of being on my own; having the time and space to
think about what my close encounters with death and life had made of me.

I could tell by the way my mother told the doctor, "We'll think about
it," she wasn't going to let me go. The conversation that followed went some-
thing like this:

"I want you home in our apartment with me. I can take care of you here
in Paris."

"What about Clare? If you're looking after me, you won't be able to find
out what happened to her. We owe her."

"What about what I owe my daughter?"

"I wouldn't be alive if it wasn't for Clare. You promised me you would
do this."

"I know what promises I made." My mother was getting upset. "If
Langley ever found out I was asking questions, he'd come after you; he's
already asked about you. I can't take that risk. They're monsters."

When I was little my mother had told me there was no such thing as
monsters, but by then we all knew that wasn't true. "The monsters can't
come for me if they think I'm dead." Dying was my idea. My mother
embraced the madness of tricking the world into thinking I was dead
because it allowed her to keep her promise to God. I know it sounds hard to
believe, but some part of her believed it was the only way to keep the cancer
from coming back.

Flo didn't just not like my plan, she cursed at me for suggesting it and told my mother she would regret it for the rest of her life. That was the night Flo went out by herself and got so drunk she broke her foot. The next day, Lulu presented my oncologist with the red Porsche convertible she had promised to give him if I lived. Understandably grateful, he found it in his heart to make a small clerical correction in the hospital's computer records indicating that Chloé Quimby Clement died of complications due to cancer at 8:33 on the morning of August 18.

Flo, Lulu, my mother, and I all agreed to a strict set of rules and swore not to break them. There would be no phone calls, no letters, no emails (except for the one I had already prescheduled when I really did think I was going to die), no contact or communication of any kind that would indicate I was still alive. Lulu paid for the clinic via a Swiss bank account her accountant didn't know she had, and gave me a Visa card to draw on in case I had a problem. My mother promised to come for me "as soon as it's over." Neither one of us had any idea just what "it" would involve. We agreed she would return no matter what, mid-November at the latest. Flo took me to the clinic in Switzerland via train, and my mother and Lulu flew back to America to shop for my tombstone.

In the old days, the Rothman Clinic was what they called a sanatorium. An hour outside of Geneva, it was a cross between a hospital and a hotel. My room had a balcony and from it I could see a forest groomed of dead wood and a mountain called Mont Pèlerin. I swam in a pool heated by thermal springs and walked with an attendant by my side across flowered meadows. And though I knew Switzerland had its share of killers and perverts and ugliness, I enjoyed the illusion that since I was dead nothing bad could happen to me.

I also enjoyed my tutor. A French-Moroccan scholarship student at the University of Geneva. He had a one-dimpled smile and a way of looking at me when I was doing math that made me feel as if I were lying under a heat lamp.

My body remembered what it was like to be hungry. By the end of that first month I had gained eleven kilos and could hike for an hour before feeling the need to turn back. By then, my tutor was walking by my side through the groomed forest, and one day instead of turning back, we lay down. When we got up, I knew for certain I was alive.

By the start of October, my blood work came back better than fine. The mountain air had cooled by then and tingled my lungs as my daily walk turned into a jog. I was doing so well the doctors let my tutor take me to a Hitchcock retrospective to see Notorious. *As I was getting dressed, I looked from my balcony and saw my tutor waiting in the square across from the clinic by a statue of William Tell. As I came out of the gate a few minutes later, he mimicked the pose of the archer whose aim was so true he defied a tyrant by splitting an apple perched on his child's head. Cell phone in hand, I laughed as I snapped his picture.*

It wasn't until we got to town and sat down for a coffee before the movie that I looked closely at the photograph and noticed a man standing just behind my tutor, staring straight at me. As I enlarged the image with two fingers, the stranger came into sharper focus and I realized I had seen this man before. He had grown a beard, but he was still the second most handsome man I had ever laid eyes on. His appearance was nothing more than a reminder of how small the world was until the film broke in the third reel and reality intervened.

When the lights came on, I ran out to get a Coke. The stranger in the gray suit was standing in the lobby with his back to me talking on his cell phone. All I heard him say was, "The women are fucking with Langley. The daughter's alive. . . . I'll take care of them as discussed."

CHAPTER 57

The women slept back-to-back on beds of pine needles hidden in the darkness just behind the tree line. They kept their sleeping bags unzipped so hands and arms were free to reach for the shotguns that lay beside them. Ephraim had programmed the system so that when the game cameras were triggered their cell phones would vibrate and the intruder and the coordinates of his location would appear onscreen. They slept with their phones in their breast pockets. That first night, the alarm alerted them to the presence of a buck whose right antler was tendriled with a spiral of wild grapevine, but nothing that walked on its hind legs.

The temperature dipped, and when daylight woke them the dew had turned to frost. The last time Evie had camped out she had been half-girl and Buddy had been by her side. Rolling her head to work out the kink in her neck, Evie muttered, "I forgot how hard the ground is."

Lulu got on her knees and stretched yoga-style. "Christ, I haven't been this stiff since I passed out at my birthday party and woke up in the morning on the bathroom floor with my clothes on backwards."

"What birthday was that?"

"Last year when I turned thirty-nine." The women's laugher was interrupted by the distant bark of shotguns being discharged in rapid succession. It was official—hunting season had begun.

That morning was spent figuring out where they might run if it came to that. They stretched barbed wire taut throat-high between the trees on either side of a warren of alternative escape routes and hoped if they found themselves running down them they would remember to duck.

In the afternoon, they took pick and shovel back into the cabin and finished digging the pit they told Clinger was going to be a root cellar, and spiked the bottom of it with broken bottles before covering it with a tarp.

In the evening before they left the cabin to bed down in the woods, they built up the fire in the box stove in the hope that a trail of woodsmoke curling up from the chimney in the moonlight would make Langley think they were at home. In case he and his Lost Boys peeked in the window before entering, they padded their bunks and arranged a blond and red wig on the pillows to make it seem as if they were tucked in for the night. When all that was done, they collected their shotguns and sleeping bags and silently climbed out the window rather than exiting through the front door and risk falling into the man-trap they had dug.

Lying on their backs staring up at the constellations in the firmament, Evie made out Orion's Belt, then the starry huntress Artemis looming over them. Recalling a story from Greek mythology Flo had told her about Artemis killing Orion for trying to rape her provided no comfort, but did put what the women were doing on the Cat's Tongue into perspective.

Lulu yawned. "You know what's fucked up?"

"All sorts of things, but what in particular?"

"I'm sort of looking forward to them coming."

The game cameras should have alerted them, but they didn't. Their cell phones did not vibrate against their breasts to warn them of the approach. An hour before dawn, Evie woke up with a gasp. He stared down at her expressionless and still, waiting to see if she reached for her gun or tried to run. Evie closed her eyes, and when she opened them again the catamount was gone.

CHAPTER 58

I had no idea why the handsome man in the gray suit had been watching my mother and me four months ago in New York City, stalking us even before Clare had died, or who he was talking to on his cell phone in the lobby of that theater. All I was certain of was that the monsters knew I was alive and they had found me.

Fear gave way to sheer panic as I heard him say, "I'll take care of them as discussed." I backed away from him as if he were radioactive and darted back into the theater. As I ran down the aisle in the dark, Notorious flickered onscreen. My tutor thought I was being romantic when I collapsed next to him and grabbed hold of his hand. Cary Grant was rescuing Ingrid Bergman; I knew I would have to rescue myself.

When we came out of the movie, the man was standing at the trolley stop across the street. My tutor wanted to walk me home through the groomed wood where we had lain down more than once by then. I said I was tired and insisted on him taking me back to the clinic in a taxi. He didn't know I was supposed to be dead. He asked me what was wrong and I answered, "You wouldn't understand." I didn't; how could he?

I didn't know they called themselves Lost Boys or that my mother and Lulu had a plan, but I realized there was no hiding from these men. Safety was an illusion. Suddenly the night watchman at the clinic gate seemed suspect. The balding doctor who rode up in the elevator with me to my room looked perfectly normal and respectable, but so did the men my mother had photographed with Langley in the street outside Clare's office. Lulu had told me their names and I had googled them while still in the hospital in Paris. Weirder than being sure they killed Clare was how they all seemed like the kind of strangers you'd turn to if you were alone and needed help. Paranoia suddenly seemed like common sense. I locked my door only to wonder how *many men in the clinic had a passkey. I was on the third floor. Closing the curtains to my balcony, I imagined how easy it would be for me to fall.*

I thought of calling the police, but what would I tell them? My life was in danger because a man I had no name for and who had once stared at me and my mother in New York had shown up in Switzerland? That the woman who had saved my life had been murdered by men who were monsters? They would have sent me to the staff psychiatrist.

Desperate to do something that would make me feel safe, I texted my mother the photo of a man who no longer seemed handsome and messaged, "Langley knows I'm here. He sent this guy after me. I'm scared. What should I do?"

I needed to hear her voice. I had to warn her they were after us. I called her cell phone, but all I got was a prerecorded promise. "Leave a message and I'll get back to you as soon as I can."

I tried to call Lulu next. Flo after that. Neither picked up their cell phones. I left more messages and waited for the women who were my anchor and lifeline to call me back. I did not know that there was no cell phone reception within a radius of three miles from the Cat's Tongue, or that Flo had left her cell phone at the Quimby cabin when she dropped by to pick pumpkins. Desperate to contact them, I called the international operator and tried to get a call through to Valhalla. The number was unlisted at the owner's request.

I fell asleep waiting for instructions that did not come. By morning I had made up my mind. It was Sunday: no tutoring, no physical therapy. I dressed as if I were going jogging, put a change of clothes, my passport, and the Visa card Lulu had given me in a small knapsack, and set off toward the woods.

Out of sight, I doubled back to town. 7:30 a.m., I was changing in the train station restroom. I bought a round-trip ticket to Geneva in the hope that if anyone checked, they'd think I was coming back.

CHAPTER 59

T hat same Sunday, Peter Shandley was culling the collection of silver-framed photographs of happy times with his late wife. It was depressing to see her smiling under glass. It also put him off his game; the Beast was dating again.

He deposited the memories of his old life in a Tupperware bin destined for his storage unit in the basement and set the sterling frames aside to be filled with magic moments yet to come. He was trying to decide whether proper respect demanded one or two photos of Clare in the living room he rarely used when Reynolds called. "We need to talk . . . alone," was all he said over the phone. In twenty-four hours the Lost Boys would fly up to the Mohawk Club in Win's floatplane to shoot grouse and woodcock and have engine trouble that would force them to make an emergency landing on Dog Pond.

Peter went to the dirty laundry hamper, took out a rumpled shirt and wrinkled pair of pants. Putting them on, he poured himself a glass of bourbon, gargled, and then spit it out into the sink. As an afterthought, he dribbled a bit of whisky onto his chest. It was important the others think he wasn't doing well. As he listened to Reynolds playing his piano in the penthouse above, Shandley reminded himself of all the things he didn't want his fellow Lost Boys to know he was thinking.

Reynolds's wife, daughter, and dog were at a horse show in Maryland. The servants had Sunday off. The conversation he was about to have would be tricky. He waited for the doorbell to ring with the same sense of anticipation he'd felt on the football field just before the referee blew the whistle to start the game.

Reynolds's living room was littered with silver-framed photos not unlike the ones Shandley was taking down. Nearly all the pictures were of his wife, Helen, and their daughter winning things—tennis tournaments, horse shows, golf championships. It amused Reynolds to think his wife had gotten just what she wanted from their marriage. She felt like a winner.

Peter was at the door now, and as Reynolds shook his hand he smelled the booze. He considered saying something, then decided it might make things easier. Remembering that he wanted Reynolds to think he had been on a bender, Shandley asked, "I have a wicked hangover. You mind if I have a beer?"

As Reynolds handed him a Beck's, the doorbell rang and Ken Strauss walked into the room.

"I thought you wanted to talk alone." Strauss said what Shandley was thinking.

Reynolds came to the point. "By that I meant without Langley in the room."

Shandley asked the obvious, "Why?"

"It appears Win has been less than straightforward with us about why these women are fucking with him and, by association, fucking with us, which leads me to suspect he's been lying to us about other things. There's a disturbing pattern to Win's behavior. I've had my suspicions for a while, but now . . ." Reynolds winced as if it hurt him to say such things.

Strauss and Shandley were caught off guard. Reynolds had known Langley longer than either one of them—they were genuinely close; not just Lost Boys-close. Rural childhoods, both college jocks who wet their beaks with culture. Langley and Reynolds seemed cut from the same cloth, whereas Strauss and Shandley were city boys and had, in fact, been jealous of Reynolds's friendship with their mentor. Both were wondering what had happened and how they could make the most of it without Langley finding out. The truth was, Langley scared all three of the men.

Reynolds handed each of them a copy of the nondisclosure agreement Langley had signed with Lulu when a bullet put him in the hospital seventeen years ago. Both men quickly read between the lines of the legalese. The hunting accident wasn't an accident. Clearly, Evie Quimby had shot Langley because he had done something to her, and he agreed not to have the girl charged with attempted murder in return for Lulu's silence.

Strauss did a good job of pretending he wasn't surprised. He sat back and cleaned his glasses. "How did you come by these documents?"

"A Lost Boy who prefers to remain anonymous thought we should be aware of Langley's history with these women." In fact, Reynolds had been in possession of the nondisclosure agreement ever since Langley dictated it to him over the phone from his hospital bed the morning after Evie shot him.

"What did he do to the women?" Shandley tried to sound more upset than he was.

"This is pure speculation, but I once heard a story from a guy who went to college with Langley about an incident that almost got him kicked out of—"

"Stop dicking around and get to the point," Strauss snapped.

"Langley drugged his girlfriend, and while she was unconscious he shaved her pussy and put things in her."

"What a fucking pig." The Beast was gentle when it came to sex.

Strauss closed his eyes and shook his head *no*. "Unbelievable . . . and sick." The truth was, imagining it turned him on, but he kept that thought to himself. "He did this to Quimby and Mannheim?"

"Who the fuck knows. The point is he's out of control. He's a liability and always has been. We became Lost Boys to pick low-hanging fruit that in all likelihood would have been picked more ruthlessly and painfully if we had not been involved. We never hurt anybody. We love our wives. Sure, they're pains in the ass sometimes, but that's marriage. Peter, you did everything you could to help your wife. What happened to Clare was tragic, but it wasn't your fault. With Langley it's different. He has a thing with women that's darker than strange."

Shandley's face flushed at the mention of his wife's name. "Why did these women put my wife's name on the tombstone?"

Reynolds closed the keyboard. "Because they think Langley killed Clare and I'm beginning to think they're right." Strauss began to sweat. Reynolds had opened a can of worms there would be no closing. Reynolds pushed on. "The women can't prove it, and neither can I for that matter, but I think he pushed poor Clare off your terrace. Those women are trying to goad Langley into incriminating himself by doing something crazy, and that puts us in a very dangerous position."

Strauss, having purchased the LSD that Walter had slipped into Clare's coffee, suddenly saw the brilliance of what Reynolds was doing and gave a faint nod of approval. When Shandley warned him that Clare was planning on getting a new lawyer and replacing her trustees, they had all agreed that engineering a drug relapse worthy of intervention would be the quickest way to get Clare under control again.

Shandley turned to Strauss. "What do you think?"

Strauss thought long and hard before he answered. "Look, I love Win like a brother, but like Reynolds I've had my suspicions for a while that Langley was involved somehow in Clare's death. I mean, you hate to think someone you know is capable of such a thing, but . . . it all adds up. Langley was the attorney for the buyers of all the real estate we sold on the cheap. It's a nightmare to think of, but we need to face the reality that Langley might have been in the apartment that night and pushed her."

Shandley pretended he was stunned, then exhibited just the right amount of rage by hurling a Venetian glass ashtray across the wall. Strauss got out a dustpan. As he swept up the shards of glass he said, "The question is, where do we go from here?" The three men looked at each other, each wondering what the other two really knew.

Shortly less than an hour after Reynolds, Shandley, and Strauss shook hands and parted ways that evening, a Lufthansa flight from

Geneva landed at JFK with Chloé Quimby Clément on board. The clinic had her US passport, so she handed the customs agent her French one. When he asked the purpose of her visit, she simply said, "Family reunion."

She took the shuttle bus to the same Holiday Inn she and her mother had stayed in. Putting it all on the Visa, she room-serviced a burger and fries and ordered a limousine to pick her up at 7 a.m. She had still not heard from her mother.

CHAPTER 60

The only thing out of the ordinary for Flo that Monday morning was that instead of being woken at dawn by bad dreams, she was yanked out of sleep an hour ahead of schedule. It was the same witch's brew of anxiety, panic, and helplessness that had haunted her since March 17, 1981. Flo understood her daughter's terminal hate for Langley and the rest of them as few mothers could. She felt it in her bones and the hollowness of her womb. As she lay in the darkness of Valhalla's best guest room, the memories of what had been done to her forty years ago returned so fresh and raw she felt as if she were still lying on a mattress soaked in her own blood.

Flo knew about monsters. She had told Evie that she had been raped, but she left out the fact that she was six months pregnant and that the perpetrator was an ex-boyfriend. Fueled by jealousy, PCP, and male vengeance, after he sexually assaulted her he did the only thing worse than killing her outright. Flo could still feel the steel cutting into her and Buddy's unborn child. Rangeley got it right when they surmised that Buddy and Flo were running from something, but the scars on her midriff were inflicted by an ice pick, not a gun.

Flo had also never told Evie that three weeks later, the man who stabbed her disappeared in the forest with a bullet in his brain.

For a very long time, Flo had known that all she and her husband had accomplished with their revenge was doom themselves to a life spent hiding in the woods. As Flo watched the sunrise, she considered the possibility that she had used Buddy to punish both her monster and herself, but that thought just left her feeling like what she was: a seventy-four-year-old woman with arthritis losing a battle with her regrets.

If Buddy had been lying next to her, he would have distracted her from this line of thinking, but her husband had not filled that empty place in her bed for a long time. Flo needed no reminding that Buddy was in prison, would not get out for thirty-seven days, and her daughter was camped out on the Cat's Tongue, trying to trap a monster of her own.

Flo slept with a portable shortwave radio on the bedside table. The Israeli who sounded like Omar Sharif had shown her how to use it. Tuned to the frequency Evie used when she dialed in each evening at 6:30 to let her mother know she was still alive, Flo had woken up twice during the night, thinking she had heard a call for help that turned out to be nothing but the sound of mice running in the attic.

The plan was that as soon as Langley and the Lost Boys engaged in behavior criminal enough to get them convicted of conspiracy to commit murder, the women would radio Flo and Sheriff Colson for help, which would hopefully arrive in time to prevent the charges from escalating to murder in the first or Evie and Lulu having to commit manslaughter to stay alive. No one in Valhalla knew about the radio. During the day, Flo carried it with her from room to room in a canvas tote bag.

A screech owl cried out as it searched for a live breakfast at first light. Flo gave up on falling back to sleep and got up to face the day. Pulling on her clothes, she made up her mind to call Dill and tell him everything, but by the time she got her boots laced, she realized the sheriff was as powerless as she was to stop the forces at play.

Dill had no grounds to arrest Evie or Langley. Lulu and her daughter could camp out on the Cat's Tongue for as long as they liked, waiting for trouble to come their way. Telling Dill what the women were planning and what they suspected Langley of having done might cause enough of a stink to force them to move out of the cabin, but bringing in the law would only put off the inevitable, not prevent it. As Buddy said when she visited him in prison the week before, "At least up in those woods Evie's got home-field advantage." Flo left before visiting hour was over that day.

Putting the shortwave in the tote, hiding it with a skein of green yarn and the half a sweater she had knitted for Buddy, she headed down the back stairs of the empty Great Camp, cursing Lulu for building the cabin, and railing against Chloé for coming up with the idea of putting her name on a gravestone. Flo was angry at the whole world by the time she got to the kitchen.

Throwing kindling and logs into the kitchen fireplace, she shouted at the flames as if her daughter were in the room. "Why can't you just pick up the pieces of your life and move on?" Part of what infuriated Flo was that she had already asked that question and Evie's answer still galled her. "I promised God if Chloé lived I would do something to fix this thing."

Flo told her daughter, "Screw your promises and stop asking for trouble. You don't believe in God any more than I do."

"I know . . . but what if we're wrong?"

~ ~ ~

The air was crisp and tart as a fresh-cut apple up on the Cat's Tongue that morning; the sky a cloudless blue void predicted to suck a storm down from the north in the evening. If it weren't for blackflies and the Lost Boys, it would have been a perfect day. Lulu hung a blanket that had been left out in the rain over the clothesline while Evie checked the charge on the radio. Double-knotting climbing ropes to the foundation of the cabin, Evie and Lulu strung lines through ringed pinions hammered into the tip of the granite tongue. Shouldering backpacks and shotguns, the women descended spider-like down into the treetops below.

Halfway down the mountain, they heard the distant two-stroke whine of an ATV coming in their direction across Mohawk Club property. Evie pumped a live round in the chamber, Lulu did the same, and the women fanned out. It was the obvious approach for Langley to take. What they would do next depended on which route the Lost Boys took up to the cabin. They were more nervous than they expected. Fifteen minutes later, three hunters in Mohawk Club shooting vests and a bird dog emerged from the forest. Evie and Lulu were both relieved and disappointed when the men got close—Langley wasn't among them.

The dog raised a trio of grouse. Shots were fired. Feathers dusted blue sky and crippled birds fell; wings still flapping, the dog dropped them at the hunters' feet. After they wrung the birds' necks, one of the men unzipped his fly and pissed on one of Lulu's "No Trespassing" signs.

The women ate their lunch out of sight behind a pair of boulders just behind Dog Pond. Pausing every few bites to check the tree line on the far shore, Lulu and Evie worried aloud about what they might have overlooked or forgotten to do that could get them killed.

Mid-afternoon, a hatch of insects appeared on the stillness of the pond and fish began to rise. Evie took a four-piece fly rod out of her pack and tied on a Royal Coachman. Six casts later, they had a pair of rainbows for dinner. Squatting at the water's edge, Evie slit open their bellies with the tip of her Buck knife and used the back of her thumbnail to scrape out the entrails. She was wrapping them in ferns when Lulu pointed her shotgun toward the far end of the pond where the state forest began and whispered, "There's someone moving back in those trees."

Shotgun in one hand, binoculars in the other, Evie watched a shadow step out into the sunlight in the shape of a man. He waved, and a voice echoed across the water, "I told you I might drop in."

The dog lover had a heavy pack on his back and a fly rod in hand. Biscuit was not with him. Lulu gave Evie a smirk. "You want me to stay on guard while you go for a quickie?"

Evie blushed. "I'll get rid of him." Putting down her shotgun, Evie cupped her hand to her mouth and shouted, "Meet you at the head of the Cascades." She pointed to a spot equidistant from them where the stream of that name tumbled down from the corner of the spring-fed pond.

Walking quickly, the pebbled shoreline crunching beneath her feet, Evie was embarrassed by how happy she was to see him. She was disappointed he greeted her with a hug rather than a kiss. The size of his pack surprised her: sleeping bag, what looked to be a tent, he had to have sixty pounds of gear on his back. "You see your catamount yet?"

"As a matter of fact I did."

"So, you're all done?"

"Unfortunately, I didn't get a photograph."

He glanced up at the Cat's Tongue. "Cabin looks cozy."

"Look . . . I'm sorry I can't invite you to stay. It's one room. And my friend and I still have a lot to do."

"I get it. No men."

"Another time."

"You can count on it." The dog lover smiled. "Well I hope you can at least find it in your heart to show me a good pool to drop my fly in."

"Absolutely." Evie called back to Lulu. "Be right back."

Lulu replied with a dirty laugh and waved Evie on.

He followed as she led the way down the rutted path that dropped down along the side of the Cascades. The rush of falling water made it hard to hear what he was saying. Something about having just flown back from a business trip and jet lag and hoping it didn't rain. Her cell phone vibrated against her left breast and Evie paused to show him a live feed of the same she-boar she had seen earlier snacking on a snake, now grunting hungrily into the lens of the camera three hundred yards west of the cabin. Shouting over the white noise of the Cascades, he asked questions about the game cameras and commented, "Very James Bond."

A quarter mile down, Evie led him out onto the slabs of granite that formed a natural spillway above the second pool. The stones were slick with moss. The stream surging between slabs, Evie pointed to the pool in the green hollow below. "This is my favorite spot."

He put his hand on the small of her back, brought her close, and shouted above the watery din, "Then it's my favorite too." His breath smelled of peppermint as he told her, "Don't forget, we have a date in Paris on Thanksgiving."

"I'll remember." She wanted him to kiss her goodbye, but he didn't. Fly rod in hand, he crossed over to the far side of the stream and waved as he disappeared down among the jumble of car-size chunks of stone the glacier had left when it finished making the falls. When he didn't reappear below her, she guessed he was more modest than she expected and was changing his clothes and putting on his waders behind a rock.

Curious to see how he cast a fly, Evie leapt silently from stone to stone, back to her side of the stream, and slipped down through the pines on the seat of her pants to the edge of the pool fifteen feet below.

No longer in the shadow of Kettle Mountain, Evie's cell phone came alive. Suddenly picking up a signal, it began to ping text messages that had been waiting for her in the ether. Seeing they were all from Chloé, Evie forgot about the man changing into his waders.

Her daughter had sworn she would stay silent as the dead unless there was a life-or-death emergency. Evie's heartbeat surged and panic rose in her throat. When the first text turned out to be a snapshot of some guy clowning in front of a statue in Switzerland, dread was replaced by anger at her daughter for scaring her.

Evie was thinking, *You little idiot*, until she read, "Langley knows I'm here. He sent this guy after me . . ." When she looked closer at the photo her daughter had sent her, she saw that the man she had hoped would kiss her goodbye was standing in the corner of the frame.

Frantic at the sight of all the messages Chloé had left and she had failed to answer, Evie bit down on her fears and pulled out the .32-caliber revolver from the pocket of her coveralls. She was tired of men making her feel stupid.

Scrambling back up to the top of the falls, hammer cocked, finger on the trigger, she crossed over and took aim at the spot where he would step out from between the rocks. Evie wondered why he had not pushed her from the top of the spillway when he had the chance. It would have looked like an accident, unlike the violence she intended to inflict on him. Her first shot would be crippling. Once he talked, she'd put him down for good. Evie would not make the same mistake she had with Langley. In her mind, it was already a done deed. Gun in one hand, she pulled out her cell phone to hear the messages Chloé had left. She was telling herself her daughter would have gone to the police, had to be safe, alive, when a herd of does suddenly bolted down through the pines halfway up the hillside.

Looking up and over, she glimpsed the man running toward Dog Pond. He had exchanged his fly rod for a scoped rifle. Desperate to call her daughter, but knowing Lulu was alone and would never see the man coming, Evie ran.

Scrambling back up the narrow trail they had descended, Evie angled up into the forest hoping she could cut the distance between herself and Lulu. Toe catching on a rotten log, she sprawled face-down. Still clutching the pistol that would be useless at more than twenty feet, Evie watched her cell phone clatter down into the Cascades. Gathering herself up, she ran on, all the time wondering when she'd hear the crack of the rifle and know she was too late to make a difference.

She stumbled out of the woods onto the pebbled shoreline of the pond, two hundred yards away from the spot where she had left her friend. Seeing Evie running, Lulu stepped out from between the boulders and shouted, "What's wrong?"

Evie's lungs burned as she screamed, "Get back." The rounded rocks of the shore made it hard to run. Evie wondered which one of them he would shoot first.

But the silence of that afternoon was not yet ready to be broken by the crack of gunshot. Pulling Lulu behind the rocks, Evie gasped, "He's one of them."

Lulu kept bombarding her with questions she couldn't answer until Evie barked, "Shut up and listen. I don't fucking know anything apart from that the bastard went to Switzerland and saw Chloé. I was an idiot to think we could get away with this." The game cameras showed no sign of an intruder. Shotguns raised, safeties off, the women began working their way back up to the Cat's Tongue. Lulu wouldn't stop talking. "As long as Chloé's at the clinic, she's safe. . . . I'll get bodyguards for her . . . we'll get through this." Evie knew talk wasn't going to keep them alive.

In full retreat, they did not stop at the cabin. Ducking under the barbed wire they had stretched between the trees, the women hurriedly rolled the electric dirt bikes out of the thicket of pine. When they tried to start them, all they got was the dim glow of a light that indicated the batteries were drained. They had left the bikes charged. The man had been there and made sure they could not run away. Looking slowly around her, all Evie saw were breaks in the forest where a man with green eyes would have a clear shot at them. Lulu demanded, "What the fuck are we going to do?"

Evie heard the panic in Lulu's voice and could feel herself giving in to it. She was certain of only one thing: that if she died on that mountain she would not be able to protect her daughter. Evie slapped herself on the face hard enough to taste blood. Lulu looked at her like she was crazy. "What are you doing?"

"Waking the fuck up." Commanding her brain to focus, fighting the adrenaline rushing through her, Evie forced herself to think like the men who had come for her—shooting would be a last resort. They would make it seem as if Lulu and Evie fell or drowned or . . .

That line of logic was interrupted by the sound of a plane flying low overhead. The women looked up just as Langley's black-and-red floatplane dropped out of the sky. Skimming the treetops, it skidded across the surface of Dog Pond. The women ran to the cabin and stopped short when they saw the front door ajar. The tarp inside the front door had been pulled back. The pit they had dug and lined with broken glass lacked a victim. More importantly, the shortwave radio was gone.

Bolting the door and shoving ammunition into their pockets, Evie and Lulu watched the floatplane taxi to the near end of the pond. Killing the prop, it glided toward the shore. Reynolds was the first out, then Shandley, then Strauss. Langley handed out the shotguns and joined the hunting party.

Flo was in Valhalla's kitchen, trying and failing to turn her pumpkins into pie. The memory of Evie and Lulu unearthing Buddy's
guns in the garden distracted her. She got the filling cooked and was
just starting to knead the dough for the crust when the pointlessness of
making pies for a family that wasn't there hit her. Throwing the whole
mess in the garbage, she sat on the back steps and lit one of Buddy's
cigars. Shortwave in the tote bag beside her, all Flo could think was,
What a waste.

Lunch was a BLT eaten with the maids, who told her in more detail
than she would have liked how Scrotum's mom's urinary problem had
gotten so bad, she was reduced to wearing adult diapers 24/7. Flo
tried and failed to sound sufficiently sympathetic, announcing tartly
to the lunch table, "Well, all I can say is if I end up in diapers, I hope
someone has the kindness to help me shoot myself." By then, trying
and failing was what life seemed to add up to for Flo. She was not bitter
so much as unreconciled to defeat.

Feeling unfit for human company, Flo encouraged the staff of the
Great Camp, both those who worked indoors as well as outside, to
knock off work early so they could all drive up to Paul Smith's College
and watch the Townsend County Catamounts play in the regional
finals of the girls' lacrosse league; Hank Clinger's daughter was the
goalie. He had tried to talk Flo into coming, but lacrosse, like so many
parts of her life, conjured mixed memories.

As she watched the caravan of pickups and SUVs drive off for
the big game, Flo recalled that when she was a girl on the reservation, lacrosse was closer to a religion than a sport. "A medicine game
for men only," was what her mother told her. Girls weren't allowed
to even touch a lacrosse stick. Once, when she picked up her uncle's

stick, ran out among the boys, and scored a goal, her mother spanked her with a hairbrush. The stick was burned because she had robbed it of its power. Sticks were made of gut and hickory back then. Flo was not thinking about lacrosse when she muttered, "Everything and nothing changes."

Alone in the elegant sprawl of Valhalla, Flo spent the afternoon sitting by a cedar log fire in the library. She made a stab at finishing the other sleeve of the sweater Buddy would not be permitted to wear until he got out of prison, but mostly she stared at the shortwave in the tote bag, waiting for bad news.

Flo dropped stitches and forgot to purl; her fingers struggled with the knitting needles. Rheumatoid knuckles, hands ticked with liver spots, she felt as if her body had been stolen while she wasn't looking and she was trapped in the flesh of an old woman that wasn't her. Wondering if that was the kind of fantasy that passes through the brains of all seventy-four-year-olds just before dementia sets in, Flo next found herself thinking about all the promises she had made and broken. Not to God, but to herself.

Most she could write off as *life got in the way*, but one promise she had reneged on troubled her profoundly. As the fire hissed and spat coals, she recalled the day she and her husband drove home with Baby A, the port-wine birthmark making her all the more special to Buddy. They were still trying to decide what to name their foundling daughter when Flo whispered into the perfect whorl of their sleeping infant's tiny ear, "I will always be there for you."

Knowing that all mothers make promises they know they cannot possibly keep did not make Flo feel better about sitting by the fire while her daughter was up on the Cat's Tongue waiting for monsters to appear.

Flo heard a car door slam. From the sound of the footsteps coming down the long wooden porch outside, she knew bad news was on its way. What Flo wasn't prepared for was hearing it come from Chloé's mouth.

Chloé came through the front door, frightened, angry, and confused. She was a fifteen-year-old who had spent the last forty-eight hours calling the women who had promised to be there for her and getting no answer. On the eight-hour drive up from JFK, Chloé had told herself she wasn't going to cry, but halfway through recounting the chain of events that had forced her to come back to life, she began to weep.

Flo felt worse than pathetic as she explained that she hadn't been able to get Chloé's messages because she had left her cell phone at the Quimby cabin. Not wanting to add to her granddaughter's fears, she was vague as to why Evie and Lulu were camped out on the Cat's Tongue with no cell reception. Though Flo had no belief, much less faith, in the Almighty, when Chloé told her about the man who had tracked her down in Switzerland, how she had overheard him talking on the phone telling somebody he'd "take care of them," Flo found herself calling out, "Oh God. . . . No."

As soon as Flo heard the man had green eyes, she knew he was the dog lover Lulu had been teasing Evie about. Keeping that to herself, Flo sent Chloé up to Lulu's room to put on a sweater and find some boots to wear. Trying to raise the women on the shortwave but getting no answer, Flo told herself there was no need to panic. Evie and Lulu were probably outside the cabin. It wasn't yet five—they'd call in at 6:30. Then she dialed the sheriff's office on the landline and asked to speak to Dill. If he had been there to take her call, things would have turned out differently.

The dispatcher told her Sheriff Colson had taken the night off to watch the girls' lacrosse game and the deputy on duty was out en route to a car wreck on Route 3. The dispatcher tried to help. "If you could tell me the nature of your problem, Mrs. Quimby—"

Flo cut him off. "You find Dill and tell him to get in his car and drive to Valhalla now. He'll know what it's about." Flo felt old, useless, and, even more terrifying, responsible for bringing her daughter and Lulu home alive.

Being back at Valhalla made Chloé feel safe until she went downstairs and found Flo loading a deer rifle. "What's that for?"

"A man who can follow you to Switzerland can follow you here."

Chloé clung to Flo's side as the old woman moved through Valhalla, rifle in hand, locking windows and bolting doors. Eye on the gun, Chloé asked, "You really think you could kill someone?"

"Unfortunately and fortunately . . . yes." Buddy had dug the shallow grave, but Flo was the one who put the bullet in the monster's head.

CHAPTER 62

Langley and the men came up onshore and convened at the mouth of the trail that cut between the granite slabs and ran steep and narrow, straight up the mountainside to the Cat's Tongue a half mile above. Evie knew it would take them an hour to make the climb. Lulu stood in the back of the cabin by the small window that looked down the face of the mountain while Evie peered out the front window, eyeing the tree line behind. Her eyes and the barrel of the 12-gauge moved as one. It was the fifth man, the Lost Boy whose name wasn't Marcus, who worried Evie the most. She'd seen the way he moved through the woods. He was agile, fast, and held his gun like a soldier, not a hunter.

The light was golden, but the temperature was dropping fast; the draft coming in between the logs told her it had to be close to freezing. Evie was sure that the man who had made a date with her in Paris he had no intention of keeping was close by. The long-barreled black sniper rifle she had unearthed with the rest of her father's weaponry was loaded now. It fired .50-caliber bullets—the kind used to shoot down planes and pierce armored plate. More cannon than rifle, she had not shot the gun since she was sixteen. Buddy was not exaggerating when he said it could drop a deer or anything else at a half mile. But neither the long arm of the sniper rifle nor its lethal ballistics made Evie feel remotely safe.

With the fifth Lost Boy out there, the cabin was a trap and she had no idea how to get out of it without worse happening to them. Still watching the forest, Evie called out over her shoulder, "What's Langley doing now?"

"He's fucking lighting his pipe." Lulu watched them through binoculars. "The others are just standing there talking and pointing up at us." The men cradled shotguns that cost as much as a car; Side-by-Side Purdeys and engraved Benellis—sportsmen's guns. Anyone watching would have thought the men had dropped in to bag wood-cock in the gloaming.

What didn't make sense to Evie was that they had flown in so late in the day. The shadow of Kettle Mountain was creeping across the pond. Sunset was an hour away, max. Landing a floatplane on Dog Pond in daylight was asking for a crash; taking off after dark was a death wish. Evie didn't understand Langley's thinking until Lulu relayed, "Langley's wading back out to his plane."

"Is he taking off?"

"He's opened the bonnet and checking out the engine. . . . Looks like he's trying to fix something."

Evie propped her shotgun on the windowsill so it looked like somebody was there to pull the trigger. Grabbing the sniper rifle, she scurried to the back of the cabin. Shouldering the heavy gun, breathing in the smell of the Cosmoline Buddy had embalmed it in to prevent rust, she put her eye to the sniperscope and Langley jumped into sharp focus.

Crosshairs on him, she fantasized about pulling the trigger. The magnification was such that she could see Langley had nicked himself shaving that morning just above his Adam's apple, but she had no idea what he was doing to the plane until he stepped back and she saw a trickle of liquid dripping down between the pontoons. As Evie watched the iridescent purple-blue sheen of aviation fuel spread out across the surface of the pond, she understood. "He's making it seem like he landed here because of a fuel leak."

"Why do that?" Lulu could see the oily slick through her binoculars.

"Emergency landing explains why they're here and how they happened to come up to the cabin and find our bodies."

Evie swung the sniper rifle back toward the men onshore. In the cold, the condensate of whatever was being said billowed out of their mouths like smoke from a manhole. Evie was trying to read Strauss's lips when she realized Reynolds wasn't there. Squinting through the scope, she followed the trail up the mountainside. She was looking for Reynolds when she spotted the man with green eyes. He had changed into full camo and was almost invisible as he cut through the pines below them. He paused in the shadows and pulled out an iPad. Before she could figure out what he was doing, he moved on down the hillside and disappeared.

"Where the fuck is Reynolds?"

Lulu pointed. "He's pissing behind the rocks." Evie could see him now. All five of the Lost Boys were below them. Evie knew she would not have this opportunity again.

Langley was wading back to shore. As Reynolds handed him his shotgun, the roar of the sniper rifle screamed down from the cabin. A rock the size of a man's head just to the left of where they were standing exploded. Langley was the last to scramble between the boulders. Evie had them where she wanted them for now.

Reynolds said what they were all thinking, "That didn't sound like a normal hunting rifle."

"It wasn't." They were all scared, but Langley liked the feeling.

The muzzle blast of the .50-caliber rifle fired inside the tin-roofed cabin was deafening. The brain-rattling bark of the gunshot echoed painfully inside Lulu's head. The flat menace in her friend's eyes was almost as frightening as the Lost Boys. Lulu slapped the look from Evie's face and shouted, "What the hell are you doing? You shoot them before we get proof they came here to kill us, we're just two crazy women with guns who murdered some fucking hunters."

"I wasn't trying to hit them. Just keep them from coming up until dark."

"The game cameras haven't pulled up shit yet. What if they get back in the plane and leave?"

"They won't go until they're finished." It was the one thing Evie was sure of.

Lulu's hands were shaking; Evie put down the gun and took hold of them. "You leave now, you'll be halfway down the back side of the mountain by the time they come out from behind those rocks. By then your cell phone will be able to pick up a signal. You'll call the Sheriff's Department. Tell Dill to get the state police helicopter and—" Lulu shook her head and said, "No." Evie acted like she didn't hear. "Clinger parked the pickup by the fork in the logging road, it will be easy to find." Evie handed her the truck keys.

"Either we both go or I'm staying." Lulu suddenly looked like a fifty-year-old child.

"If you don't get Dill up here, we're both dead."

"Come with me. We'll get in my plane; fly somewhere they can't find us . . . I'll make sure we're all safe."

"We know too much. They'll track us down. We've got to end it here."

Lulu thought about all that for a long moment, hugged her awkwardly, and ran for the tree line.

Evie stood in the doorway watching her friend disappear into the pines that crested the mountain, then stepped back into the cabin and bolted the door. She jumped when one of the game cameras suddenly came alive and a mink sprang to life on a monitor, yelping as it wrestled a hen pheasant into a thicket of thorns.

Picking up the remote control, Evie switched on the game camera she had hidden between the granite slabs down by the pond. The men weren't close enough to the camera for the wide-angle lens to capture them, but the microphone picked up their voices. She heard a cough followed by, "Jesus, it's cold." Then somebody else said, "Where the fuck is Dolenz?" She had wondered what the man with green eyes' real name was.

"Why doesn't he just do it?" That sounded like Clare's husband. As Evie watched the mink lap the blood from the neck of the now headless pheasant, she wondered what "it" was going to be.

The next voice was Langley's. "It has to be done correctly to be convincing." That was all she heard. Without warning, the mink and its dinner vanished and the monitors all went dark. It had to be Dolenz. It meant he'd cracked their surveillance system and turned off the game cameras because he was getting ready to kill her.

Evie threw the remote at the blank screens and wondered what form the accident the Lost Boys were planning would take. Slamming closed the heavy shutters, she snatched up the sawed-off shotgun, stood in the middle of the room, and eyed walls and ceiling as if they were the enemy.

Listening for footsteps, waiting for the worst, Evie felt the same sense of paralyzing dread she had experienced in a girlhood inhabited by Morlocks. The vast and terrifying assortment of bad things that could be done to her by the men filled her with vertigo. It suddenly occurred to Evie how much of her life she had wasted in fear of men doing things she did not want, ask for, or invite. She was tired of waiting for men to decide when, where, and whether they would do their worst. Death might be inevitable, but it would be on her terms.

CHAPTER 63

As darkness fell, Evie's scream echoed down the mountainside. Langley looked up and saw flames licking out the windows of the cabin. He thought he heard a distant cry of "Help!" but it was hard to tell. Fresh-cut timber fanned by the wind, the fire engulfed the cabin in a matter of minutes. When the flames reached the women's stockpile of ammunition, shotgun shells exploded in rapid succession and .50-caliber bullets rocketed intermittently into the twilight. Langley stood up to take in the pyrotechnics and practiced one of the lines he planned on using in the days to come. "Alcohol stoves are a terrible fire hazard."

Reynolds, Strauss, and Shandley said nothing. Each was thinking about the plan they had made Sunday afternoon to limit their exposure by removing Langley from the equation. They weren't looking forward to it and had no interest in telling the larger community of Lost Boys of the decision, but all agreed that Langley was out of control. They had to protect themselves. After they were sure the women were dead, they would drown Langley in the pond. Tragic accidents all around.

Langley lit his pipe and took charge. "We'll meet Dolenz on top, make sure there's no incriminating evidence, then we'll come back down, get on the radio, and let the sheriff know about the fire." The gap between the boulders was narrow, barely wider than a man. A .50-caliber ignited by the heat of the fire ricocheted off the shoreline. The men were lined up, Shandley in front, Langley in the rear. "What are you waiting for, Shandley?" Langley sounded impatient.

"I don't feel like getting hit by a stray bullet."

"If you're scared, I'll go first."

"Fuck you." Shandley flashed on Langley pushing poor Clare

off the terrace. Reynolds had shown him how Langley had gotten into the building without the doorman seeing him; taken him down to the parking garage in the basement and demonstrated how Langley must've slipped past the security cameras unnoticed.

Shandley was looking forward to watching Langley drown as he bolted up the pathway between the rocks, shotgun in hand. Three strides later, his right foot came down on the cattails Evie and Lulu had laid across the hole they'd dug between the boulders. By the time he could scream, his ankle was shattered and his leg broken just above the knee. "My fucking leg! Get me out of here!"

As Reynolds and Strauss pulled him up and laid him out, they exchanged a concerned look. Ken said, "This is going to make things more difficult."

Reynolds answered, "We'll have to improvise." Shandley had been the one who agreed to drown Langley.

Langley had his own plan. Pushing the men aside, he abruptly grabbed Shandley by the collar and started to drag him toward the shoreline. Shandley shrieked in pain and grasped at his broken leg. "What the fuck are you doing!" Langley said nothing.

Shandley screamed at his conspirators, "Stop him! He's crazy! What the fuck are you waiting for?" Strauss and Reynolds rethought the odds as they watched Langley pull Shandley into the shallows. From the expression of their faces you would have thought they were looking at the Weather Channel, but the truth was they were scared, especially after Langley put a boot on the screaming man's chest and pushed him under.

When Shandley stopped struggling, Langley explained, "Had to be done. He was a threat to all of us." Langley left the body bobbing at the edge of the pond and picked up his shotgun.

Ken staggered back from the corpse. "Jesus Christ! Why did you kill him?"

Langley cradled his shotgun. "Somehow Brother Shandley got it into his head that Clare didn't jump, that she was pushed."

Reynolds sounded calm but he wasn't. "How the fuck do you know that?"

"Last night Shandley came to my house. He pounded on the door and accused you two of murdering her. I tried to convince him he was being paranoid but—"

Strauss jumped to his own defense. "How could Shandley think I pushed her? I was with him in his office when she went off the terrace!"

Langley sucked on his pipe. "He accused you of deliberately keeping him late at work so Reynolds could let himself into the apartment when Clare came home." Shandley had told Langley no such thing.

"Why didn't you warn us?" That was Reynolds.

Langley smiled. "I was waiting for the right moment."

Strauss considered the possibility that Langley might have decided to get rid of all his problems at Dog Pond that evening and felt it time to point out, "As long as the three of us stick together, we have nothing to worry about."

"It's good we have each other's backs." As Reynolds clicked the safety off his shotgun, he considered shooting Langley then and there, but decided it would only complicate things. With Clare, he had had no choice. He had used a sock weighted with four rolls of pennies to knock her unconscious, then seeded the apartment with photographs of the baby she had left on top of the car to make it look as if lingering grief over the death of her child had finally pushed her over the edge. He waited until it was dark to carry her out onto the terrace and drop her from the twelfth floor.

Langley looked down at Shandley's lifeless body. The dead man's jacket had come unzipped in the struggle, revealing a 9-millimeter pistol stuffed into his waistband. Langley shook his head in disappointment. "I told him specifically shotguns only. He was never a good listener." Langley pocketed the pistol with the air of a teacher confiscating a pack of cigarettes. "Just so we're all straight on this, we saw the fire, Shandley broke his leg, we left him here while we went up to try to help the women. When we came back down we found him float-

ing. Apparently, he tried to go back to the plane to get out of the cold."
Reynolds and Strauss nodded nervously. Langley went on, "We'll
take separate trails up the mountain."

"Why?"

Langley smiled. "The women knew we were coming. Dolenz took
out the cameras, but chances are there are other traps—we don't want
to get caught in the same one." The men fanned out. Langley to the
left, Strauss in the middle, then Reynolds on the far right.

As Langley headed up the mountain, he replayed Evie's screams in
his head and indulged the fantasy that she was calling out to him specifically when she cried out, "Help!" He liked the idea that he was on
her mind at the end.

In fact, he was indeed still very much on Evie's mind. She had set
the fire herself: doused the inside of the cabin with alcohol from the
cookstove and spiked it with lighter fluid. Slinging her pump gun
across her back, she tossed a match. Sprinting to the tip of the granite
tongue, Evie grabbed hold of the rappelling line and jumped. Langley
heard her scream and looked up at the flames a heartbeat too late to see
her drop, spider-like, down into the trees below.

As the cabin burned in the darkness above, Evie had pulled on
Buddy's old night-vision glasses just in time to witness Langley calmly
drowning Shandley under the heel of his boot. She wondered which
one of the males the pack would turn on next.

Shotguns in one hand, flashlights in the other, the Lost Boys began
their climb up into the darkness. Through the distortion of the infrared lenses, Evie saw only the blur of body heat, glowing red-and-blue
blobs lumbering up the mountainside. Langley would not leave until
he had seen her charred corpse in the burning cabin, and when he
didn't, they would hunt her down.

The different trails the men were on converged just below where
she was standing. If she didn't move by the time they got there, she
would be dead. The problem was, she had no idea where Dolenz was
on the mountain. If she moved and he saw her, she would also be dead.

Fighting the panic that was bleeding into her brain, Evie considered options. If she ambushed them, she might be able to kill one or two, but with Dolenz out there, they'd get her eventually. It was possible she would be able to slip past one of the men, but not all four. Even if they didn't see her, they'd hear her moving through the deadfall between the pines. With shotguns, one of them was sure to hit her. The Lost Boys would prefer for her to die in a fire, but at this point, they would not hesitate to shoot her. Given her history with Langley, it would be easy for them to claim self-defense. Evie could already hear Langley explaining, "When Miss Quimby shot me all those years ago, I naturally assumed it was a hunting accident, but it seems even then she harbored some fantasy I had abused her in some way. She was never mentally stable. When we tried to help her put out the fire, she began shooting. It's regrettable, but she left us no choice."

Evie was imagining herself lying gutshot on the forest floor and Langley looking down on her when she caught sight of a glimmer of body heat behind the jumble of toppled pine and fallen rock where the three trails merged into one less than twenty feet from where she was standing. Dolenz?

Raising the pump gun to her shoulder, she had her finger on the trigger when a doe bolted out of the darkness. She heard Reynolds shout, "What the fuck was that?" and Langley answer, "Relax. Just a deer."

By then, Evie had her belly to the ground. Crawling down to the tangle of jagged stone and dead pine, she burrowed into a crevice that smelled of badger. The men couldn't kill what they couldn't see. Her head less than three feet from where the men's paths would converge, Evie told herself they would be looking up at the fire when they passed. She'd wait until they made the final ascent to the Cat's Tongue to move on down the mountain.

Lying there, Evie considered the possibility that Dolenz might come out of hiding and join the men when they got to the top of the trails. At close range, if she got lucky she could take down all four of them with oo buck. It wasn't crazy to think she might have enough time to get off two shots before they fired back, just wildly optimistic.

Evie looked at her watch. It was seven minutes after six. Another ten, fifteen minutes, Lulu would be far enough down the back side of Kettle Mountain to pick up a signal on her cell and she'd call Dill. All Evie had to do in order to see Chloé again was keep breathing until the state police helicopter landed.

The glow of the flashlights was getting closer. The men were calling out Dolenz's name. Evie was confused that he did not answer until she looked up and saw him standing beneath the Cat's Tongue a few feet from where she landed when she had rappelled down into the pines. The night-vision goggles strapped to his head made Dolenz look like a cyborg as he scanned the darkness.

Suddenly pulling off his goggles, Dolenz crouched down and studied the footprints she had left in the spongy carpet of pine needles. Looking up, he saw that there was just one line dangling from the rock outcrop above. The man with green eyes did not answer the men's calls because he knew she was alive and armed and didn't want to give away his position. Evie watched as Dolenz silently turned and disappeared back up into the pines. A moment later, he called out to the men below, "I'll meet you at the top."

The temperature had dropped below freezing by then. Her fear had crested and a grim calm had taken its place. Cupping her hands over her face so the vapor of her breathing did not give her away, Evie lay still as a fallen statue. As the cold numbed her, she imagined she was made of stone.

CHAPTER 64

D ill was off duty but still in uniform, an hour and a half's drive north of the Cat's Tongue. He sat in the bleachers next to his husband Jan, watching a girls' lacrosse game get out of hand. The crowd packed into the field house was three-beers rowdy and the score was tied. At that moment, Clinger's daughter's nose had just been bloodied and most likely broken by a slash that wasn't called. Jan was cursing the referee in Dutch. Three rows down, fathers of opposing players were calling each other "pussy" and "cocksucker," which Dill thought was rough talk for a girls' sporting event. He had already told them once to sit down and shut up. Unlike most county sheriffs, Dill found no satisfaction in arresting people for doing things he warned them not to do.

Sheriff Colson was getting up to go down and confiscate the beer that was fueling the belligerence between the dads when his dispatcher called to give him a rundown on all that had gone wrong in Townsend County since he had punched out. The driver of an unregistered pickup that had gone off the road on Route 3 had been extracted from his vehicle and was on his way to the hospital in Speculator. A float-plane was forced to make an emergency landing in Dog Pond; pilot and passengers were safe and arranging their own transport out. And one of the Morlocks had been picked up for violating a restraining order his girlfriend had taken out after he had shot two of her dogs.

Sheriff Colson listened to the litany of misfortune with an eye on the fathers, who now had their fists cocked back and were arguing about who was going to kick whose ass. Dill was about to hang up and address the trouble at hand when the dispatcher added, "Oh yeah, and we got a weird call from Flo Quimby."

"How weird?" The sheriff was well aware that the dispatcher, like most of Rangeley under the age of thirty, grew up convinced that Flo collected roots and berries for the sole purpose of practicing witchcraft.

"Flo got on her high horse and ordered me to tell you to drop whatever you're doing and drive down to Valhalla ASAP."

"What's the problem?"

"Wouldn't tell me. Said you'd know what it was about."

When Dill told his husband why, on their "date night," he suddenly had to go back to work, all he said was, "It has to do with Evie Quimby." Jan told him, "I understand," but Dill knew Jan didn't. He couldn't. Dill himself did not understand the strange obligation he felt to help Evie. Help her in spite of the fact that she did not want his help or trust him with the truth about the constellation of misfortune and hurt that had forced her to leave all those years ago and now had brought her home.

The fight he had seen coming three rows down broke out into an eye-gouging brawl just as he left the bleachers. A woman grabbed hold of his uniform and pointed to his badge, demanding, "You're not going to stop it?"

Sheriff Colson told her, "They're not in my jurisdiction." But Evie Quimby was. He was walking fast to his cruiser when the dispatcher rang back and patched through Lulu Mannheim.

As she stumbled in the darkness down the back side of Kettle Mountain, hyperventilating panic, Lulu's voice was frantic and scared. The la-di-da was replaced by uncommon terror. The connection was spotty; Dill could only make out every third word. *Langley . . . men . . . guns.*

He kept repeating, "Slow down and say that again."

She was crying. None of it made any sense to the sheriff until he heard, "It was Langley who raped Evie."

Reeling at how blind he had been, Dill began to run. Jumping into his cruiser, he screeched out of the parking lot and headed south. Siren

wailing, lights flashing, he radioed the state police. The rescue helicopter was on its way back from a boating accident on Racquet Lake.
It would be gassed up and ready to fly in an hour. Calling in his deputies, he told them to meet him at the airport and to bring assault rifles
and bulletproof vests.

By then Flo and Chloé had taken the shortwave, deer rifle, phone,
and themselves up to the little octagonal room at the top of the four-
story shingled tower that had been added onto Valhalla in 1910. Reach-
able only by a steep and narrow spiral staircase, Flo was confident that
in spite of her age and arthritis, it would be impossible for a man to get
to the top of the stairs if she wanted him dead.

Having no way of knowing what had already transpired on the
Cat's Tongue, Chloé and Flo were still thinking Evie would call on
the shortwave at the usual time. They'd be able to warn her about the
man with green eyes, and Evie and Lulu would get on their electric
dirt bikes and ride away to fight another day.

In a tower on a moonless night, accompanied by a loaded gun, a
shortwave radio, and a white-haired old woman with feathers braided
into her hair, Chloé felt like she was in a fever dream, toxic as chemo,
as she listened to Flo tell her what Evie had discovered about the Lost
Boys. "How many men are part of this fucking thing?"

"You mean card-carrying Lost Boys or just men who have a hate
hard-on in them for women?" Flo lit one of Buddy's cigars.

Chloé's knowledge of men being limited to a debater and a Moroc-
can tutor, she suspected Flo of being prejudiced. "You don't think
much of men, do you, Flo?"

Flo shrugged. "The trouble with men is that sometimes you don't
know what's really inside them until they've already hurt you."

The phone rang at 6:27 p.m. Chloé picked up and heard, "This is
Sheriff Colson, I need to talk to Flo Quimby."

"Is my mom okay?"

Having stood before Chloé's gravestone, he was startled to hear
the girl's voice. Chloé started to explain. Doing thirty mph over the

speed limit down a dark country road, he cut her off. "I'll get a statement from you later. I just wanted you to know that we're aware of the situation your mother's in and we're going in by helicopter."

"Situation? What are you saying? What's happening?"

Flo was listening in when Dill said, "I promise you, I'm going to bring your mother home safe." Then he hung up. Flo knew all about making promises you can't keep, but kept that shard of wisdom to herself.

"You think my mother's all right?"

Flo looked her granddaughter in the eye and forced a smile. "Yes. I truly do."

Chloé remembered her mother telling her back in Paris, *The hardest part of being a mother comes when your child asks you questions you think you have to answer with lies.*

Lulu called five minutes after that. She had found the pickup truck Clinger had left and was careening down the logging road six miles north of Valhalla. When they heard her sob, "There are five of them there; they have guns. Evie made me go for help," all they could do was hope for the best and imagine the worst.

Sheriff Colson was still a half hour away from the airport when the first snow flurries appeared. By the time he got to the field, there were three inches on the ground and the wind was gusting to 40 miles per hour. The helicopter couldn't take off until the storm blew through. Dill considered going in on snowmobiles, but the trees grew so close to one another in the forest surrounding Dog Pond, they would have had to hike the last five miles uphill on snowshoes. At best, they wouldn't get there until sunup. Everyone knew in their hearts it would be over by then.

CHAPTER 65

S now had not been on anyone's radar. Meteorological reports had promised heavy rain starting between 2 and 4 a.m. the following day. Langley thought the timing of inclement weather perfect: rain would wash away any evidence inadvertently left behind that might indicate foul play. The arctic air mass that descended seemed to come out of nowhere. High winds rapidly turned the first snowfall of the season into a full-fledged whiteout. By 7 p.m. that night, everyone on Kettle Mountain was operating blind.

As the snow swirled around them in the darkness, Langley, Strauss, and Reynolds quickly lost sight of each other. None of them were dressed for the weather. Crystalline flakes bit at their faces and eyes. Flashlights were useless. Ice and the incline made it impossible for them to keep their footing. They were unable to see more than an arm's length ahead of them, and their pace slowed to a crawl. Sliding up the slippery slope of trails taken out of mutual mistrust, each of the Lost Boys was locked in his own private, paranoid world. It was only the glow of the burning cabin up above that kept them on course. There was no turning back now.

Evie knew the helicopter wouldn't be taking off, much less land- ing, until the snowstorm had blown through. She would have to save herself. Shrouded by a blanket of snow, she couldn't see the men, but she heard them cursing each time they tripped in the cold, impenetra- ble night. Langley sounded furthest away. He'd left the trail and cut around to the left, calling out, "The footing's better over here between the trees." Reynolds bellowed back, "I'll stick with the trail I'm on." From the sound of his voice, Reynolds was close.

The cold of the ground below her and the snow on her back were draining her body heat. Her feet were numb up to her thighs and she could not feel the fingers that gripped her gun. Evie was just beginning to consider the possibility of freezing to death when she heard the crunch of Reynolds's boots in the snow.

His right foot stomped down so close to her head it knocked a dollop of powder from the top of her stocking cap. She could hear him panting as he paused to catch his breath. If Reynolds looked down, he would see her. Knowing that thinking about Chloé would only get in the way of staying alive, Evie had kept her daughter out of her mind until then. As Reynolds lowered the barrel of his shotgun toward her head, she surrendered to a memory of Chloé telling Flo that her tea tasted of dust bunnies. Evie braced herself for the never-ending silence that would follow the roar of a shotgun discharged into the back of her head point-blank. Instead, Reynolds hacked up phlegm, spat, and moved on. Evie should have known. Flo always said, *Bad things never happen the way you expect them to.*

Evie waited for a full five minutes after Reynolds passed before she pulled herself out of her burrow. There was snow in the barrel of her shotgun. Taking off her gloves to clear the muzzle, she heard Reynolds shout, angry rather than injured, "Fuck me!"

Snow fell from the boughs of the pines up above her as he tumbled downhill in a wash of powder. Sliding on his ass, gripping his shotgun with both hands, Reynolds came out of the white whirl staring straight at Evie. She fumbled for her gun, but there was no time. He already had his shotgun to his shoulder. Diving for her burrow, she screamed as he fired both barrels.

When she closed her mouth, the screaming didn't stop. Evie looked up and saw Strauss stumbling out of the whiteout. His face was a mask of blood. The second barrel of Reynolds's 20-gauge hit him straight between the eyes. Bird shot at a distance of thirty feet, the wound wasn't necessarily lethal, but was guaranteed to leave him blind for life. Strauss charged forward screaming obscenities, firing blind from his 28-gauge pump. Reynolds was just reloading his

Purdey when the third and fourth rounds out of Strauss's shotgun hit him in the chest and groin. He wasn't dead yet, but he would be soon. Evie wasn't sure if the two Lost Boys had shot each other on purpose or by accident.

Ken pulled the trigger of the empty gun and wailed, "Win, I'm hurt." Langley couldn't hear him, but even if he could he wouldn't have said anything. Strauss fell to his knees and began to weep. Reynolds struggled to keep his small intestines from falling out of his stomach and gasped for breath.

Evie reeled back from the blood. Instinct screamed, *Run*. From Dog Pond down along the Cascades, it was just two miles to the guide camp. She might be able to make it before hypothermia set in and she lost all sense of direction. The guide camp wasn't insulated, but there was a cast-iron stove. If she couldn't find firewood, she'd be able to break up the furniture, strike a match, light a fire, get warm. In her brain the decision was made, and yet she did not run.

Evie stood her ground and stared at the blood leaking out of the men until it ceased to frighten her. There was no running for Evie, but not because she was brave or principled. What ruled out retreat was hate tempered by the certainty that if she ran away, Langley and Dolenz would walk away. They would give each other alibis; blame everything on the dead men. She tried to remember what the microphone on the game camera had picked up before Dolenz pulled the plug; something about *It has to be done correctly to be convincing*. She knew that wasn't going to get Langley convicted of shit. If she had to finish it on their terms, so be it.

As the snow swirled around her, Evie dropped her pump gun to the ground and picked up Reynolds's double-barreled Purdey, collected a handful of 20-gauge shotgun shells scattered around his body, and reloaded. She would make it look as if Reynolds killed Dolenz and Langley. It took a moment for Evie to realize there was something far crueler she could do than killing them outright, but she got there eventually.

~ ~ ~

Up on the Cat's Tongue, the falling snow had slowed the fire. The charred remains of the cabin hissed and sizzled as snowflakes landed on burning beams and flickering flames. One wall had already collapsed and a corner of the scorched tin roof had given way. Smoke and steam billowed out into the night. As Dolenz waited for Langley, he took off his gloves and warmed his hands by the blaze.

Dolenz was the only one prepared for the possibility of snow. Risk management being his specialty, he had analyzed a century's worth of weather reports for that day. Snow was unlikely, but not impossible. While the women were down at the pond that morning, he had stashed cross-country skis in the woods just back of the cabin. After he was finished with his Lost Boys business, it would be all downhill for him. In an hour he'd be getting into the outboard he'd left on the bank of Mink River near Indian Rock. An hour after that, he'd be coming ashore on the south end of Lake Millicent where the county road ran twenty feet from the shoreline. Then he'd get into the four-wheel-drive truck he had hidden back in a stand of aspens and be on his way to Dorset, Vermont. A Lost Boy had a horse farm there, and if need be, he'd testify that Cal Dolenz had never left the property.

Dolenz waved when Langley finally staggered up on the ridge, and noted that Win was limping slightly. No greetings were exchanged. Langley handed Dolenz his shotgun and began to kick through the edges of the smolder looking for women's corpses that were not there when the shotgun blasts echoed up from down below. "What the fuck was that?"

"I'll check it out." Dolenz pulled down his night goggles and peered over the edge of the Cat's Tongue. Strauss's and Reynolds's bodies still had heat, but Dolenz could tell from the way they were sprawled out in the snow that they were either dead or dying.

Langley peered into the flames, looking to confirm the kill.

Dolenz's voice was barely audible over the crackle of the fire when he called out, "It doesn't matter, Win."

"What are you talking about?" Langley understood when he looked up and saw Dolenz's rifle pointing at his face. It was only then that he noticed it was the kind of rifle game wardens used in Africa to anesthetize wild animals. He did not know that the hypodermic dart the gun fired contained enough digoxin to make it appear as if he had suffered a sudden massive heart attack, but he got the idea when Dolenz said, "It's painless." As he said it, Dolenz imagined Evie scrambling down the mountain and hoped she didn't freeze to death.

Dolenz towered over Langley. Forty pounds heavier, twenty years younger, besides the tranquilizer gun, he had Langley's shotgun— there was no fighting back. The pistol Langley had taken off Shandley was inside his zippered jacket. By the time he got it out, he would be dead. If he ran, he would be dead. What bothered Langley the most was not the dying, but the fact that he didn't see it coming. His bad legs ached, wind teared his eyes as he put it together. "You didn't set the fire; she did."

Dolenz nodded. He wanted to be done with it, but Langley had brought him into the Lost Boys, recruited and mentored him; he thought an explanation was owed. "Your friends voted. It was unanimous."

Friends was how Lost Boys referred to the others of their ilk whom they knew by face and name. But the chain of obligation extended far beyond those you were personally acquainted with. Debts owed and, in turn, owed to you were collected, traded, and repaid with dividends by strangers you would never meet or know, and more importantly would never be able to identify, except to say with certainty that they were either a husband or widower of a very, very rich woman. Those friends had instructed him to permanently retire Shandley, Reynolds, and Strauss along with Langley, but serendipity had already taken care of the first three.

"Why kill me and let the women go?"

"Without you and the others, the women can't hurt us."

"You don't know Evie fucking Quimby."

Dolenz smiled. He was neither quitting the Lost Boys nor in love with his blind wife. He had told Langley that to distract him with a motive too embarrassing to be suspect. He did, however, know Evie Quimby, and found her determination to stay alive seductive. Unaware that she now knew who and what he was, he was still toying with the idea of actually showing up in Paris on Thanksgiving and treating her to a good time. He wouldn't do it, but liked thinking about it. Like all Lost Boys, the man with green eyes thought his secrets made him safe and strangely sexy.

Dolenz was pulling the trigger when the front wall of the burning cabin suddenly gave way. The dart went wide with a hiss of compressed gas as the near corner of the roof crashed down in an explosion of glowing embers and smoke. As Dolenz reared back from the fiery splash of spark and burning coals, Langley leapt into the swirl of smoke and ash and ducked back into what was left of the burning cabin.

The tin roof was red-hot and heat rose up in rippling waves, blistering his face. The rubber bottoms of his waterproof boots were just beginning to melt when he burst out of the other side of the firetrap and staggered into the pines. Dolenz calmly reloaded. He would look for the spent dart later. As long as the snow kept falling, he had time.

Moving at a trot, Dolenz circled around to the other side of the fire. Pausing to pick up Langley's tracks, he had just begun to run when he saw Evie coming out of the darkness. She was smiling; it amused him that she seemed relieved to see him. He didn't understand why she was holding Reynolds's shotgun by the barrel like a baseball bat until she brought it down on his right arm and he felt the bone break. Then he heard her scream, "Fuck you," as she raised it up above her head again, this time connecting on the base of his skull. Stunned, he collapsed forward. By the time he regained consciousness, Evie had tied his hands with a length of climbing rope and was in the process of securing his feet.

Not shooting the man with green eyes wasn't an act of mercy. When she was down below, walking away from Reynolds and Strauss—one dead, the other blinded by blood—she remembered something Buddy had told her the first time he made her kill an animal caught in a trap, but not yet dead. *The cruelest thing you can do to a wild animal is capture it alive.*

Dolenz was just beginning to struggle when Langley came out of the trees behind them firing Shandley's pistol. The bullet entered just below Dolenz's left eye and exploded out of the top of his head. Evie was reaching for the shotgun in the snow when Langley pistol-whipped her across the side of her head. Sprawling her facedown, he pressed his advantage, kicking her in the ribs, stomach, and crotch. Once he saw she was helpless and unable to stop him from doing as he liked, Langley seemed satisfied.

Grabbing her by the hood of her parka, he began to drag her out onto the Cat's Tongue. He was already thinking about how he would explain the bloodbath to Sheriff Colson. *The women fired at us with a .50-caliber sniper rifle. Dolenz, a decorated veteran of the war in Iraq, snapped and went after her. The cabin caught fire. Evie fell while try-ing to escape.* If Lulu Mannheim said anything else, he'd sue her and take Valhalla.

Evie wasn't privy to the thoughts raging in Langley's head any more than she knew the thinking of any man's brain, but she had regained her senses enough to realize that when he finished dragging her to the tip of the Tongue, he was going to push her off.

The wind howled; the stomping made it hurt to breathe. Langley stood above her and, arms outstretched to balance himself, brought his boot back to kick her off the lip of the precipice. Unwilling to die letting the monster think he'd won, Evie grabbed hold of his leg and pulled him with her.

Snowflakes falling with her, Evie felt as if she were floating in a snow globe that was being shaken. Crashing down through pine boughs thick with snow, she heard branches snapping, slowing her fall, delaying impact just long enough for her to wonder how much more time she had left before she hit the ground.

Then there was a great, cold whoosh of white and a thud that drove the air out of her lungs. Gasping for breath, inhaling frost, it took Evie a long moment to realize a snowdrift had saved her life. Broken ribs cut into her, sharp as a knife; being alive hurt. All she wanted to do was lie there and not make it worse, but Evie knew if she did not get warm she would freeze to death, and forced herself to open her eyes.

The same pine boughs and powdery snowdrift that had saved her life had spared Langley's. He was still clutching the pistol and it was pointed at her. The thing that didn't make sense to Evie was that Langley looked even more terrified than she was. The wind shook the snow from the pines and a great swirl of white surged over her. Langley fired once and it was over. The end came fast. Like all bad things, it didn't happen the way she had expected.

CHAPTER 66

Nonoe of us went to bed that night. Clinger had talked to the sheriff by then and had stationed gamekeepers with guns around the Great Camp. It didn't make us feel any safer.

Flo and I came down from the tower and huddled with Lulu in the library. Exhausted from her frantic scramble down the back side of the mountain for help that wouldn't get there in time, Lulu snorted an old prescription of diet pills so she could stay awake. We took turns blaming ourselves for my mother being out there on the Tongue, facing the men and the storm by herself. I dozed off once, thought I was having a bad dream, only to discover the nightmare was real life.

The snow started to taper off around 4 a.m. Dill called to let them know that if the weather held, they'd be able to take off in an hour. Clinger had put chains and a plow on one of the four-wheel-drive pickup trucks. When Lulu told the sheriff we'd leave now and meet him at the helicopter, Dill made it clear that wasn't going to happen, "I know how you feel, but you can't be part of this. Besides the fact that it's against regulation, the helicopter's overloaded as it is."

Lulu snapped back, "You don't know how I feel. And fuck your regulations," then chartered a helicopter of her own.

We were in the air ten minutes after Dill took off and flew in low over Kettle Mountain just as the sun was rising. When Flo spotted smoldering timber and a collapsed roof, she started to weep. I shouted, "It doesn't mean she's dead." Lulu looked down into the misty snow-white stillness of the forest that loomed below and winced as if she'd just been hit with something hard.

As we passed above the burnt-out cabin, I kept telling myself that any second my mother would hear the racket of the helicopter overhead, step out from between the snow-laden trees, and wave up to me, but as I peered out the window, all I saw was a reflection of my own despair.

Hovering over the summit, the helicopter began to descend. Buffeted by a gust of wind, it yawed and dropped, skittering sideways. The pilot shook his head and shouted, "Can't do it. Too much wind. I try to put down here, we'll slide down the mountain."

Circling, we landed on the shore of Dog Pond next to the blue-and-white state police rescue helicopter. The sheriff had flown in three deputies, a paramedic, a dog handler, and a massive black Lab experienced in finding the lost, the living, and the dead.

Dill was angry but not surprised to see us. "SHERIFF" spelled out in fluorescent yellow on his parka, mirrored sunglasses, assault rifle slung across his back, he looked different from the man who had dropped the keys in the parking lot so we could break into the town hall. He wasn't that Dill today. He was Sheriff Colson and he made it known. "I'm letting you accompany us against my better judgment. You don't follow my orders, you're out of here. You disturb evidence in any way whatsoever, you're under arrest. Understand?"

The pond was crusted with ice and there were ten inches of snow on the ground. Langley's floatplane had blown off its moorings and was washed up on the far shore. Bright sun and harsh blue sky, there was glare everywhere I looked. The dog was barking and scratching at the thin shelf of ice that had formed along the shore. When the deputy brushed away the snow, we saw the tip of Peter Shandley's nose and the toes of his boots protruding from the ice. Sheriff Colson called out, "We'll get him later," then sent the helicopter back to Rangeley to pick up the county coroner.

I had never seen a dead person outside of the hospital. It's different when you know they died trying to kill your mother.

I fell twice putting on the snowshoes Lulu had brought for us to wear, then tripped over the ski poles that were supposed to help us keep our balance. The sheriff glared at me and asked Flo, "You sure the daughter's up to this?"

Flo answered back, "Are you, Dill?"

The dog ran back and forth between the three different trails that cut up the mountainside. Unsure which man-scent to follow, the Lab sniffed the air, suddenly barking in a different tenor than before. The handler thought I couldn't hear when he whispered to the sheriff, "Dog smells blood." I called out, "Mama," but all I got was an echo. The dog loped up the trail furthest to the right, nose to the ground, barking mournfully.

As we followed the animal up the mountainside, the morning turned warm. Wet snow made the snowshoes heavier and the climb harder. It was pushing 40 degrees by the time we saw Reynolds and Strauss. The dog chased away a blue jay picking at the edges of the hole in Reynolds's stomach. As soon as I saw it, I closed my eyes, but once you have seen something like that, there is no forgetting.

A few feet away Strauss was sprawled out on his back. The men lay in an open spot on the mountainside and most of the snow had blown off the carnage. Shells spent and unfired were scattered around the corpses and there was a shotgun lying on the ground. Strauss's face was lacerated by bird shot and darkly caked with blood. Mouth open, lips pulled back in a frozen scream; the paramedic suggested that Strauss died of exposure rather than the wounds that disfigured him. I looked away only to notice that Reynolds didn't just have a hole in his stomach; his crotch was a mass of red pulp.

More harrowing than the splatter and gore of the battlefield was the realization that I, as much as the dead men, was responsible for what happened to my mother. If I hadn't insisted she pay my debt to Clare, go back and find out the truth about these men, she would be alive and well and with me in Paris. I screamed, "Why are we fucking standing here?" I was yelling at them, but mostly I was screaming at myself.

Dill would have sent us down the mountain then and there if the dog had not suddenly started to bark again. As the black Lab signaled the smell of death further up the mountain, we resumed our climb. Pushing off hard with his poles, Sheriff Colson moved with grim urgency. I could tell from the stunned expression on his face, in his mind he had already uncovered my mother's body. Snowshoes caked with ice, legs aching, I struggled to keep up.

The dog had found something up in the tall pines directly below the Cat's Tongue. Icicles hanging down from the lip of the rock outcrop sixty feet above us gave the landmark a set of fangs. Suddenly Dill stopped and said, "Oh Christ." There was blood and pink bits of flesh splattered across the broken boughs of a pine tree. The black Lab was pawing at a deep drift of pink snow. Dill shouted at the handler, "Get that dog on a leash." Falling to his knees, he took the dog's place.

As he dug deeper, the snow turned red. The deputy tried to pull me away. I told him not to touch me. All Sheriff Colson found at the bottom of the drift was a pool of frozen blood.

Samples of crimson slush and small shreds of skin and muscle were collected for DNA testing. The sheriff huddled with his deputies. I heard one of them say, "That much blood, couldn't go far." Dill and his men took the baskets off their ski poles and used the shafts to probe the drifts large enough to conceal a body. Numb to everything but hopelessness, we watched and said nothing. Dill seemed more puzzled than optimistic when they failed to find a corpse in the immediate vicinity. He muttered, "Let's see what we got on top," and we began to move again.

I can't remember anything about the climb up to the Cat's Tongue except that the incline was so steep and the snow so deep, the dog had to be carried partway. By that point, the snowshoes had worked my feet raw inside the boots I had borrowed from Lulu. When I got to the top, I could barely stand. The dog was lunging through the snow toward the blackened ruins of the cabin. The sheriff and the two deputies struggled along a few feet behind.

Lulu was in front of me, and when she suddenly paused to catch her breath, I stumbled into her and tripped. As I pushed myself up, my right hand closed on something round and hard that had a face. When I looked down, the man with green eyes was staring up at me, only now he had a bullet hole in his cheek and his eyes had lost their shimmer.

Dill and the deputies turned back from the cabin when they heard me scream. The dog handler was the only one who noticed that the Lab's bark had changed pitch again. "He's onto something that's moving." The dog pivoted in the snow, tilted his black snout into the breeze, and growled;

as his hackles rose, he charged into the woods. Dill said what we were all thinking: "Langley might still be alive."

The deputies unslung their rifles and followed after the dog up through the wall of pine behind what was left of the cabin. The sheriff's radio crackled. The whine of state police skimobiles was on the mountain below us. We left Dill shouting instructions into his radio and pressed on to the cabin. He called out, "Wait! Don't go in there." We did not listen. Each of us told ourselves we were prepared for the worst. People say that, but they never are.

Two of the cabin walls were completely collapsed, and a third partially. The tin roof dangled precariously from the one sound corner of the building and shifted in the wind as blackened rafters continued to smolder beneath. A thin finger of dirty smoke trailed skyward. As we peered into the charred rubble, the cabin groaned, and the roof fell another foot closer to total collapse. Ash billowed up in our faces and we stepped back, eyes teared as cinders flew. Dill was running toward us shouting, "Don't go in! The roof will collapse on you."

I got down on my knees and started to crawl inside. Dill was pulling my feet when I caught sight of a blackened hand I knew to be my mother's. Not ready to let go of her, I grabbed hold of her scorched wrist. As Dill yanked me out of the rubble, I dragged her body with me.

A singed wool blanket sodden with melted snow was wrapped around her face like a shroud. I was afraid to pull it back. Flo reached down and gently peeled off the woolen death mask, then Lulu began to wash the soot and blood from my mother's face with a handful of snow. There was no talking, only tears.

PART IX

TRUTH
BE TOLD

There are different versions of what happened before and after Evie Quimby was pulled from the burnt-out cabin. The more sentimental souls in Rangeley will tell you it was the sound of her daughter's crying that brought Evie back to life and opened her eyes. Others insist she was revived by the shock of Lulu washing her face with icy snow. What wasn't open to debate was that Evie came out of it alive. As to the chain of events leading up to her resurrection, everyone agreed on only one thing: Evie Quimby was lying about all or part of it.

Fact incontrovertible was that after she fell from the rock outcrop the night of the storm, though concussed with a detached retina and two cracked ribs, Evie found strength enough to drag herself back up to the cabin. Equally impressive, she possessed the presence of mind to take a wool blanket stiff with ice from the clothesline, wrap herself in it, and crawl into a bed of ash and embers hot enough to keep the cold from killing her. Singed, blistered, but not cooked to death, Evie suffered second-degree burns on her right arm and leg.

Open to debate was the brief exchange of words Sheriff Colson and Evie had on the mountain when she briefly regained consciousness after they pulled her from the smoldering cabin. The paramedic had placed an IV drip into her arm. The dog had lost the scent in the forest and the deputies were back when Dill bent close to Evie and asked, "Where's Langley? What happened to him?"

How Evie answered that question was at the heart of the controversy over what really occurred up at the Cat's Tongue. Sheriff Colson was the only one who heard what Evie whispered in his ear. When his deputy asked, "What did she say about Langley?" all Sheriff Colson had to say was, "She's delirious."

All present would later testify that as they lifted Evie onto the stretcher, a 9-millimeter pistol that somebody had used to put a hole in the head of the man with green eyes fell out of the pocket of Evie's coveralls. The sheriff sent Flo, Lulu, and Chloé back in the helicopter with Evie and the paramedic. Dill and his men hadn't slept in over thirty hours. It was two in the afternoon. He ordered his deputies, dog handler, and the exhausted Lab home. Sheriff Colson's decision to linger on the Cat's Tongue by himself would later be scrutinized.

Once he was alone, Dill pulled back the roof and kicked through the muck of charred wood and melted snow in an attempt to get a clearer picture of what actually occurred. Based on what he found, he realized that trying to help Evie without breaking the law would be impossible.

The sniper rifle was scorched, but still operable. Buddy had shown it to him the night of Evie's seventeenth birthday. Doing his duty, he carefully collected it and the brass casings of the twenty-some rounds of .50-caliber ammo discharged in the heat of the fire. Sun shining, the air suddenly still and sweetened with the sound of songbirds, Dill paused to think about the police report he would have to file when he got back to his office. Bone-weary but determined to walk an extra mile to see that justice was done, he trudged down the back side of the mountain and hurled the incriminating evidence into a beaver pond. Evie already had enough questions to answer without having to explain why she had a gun up there designed to kill men at a great distance.

They flew Evie to the hospital in Albany. She was admitted suffering from exposure, burns to the right side of her body, trauma to head, torso, and lower abdomen. Blood in her urine, double vision in her right eye, and a headache that made her vomit; while doctors worked on her with detached urgency, Evie slipped in and out of consciousness.

The trauma team was relieved when X-rays and magnetic resonance determined that her injuries, though numerous and painful,

were not life-threatening. As a bearded resident sporting a Sikh tur-
ban cleaned and bandaged her burns, he promised, "When you heal,
you'll be as good as new, Miss Quimby. I promise." Evie knew restoration didn't work that way.

Heavily sedated, she slept for thirteen hours and woke up the
next morning to the discomfiture of a catheter being inserted into her
urethra. The unpleasantness of the invasion jarred loose the long-
suppressed memory of something Langley had done to her in the
guide camp. Evie shrieked, "Get your hands off me!" Jerking her legs
back in a spasm of protest, Evie kicked and flailed with closed fists
at a ghost that wouldn't stay dead. It wasn't until a frightened nurse
shouted for an orderly that Evie snapped back to the here and now and
remembered she was in a hospital.

Chloé, Flo, and Lulu were down the hall talking to the lawyers
Lulu had flown up from New York that morning. The lead counsel
was the same attorney who had told Lulu not to sign the nondisclosure
agreement with Langley seventeen years ago. He had called Sheriff
Colson as well as the state police notifying them that his client Evie
Quimby was not physically capable of making a statement at this time.

When they heard Evie scream, the women ran to her. The nurse
had a bloody nose and started talking about filing a lawsuit. The lawyer invited her to have a cup of coffee with him and discussed the
financial benefits of not doing any such thing.

The women told Evie, "You're safe . . . they're all dead . . . it's
over." Evie wanted to believe them, but that proved difficult. Ten minutes later there was a knock on the door. A man in a cheap suit offered
a bouquet of flowers that looked like they had been stolen from a grave
and identified himself as a reporter. As Lulu pushed him out of the
room, he shouted, "Why'd you kill the men?" Evie knew it was just
the beginning.

The previous day, the afternoon edition of the *New York Post*
featured a headline that read MOUNTAINSIDE MASSACRE: FOUR MEN
DEAD, ONE MISSING, MYSTERY WOMAN LONE SURVIVOR. The morning

edition followed it up with BILLIONAIRES' HUNTING TRIP TURNS INTO BLOODBATH; WOMAN FOUND IN TORCHED CABIN LINKED TO VICTIMS. In fact, none of the dead men were billionaires, unless you counted the assets of their wives as their own, which each of them in their Lost Boy way did, though that point was not made.

The two-page article inside succeeded in painting an ugly picture. The basic facts were correct. Four men, all old friends, en route to the Mohawk Club in a private seaplane, landed in a remote pond on an eighteen-thousand-acre estate called Valhalla. There, either by accident or by design, they met an old acquaintance who appeared to be camping nearby. Snow fell, and by the next morning, three of the five men had been shot, one drowned, and one was missing and presumed dead.

It was the details, cherry-picked to add sizzle, pathos, and color, that led the reader to jump to the most obvious and homicidal conclusion. Tabloid journalism at its best, the article let the reader know that a membership at the Mohawk Club cost two hundred thousand dollars, and there was a photograph of one of the dead men's grieving wife and orphaned children climbing into a limousine. The article also noted that Lulu Mannheim, owner of the estate where the crime occurred, appeared in a threesome on a sex tape that can still be seen on YouTube, and was once engaged to a man who drowned himself wearing her wedding dress.

Likewise, the *Post* made much of the fact that the woman found in the burnt-out cabin had, at age seventeen, "accidentally" shot the still-missing and presumed-dead Win Langley. The paper concluded by drawing its readers' attention to the doubly strange coincidence that Evie Quimby was the long-lost twin sister of the fabulously wealthy Clare Loughton, who, besides committing suicide five months earlier, was the wife of the hunter who somehow managed to drown in less than two feet of water. The tabloids didn't come out and call Evie a murderess; they didn't have to.

The *New York Times* offered a more discreet indictment on page

20 under a boldface caption that read "Four prominent businessmen killed in Adirondacks. Wealth adviser Win Langley missing. Foul play suspected." No matter how you served up the news—plain or extra spicy—it was the kind of story the people loved to follow. Not surprisingly, the TV news teams pouring into Townsend County were eager to put their own spin on the bloodletting. It had something for everyone.

When Sheriff Colson called in to the hospital to check on Evie, Lulu filled him in about the Lost Boys. Dill heard her out, then asked if she had any proof. When she told him, "No," and launched into a rehash of what some rich old lady in Florida had said, he cut her off. "Don't say anything about her or the Lost Boys or Clare Loughton's death or anything else," which was just what her lawyer told her when she threatened to go out and talk to the press. Before Dill hung up, he had one more question. "Evie say anything about Langley?"

Lulu answered, "Just that she'll talk about it when she's ready. She says she needs time to separate her thoughts from her feelings."

"What the hell does that mean?"

"Flo says it has to do with *Pride and Prejudice*."

CHAPTER 68

D ill was back on Kettle Mountain the next morning. A warm rain the night before had melted the last of the snow and it was still drizzling. He, three of his deputies, and six state troopers were fanned out across the north face. Eyes to the ground, mud sucking on their boots, they worked their way up through the sodden forest looking for evidence that would explain the holes in the newspaper accounts of the loss of life. State police had a pair of cadaver dogs working, but Langley's body refused to surface.

Evie's sawed-off Winchester shotgun was discovered near where Strauss's and Reynolds's bodies had been found. Dill did not volunteer that the gun belonged to Evie, but made sure it was officially noted by both a state trooper and one of his deputies that the Winchester was fully loaded. He hoped for Evie's sake that when the gun was tested, the results would indicate that it had not been used on Reynolds, Strauss, or Langley, if and when his body ever turned up.

Directly beneath the Cat's Tongue where the sheriff had dug into a drift of blood-drenched snow the day before, he found an iPhone. Given that cell phones had been found on the bodies of the four dead men they had already collected, Dill figured it belonged to either Evie or Langley.

Except for not finding Langley's body, the investigation was pretty much what Dill expected until he got to the summit and found the rifle that fired tranquilizer darts. He was just bagging the dart gun when a senior state police investigator by the name of Gerber arrived. Square-jawed, built thick as a porta-potty, Gerber was an intimidating body mass that smelled of Brylcreem and reminded Dill of a G.I. Joe doll.

They had met professionally once before in the course of investigating a fire one of the Morlocks had started cooking methamphet-amine in an ice-fishing shack out on Lake Millicent. On that occasion, Gerber, a born-again Christian who had taken Jesus into his heart, felt obliged to counsel Sheriff Colson, off the record, that homosexuality was an abomination and Dill was at serious risk of spending eternity in the lake of fire.

Dill was less bothered by Gerber's interpretation of scripture than the way he handled evidence. Dill didn't know if Gerber was corrupt or simply inept, but given that the Morlock making crystal meth had been Gerber's cousin, it bothered Dill when Gerber's boot acciden-tally kicked all incriminating evidence through a hole in the ice.

Aware of the fact that he had done the same thing for Evie, he tried to keep it professional if not cordial as he brought Gerber up to speed. "I found the tranquilizer rifle approximately four feet from the head-shot victim we discovered yesterday: a Mr. Callum M. Dolenz from California. Our assumption is that it belonged to him. His wife said he was here fly-fishing. The obvious question is what's a fisherman doing with a tranquilizer gun?"

Gerber looked at the rifle inside the clear plastic evidence bag. "It's a glorified air gun, not a firearm. In most states you don't need to show ID to purchase. Tranquilizer rifle could belong to anybody. The women were up here thinking they were going to find a mountain lion. Probably belongs to them."

Rather than tell Gerber he was wrong, Dill suggested, "I think we'll have a clearer idea of how it figures into what happened here when we check the fingerprints and find out what kind of drug these darts contain."

"I have a buddy who's a game warden. Got a rifle just like that. I'll have him check it out for us." Gerber reached for the evidence bag. Sheriff Colson shook his head *no*.

"I appreciate the offer, Gerber, but I've already called the FBI. I'm going to give all the evidence we've gathered to the Bureau; let their technical people check everything out." Dill hadn't called the FBI. He hadn't even thought of it until he saw the way Gerber reached for the evidence bag.

"The county prosecutor sent me here specifically to take physical possession of everything pertaining to this case." The county prosecutor was married to Scrotum's sister.

Dill saw where this was going and lied. "Too late. I've already filed the paperwork with Federal."

"Why are you making this so complicated?"

"I want to make sure we get it right."

"You have any idea why your old girlfriend decided to shoot all these men?" Gerber had read the *Post*.

"I don't think it happened like that."

"How do you think it happened?"

"I'll let you know when I'm ready to make a statement."

"The prosecutor got a call from a US senator and a congressman about what happened here. They want to see justice done. These men had families."

"Evie has a family."

"Just so you know, the prosecutor and I are both going to be there when you question Quimby. Judge wants me to take her passport."

"That would be against the law."

"Won't be once we charge her with murder. All that Mannheim money, private planes—flight risk."

"Why are you so eager to convict her?"

"You mean besides the fact she thinks she can get away with shooting a bunch of men?" Gerber thought more about it. "Quimby always thought she was something special, that the rules don't apply to her."

"Do those rules include that women aren't supposed to fight back?" When Gerber responded by spitting in Sheriff Colson's general direction, Dill called out to his deputy, "Don't let Officer Gerber drop any evidence through a hole in the ice."

That afternoon, Dill logged in the evidence that had been gathered from the mountainside. Tranquilizer rifle, five shotguns, 9-millimeter pistol, cell phones, and the laptop they found in Dolenz's backpack. Uncertain whether he was being paranoid or smart, instead of storing it all in the evidence locker, Dill put everything pertaining to the homicides in a closet in his office which only he had the key to. Not at all sure the truth would set Evie free or lead to anything resembling justice, Dill put an official request in to the FBI for technical assistance and lab work in connection with a multiple homicide.

When Dill left work that night, there were bright lights and TV cameras in his face. Reporters shouted and called out questions. "Have you found Win Langley's body yet?" got a "No, ma'am."

"Why did Evie Quimby pretend her daughter died?" received a "I have no comment to make about that at this time."

"Is it true Quimby has a history of mental illness?" and "Do you have a suspect?" were thrown at him at the same time.

Dill put his smoky hat on and laid down the law. "My department is working around the clock in conjunction with the state police, and all I can say at this point in time is our investigation is ongoing."

CHAPTER 69

Evie ignored the advice of both her doctors and her attorneys and checked herself out of the hospital at noon the following day. Langley's body was still unfound. The swelling in Evie's jaw and face had gone down enough to make talking easier, but on the subject of Langley, specifically the whereabouts of his corpse and the manner of his death, she remained catatonic. It seemed to Chloé that her mother was saving her strength, collecting her thoughts and feelings for the attack she knew was coming.

The lead counsel for the women's legal team had more than a few friends who belonged to the Mohawk Club. They had not hesitated to reach out and tell him in explicit terms that they took personal offense at four of their members being killed off while hunting grouse. The membership worked their phones, favors were called in, men with influence were using it to make sure whoever was responsible paid dearly. The bond among the members of this extended old boys' club went far beyond a shared interest in hunting and fishing; all agreed that Evie Quimby was guilty. It was made clear by one and all to the county prosecutor that if he had any aspirations of remaining in office, arresting Evie Quimby would not be enough.

By then reporters had discovered that Evie's father had burned down a cabin with a member of the Mohawk Club inside. Flo called the prison to see how Buddy was doing. She was told that her husband had been placed in isolation for taking part in a fight stemming from comments made about his daughter. It had not been decided whether he would be punished with additional time on his sentence. Buddy had been scheduled for release in thirty-four days. Flo took it hard.

The women got back to Valhalla at 2 p.m. that afternoon. The snow had knocked the fall color from the hardwoods around the

Great Camp. Tree limbs looked skeletal. Gardeners were out on the frostbitten lawn raking and burning leaves. Evie took the stairs up to the porch one at a time. Each step reminded her of a different place she hurt.

Lulu had called ahead and told the maids to make up a daybed for Evie in the living room. The fireplaces at either end of the elegant room were ablaze. It was Chloé's idea to have the statue of the stone girl moved down from the landing into the living room. When Evie saw her shadow dance in the flicker of the fire, she touched the cracks she had mended long ago with dental cement and laughed for the first time in five days. "She's holding together better than me . . . but what's she doing down here?"

Chloé handed her mother a cup of tea. "I thought she'd remind you of something you need to remember."

Evie winced as she adjusted herself on the pillows. "What's that?"

"You can fix anything."

"We'll see about that." There was a kindness in the silence that followed as the four women watched the clouds roll across the black mirror of the lake.

The lawyer was in the library on the landline to the state attorney general when Dill's cruiser pulled into Valhalla unannounced. The maid showed him into the living room. Hat in hand, he didn't bother with hello, he just looked at Evie and said, "There's some things we need to talk about."

When the attorney caught sight of the uniform, he burst into the room at a trot. "Stop right there! You can't come in and harass my clients. Physicians for Miss Quimby and Miss Mannheim have notified you in writing that neither of these women are in any condition to—"

Evie cut him off. "It's okay, Sheriff Colson and I are old friends."

Lulu offered Dill a cup of coffee, but he wasn't interested. "I wish I could give you more time, but the county prosecutor wants you both to come to his office at eleven a.m. tomorrow morning for questioning in regard to the deaths of—"

It was the lawyer's turn to interrupt. "I just got off the phone with the attorney general. Time and place for questioning has yet to be determined."

Evie waved him off. "Eleven is fine. I want to get it over with."

"Bad idea." The attorney started to whisper something in Lulu's ear.

Dill gave the attorney a look that said *Get lost*. "I'd like to speak to Evie without you here."

The attorney laughed. "I bet you would."

"What are you doing, Dill?" That was Lulu.

Dill looked at his feet. "Something I probably shouldn't."

Lulu pointed to the door and the attorney left the room. Dill came to the point. "You've got to tell me the truth about Langley. I'm not going to repeat it or use it against you."

Flo lit one of Buddy's cigars. "That's what the police always say."

"I'm trying to help you. Christ, I already threw your damn sniper rifle in the beaver pond. If I don't know what really happened, I can't protect you."

Evie looked at Dill as if she felt sorry for him. "When Chloé pulled me out of the cabin, I told you what happened."

"No one will believe that."

"You want me to lie?"

"Yeah, basically."

"What's wrong with the truth?"

"It'll send you to jail."

CHAPTER 70

The search for Win Langley's remains continued on Kettle Mountain. There was already grumbling that with the overtime and transport in and out by helicopter, the county would not have enough money to salt the roads that winter. More than a few locals had suggested that the Mohawk Club should pick up the check, though all in all, with reporters and TV news crews eating in local restaurants and checking into motels on the lake, the homicides were a boon to the economy of the Sister Lakes.

Sheriff Colson did not join the search party the next morning. Instead, he stared out his office window and waited for the FBI to arrive. He was fearful of the lies he had asked and finally ordered Evie to tell under threat of perjury at 11 a.m. in the county prosecutor's office. Dill was surprised that the FBI office in Albany had volunteered to drive up to Townsend County to pick up the evidence he had collected on Kettle Mountain, rather than him arranging transport. The Bureau was not known for being so obliging.

Just before 10 a.m., an unmarked blue Ford pulled into the parking lot the Sheriff's Department shared with the Sister Lakes Correctional Facility. Dill's experience with federal law enforcement was limited. The driver was rank and file, pushing fifty, but the man who got out of the car with him was something altogether different. He was thirty at most, boyish yet dead serious. Straight-backed, six feet six inches tall with unnaturally long arms, he wore a crisp dark blue suit, silk necktie, white shirt, and black lace-up shoes as polished as the rest of him.

Before Trevor Knox set foot in his office and handed him his card, Dill knew he was not the kind of agent sent to pick up evidence.

Knox's card indicated that he was an attorney for the FBI with an office at Federal Plaza in New York City specializing in fraud, illicit finance, white-collar crime. "Sorry you didn't get a heads-up I was flying in. It was a last-minute decision. The Bureau's had some calls in relation to what at this point has to be considered a possible multiple homicide. Given the prominence of the victims within the financial community and the potential impact their sudden deaths might have on market prices of publicly traded fiscal institutions, I wanted to sit in when Miss Quimby and Miss Mannheim are questioned this morning." The FBI lawyer's eyes were wide open and unblinking as he stared at Sheriff Colson searching for a tell of anxiety.

Dill smiled like a hick and replied, "Hey friend, I need all the help I can get on this investigation. It's important to everyone we do this right." The room was cold, but Sheriff Colson was sweating. Telling Evie to lie to the county prosecutor, who, besides being dim enough to marry Scrotum's sister, had graduated second from the bottom of his law school class at Buffalo State, was one thing; deceiving an FBI lawyer who looked like he'd gone to Yale Law, because he had, was another.

The windbreaker asked for a cup of coffee. When the sheriff's dispatcher brought it in, he suddenly pointed at Trevor Knox. "You're the Stork Man!"

"Long time ago."

It took Dill a moment to get up to speed and discover that Knox had been an honorable-mention All-American basketball player at Cornell. Trevor Knox was dubbed "the Stork Man" because of his long, pencil-thin legs, the wingspan of his reach, and his ability to deliver from beyond the three-point line.

Dill handed Knox's driver a list of items found in connection with the homicides. Unlocking his closet, he handed over five shotguns, one pistol, one hypodermic dart rifle, two drug darts containing unknown substances, five cell phones, and a laptop, each bagged in clear plastic. The driver checked them off one by one and placed them in foam-lined aluminum suitcases marked "FBI." After securing the latches on the suitcases with lead seals, both he and Knox then signed a receipt certifying that they had received possession of the items.

Dill ate pumpkin seeds and spit husks as he watched the suitcases being loaded into the trunk of the unmarked car. Then, getting into his cruiser, he led the way to the county courthouse, overlooking the Mink River, three blocks away.

The driver stayed with the car. Sheriff Colson and Trevor Knox took the steps at the courthouse two at a time so as not to be late. Flo was out in the hall by herself sitting in a patch of sunlight, knitting the last of Buddy's sweater. She nodded but did not say hello. Evie and Lulu, both wearing sunglasses, were crowded into the waiting area just outside the conference room where the questioning would take place.

Trevor Knox, unable to see anything but his own reflection in their dark glasses, told them flatly, "Pleased to meet you."

"I hope I feel that way when this is over." Evie told him what was on her mind straight off.

Lulu offered up a smile and commented, "I like your cuff links."

Dill hadn't noticed them before. They were amethyst, set in gold. Trevor Knox explained, "Wedding present from my wife."

Gerber and county prosecutor George Ellroy were already seated at the conference table inside. A map indicating the position of the bodies found on Kettle Mountain was propped up on an easel. The FBI lawyer sat next to Ellroy. Thirty-eight years old and pink-skinned, Ellroy had the look of a parboiled rabbit.

Dill could tell Ellroy had bought a new tie for the occasion because he'd left the price tag on it. Sheriff Colson sat as far away from Gerber and the stink of Brylcreem as he could. Evie and her lawyer sat on the opposite side of the table. A secretary named Eileen operated the video camera on the tripod that was already running. Lulu would be questioned separately afterward.

The prosecutor began by asking, "Do you mind removing your sunglasses, Miss Quimby?"

Evie obliged. Both eyes were blackened. The white of the right one was engorged with blood. The secretary volunteered, "Jesus, that must hurt." Gerber shot her a look that said *Shut the fuck up*. It was as solemn and serious as you can imagine. The only people in the room who seemed to be relaxed were Evie and Trevor Knox.

The prosecutor took a sip of water and pushed his glasses up his nose. "Could you state your name for the record?"

"Eve Quimby." Evie said it like a threat.

"We'd like to begin, Miss Quimby, by asking if you played any part in the deaths of Callum Dolenz, Peter Shandley, Kenneth Strauss, Thomas Reynolds, and/or in the disappearance of Mr. Winthrop Langley." All eyes were on Evie. Dill took a deep breath and asked God to help her lie.

Nobody expected her to start by saying, "For me to answer that question honestly, you need to understand the events surrounding the murder of Charles Radetzky in June of 2001."

CHAPTER 71

My mother was in that room for more than two hours. After it was all over, Dill sent me a copy of the video that was made of her questioning. It was not pleasant to watch, but sometimes I look at it to remind myself of her. With each viewing I learn something new about the woman inside my mother's skin.

She told the truth unvarnished; told it with all its discrepancies, contradictions, lies, anomalies, brutality, greed, and perversion. She made no effort to avoid self-incrimination. Sheriff Colson would later confide, "It was like I was watching your mother set herself on fire."

When she started to explain how and why Langley killed Charlie and put his body in a wedding dress, Gerber cut her off. "Do you have any witnesses to this so-called murder that happened seventeen years ago?"

"No."

"Any new evidence to prove Radetzky didn't commit suicide?" Gerber enjoyed pushing her into a corner.

"No."

"So you don't know what happened?"

Dill watched incredulously as my mother poured gas on the fire and told the state policeman, "I recognize you now. They used to call you 'the Laugher.' You and your cousin tried to pull me into the back of a truck once."

Gerber's cheeks flushed. "We offered you a ride. We were trying to be nice."

"No you weren't."

The county prosecutor quickly got the questioning back on point. "You and Mr. Langley had a complicated history. Would you tell us about the deer hunting accident you were involved in?"

My mother caught him off guard when she answered, "It wasn't an accident."

The secretary operating the video camera can be heard in the background of the tape muttering, "Oh my God," as my mother detailed how Langley drugged her, shaved her pubic hair, and filmed himself raping her both vaginally and anally while she was unconscious.

When Prosecutor Ellroy asked, "Why didn't you report this alleged rape to the sheriff?" my mother replied, "I did, after I shot Langley." And then explained how the tape recording she had made of Langley confessing to the rape—which she openly admitted she had obtained in return for not letting him bleed to death in the snow—was later thrown off the Mink River Bridge by the former, now deceased, county sheriff Billy Dunn.

By then her lawyer was already on his feet announcing, "I'd like to stop this interview now and speak to my client privately."

Dill wore an expression on his face usually reserved for train wrecks as he watched my mother wave her lawyer away and calmly assert her right to tell the whole truth and nothing but the truth. "I want them to know."

Her voice never wavered, nor did she give them the satisfaction of seeing her shed a single tear as she laid out the chain of misery Langley and the other dead Lost Boys had inflicted on women.

Ellroy kept interrupting. "What possible motive could five wealthy and highly successful men have had to kill Clare Loughton?"

My mother didn't know that Clare had made the fatal mistake of telling her husband she was going to replace Ken Strauss as her foundation's attorney and bring in new trustees, but she got it right when she said, "Clare Loughton was worth over seven hundred million dollars, and at the time of her death was on the verge of discovering that the men who died on Kettle Mountain and their friends had been stealing from her for years."

Financial fraud was the FBI lawyer's specialty. "Did Miss Loughton tell you she had suspicions that her assets were being exploited for personal gain by Langley, Reynolds, Strauss, and Shandley?"

"No."

"Then why do you think these men were guilty of taking advantage of their position of personal and financial trust."

Dill looked like he was going to cry when my mother volunteered, "Because that's what Lost Boys do."

The county prosecutor barked, "What the hell are Lost Boys?"

"It's an organization, a conspiracy of men who help each other marry *very wealthy women so their friends can steal from their wives.*"

Except for Dill, the FBI lawyer was the only one of the men who seemed to be taking her seriously. "How did you hear about this organization's existence?"

"A woman who was married to a Lost Boy told me. Her name is Ida *DuBorg. She lives on Ascension Island, Florida.*" You could tell by their *faces that Ellroy and the state trooper weren't expecting her to have a name.* Trevor Knox was interested. "Why did she tell you and not the police?"

"She was protecting her husband."

"From whom?"

"Me."

The prosecutor and Gerber let her digress in the hope of gaining enough information to charge her with murder one, as opposed to letting her off easy with manslaughter. From start to finish, Trevor Knox stared at my mother as if she were a creature in a zoo he had never seen before and did not know existed.

Her attorney had given up trying to prevent my mother from further incriminating herself by the time she got around to explaining why she felt obliged to expose men who preyed on women. "They're symptomatic of something larger," *my mother said.*

The prosecutor's nose twitched as he baited my mother. "So you went up to the Cat's Tongue, built that cabin to trap the men you accused of doing all this."

"Yes."

"But if you didn't know Mr. Dolenz was part of this so-called con-*spiracy at that point, what did you think when he suddenly showed up at* Dog Pond?"

It can't have been easy for my mother to answer truthfully. "I thought he *liked me. We had plans to meet in Paris for Thanksgiving—*"

Gerber interrupted. "Is that why you shot him in the head?"

"I didn't shoot Dolenz, Langley did."

Gerber yawns on the videotape then and looks at his watch. "Why don't you save us some time and just admit you killed Langley and tell us where his body is?"

"Because I wasn't the one who killed him."

The prosecutor jumped in. "Since everybody else on the mountain was dead but you, who did it, then?"

On the tape, you see Sheriff Colson shake his head no, just before she told them, "A catamount jumped him just as he was about to shoot me. Dragged him off into the snow by the neck."

Gerber laughed out loud. "You're telling me a mountain lion ate him?"

"I hope so."

The prosecutor wheezed exasperation. "You don't expect us to believe that, Miss Quimby, do you?"

"I lowered my expectations of men the day Mr. Langley raped me." My mother stood up then and announced, "If you have any other questions, you know where to find me," and walked out of the room. The secretary working the camcorder was so rattled, she forgot to turn off the camera.

Trevor Knox stared at the empty chair and nodded as if still listening to what she had said. Gerber wanted to arrest her before she left the building. The prosecutor looked to Knox. "You don't believe all that stuff about the Lost Boys, do you?"

Trevor Knox didn't have to think about it. "I want to talk to this DuBorg woman. Then, once we see what's on the smartphones and the computer, get fingerprints and ballistics on the weapons, we will go wherever the evidence takes us." Knox had a sheet of paper and a pencil in front of him, but he had made no notes. He let everyone know he was done when he crumpled up the foolscap, cocked his hands back as if he were about to make a three-point shot, and tossed it into the wastepaper basket at the end of the room. The video goes dark then, but it wasn't over.

CHAPTER 72

When Sheriff Colson left the courthouse, Evie and the women were standing in the parking lot by a black chauffeured Suburban and a bodyguard. Dill had posted a deputy in advance to keep the TV crews behind the chain-linked fence. The lawyer was still upstairs working out the details of having Lulu's questioning put off until the next week. The case had changed. The prosecutor wanted Evie and Lulu charged and tried separately. It was after 4 p.m. and the light was fading fast. Lulu and Flo smoked. Chloé cried and Evie hugged her and said, "Everything's going to be okay, I promise."

Dill came just close enough to ask, "Why?"

"Because I want it to stop." Evie was talking about something larger than the Lost Boys.

Sheriff Colson got back in his cruiser knowing that he had no idea how to protect Evie Quimby from being Evie Quimby. Feeling helpless, he pulled back his fist and was about to punch out the dashboard of his cruiser when Trevor Knox knocked on his window. "I was thinking of grabbing something to eat before I fly back to the city tonight. Want to join me?" The driver had turned the unmarked blue Ford around.

Dill wasn't hungry but said, "Sure, why not, I could eat," in the hope that Knox might give some indication of what the FBI had in store for Evie. Dill was about to suggest a restaurant down the street when Trevor Knox rubbed his hands together and reminisced, "You know I caught my first trout on a fly down on Lake Millicent. Is the Rangeley Inn still open?"

Dill led them down to Rangeley, one eye on the road, the other on the unmarked car behind him, wondering why the FBI lawyer wanted his company. Having personally installed a "No Parking" sign in front of the Rangeley Inn in order to give himself easier access to bar fights on Friday and Saturday nights, Dill pulled into the parking lot by the town dock, a half block away, and the unmarked car slid into the space next to him.

It was dark, but the stars were not out yet. It being a weeknight in mid-October, the streets were empty. Thunder foretold rain coming down-lake, and jack-o'-lanterns grinned from porches across the street.

The driver ordered the Rangeley Burger, which came with both fried onion rings and French fries. Dill and Knox had the trout. Non-alcoholic beer was imbibed. The men talked football and Dill pretended he enjoyed the game. He waited until the meal was over and the driver went to the men's room to ask, "Off the record, what do you really think about what Evie Quimby had to say today?"

Knox considered the question as he picked up the check. "I think there just might be something to her accusations about these guys. I also think she killed Langley."

"What about the woman in Florida?"

"I put a call in to her on the way down here."

"What she say?"

"Her housekeeper told me she passed away a week ago."

It was raining when they left the restaurant. The men jogged toward their cars. The lawyer, cell phone to his ear, was calling home. Dill heard him say, "How's my gorgeous wife . . ." just as the driver stopped short and shouted, "What the fuck?!" The unmarked car was gone.

Sheriff Colson and the FBI man stood in the rain looking for a blue Ford that was not there. Dill asked the driver, "Did you lock it?"

"Of course I fucking locked it. There was evidence in the damn trunk."

Knox cursed quietly and glared at Dill. "Is there anybody in your town stupid enough to steal an FBI car?"

"More than you would imagine." Dill's first thought was the Morlocks, but even they weren't that stupid.

Three hours later, the unmarked car was found on fire a mile up a logging road on Saddlers Mountain. Trunk open, tires melted, the five shotguns, one pistol, one dart rifle, two hypodermic darts filled with unknown substances, five cell phones, and the laptop Sheriff Colson had turned over to the FBI were gone.

The following morning, the state police and FBI appeared out of the fog and descended on Valhalla at 6 a.m. Uninvited, unannounced, and armed with a warrant, they came in the back way so the women would have no warning. Flo was the only one up when Gerber and the driver whose car had been stolen the night before pounded on the front door.

Evie's lawyer had told her an arrest warrant would probably be issued that day, but he had assured her she would be allowed to turn herself in rather than be hauled off in handcuffs. When Evie looked out her bedroom window and saw the police cars and men with guns, instinct told her to run, but there was no hiding from what was out there. Standing trial was the only way for her to nail Langley's ghost in his coffin.

Evie was pulling on her jeans when Gerber and a state trooper burst into her bedroom and shoved a search warrant in her face. Lulu was on the phone to the attorney who was staying in a motel near the courthouse. Flo was shouting, "I'm going to sue your ass." Chloé cursed them in French. The driver, in a cold rage over the theft of his unmarked car, let spittle fly as he bellowed, "If you attempt to interfere in any way with these officers, you will be arrested."

The women had no idea what the men were looking for. As they retreated to the kitchen, they saw state troopers and field agents fanning out among the outbuildings, flashing warrants in the faces of the employees who lived on the grounds.

Sheriff Colson was not informed of the raid until he got to his office that morning. State police had kept it a secret, correct in their suspicion that he would have warned the women. Evie had no idea what was going on until Dill arrived an hour later and told them about the unmarked car being stolen, and said that all the evidence pertaining to the homicides was now missing.

"Why the hell would they think we'd want to steal it?"

"No evidence, no case. They can't take you to trial."

As Dill watched the FBI and the state police drive away, he told the women, "If any of you had anything to do with stealing that car . . . make my life easier and keep it to yourself."

As the others celebrated, Evie went onto the porch by herself and stared at the fog that refused to burn off the lake. She was the only one who was disappointed she would not get a chance to stand up in court and tell her truth.

Flo cooked breakfast and Dill stayed, mostly to keep an eye on Evie. Ignoring her eggs, she gazed out the window as rain began to fall and asked, "What was the name of the FBI lawyer?" When he answered, "Trevor Knox," Evie nodded thoughtfully and quietly excused herself from the table, saying only, "I think I'm going to be sick."

Sheriff Colson found Evie in her bedroom staring at her laptop. "They won."

Dill didn't get it. "What are you talking about?"

"He's one of them."

"What?"

"The FBI lawyer is a Lost Boy."

Dill didn't understand until he looked at her computer screen. She had brought up a copy of an article in the *Houston Chronicle* published two years earlier announcing the marriage of FBI lawyer Trevor Knox to Miranda Ayres Stillman. There was a photograph of the happy couple on the church steps, and in the article it was mentioned that the bride's late father was the founder of the largest privately held energy company in America and owner of a professional baseball team.

It proved nothing, yet Dill knew Evie was right.

"How'd you figure it out?"

"The gold and amethyst cuff links from the wife."

"What are you going to do now, Evie?"

"Pick up the pieces, try to put them together as best I can."

The next day, Sheriff Colson called off the search for Win Langley.

CHAPTER 73

Three of the five Lost Boys killed on the Cat's Tongue left very rich widows. After their funerals, against the advice of their attorneys, Lulu and Evie sent each of the wives a condolence letter detailing their reasons for suspecting that their husbands were not what they seemed to be and alerting them to the likelihood that their own considerable fortunes were being mismanaged by highly respected thieves. It was awkward, but in their opinion the only right thing to do.

Ken Strauss's widow called Evie in the middle of the night, drunk and raging. "I hope you and everyone you've ever loved gets fucking cancer and dies." Reynolds's widow took the high road. Upon encountering Lulu by chance at the opening of an art exhibit at the Gagosian Gallery, she tossed a glass of wine in Lulu's face and let it go with, "Bitch." The letter they sent to Dolenz's widow in California received no response.

Evie's and Lulu's attorney reluctantly made a formal complaint on behalf of his clients to the FBI accusing Trevor Knox of orchestrating the theft of an FBI vehicle that contained evidence of a criminal conspiracy involving fraud and the murder of Clare Loughton. The Bureau responded six weeks later indicating that after completing a thorough internal investigation, the agency had concluded that the accusations of corruption, evidence tampering, and murder made by Miss Quimby and Miss Mannheim had no basis in fact.

CHAPTER 74

E vie had been back in her restoration studio on Rue Daguerre for almost six months. In her absence, a pipe had burst and the roof had sprung a leak, but her enterprise had survived.

Evie had things to be happy about; big, small, and priceless. Chloé had been cancer-free for a full year. Lulu had bought a penthouse three blocks away. Buddy was out of prison and he and Flo were at that very moment in Paris being pampered in Lulu's guest room. A French psychologist she met at a Babylonian exhibition had taken her out to dinner once a week for the last two months, and her body was alive enough for her to consider the possibility that it might be safe to lie down with him in a darkened room.

Part of that safe feeling came from the fact that Dill had called to let her know that the femur and lower jaw of a white male around the age of sixty had been discovered by a rock climber in a cave on the back side of Kettle Mountain. Dental records saved the county the cost of DNA testing. There was no doubt about it being the remains of Win Langley. The bones had teeth marks indicating that some manner of wild thing had dragged him to a dark place and fed upon him, but forensic analysis could neither confirm nor deny it was a catamount. That didn't matter to Evie. The important thing was that Win Langley was dead and gone.

She had work. The here and now of her life distracted her, but the Lost Boys still haunted her. Not the dead ones, the ones who were still out there. And not just the ones who were married to rich women. The Lost Boys were just a subspecies of Morlocks, and it seemed to get clearer by the day that Morlocks were everywhere.

Evie was bent over one of their recent victims that afternoon. A neoclassical nude Aphrodite that had been minding her own business atop a fountain on the outskirts of Paris had been vandalized with a claw hammer. Her right breast was shattered and her head severed. The perpetrator claimed that her nakedness provoked impure thoughts in men and God told him to strike her down.

Besides being a religious fanatic, the Morlock who did this was a former mental patient. A woman who witnessed the attack tried to stop his madness. With the same hammer he had used on Aphrodite, he hit her twice, first in the face, then at the base of her skull. Like the statue, the woman would never be the same.

As Evie laid out the broken pieces of the marble statue on her worktable, she found herself thinking, not for the first time in her life, how much easier it is to fix things than people. Magnifying goggles on, she was puzzling at how it all fit together when the doorbell rang. She was not expecting anyone. Since she had come back from America, she worried about who she opened her door to.

Evie put her eye to the peephole in the steel door that opened onto the street. A woman wearing dark glasses stared back at her. She looked to be about thirty-five; pale, freckled, barely five feet tall, the way she bit at the corner of her lip told Evie she was nervous. The truth was that Evie would not have unlocked the door if the woman was not so pretty.

Evie heard an American accent when the stranger explained urgently, "I should have called to make an appointment, but I can't wait and it's important. I need something fixed." It wasn't until she opened the door that Evie saw the woman was gripping a leather harness attached to a large yellow Lab and realized that the woman wore dark glasses because she was blind.

As she guided the sightless stranger to a stool, it occurred to Evie that, unable to see herself in a mirror, the blind woman had no idea how beautiful she was. "What sort of restoration are you interested in?"

"It's complicated . . . you see, I'm Mary Dolenz. My husband was one of the men killed on Kettle Mountain." Evie reeled back as if a door to a furnace had just been thrown open in front of her. The seeing eye dog was Biscuit.

"What do you want from me?"

Mary Dolenz's right hand was reaching into her canvas tote bag. *Gun? Knife? Claw hammer?* "When I got your letter, I thought a lot about what it would be like to kill you; what I'd say as I listened to you beg for mercy. . . ."

Evie, imagining the worst, was reaching for a chisel to defend herself with when the blind woman pulled a leather-bound notebook out of her bag and blurted out, "It contains a record of transactions, profits from secret partnerships, the names of other men like my husband."

As Evie flipped numbly through the pages of the ledger, the blind woman muttered, "I found it in the bottom of the trunk where he kept his fishing equipment and asked a friend to read it. I was hoping my husband might have jotted down something about me that I could hold on to." She sobbed for a moment, then, pulling herself together, confessed, "He made me feel special . . . like sunlight was on my face. Sometimes I think if I wasn't blind I would have seen that it was all a lie."

"We've all been blind."

Evie put the notebook aside. Lulu would help her figure out how to make use of its contents. After she and her visitor had talked for a while, Evie led Mary Dolenz over to the damaged statue of Aphrodite laid out on her workbench. Taking the sightless widow's hands in hers, Evie showed her the parts of the woman that could be salvaged as well as what was broken beyond repair and would have to be made new.

THE END

ACKNOWLEDGMENTS

I am indebted to Starling Lawrence for his astute editorial eye and want to thank him and everyone at W. W. Norton for their support and enthusiasm. I would also like to convey my gratitude to my friend and agent Zoë Pagnamenta for her wise counsel over the years, and to Carole DeSanti for all she has taught me about storytelling.

Early readers Gretchen Johnson, Tom Mangan, Tom Cohen, Richard E. Grant, and Griffin Dunne—your insights and encouragement were invaluable. Charlotte Wells and Tim Delaney—your input was a huge help.

I also want to express my appreciation to my brother, Dr. Richard Wittenborn, for the many hours he spent answering medical questions, and to Irik Sevin for sharing his memories of Wall Street circa 1982. And a special thank-you to Sylvie Chantecaille for a conversation that sparked my imagination.

Much of the novel is set in New York State's Adirondack forest—my appreciation and understanding of the wonders of this six-million-acre wilderness were illuminated by *An Elegant Wilderness: Great Camps and Grand Lodges of the Adirondacks, 1855–1935,* by Gladys Montgomery, and Paul Schneider's *The Adirondacks: A History of America's First Wilderness.*

Most of all, I would like to thank my wife and daughter for opening my eyes to the omnipresence of male violence toward women and the pernicious shadow it casts over all our lives.

461